Emerald Idol

Hank Fielder

Dreamspinner Press

Published by
Dreamspinner Press
5032 Capital Circle SW
Ste 2, PMB# 279
Tallahassee, FL 32305-7886
USA
http://www.dreamspinnerpress.com/

Emerald Idol
Copyright © 2012 by Hank Fielder

Cover Art by Paul Richmond
http://www.paulrichmondstudio.com

ISBN: 978-1-61372-612-9

Printed in the United States of America
First Edition
August 2012

eBook edition available
eBook ISBN: 978-1-61372-613-6

This book is for Ricky Bruce

My thanks to Elizabeth North and everyone at Dreamspinner Press. I will always be grateful for the love and encouragement I receive from my dear friends and for the help from my beloved family and guides here in this world and in the great hereafter.

I will go to the bank by the wood
      and become undisguised and naked.

                    Song of Myself
                    —Walt Whitman

Chapter 1

THE message popped up on Nick Davanger's phone with the soft, gentle ringing of a distant church bell. He held the sleek and powerful black device in his strong hand, which was the color of café latte. A simple band of white gold gleamed on his ring finger. Nick narrowed his gemlike green eyes as he scanned the glowing screen.

Nick had been feeling pleasantly contemplative as the limo rushed through London traffic at twilight toward Heathrow. Then the phone interrupted his photo viewing, signaling this fateful incoming message. Snowflakes blew against the dark windows.

He'd been looking at pictures of Rusty from about a year ago. And of Wolfy, his new puppy, at their cottage in Ireland. Wolfy was at that time a mere eight weeks old. Each photo tugged at his heartstrings in its own way. A rustic kitchen, bursting with flower-filled vases and shiny pots and kettles. Wolfy chewing on a big soup bone tied with a red ribbon. A window view of soft green hills rolling down to the blue sea. Rusty in his pine chair in the garden, in one of the last pictures ever taken of him. Even after all this time, it was hard to believe he was really gone, dead and buried in that green land he loved.

Nick opened the message, and a photo appeared. What he saw on the screen made his heart skip a beat: a full-color photograph of a stark-naked young man.

The guy was posed seductively on his back, with his legs and feet in the air. The spread legs left nothing to the imagination. Despite the peroxide-blond highlights on the dark model's head, the handsome young face was shockingly familiar. It was Nick, in a picture from a series shot more than twenty years ago.

From tougher but more adventurous—or plain reckless—times in his youth. When he was an unknown American exchange student fresh in London with just a few English pounds to his name. Before pop stardom. Before everything.

He hadn't thought about these photos, or those times, in a long time.

Of course he knew these images were out there; they'd been published in a seedy English porn magazine, now long extinct. A few devious others must have known of these pictures too. That was now obvious. But Nick hadn't seen or heard from any of those people—former friends, colleagues, acquaintances—in years, on either side of the Atlantic.

Nick glanced up at the driver, who seemed very far away in the luxurious limo. Merton was long past sixty but a skilled chauffeur, and his eyes were aimed on the dark road ahead. Nick was alone in the comfortable rear compartment, his long legs outstretched, his Louis Vuitton travel bag at his feet. He poured a stiff whisky into a heavy Waterford Crystal tumbler from the car's built-in enamel cabinets. From the ice bin of the compact wet bar, he scooped with his fingers two crystal-clear cubes and plopped them into his drink.

He drank down the warming liquor.

His homecoming to America might become as bumpy as his departure from the States, he thought. A departure made so many years ago.

If he'd fought his way over many a rocky, winding road to find himself, to find a measure of lasting peace, he also had to admit that he still didn't completely understand who that *other*, younger Nick in the photo had been. That pain-filled, hope-filled lost child who had run to England from America so long ago with a dream of fame in his heart. A confused, mixed-race young man desperate for attention, for love, and sex, and money, and riches—vast riches. For glory at any cost, for fame on a grand scale—or a completely debased one, if that was what it took.

His art, if he dared to call the successful memoir he had published art, was at least in part a search through long-ago journeys he'd taken without maps or guides.

And now someone—who?—was sending him a threatening reminder of his secret past. He took a long, slow breath.

He touched the side of his travel bag. In addition to his toiletries, shave kit, some clothes and some magazines, he never went anywhere without two books, his touchstones. One was the *Oxford Annotated*

King James Bible. The other was *I Know Why The Caged Bird Sings* by Maya Angelou.

Nick opened his eyes and looked at his reflection in the smoky glass between the passenger compartment and the driver's seat up front.

Nick's short-cropped hair was still black and dense, with just a bit of gray, and neatly groomed against his handsome skull. He looked every inch the successful man of color—businessman, entrepreneur, musician, writer, star.

Star?

Looks could deceive, he knew. And how many people these days really remembered that he had been a pop star once upon a time? Before he'd written his recent book, he was barely remembered as an eighties "one-hit wonder," despite that the record had been a worldwide smash.

He'd been many things. Some he was proud of. Others—*well*, he mused, *let that be for now.*

At six feet tall, Nick was as fit and muscular as he'd been in his twenties—better, really, with a much healthier diet and lifestyle. His immaculate gray wool suit flowed over muscles like sculpture. His black Prada shoes gleamed in the faint light of the luxury vehicle. The Swiss watch he wore was valued at slightly more than the cost of a couple of years of private college tuition. His cashmere socks and scarf and his silk drawers alone would have been equal to a month's wages earned by the grandfather who had reluctantly helped raise him. He barely resembled that poor kid of twenty-one in the photo, he told himself.

But it *was* him.

The shining crystalline-green eyes were the same. His emerald trademark.

He was already thinking about how he could explain away the possible resemblance, if confronted about it. Effects could be photoshopped, as everyone knew. The Internet was awash in fake celebrity nude images.

This one, of course, was not a fake.

Whoever sent it sure as hell knew that.

He tried not to let panic kindle in his chest. He needed to take a few more deep breaths before he read the message that was attached to this photo.

It sure as hell wasn't gonna be good news.

ONLY moments before the shocking message arrived, Nick had been looking happily at a shot of Wolfy, his poodle-mix puppy.

Wolfy had preceded him to Los Angeles, taking a special flight in which pampered animals were welcomed into the cabin with their caretakers and padded crates. Susie Billings, who had long been in Nick and Rusty's trusted employ, was only too happy to accept the assignment and serve as Nick's aide in LA. Now Nick wished he'd taken that flight himself with Wolfy, instead of a later one reserved for rarefied human beings who slept in comfortable fold-down podlike beds in what Nick thought of as the ultimate in luxury. But he reminded himself that it would only be a matter of hours, about a day in total, until both he and Wolfy were comfortably ensconced in the rented Hollywood Hills house where they would spend the winter, and where Nick would begin the rehearsals for his one-man stage performance based on his bestselling memoir.

The memoir was a surprise hit. It was also a door to a new life, a chance to begin again. Slowly, and much more calmly than last time, the world was turning to take notice again of the one-time heartthrob.

Against considerable odds, Nick and Wolfy and Susie were off on an adventure of reinvention.

Los Angeles was going to provide yet one more of the "second chances" he'd all but given up on back in a dark, tough time when he'd dared not hope too hard for happiness.

Nick cleared his throat and sat up in his seat, his thumbs on the phone's controls. Yes, the Lord worked in mysterious ways, he thought; and sometimes His universe threw curveballs.

Remember your accomplishments, not just your failings and human mistakes. Those had been his friend Marisa's orders to him when he was so young it seemed he had nothing but failings, and few if any successes to be really proud of. The legendary Marisa Tambov knew what she was talking about, because she had been there. Now she was waiting for him in Los Angeles.

Nick's memoir, frank as it was about his confused mixed-race childhood and his coming to terms with his blackness, his white family, his sexuality, and of course his single "one-hit wonder" record of the eighties, had by necessity left out so very much of his journey.

Things like the nude sex picture someone had just mysteriously sent him, and how such pictures (oh yes, there were others) had come to be.

Well, he thought with his devilishly handsome wide grin, *you gotta save something for the sequel, right?*

Boldly, Nick started to read the message from a stranger. His smile faded. He knew that his life was about to change again. Just not in the way he'd hoped.

NICK read the message sent to his phone, and then reread it several times as tension twisted in his gut.

This time I need £100,000, Nick. Times got tough. You understand. Don't try to trace this message or call the cops. You have plenty of resources, we know that, from last time. But that money is nothing compared to what I have of yours. Sincerely, Smooth Criminal.

It made Nick doubly angry that the anonymous criminal used a Michael Jackson song in his message. How dare he!

But that was a clue, right off. Whoever sent the picture and this dirty threat *knew Nick*. He—or perhaps they, if there was more than one of them—knew it would push Nick's buttons to mention Michael.

Nick had to breathe slowly.

In the dark of the limo, he remembered, almost despite himself. The pop star he'd ached to be as a kid had a very direct link to the Jackson Five. One memory in particular was bittersweet. It crystallized something in him.

The memory rushed back unbidden.

A LONG-ago scene from his childhood. Nick's grandparents' modest gray clapboard house on the West Side of Chicago, before they'd retired and taken him (still a small boy) to the northern Wisconsin town of Appledale. The town where the couple had met so many years before. A white town, of course. A rural "farmette" where Grandpa and Grandma, Mama's folks, had scratched out a living.

He'd been left there with them. In the night. His mother had gone missing again, and his grandparents were left to raise him. As for his father? Nick couldn't remember ever even seeing him. Among these rural white folks, he was not spoken of, except rarely, and then only as "that man," or once as "the colored man," and never referred to by any name, at least never in front of Nick.

Mama was only slightly less a stranger. And then she was gone. Long gone for long, long stretches.

There must have been reasons. But whatever they were, they were not considered fit for Nick's ears, even when he grew to become a precocious cute little boy prone to asking uncomfortable questions.

Punishment came swiftly. Whippings were bad, and a steady rain of disapproval without explanation came down harder, and, in many ways, painfully worse.

A part of Nick was in hiding, even if he didn't yet know about that damaging strategy of survival. Yet his grace and enthusiasm were somehow stronger, and nobody anywhere could keep that Nick down.

One afternoon, Nick had come home with a poster of the Jackson Five he'd won in a school-wide drawing competition. He taped the poster to his bedroom wall, above his bed. The room, like the little house, was spare and modest. He had only one window that overlooked a lonely gray stretch of highway. The bed wasn't much more than a lumpy army cot. Nick was proud of that poster, to the point of being in love with it. The night Nick had mounted it on his wall with Scotch tape, his grandfather discovered it and became enraged. The old man tore down the poster and ripped it in half and crumpled it up. Scared the hell out of Nick. Grandpa's face was red and full of contempt. It didn't make any sense to Nick, and if he hadn't been so scared, his own anger would have come bursting out too.

"You don't need to get mixed up in that," the old man had scolded, the bald spot on his head turning bright red, wisps of white hair floating like angel feathers. "You're not like *those people.*" He jabbed his finger at the ruins of the prize poster.

Those people? The Jacksons? Nick would have loved nothing better than to be thought of as remotely resembling them. There was something in his grandfather's statement that had chilled him, though. The violence of it had startled Nick, a pretty sensitive kid. He was just ten.

"But… am I *kinda like* them?" Nick asked in a tremulous voice.

"You're mostly white!" the old man barked. Nick's grandmother, who had come over to the bedroom doorway to see what the stir was all about, turned tail quickly, wiping her hands on a dish towel. "Your mother is as white as we are," the old man snarled.

Nick felt it was one of those moments when maybe he was a little more mature than his years, and a little closer to a dangerous truth than might be good for the well-being of his oft-whipped round bottom. It emboldened him to find out something. He decided—if such an impulse could be called that—to hazard a chance.

"My skin is darker than yours, though," Nick said in a trembling voice. "What color was my daddy?" He knew full well the answer and yet had to hear it—burned to hear it—said aloud.

"Your father abrogated his claims to you when he disappeared," said Grandfather Davangere (Nick would drop the final E from his name years later on the advice of a talent agent). "Anyway, I never laid eyes on him, so I haven't a clue what he was like or what he looked like."

"Did he have green eyes like me?" Nick asked.

"How should I know?"

"Ain't nobody else in this family got green eyes," Nick mumbled.

His grandfather slapped Nick hard across the face, surprising him.

"Don't you talk that… *colored talk*! Use proper English grammar and talk like an American boy, like a white boy! That's how we're raising you, no matter that you might be a shade or two darker and a might *less* than your own people!"

Nick was a spunky kid, and he had been provoked, even if he was frightened of his hard-ass, farm-raised white grandpa.

"But you told your friends at the grocery store I was *Spanish,*" Nick taunted through his tears. "I heard you say it! You lied, Grandpa! I ain't Spanish. You keep me locked up on summer days so my skin won't get any darker! You're ashamed of me!"

"We're not ashamed," his grandmother cried. She'd come back, apparently unable to bear the tension any longer. She came swooping in between the males of her household. She looked at her husband. "Leave Nick be," she admonished. "He's as good as anyone, and I won't stand for him being told he's any less. He can be whatever he wants to be!"

The old man laughed sarcastically.

"He can't *be anything,*" the old man hissed, "but what he is." Nick didn't know what his grandfather meant by that. But it didn't sound kindly.

Grandpa walked away, mumbling, "You can hide some things, and he does, but you can't hide your face or your skin color...."

One time Nick would never forget, the only black girl in the whole school, Patty, had summed up this part of Nick's lot in life more succinctly. "Mama white, daddy black," she'd said, her own skin the rich color of strong coffee with just a drop of cream. "That makes you a mule."

A mule?

Nick found that very curious. Certain words arrive in a shower of acid. Shock you at first, and then start to corrode and burn, leaving ugly holes behind.

They were six years of age. Patty left at Christmas break and never came back. Her words never left him.

Six is a funny age to begin to learn to hide yourself. Six is an age when you might believe almost anything.

No matter how untrue.

NICK'S grandfather retired from the building trades in Chicago, in which he had never really prospered. His grandparents moved Nick with them up to Wisconsin, to Appledale, to the old family farm. Nick grew and at last entered high school and made every attempt possible to be like all the other kids—sports-crazed (Nick loved baseball), clean-cut, and... white.

Nick was "just a little"—or maybe more than just a little—off-white, and his hair was black or nearly so, and was more on the wavy side than the nappy side. He parted it on the side. He wasn't really fooling anyone.

He was different in more ways than one, so he tried to compensate for that among his peers.

They looked at him, all right. They knew he was a little different. But he could talk just like they did, and as he grew he became good at sports and at drawing funny cartoons and even halfway decent portraits. He could sing, dance better than most of the kids, and was considered downright talented. He made friends. He also started to come into his own good looks, and that drew attention, as well as envy.

If Nick felt a little paranoid sometimes, he just put the energy into his games, into his drawings, into fitting in like everybody else.

Damn if he didn't believe he could.

Chapter 2

NOW Nick hit *reply* on his phone. The limo was entering the lanes that led to the various gates at Heathrow. Long, long way from Chicago; long, long way from the rural Wisconsin farmette he had been thinking of in his little reverie.

And a helluva long way from the time a young man named Nick Davangere first set foot on this "foreign" soil, jolly old England, where he was so eager to make the world take notice of him.

He angrily texted, *Go to hell, Criminal. You can't prove who that is in the photo. Garbage like this is all over the Net. You've failed, and if I catch you, you'll meet justice.*

He hit Send.

In line to check in for his international flight, another message came up on his phone from the same anonymous "private" sender. Annoyance turned into anxiety. And then sweat. This time there were two pictures, then two more came in.

Nick moved slightly out of the line, turning his back so no one could see these photos when he looked at them.

The first shot was of Nick, age twenty-one, nude, from behind. The second shot was a variation of the first, bent over. His balls were clearly visible between his legs. The third shot surprised Nick. He'd never seen it before. In fact, it shocked and angered him. It had obviously been taken by someone spying on him, a long time ago. Spying on a beach at night. A Los Angeles area beach! Spying on a scene of moonlit lovemaking that in the photo looked like an utterly explicit sexual act from a pornographic magazine.

The passengers in front of Nick moved forward, and he turned back into his place in line.

He stared at the photo. Who was he with on that long-ago night? A terrible jolt of recognition pulled Nick up short. Both faces in the photo were clearly identifiable. The other guy's face was clear in the frame. Somebody he hadn't thought about much in years. His name rang silently in Nick's head. A famous somebody—very famous. His naked body in a very compromising position intertwined with Nick's. Nick almost didn't hear the ticket agent calling him forward.

"Huh?" he said, looking up.

The agent's lipstick frown changed to a smile of recognition.

"Mr. Davanger?" she sang in her mellifluous English accent, taking his ticket and identification. She scanned it. "I thought so! Saw you on *Good Morning Britain* the other day. I can't wait to read your memoir." She typed rapidly on her keyboard and continued speaking. Nick judged her to be about forty-five, her hair dyed brunette and styled in a businesslike bob. "I'm a fan from way back," she said with a knowing nod. She hummed a couple of distinctive notes from "Wonder What," the single pop tune he would forever be linked to, and then she blushed and laughed at her own pluck.

Nick smiled politely.

"You're all set, Mr. Davanger," she said, handing him his boarding pass. "But would you mind... terribly?"

He took the slip of scrap paper and pen she held out toward him.

"Of course," he said, signing his name with a flourish of her pen.

She beamed.

"You're even more handsome in person," she said. "And those emerald eyes! Just like on TV. You really are an emerald idol," she said, parroting another cliché that had once been chained around his neck by the media machine of pop fandom. For one year, 1982, it seemed like he'd been everywhere in Britain with that song, with a softer follow-up in the States. Then came the worldwide smash. It was as if for one moment, everyone on the planet knew that tune. The world seemed to grow smaller, at least for a time. Then it—pop stardom, flash fame—seemed to end for him completely. Revivals of the eighties would be a long way off, and a long time coming.

Whatever happened to Nick Davanger? Well, a lot. If he seemed to disappear from the media's glare, the song had a way of coming back to life from time to time.

The soundtrack from a recent movie, set in the eighties and featuring a whole bunch of catchy eighties dance tunes, including his hit, had made the song popular for a new generation. Young people all seemed to know the lyrics again: *"Wonder what it would be like/To be with you/All night/It would feel so right/I know it's true."* Old and young seemed to love those kinds of songs, great old songs like "Tainted Love" by Soft Cell and "Don't you Want Me," by Human League, even songs by more obscure eighties bands from Britain, like Haircut 100 and ABC. Now "Wonder What" was even turning up in TV commercials and oldies compilations, and was one of the most downloaded songs (legally and illegally) of the MP3 era. It seemed like everybody had it on their iPod playlists.

Because he'd found his moment of fame there, some people still thought he was an Englishman of sorts. Why not? Nick's unpindownable identity was one of the myriad stories he'd spun into his memoir, and now an evolving one-man play.

Another ticket agent beamed at him with a pretty smile. Her red curls flowed like a halo around her plump, freckled face. "The emerald idol himself," she gushed. "Sign my notebook too?"

Nick nodded and signed. He handed it back to her.

"I don't recommend worshiping false idols," Nick said with a joking smile. "I'm just a humble sinner like anybody else."

IN THE VIP lounge, Nick took an out-of-the-way table and ordered a glass of white wine. He'd not planned to consume any more alcohol and rarely drank at all these days, the steadying scotch in the limo notwithstanding. But his nerves were freshly frayed. How on earth would he summon the nerve to perform a one-man spoken-word show, based on his memoir—before a live audience of thousands, night after night in LA—with this blackmail message hanging over his head?

He'd already signed the contract, and he sure knew well what that meant. The set was built, the crew engaged, and the posters and media packets sent around, generating buzz nationwide, with lots of attention directly on him.

Nick didn't need a crisis of confidence right now.

The bloody blackmailer had timed the strike just right, he had to admit. But he would yield nothing more, he thought angrily.

He flipped again to the photos sent to his phone: two young men, their faces clearly visible, engaged in an intimate act that brought back strong feelings—and mixed emotions.

The familiar face of one of America's most respected baseball players, Paul Tolanaro, was tilted back in ecstasy. He was butt naked. Most of his erect penis was in Nick's mouth. Paul's hand was on Nick's dick.

How had someone been able to take these clear pictures without him knowing about it? Nick knew the year was 1984, the place Los Angeles. It was the summer of the Olympics. But even then there were ambitious and ruthless paparazzi with telephoto lenses. And Nick had been famous by then. So was Paul, a rising star in Major League Baseball. They had both been twenty-four and caught up in the glamor of their incredible respective areas of success—Nick the new shining pop prince and Paul an Olympic athlete on the American baseball team. The encounter had been one of Nick's boldest and wildest, and if he were honest with himself, he'd never quite gotten over Paul.

Paul was six feet of dynamite, muscle, and intensity. A sexy shade of milk chocolate, with a Latin beat.

But Paul had ended it before "it" had a chance to begin. He went on to glory in the Major Leagues, married, had four or five kids, and was now one of the most recognized commentators in sports, with reams of endorsements. An outspoken conservative, he had been recruited for years to run on the Republican ticket.

Because Nick had really loved Paul and respected him, he'd promised to follow his wishes, however painful they had been at the time, and ever after.

Paul had asked Nick to never contact him again.

Actually, it was more a threatening directive.

Nick read about Paul in the media from time to time. And he honored Paul's wishes. After all, it wasn't as if Nick had been carrying a torch all these years. He'd been with Rusty.

Paul was a bittersweet memory. Rusty had been Nick's *life*, in good times and bad, sickness and health. *Till death do us part*, but without a ceremony, a license, or the recognition of the law.

And now Rusty was gone, passed on. His presence was with Nick always. But the warmth of his human touch—that could only survive in memory.

Nick flipped to the next picture he'd been sent.

The blackmailer sure had his attention now. This shot was even more intimate and revealing.

Paul's face was pressed between Nick's bare legs. Paul's slick pink tongue could be seen, and his face was contorted with pleasure. Nick's dark hand had a tight grip on Paul's thick cock. A rope of white semen was shooting forth from its purple head, frozen in the stop-time of the moment of orgasm. A long time ago.

"Whew," Nick said now. He shook his head almost in disbelief.

Nick knew that obviously the pictures had been taken in secret. But by whom? Someone from Nick's camp? The entourage of international entertainers performing at the games? Or someone from Paul's crowd? An opportunist? A kinky acquaintance?

Or a stranger?

That didn't seem possible, but this had all happened so long ago. It left Nick with an eerie feeling.

Someone had kept the secret—until now.

Nick's mind reeled from the possibilities. He'd been blackmailed once before. He knew the horrendous feeling of violation and powerlessness. This time the blackmailer had pictures shot in America. The previous extortion had been based on poses shot back in London's Soho neighborhood, where Nick had known more than a few wild moments.

If Paul Tolanaro knew he and Nick had been spied on that night on the beach, and that these outrageous pictures existed, what would he do? Was it possible he did know somehow?

Nick didn't think so. The previous episode, in which he'd been blackmailed over pictures, hadn't involved Paul or anyone else but him.

There was a terrible note of familiarity about it all. The blackmailer was someone from Nick's past, Nick was certain. Just like the first time. The criminal was not someone from Paul's world.

Could Nick tell Paul about this now? Warn him? Wasn't he obligated to do just that? These pictures would probably ruin Paul Tolanaro with scandal.

But Nick figured if he even so much as tried to contact Paul, he could end up making matters worse. And of course there was that promise he had made to never try to reach Paul again.

Maybe it would be best if he just paid the fuckin' blackmailers, he thought, as he had done the first time it had happened. But he sure as hell didn't want to.

Nick looked at the new message that followed the latest batch of pictures from the busy blackmailer. He steeled himself and read.

It's not just about you, Nick. As you can see, it's also about your old friend in the photo. Tolanaro. Figured you'd remember that face. You can save him—or destroy him. Think about it, and get the money ready for a drop in LA on our say so. But don't wait too long. And don't call the cops. SC.

Caller ID naturally only showed the words *Private Number*.

Where were the messages originating from? London? Or California?

Nick flipped the phone off. His temples throbbed. He left his wine untouched.

He boarded the aircraft and got himself situated. After takeoff he made himself comfortable in the ample seat allotted him. The seat folded out smoothly into a comfortable bed, complete with two fat, fluffy down pillows. Nick slipped off his shoes. He unbuttoned his shirt and pulled a soft beige cashmere blanket to his chin. And then he simmered and thought about what to do.

He turned his international phone on. Using the reply function, he sent a text message to the blackmailer.

I should know who you are by now, and chances are one day I will find out. You are taking a terrible risk, friend. You don't have to go down this road. You should also know that the photos will be assumed to be fakes. Still, you're right. I wouldn't want to put an old friend though the hell you would so cavalierly inflict on innocent people. I could take the abuse. Something tells me that in the end, my old friend could too. So I might just decide to tell you to piss off, mate. And then come after you with everything I've got. You think about that.

He hit Send.

The reply came in less than five minutes. Nick read with bleary eyes.

A new photo opened. He was confused at first. He'd never seen this shot of Wolfy before.

I have something else of yours, Nick, and believe me you don't want me to have it.

Nick felt his throat tighten. For the first time, this caper felt truly dangerous, truly evil. He read on.

Nick, I don't doubt you know all about what goes into making a fake, as you have been one of the biggest fakes who has ever lived. Your whole life is damn fake.

Who the hell does Nick Davanger think he is?

The photos of you and Tolanaro have been authenticated. Believe me. And the beloved possession of yours I mentioned, which you blithely let out of your sight, sending him off to his sunny new home in Los Angeles ahead of you, is also now in my grasping hands.

And I'm in a foul mood, "friend." I wouldn't mind hurting something. Something really innocent. Innocent, in a way you are not. Just look at those dirty pictures of yourself! Innocent? Showing your filthy naked body, your hard dick out, ass spread, even your asshole showing! You call that innocent?

Have the money ready and stand by for further instructions.

Nick shivered, a coppery taste of fear in his mouth.

The bastard had Wolfy.

Chapter 3

1982

SOHO was a good thirty minutes ride by Tube from the youth hostel in Hammersmith. Peacehostel, in the very urban old London suburb of Hammersmith, was a charming, crumbling, red-brick storybook Victorian mansion. Its five poorly heated stories housed fifty American college students, five to a room. It had stood through time on a magically pretty leafy corner, its five chimney pots pointed into the gray overcast sky, its winding cobblestone paths led through overgrown gardens protected within a low pink-brick wall.

Soho, in contrast, was in the thronging heart of old London, and by day it seemed almost quaint, if grimy—a miniature town with rain-slick, gleaming, narrow streets and dark, dingy alleys. Soho at night seemed a world away from Peacehostel, which was like a haven, day or night.

Taking a late Tube to Soho, Nick—at the tender age of twenty-one—thought more than once of returning to the safety of the hostel. His heart raced the whole way.

Only a few weeks before, he'd seen Peacehostel for the first time. His new temporary home, once stately, now decayed, stood humbly on its street of aged grand homes, dusted with sparkling January snow. Two college professors from the University of Wisconsin at Stevens Falls served as visiting chaperones for the "semester abroad" study group: timid, bespectacled Mr. Collins and rotund Mrs. Frederick, both in their late fifties. The live-in manager of the house was a kindly Londoner called Raymund, originally from Nepal.

Ray had early on warned the assembled semester-abroad students to stay away from Soho, especially at night. "They will kill you for ten pence in that den of thieves," he told them in his charming accented English. The snickers in the room suggested something else. Soho was a notorious sex district, filled with strip clubs, live sex shows, and attractions for every and all proclivities.

Young Nick Davangere (that final E still firmly in place) was intrigued. And so he soon decided to do something about it.

Now, less than a month since his January arrival in London, Nick prepared to take the stage at one of Soho's most notorious gay fleshpot bars, a place called Sodom X. From the gloomy hallway behind the stage, Nick could hear the thumping disco music and smell cigarette smoke and beer.

His heart had pounded on his journey all the way over to the narrow, neon-lit streets where strip clubs and leather fetish shops were crammed side by side, signs glittering and flashing and blinking in lurid colors, one after the other.

The signs said things like "Nonstop Erotic Cabaret," which happened to be the name of a hot new album by a group called Soft Cell. The song "Tainted Love" was everywhere that winter.

In every window were lurid nude photos, mostly of women. But here and there were the gay "cabarets," porn shops, and film houses.

A big sign said "Dirty Pictures," and below it was a young white man with blue eyes with dark circles beneath them; he was nude, holding his hard dick and leering into the camera. The dick was barely blacked out with a censor bar.

The human body, Nick knew, was not a dirty or tawdry thing, or a piece of meat. Or a piece of merchandise. And yet here, a kind of alluring darkness spiced the sensation of illicit desires. Sin was in the air. The body on display, exhibited, lusted over, exposed, given and taken, bought and sold—the feeling was intoxicating.

Right now, standing backstage, Nick felt like a ballsy kid, ready to be bad. The twinges of guilt he felt added a weird spice to his erotic thrill. This was not something he would ever do back home in America.

This was an exploration of his own body, and male bodies were his chief interest, whether in the high realms of classical art so abundant in London or in a low fleshpot like this, where his penis strained and ached with desire.

The body, sacred. The body, profane.

In his art history course at a famous museum near Pimlico Station, Nick had gained a deepening appreciation of the naked human form as an artistic image from antiquity onward.

Whereas in America naked images seemed the reserve of the female form almost exclusively, here, male images were everywhere.

All you had to do was look at photos of the David or all the endless depictions of Saint Sebastian, naked, tied to a tree, and bleeding from the arrows stuck into his martyred flesh.

But here in Soho, at night, the flesh was real and hot as hell.

Nick had always felt horny about acts of naked exhibitionism. He was a long way from his rural Wisconsin home, and his sexual experience was limited. But he loved being naked. An incident when he was about thirteen, skinny-dipping with an older neighbor boy and then running free through pine woods with him, had given him an incredible, indelible thrill.

That love of nudity had never left him.

He fantasized about nudism and read about nudist camps where everything was on constant display. He didn't quite believe it when he'd read that such nudity was not considered to be sexualized. He was certain if he were to visit one of those places, he'd have a raging hard-on the whole time. Of course, he'd yet to see those famous Diane Arbus photos of drab middle-aged nudist couples sagging on their boring sofas in the plain rooms of rural cabins.

The nudist "camp" he fantasized about was full of handsome bucks like the guys on his softball team and the wrestlers back at college, as well as older guys who kept in shape. Coach types and military types.

Back at UW-Stevens Falls, he'd enjoyed the anonymity of the open "gang" showers at the big gymnasium. Guys who walked around the locker room nude were a common and exciting sight. Nick liked showing himself in the communal shower, and he loved it when he could feel eyes moving surreptitiously over his muscles and his most private parts.

But a shower was not a transgressive place in which to be naked. It sure wouldn't be a great place to sport a hard-on. The excitement of commercial exhibitionism meant taking such exposure to a higher level—or maybe a lower one? Nick had never been interested in "flashing," that is, showing himself to an unwilling or unsuspecting person. He liked the equation of eager voyeur and turned-on exhibitionist. And now he had found the place to bring this fantasy to life, along with the opportunity of relative anonymity.

It was a risky, daring shot at fulfilling a longstanding fantasy thrill of his.

One of his favorite masturbatory fantasies was of being naked in front of a crowd of horny onlookers. He'd imagined himself jerking off, being watched, being wanted.

The act itself would be satisfying to him, he believed. Because it was bad, it was nasty, and it was wrong. But it was tied up with another desire, a deeper one, maybe. The desire to be celebrated, to be a kind of iconic image or a star, even if a naked one. It played into other ambitions he'd nurtured in secret.

Maybe, he thought, absently touching his penis, that was the key to all of it—a desire to be a star, looked at, wondered about. Loved. But by total strangers.

He played around with fantasies of being a rock star in a band like The Cars or maybe even an edgier group like The Clash or U2. But rock-star fantasies were pretty standard, he decided. Were stripper fantasies like that? Or even porn-model fantasies?

But Nick's dream life didn't end there.

Maybe he'd be a famous writer like Stephen King. Or a movie star. Or a painter like Andy Warhol.

He just had to be *something*!

And he held on to that unlikely fantasy of being "discovered." Walking around the snowy streets of London in February, hearing "Tainted Love" everywhere he went, and "Don't You Want Me," he imagined himself being approached by a talent scout.

It was a silly sort of daydream, he knew.

But some daydreams you could make real.

This night, backstage in Soho, *was real*.

He was about to make a dream come true, even if it was in utter secret. Even if it was dirty. Even if it was reckless and wild.

The music blasted. The spotlights spun around behind the curtain. Nick folded his pants and shirt, then set them on a rusty metal folding chair. He pulled his socks off. The cold floor felt gritty under his bare feet. On second thought, he put his socks and shoes back on.

These were the heart-pounding moments before you go out on stage for the first time to dance stark naked before lusting strangers.

And show them everything.

THE music faded, and a sweating, glittery, young nude blond guy in white sneakers exited the shadowy stage across from Nick. Nick couldn't see him clearly with the stage lights turned down.

The guy looked just average, as far as Nick could tell, and a bit on the skinny side. Nick knew that he looked pretty good in comparison. Probably not what the audience at this place was used to seeing or what they were expecting. Nick was fit and athletic. He had natural muscle tone, smooth jutting pectorals, long sturdy biceps, and a compact round bottom. His legs were long and beautifully formed. Nick was not especially vain, though, and was more likely to consider with shyness the zits (or "spots" as the English called them) and other perceived flaws on his skin than he was his classically handsome, sexy form. In the looks department, Nick could stop traffic even fully dressed. Now he just needed to convince himself to "become" that confident, cocky young man who could actually carry off an act of pure sexual exposure.

Inside, he felt nervous as hell. Sexual tension mingled with stage fright as he thrilled to the boldness and risk of what he was about to do.

Just remember, he told himself as beads of sweat trickled down his bare sides, this is a performance, an *act*. So be an actor. And get off on it!

He'd sort of changed into this wild man he was creating for the stage, at least physically.

He had already had the tips of his wavy brown hair bleached a punkish peroxide blond, and the sides and back buzzed. At the Vidal Sassoon salon, you could get your hair cut for free by student apprentices. He'd gone in a day before and selected the wavy, spiky cut he felt would look good in the rock clubs he'd been checking out with a couple of fellow students. These new friends from Peacehostel were heavily into punk music, which Nick liked. But the new electronic dance sound of Human League and especially Soft Cell really intrigued him too.

The hair-stylist students at Sassoon were all Asians, but their supervisor was a squat English "poofter" type with lavender-streaked brown hair. It was his idea to give Nick that spiky blond color.

The instructor, called Alistair, seemed to like Nick.

Alistair was funny, though not sexually attractive to Nick. Yet Nick was flattered to have a potential English friend.

Alistair took Nick to a pub afterward, and they had a few pints together. Then, on another outing, Alistair paid for Nick to get a gold earring in his left earlobe. Nick had declined the offer several times, not wanting to lead Alistair on. Yet Alistair insisted, and also insisted they were just friends and it gave him pleasure to purchase a little "bauble." Alistair had an ulterior motive that was completely obvious to Nick.

Finally one night after having a bit too much ale, Alistair propositioned Nick.

"Who says I sleep with boys?" Nick said at the Tube station at Piccadilly.

"Who says you don't, is more like it," Alistair said tartly. "You ought to see my flat in Chelsea. It's not too late to change your mind."

Nick shook his head.

"Thanks for the pints," Nick said.

"You think you can do better than me?" Alistair hissed. "You talk a good game, but I think I see a little *wog* behind that all-American smile."

Nick's eyes narrowed. He was a lot bigger than Alistair. And although he didn't know what a "wog" was, he felt like giving Alistair a hard shove.

"You want some money?" Nick asked. "I didn't ask for this earring, you know."

"You accepted it," Alistair replied coldly. "You're either very stupid or very venal. I think it's both."

Nick felt ashamed and angry. And also aggressive. He simply reacted before he really thought about what he was about to say.

"Yeah, well, fuck you Alistair, you little cocksucker!" Nick shouted. As he turned down the stairs toward the Tube platform, he heard Alistair cackling.

"Now *that's* calling the kettle *black*," he said, laughing.

Nick felt insulted, but he wasn't completely sure why. He had not accepted himself as gay yet. It shocked him to hear it verbalized—much less hurled back at him as an insult. He knew he liked men's bodies, and he had fallen hard for his roommate back in his freshman year in college, more than three years ago. But he liked girls too, didn't he? And they liked him. So what difference did it make if he liked to experiment with his sexuality?

This was London.

It was time to try everything.

And here he was, doing just that. The hard-faced manager of Sodom X gave Nick his cue to take the stage.

THE music pounded.

"You're on, big boy," said the manager, a tiny man behind his sunglasses and thick black moustache. Nick's "boss," he supposed. He'd answered the phone when Nick had called, responding to an advert in one of the gay papers. The "audition" and the performance—tonight—were one and the same. Though at Nick's "interview," the manager, called Monty, had asked Nick to pull his pants down completely, when he'd arrived for "work." Apparently Nick had more than passed muster. At least as far as Monty was concerned.

Now Nick was about to get his first chance to strip for pay

To the familiar opening strains of "Don't You Want Me," Nick walked out into the purple spotlight. The black stage was tiny, beat-up, and strewn with bits of glitter and fraying bits of tape. Beyond the purple-and-red lights bathing him, he could sense a crowd of at least fifty people in the shadowy club. Some were propped on stools at a bar. Others sat alone at tiny tables where red candles glowed and flickered like outer planets. Faces were dimly lit or nearly black in the shadows and clouds of drifting smoke. It seemed, naturally, that all the patrons were men.

He wore nothing but white Fruit of the Loom briefs, white socks, and his "trainers," that funny English word for what Americans like Nick called tennis shoes or sneakers.

Nick felt sweat trickling down his sides from his armpits. He'd wondered if stage fright would actually end up making the experience a turn-off, and perhaps shrivel him up.

Instead, the feeling was even headier than he'd imagined in his dirtiest fantasies of exhibitionism. His cock grew hard and strained against the front of his briefs. Spit thickened in his mouth. This was going to be a wild and dirty thrill. The shabbiness of the place added to his sense of the forbidden.

Nick danced, thrusting his hips, turning, bending, playing with the elastic band of his briefs.

Wanting to be fully naked, he kicked off his shoes, which had been loosely tied for that purpose. He rolled onto his back, feeling the grit and dirt of the stage floor against his hot bare back. He peeled off his socks. The music thumped loudly. He jumped back up.

At the edge of the stage, he leaned out, shook his head, sending some sweat flying. With his back to the stage, he slowly peeled down his briefs, showing his well-formed bare ass. He stood up ramrod straight and let the briefs slip down to his ankles.

Then he stepped out of them. The music was almost deafeningly loud. The beat moved right through him.

His heart pounded wildly. Totally nude, he felt intensely excited. He loved what he thought of as the sheer *badness* of what he was doing, the dirtiness, the delicious shamefulness. He turned and shook his pelvis so his rock-hard dick bounced against his belly.

He gripped his thick cock, which glistened with precome. He knew if he wasn't careful he'd reach his climax, which he didn't want to do onstage. He heard what he thought were some appreciative grunts coming from the audience. Some coins jangled to the stage at his feet. He saw pound notes being waved by furtive hands. Five quid. Ten.

When he bent forward to take the money, hairy hands moved over and up his thighs.

The eyes he looked into were avid, serious, burning with lust.

He turned and bent and spread his buttocks for them, giving the "wink shot" that in its way was the completion of his act of sexual self-exposure. The music reached its end. Sweat was pouring off his head. He didn't want this to end. He loved this.

But then the house lights came up harshly. There was a smattering of applause. He looked out over the crowd of men, all of them middle-aged, in all sizes and shapes.

"Okay, green eyes," the little manager called from the wings. "Exit stage left. Your number is over."

In this light, Nick felt even more exposed. And he liked it. He bent and picked up his underwear and shoes and socks as men whistled. He gathered his tips from the grimy floor of the stage. Along with the wages he'd been promised, this was a sizable sum, at least for a poor college student who had "worked" for about five minutes total. Tonight, he had just this one number. If he decided to do this again, he could do several in a night.

He walked backstage, where it was darker. In a corner, he set his shoes and underwear on the shabby wooden chair where his clothes were neatly folded. Sweat was pouring off him. He stepped into the dark cubbyhole that was the WC, or toilet, and closed the door. He breathed heavily in the darkness. Grabbing his dick, he came in three strokes. He had a powerful orgasm that left him gasping.

Nick came out of the squalid toilet with sweat dripping from his hair and face. Another male dancer, this one another bottle blond in leather hot pants, brushed past, carefully stepping around Nick.

"You're a right healthy squirt," Monty said to Nick. For the first time in Nick's presence, the club manager grinned, showing brown bad teeth. "I'll give you a featured spot next Saturday." He handed Nick a twenty-pound note. "I have some other ideas for you as well. Photographer for one of the wanker mags will be 'round, and that pays decent. Fifty quid. I get a little percentage of that, and the photo goes in my playbill. What say you?"

Nick finished dressing, donning his thin parka and cap.

"Pictures," Nick said. "I don't know."

"Nobody sees 'em but old wankers, same as just took a long gander at your bollocks just now. You leave at least your socks on next time so they have a place to tuck their notes."

"I need to think about whether there's gonna be a next time, much less posing for nude pictures," Nick said softly.

In truth, the idea excited Nick. It would be sexy to show his bare ass, and more, in a magazine. Total strangers would see it… they'd thrill over his image, he knew. He understood that to be the case with such pictorials because he had worked up the nerve back at Stevens Falls to purchase a copy of the one gay skin mag sold at the college bookstore. It was called *Roughboy*. Purchasing it in public had seemed an extravagantly expensive—at nearly four dollars—and risky proposition. But he found he couldn't resist. So, in sunglasses and a baseball cap, he'd mildly shocked the older silver-haired matron who rang up his purchase. That well-hidden, well-used magazine was the only one of its kind he owned. And before his semester abroad in London, which had cost every penny he'd earned plus an additional student loan, he'd burned the copy.

But he'd jerked off dozens of times looking at the hairy, muscular nude men posing in color spreads, and in two black-and-white spreads.

Those anonymous guys were as familiar to him as any movie star he'd obsessed over. He found the poses they struck to be almost comical, certainly undignified, shameless and dirty. Yet it turned him on to think guys could be so brazen, showing themselves naked like that. He wasn't the only one who had a thing about going bare-ass for kicks.

And maybe for a little money too.

In the end, he'd tired of the models in that magazine. Tossing those images into the flames with notebooks and drawings he'd made for the school paper and other stuff he couldn't travel with, left him feeling weirdly weightless. Like he'd destroyed some evidence but also gotten rid of some shame.

Nick had never been completely satisfied with his own drawings, which tended toward the comic style he'd been raised on with his beloved *MAD* magazine and Batman comics. Even when he was made graphics editor of the student newspaper, the *Punter,* he doubted his own skills. His fantasy of becoming a great artist or a top cartoonist was quite a ways down the priority ladder of his fame-inspired daydreams. The stage or screen seemed so much more pleasing to him. On days when he felt he was really lowering his expectations, he thought he might settle for being a poet or photographer. How hard could that be?

Nick had talents, just like many young people did. And like the talented writers he knew on the newspaper, and the few skilled cartoonists, and the kids in art classes who really took their own work seriously, he was still trying to figure which of his talents to focus on.

Nick could play the guitar competently and sing fairly well. His cartoons and graphic work on the school paper were considered quite a bit better than average. The essays he'd written in a fairly demanding English course the previous semester had all been awarded As.

He also had athletic abilities. He had been recruited to play first base for the university baseball team his freshman year, though he didn't return to it his second year, deciding instead to concentrate on art, music, and writing. The practice for baseball had gotten too time-consuming, and he'd never felt really accepted by his teammates, all of whom were lily white and all of whom seemed to be straight.

Nick had talent, after a fashion. But he did not have focus. Now, on this adventure abroad, he didn't think it much mattered where his true talents lay. What mattered was his drive and his determination to succeed, to be some kind of star, and to let his fantasies loose.

That would take risks and guts (and much else). But now, zipping up his parka and putting his wages into his wallet, he decided he had, in a way, just displayed not only to an aroused and interested audience, but to himself, that he was just such a risk taker. In a funny way, he'd crossed a hurdle, he told himself.

He knew he was off to a wild start.

"I'll see you Saturday," Nick said, and he went out into the blustery night through the back "stage door." Monty followed with a smelly cigarette.

"There are gentlemen out front at the bar who'd be only too happy to get you a drink, Nick," Monty said. "They could take good care of you."

Nick shook his head.

"Not tonight."

With the little newly acquired money he'd just earned, he treated himself to a taxi home to Peacehostel in Hammersmith. The last Tube had run at midnight. That was more than two hours ago.

THE morning after his stage debut at Sodom X, Nick overslept in his freezing attic room at Peacehostel. He barely made it to the Pimlico Trident Gallery in time for his art history class.

The streets were slick with a fine dusting of hoarfrost, and Nick slid all the way along the Thames River walk in his beat-up sneakers, his red scarf trailing behind him in the wind. The fairy lights of Christmastime still twinkled in some of the shop windows and in some of the bare old trees that lined the London streets.

He felt happy this morning, remembering the previous night. London—old, merry, big, and dirty—felt like a fairy-tale city to him. And now he had a secret—and a secret life in this city. It made him feel horny all over again.

He rushed through the museum's high-ceilinged halls to his classroom.

The instructor, a dignified, quiet and buttoned-up English gentleman past sixty, Trevor Shannon, held his class in a basement room one day a week. Mr. Shannon was Nick's favorite instructor. The older gentleman was kindly, full of good humor, and incredibly knowledgeable about art. He gave fascinating lectures on the "psychosexual subtext" of the wonderful paintings he showed on his slide projector.

Nick barreled into his chair next to curly-haired Karl and one of his other favorite housemates, Roy. Both Karl and Roy lived at Peacehostel, across the hall from the cramped room Nick shared with three other guys who also took this special class set up by the semester-abroad program.

Nick's housemates eyed him a little suspiciously, probably wondering where he'd been the previous night. Everyone in the house was a stranger only a month ago. Fast friendships were fragile, Nick knew, but they seemed to be coming into bloom.

Mr. Shannon had gotten into the habit of making small talk before he began his lectures. Each presentation was concluded with a tour upstairs, focusing on a few of the paintings discussed in his lesson.

"I see you Yanks in sweatshirts heralding all of our fine institutions you've visited as tourists," Mr. Shannon said to the room in his upper-class intonations. He had a pleasant, broad face, silver mustache, tweed coat, and tie. "I spy Oxford, Cambridge, even Glasgow. Young Nick here seems to be the only sporting fellow of the bunch." Nick wore a hooded sweatshirt emblazoned with the name of his school—UW-Stevens Falls.

Nick smiled at being singled out by this distinguished teacher.

Today's lecture was deceptively simple: all about "looking" and about "seeing."

Simple words. The concepts were more complicated in Trevor Shannon's poetic explication. Or maybe the whole thing was so simple it seemed mysteriously elusive. The subject seemed apt to Nick, who wished to see—and be seen.

With his sexy secret glowing inside, he felt as relaxed as he'd ever been before in his life. His mind was keen, and he let the fascinating talk by Mr. Shannon wash over him like a tonic.

After the lecture, which ended with a story about the dreams of Salvador Dali, the class trooped upstairs to see an actual Dali painting. After that, the students were free to roam the galleries independently to look at some pictures. To "look" and to "see."

Nick was always taken by the works of David Hockney and Francis Bacon. Standing before one of the Hockney paintings, a sort of semiabstract, colorful splash of Los Angeles brilliance and sunshine, Nick couldn't imagine a scene that felt more removed from cold, gray, but oddly romantic London in winter. Trevor Shannon stepped close to Nick.

"A man taking a shower," Shannon said. "Not a bad choice of subject, hmm?" he asked. The older man's eyes twinkled.

Nick wasn't sure if Mr. Shannon was flirting or merely making an observation.

"I'd love to own a painting like this someday," Nick blurted.

"Perhaps you will be so wildly rich to do so," Mr. Shannon said.

It was a moment Nick committed to memory forever. For one day, he would own two Hockneys. He had a taste for contemporary art he would always source to this day, this moment. He would also end up the owner of a huge piece by the English artists Gilbert and George (called a "sculpture," it more aptly resembled to Nick a two-dimensional photo-collage, in greens and red with black borders like stained glass). Nick's favorite painter of all time was someone whose name he would not learn for several more years: Jean-Michel Basquiat.

Nick's collection had begun, if only in his fevered mind.

Today, Nick was just a greenhorn student of fine art, standing in one of the most vibrant galleries in the world beside an eminent art historian who seemed to be taking an interest in him.

"I hope you won't mind my saying this, Nick, but you strike me as worthy subject matter for a great artist yourself, or any appreciator of beauty. You're a diamond in the rough."

Nick felt blood rushing into his face. He grinned sheepishly. Sometimes, he knew he was growing into that beauty others seemed to appreciate. Yet he also knew he had the remnants of some acne. His clothes were shabby, college-sloppy, his posture rather lazy. And now his hair was a deliberate mess of blond spikes and wavy black roots. Sure, men would pay to see him dance naked. But to be told he was worthy of a painting, now that seemed a stretch to Nick.

He smiled, and he saw Trevor gazing into his eyes.

"The most striking green," Trevor Shannon muttered. "Yes, I recognize you."

"What?" Nick asked, confused.

"I was in the audience last night when you danced at Sodom X," Trevor Shannon said softly. "I'd have recognized those emerald eyes anywhere. They shine like the finest gems, even in those tawdry lights."

Nick was speechless.

"Are you sure you know what you're getting yourself into in places like that?" Trevor asked. There was genuine concern in his warm old eyes.

Nick shook his head. He didn't have the nerve to ask what a gentleman and scholar like Mr. Shannon would be getting up to in such a seedy club.

"I needed a little money," Nick said. Which, while true, didn't come close to his actual motivation.

"Certainly there are other places in which to make some cash and discover who you really are," Trevor said softly. "That peroxide blond in your hair… it hardly suits you. I can't be the first person to wonder just who exactly it is hiding behind that rocker façade."

"It's just hair," Nick said shyly.

"Strikes me as a bit of a disguise. But if you wish to show off, as you did last night, perhaps that's wise. Try out being somebody else before you show the world the real Nick. At any rate, I trust I could introduce you to a better class of aficionados of the male form, Nick. As an erotic dancer, you're impressive. As a model for some rather heady artists, you'd be paid perhaps a little better, and meet a finer class of person. And in a much safer environment."

"You want to paint my picture?" Nick asked.

"Not I. I'm not a painter. But I have someone in mind. There are several people you ought to meet, in fact. I have tickets to the ballet on Sunday afternoon. Would you join me? A little dinner afterward, to meet some new friends?"

Nick smiled shyly.

"My intentions are honorable," Trevor Shannon said with a smile. "I happen to be fond of you. I think you're something special. I'd like to give you a leg up, as it were, in this cold, harsh world. Let's just say I let someone down once, a long time ago, someone you remind me of. I'd like to make some amends before I die. Think it over and call me."

THAT night Nick went with Roy and Karl and another housemate, a young woman named Candy, to the Hammersmith Palais to see The

Go-Go's, a new girl group from California. The room was grand and packed with young people. Nick was excited to be at a concert and out on the town with his two favorite guys.

The music was pleasant enough, Nick thought. Pop without a punk edge, though. Nick liked something with more rawness. Still, The Go-Go's tunes were melodic, good-humored, and it was impossible for Nick not to slightly envy their stage coolness. He could easily imagine himself singing and playing guitar on that stage to a screaming audience. But how the hell could he make that happen?

He had a couple of pints of lager and felt good. As he started to relax, he looked around the crowded venue.

Despite all the spiky Mohawks one saw everywhere in London that winter, which Nick associated with the English punk rock he had come to love, the media—hosts of such popular British TV shows as *Top of the Pops* and *The Old Grey Whistle Test*, as well as writers in *NME* and other music mags, and the hip events weekly called *Time Out*—were all constantly declaring that punk was dead.

Maybe in London. As far as Nick knew, it was alive and well in the States. Nick liked California groups like X, and of course New York outfits like the Ramones and Blondie—groups that seemed to come into their own in the early eighties.

The music that had inspired him most as a kid—The Jackson Five, Diana Ross and the Supremes, and Stevie Wonder—all seemed like a thing of the past to him now. Even if he secretly craved it. Even if Michael Jackson's music on *Off The Wall* sounded revelatory to him. In Stevens Falls, people enthusiastically joined in the chanting of "Disco Sucks," and they simply lumped black music in with anything with a strong dance beat.

Nick could sense more than a little hint of racism and homophobia in that "disco sucks" routine.

Nick, passing as white (or as white as he could manage), had wanted to fit in to the point that he embraced this dubious attitude about music. His best friends were hard-rock fans. And if joining them in this exclusionary taste meant some self-loathing on his part…. Nick knew all too well how to bury his feelings.

By this time, he was already like an actor playing a part. The guy with the "tan," handsome face, twinkling green eyes, and athletic body—that's just good old Nick; he's all right. His shyness only made him more appealing to some. And sometimes a target for others.

The Peacehostel students, all white save for one Asian girl, seemed to be rock and rollers. But they'd accepted him, hadn't they? He wanted to keep it that way.

After the Go-Go's show, one of his housemates, Candy, wanted to go to a pub there in Hammersmith, within walking distance of Peacehostel. She stood on the corner outside the Palais, smoking a cigarette and dabbing at her sweat-smeared mascara with the heel of her hand.

Nick wanted to go into central London and try to get into the club called Xenon, not hang out in Hammersmith. On this particular night of the week, the dress code at Xenon was supposed to be relaxed, according to the events magazine *Time Out*. "Casual but smart," read the listing in the mag that was read by everyone in the house each week, passing through so many hands it usually ended up in rags.

Roy, who had a thing for Candy, agreed to go to the pub with her. But Nick stood his ground. Candy, who wore blonde bangs above clunky glasses that somewhat obscured her pretty, doll-like face, was clearly disappointed Nick would not be joining them.

He knew she liked him. They'd recently gone to Canterbury by bus together on a sightseeing weekend. Possibly the most boring weekend Nick had ever experienced. Walking around the slushy streets past shops that were almost all closed for the weekend (this being low season), they did little more than walk around the Cathedral and bide their time. They stayed in a small room in a B and B. The room had two small twin beds, and in the morning, Candy informed Nick that he snored.

He'd never joined her in her bed. The conversation had never even veered in the direction of such an encounter, despite the sexual tension in the room, almost all of it coming from Candy.

When they returned from Canterbury to Peacehostel, the conventional wisdom around the house had it, mistakenly, that the two had made it. Nick didn't respond to the whispers, just let them be. He found new respect among the guys, even rough and tumble Karl, whose curly head Nick had more than once found himself daydreaming about. Roy, a somewhat short boy with a powerful wrestler's compact body, was too much of a nice lug from a hick rural Wisconsin town to show any outward jealousy toward Nick over Candy. He kept his hopes up, though, where Candy was concerned.

Karl showed little interest in women, though he seemed and acted straight enough—but so did Nick. Karl, good-looking as he was, was a major subject of interest among the girls at Peacehostel. Nick was perhaps too exotic to them, at least at first. But now that Nick and Karl had palled around a bit, they were both seen as attractive and maybe a little bit unattainable, if not snobby. That added a little something to their cache.

Nick had little interest in girls at this time in his life. That interest had ended when he'd fallen in love with his male roommate back in Wisconsin. Nick figured his fate was sealed by then. The roommate, Casey, had become an unattainable enigma. Casey, a dark-haired, Italian-featured little muscle number had captivated Nick so badly it still hurt him when he thought about it. Nick carried his broken heart to London, determined to get over Casey—and get the kind of experience he had so far only dreamed about.

Karl was beginning to feel like more than just a friend.

"Well, see you later," Candy said, walking off. Roy trailed behind her. He turned and grinned and gave a thumbs-up.

"I'd like to see this club you mentioned," Karl said, showing his white teeth and dazzling smile. "Xenon?"

"Let's give it a try," Nick replied confidently. He felt warm despite the damp winter bite of the night air.

Nick liked Karl. On the Tube to central London, they laughed and talked as if they'd known each other a lot longer than a mere month. But in that month, they'd gone from the greenest of young American innocents to the kind of quick learners who read maps expertly, gained their bearings fast, hitchhiked across the countryside, and generally got around anywhere they liked, fearlessly.

They looked pretty cool together walking down High Street.

Nick smiled, thinking of his big secret. Karl would, of course, have no idea Nick was thinking sexual thoughts about him. And if Karl had any idea where Nick had been last night and what he'd done.... It was unimaginable.

At Xenon, Nick and Karl met with disappointment. Nick might have thought of the pair of them as the hottest two guys on the Piccadilly line, but the doorman was not impressed. A tall black man with an impressive afro, in a uniform, stepped out onto the street. Behind him, through smoky glass doors, a small lobby was bathed in purple light.

"Sorry, gentlemen," the big man said.

"What are you sorry about?" Karl asked cockily.

"No admittance. We have a dress code."

"The dress code is casual tonight," Nick protested.

"Casual but smart," the doorman said.

"This isn't smart?" Nick asked. He showed off his "good" hard sole leather shoes. They had once been his Sunday best, but they seemed woefully inadequate now. At least he was wise to never wear those hated "trainers" the English forbade in so many establishments where Americans were not wanted.

"You're both wearing cords," the doorman said. "No cords."

"Cords are smart, aren't they?" Nick asked. "What's wrong with cords?"

After a few moments of silence, the doorman said, "Good evening, gentlemen."

The towering doorman stood his ground.

Nick and Karl looked at one another with expressions of abject shame. Cords were apparently not "smart" enough. Though it was impossible for Nick not to wonder whether it was them and not their clothing that lacked the necessary cool.

They turned and walked away down the street.

"Fuck that fancy-ass shit," Nick said.

But he was gravely disappointed. He'd wanted to get in so badly. There might be stars and producers and who knew who else in there.

It really hurt to be turned away, and it fed into something deep and painful in Nick's heart, though it shouldn't have. That something was a feeling Nick tried awfully hard to keep icy cold and frozen.

But now the ice cracked. Rejection, even over a silly club, a club in which drinks probably cost ten pounds or more, still hurt too much.

"To hell with it," Karl said. "Let's get a beer."

"Where?" Nick asked.

"Who cares. A pub. Any pub."

They found a modest, welcoming pub with a warm fireplace. They had several pints of lager and plugged coins into a jukebox, selecting nothing but Beatles songs. They recovered their merriment and ended up playing darts, not with English kids, but with a group of students their age from California.

Karl seemed to take an immediate interest in a fair-skinned girl with strawberry-blond hair that was long and parted in the middle. Nick felt some familiar pangs of jealousy, despite himself. And knew he was being silly. He was relieved to learn the California students were only in London for one more night. Then they were off to Paris and the rest of a long, elaborate tour. Clearly the program they were attending was a lot better endowed financially than the bare-bones one Karl and Nick attended.

For a moment, Nick wondered if Karl and the strawberry-blond girl would try to make the most of her last night. But she stuck close by her friends, and when they wanted to leave, she left with them. And left Karl. He didn't really seem to mind.

As the night wore on, Nick learned more about Karl, both from the things he said and from things he didn't say.

Karl's eyelashes were long and black, and his dark eyes sparkled with merriment. When he smiled, dimples formed on his cheeks. Beer made his voice deeper, maybe worsened the congestion he'd complained of earlier in the evening. His mother, he said, was a teacher. His father worked in the construction trade, where Karl spent his summers earning tuition money. The muscles from his labor showed.

They ducked into another pub.

The more Nick drank, the warmer he felt toward Karl. He knew if he didn't watch out, he'd develop a bad crush on him, just like he had on Casey. And that had gone nowhere.

They left the pub in search of a new place that might offer more excitement. Nick was feeling good, but he was already pretty drunk. He knew he'd better slow down. He and Karl bumped into each other several times as they walked and laughed. If they weren't careful, they could end up arm in arm, singing like drunken sailors.

Nick knew they drew some attention on the streets. They made a handsome pair, one dark and smolderingly handsome, the other with skin white as ivory and shining eyes warm and dark as strong coffee.

Vanity? There was power in youth and beauty. For someone who had felt all too powerless, lost, even abandoned, this kind of power felt heady to Nick.

At a large club called "The Venue," they were frisked and metal-detecting wands were waved over them. Inside, Nick got his first glimpse of a glamorously hip rock crowd.

When no girls would dance with them, Nick and Karl took to the dance floor together (or rather by themselves, together). A couple more lagers helped.

At the bar, a stranger spoke to Nick.

"Who are you, mate?" asked a cool-looking beefy guy in dark glasses and a sharkskin jacket. This aggressive guy had an air of stardust about him. He was not handsome; in fact, his curly black hair was receding. But he was an important somebody, powerful and cool. Nick could just tell.

"I'm an American student," Nick answered, with sort of a drunken smile. "Does that mean you're through speaking to me?"

"Not at all," the guy said in a gravelly yet imperial English accent. "I'm Drake." He handed Nick a card. "It's an invitation to a party at a newish club next weekend. You're invited."

Karl tried to stay aloof, but Nick could tell he was listening.

"My friend too?" Nick asked.

Drake looked away.

"Just you, mate," Drake said tersely. "It'll be an awesome time. Never know who you'll meet. You model? Sing?"

Nick shrugged. He looked at Karl. Then he ripped the little card into pieces and let them fall like snow upon the floor at Drake's feet. Nick placed his arm around Karl's shoulder.

"I'm with him," Nick said boldly and turned his back to Drake.

"Pity," Drake said with a laugh that had a bit of sneer in it. "You'd be a hit at my friend's party, but suit yourself." He set his drink down, and Nick saw him cross the dance floor and disappear into the crowd.

"Might be interesting," Karl said.

"Maybe, but he was rude," Nick said.

But he remembered the name of the bar where the party was to be held, a place called Club View. And he remembered the time and date of the party and the address.

But he didn't like "Drake," if that was his real name. There was something creepy about him.

NICK and Karl caught the last Tube home at midnight. The glowing white moon shimmered in the black River Thames. The riverbanks were dusted in a sheen of frost. The twinkling lights of London could not have been more romantic.

In the dimly lit foyer of Peacehostel, they shared a manly hug.

Karl was kind of loaded and so was Nick. Nick felt that this was one of the moments when something might happen. Nick had known several such moments. Maybe too many.

Karl was sexy, masculine, full of good humor. He was definitely the kind of guy Nick would like to get to know a whole lot better. The kind of guy Nick would like to know naked, with their bare chests pressing together in a kiss that never seemed to end.

But Karl was straight, and Nick had vowed not to fall for another straight guy, ever again. Not after Casey.

And yet....

"Wanna watch some TV?" Karl asked, grinning. "I'm hungry. You?"

"Always," Nick said. The house had no kitchen, no fridge to raid. The food was all cooked and served in a separate building, next door, locked up except at mealtimes. Nick was beginning to miss those "American comforts" he'd taken for granted. A fridge full of food whenever you wanted something and all of his favorite records at his fingertips.

There were vending machines in the front hallway at Peacehostel, and Cadbury candy bars were just about the only selection available.

Karl treated.

They sat in the stairwell, munching their chocolate bars.

Nick couldn't help but imagine leaning into Karl's embrace and kissing those wet inviting lips of his.

Nick had kissed two guys before in his life. And gone quite a bit further with one of them. He wouldn't have minded Karl being guy number three.

But… he knew it wasn't going to happen on this night.

Nick simply bucked himself up about it. He was a gentleman. No matter what anybody else thought of him, he was a gentleman.

They both staggered, laughing, up the stairs.

"Well, g'night," Karl said, his eyes dewy.

They hugged.

Nothing happened.

They went off to their separate rooms, where their roommates were already snoring in their beds.

And by the next morning, that seemed all for the best. Nick didn't really need the complications that came with fooling around with a straight guy.

And Karl was straight.

Chapter 4

A WEEK later on a blustery night, in that memorable winter of 1982, before Nick was scheduled to travel to Cornwall by bus with Roy and Candy and Candy's new best friend at Peacehostel, a tall witty girl named Jean, Nick returned to Sodom X.

His heart pounded, just like the previous time.

He took the stage to the pounding beat of U2's "I Will Follow."

Monty had objected to that choice of song at first. Nick insisted it was sexier than the disco numbers Monty wanted to play.

Nick hit the stage in his blue jeans, no shirt, no shoes. As the song pounded, Nick lowered his pants. His hard-on throbbed and strained against his white cotton briefs.

He did a handstand that caused audible gasps from the audience. On his hands, he kicked off his pants and jumped to his feet. Then he pulled his briefs down, springing loose his hard-on.

Spinning around, he peeled down the briefs to his ankles, and then kicked them off.

Nude, he strutted and dipped. He kept his facial expression hard, but once or twice he found it difficult to suppress a grin.

The grin turned into a sexy smile, beamed out to the small crowd behind the hot pink lights.

Whistles and applause erupted.

Nick had drunk one pint of lager before going on stage. He felt good. He felt free. And he had to admit he loved the feeling of being totally naked and exposed.

It was a thrill like no other, a wild turn-on. These strangers loved him, and he gave them their money's worth.

The pound notes fell at his feet. Hands reached up to feel him.

He looked quickly around for familiar faces in the shadowy crowd. If Trevor Shannon was in the audience tonight, Nick couldn't see him.

A hand traveled up Nick's leg, to his ass.

Nick turned and smiled down at a dazzlingly handsome man. Nick's heart fluttered a bit. A handsome gentleman with silver hair returned the smile. The guy looked mature but youthful. He was well dressed, hip, with a trim beard and a sexy gleam in his eye. Nick judged him to be about thirty. What Nick considered an older man. Certainly not a furtive troll of the sort Nick might have cruelly expected in this place. This striking guy would have looked good on stage himself. He had a nice body and emanated strength.

Nick crossed the stage, leaving this admirer and finding others only too happy to hold out their tip money for him to accept with a hug.

When the lights came up slightly, Nick saw that Trevor was seated at a table in the back, near the bar. Nick looked away, pretending not to have seen his professor. But when he looked back, he saw that the handsome man with the well-groomed, longish silver hair was taking a seat beside the distinguished art historian.

Another man sat at the same table too, this one a bit older than Trevor's companion. He had a somewhat comical elfish, yet pleasant, face, and his curls were a mix of salt and pepper. He wore a pale green blazer over a soft lavender vest.

Kind of an odd ensemble, Nick thought. But interesting.

Then a fourth man came to the table and sat with the others. Nick recognized this fellow with a start. It was Drake, the man who had given Nick the invitation to Club View the other night. Nick had not forgotten the discarded invitation. He had also not forgotten his dislike for the hard-faced Drake.

Nick went backstage to a smattering of applause.

"The photographer is upstairs," Monty said, stabbing out a cigarette. "The money is good if you're into it. Solo shots. And by shots, you can right guess what I mean."

Nick smiled, though his heart raced at the thought of posing. Sweat fell from his face and ran down his sides. He wrapped a towel around his waist.

Tonight Nick used the backstage shower stall. Under a cascade of hot water, he thought about the prospect of posing for nude pictures. He knew they would not be "arty" pictures, but decidedly dirty ones.

The idea excited him. It felt risky. But was it stupid to actually be documented naked like that? Stripping in a club was one thing—basically anonymous and fleeting. Pictures could potentially be around forever.

But who would see the shots? Old wankers? And a few young wankers? With his hair cut in this style, with its punky blond highlights, would he even be recognizable?

He knew he'd eventually discard this persona—Nick the amateur, nude stripper/dancer. Discard it as soon as he was finished having fun with it and earning a little extra cash.

The photos would pay decent money and be a kick. Another experience. A decidedly rebellious one.

What could it really hurt? he asked himself. No one would ever know back home in the States. It was "now or never" time, he figured. And he had been holding himself back for an awfully long time. That repressiveness he'd imposed upon himself all through high school and college was getting blown out of the water at last. The photos might not only pay and be fun, they could also be kind of liberating.

He decided to go for it.

NICK dressed after his shower. Then he went up the narrow back stairs to a small room above the Sodom X club. The room was squalid, with ugly gray walls and a rickety single bed shoved up against a gray lace-curtained window. The curtains were shredded at the ends. The bedspread was orange and threadbare. The shag carpet on the floor was lime green, and seemed relatively new and completely revolting.

Through the window curtains, neon blinked and flickered purple and red.

"You must be Nick."

The photographer was a chubby bearded fellow with wide dark eyes and thinning strands of hair over his shiny pate. He was smoking a cigarette. He wore a canvas vest with lots of pockets for lenses and other gear, as if he were shooting for *National Geographic* in the wilds of Africa and not in a seedy bedroom above a sex-show club in Soho.

"Dirk," he said with a cockney inflection, extending his meaty hand. "I usually shoot birds, so don't worry about me thinking dirty thoughts about you." *Birds* was English slang for girls, Nick knew.

"I like girls too," Nick said, somewhat haltingly.

"Well, the blokes that beat off to a magazine called *Manhole* prefer the likes of you, so we both get paid and no harm done."

"Okay, well, let's do it, then," Nick said boldly.

Dirk grinned.

"Lie on the bed with your clothes on for a couple shots."

Nick obeyed.

"Don't smile," Dirk said. "Look hard. Mean. Like you hate me."

That made Nick laugh.

"Why?" Nick asked.

"Because that's what the market demands, mate. Okay, good. Now take off your shirt. Arms, up, let me see your armpits. Not much hair. You African? Part African?"

Nick was a bit stunned, but he simply pouted into the camera.

"I'm American," Nick said defensively.

Dirk said, "Not meaning to be nosy, no offense, just relax. Pants off now. You're a right handsome bloke if I say so *meself.*"

After a few more shots, Nick was completely nude and getting hard.

"Mm, you're really into this, aren't you?" Dirk laughed.

Nick saw Dirk adjusting his pants. A hard-on? Was Dirk getting turned on, despite what he'd said, despite how masculine he was?

"Okay, now up on your knees, arse on your heels," Dirk said. "Stroke it. Good. Now onto your side, leg up." Dirk moved in close between Nick's legs, camera clicking away. "On all fours with your back to me. Spread your legs wider. Wink at me, get it?"

It wasn't Dirk that turned Nick on. It was baring himself this way to the camera. It was crossing some invisible border. It felt powerful. It also felt submissive. Anyone could see his most intimate physical self.

That felt good too! The feeling was too weird to really pinpoint, he thought. But whatever it was, it was also probably tawdry, potentially damaging, sinful, and wrong. *It was a cheap thrill.*

But so what!

Still, there was this frightened-boy feeling in him, welling up. Even at that moment, he had a sickening premonition that somehow this sort of thing could come back to haunt him, somehow.

Someday.

Yeah, Nick thought. But not today….

This is my body! My freedom! I'll do what I damn well please, and if it feels good—and it sure as hell does!—it's my business and no one else's!

"Fuck," he whispered, shutting his eyes tightly.

Nick groaned, stroking himself faster.

"I'm gonna…."

"Go ahead," Dirk said. "Shoot on your belly. Show me the agony and ecstasy, Nick! Really shoot! Show your passion in your eyes and your mouth, in your entire face—good! Let 'em all see you come *hard*, and let me see your soul in those pretty emerald eyes of yours!"

Nick winced. He gasped.

His orgasm began, a burning eruption of ecstasy in the lens of the camera, in the eyes of a stranger. Of hundreds of strangers. Millions. *Billions!*

It felt so good, so free, so bad. Nick felt his dick spasm from the root to the tip, and a first long spurt of thick white semen shot out of him and splashed on his chest, on his left nipple. He squeezed off four more big milky shots onto his chest and belly, and he groaned with pleasure.

Spent, he took a deep breath and smiled lazily into the camera.

"Good," Dirk growled. He was still snapping away, documenting every moment of this most intimate of acts, usually done in utmost secrecy. "Now smear the come over your chest."

Nick almost laughed, but he said, "Okay. Sure."

He rubbed his semen against his skin.

"Lick your fingers," Dirk said.

"What?" Nick said. "I never do that."

"Never tasted come?"

Nick cleared his throat. "I didn't say that," he answered.

"Probably every guy has tasted at least his own come, mate," Dirk said. "You like the taste?"

"Not really," Nick said. "I don't think liking the taste of it is why people... end up with come in their mouths."

"Love's the reason then, eh?" Dirk said and snickered.

"I didn't say that, either," Nick said. "I'm not an expert."

"No one ever jizzed in your mouth?"

Nick shook his head.

"That makes two of us." Dirk winked. "I've certainly unloaded into a few throats in me day. And by the way, there are plenty of people who simply love the taste of come."

"Birds, though, as you call 'em?" Nick asked playfully. "Ladies only?"

Dirk smiled and winked again.

"On the record, of course," Dirk said. "Off... well, let's leave that one be." Dirk looked at his camera. "Done here." He removed the long lens from his 35mm camera and tossed Nick a clean white rag. Nick mopped up his belly.

"*Manhole* pays in cash," Dirk said. "Envelope on bureau drawer as you leave. Oh, and if you want to see the snaps, those sods usually go to press quickly. Find it at your newsagents wherever wanker mags are sold. I'd say they're getting their money's worth for what's in here." He patted his camera bag, then put on his cap, and zipped up his parka. "Wouldn't think they'd place you on the cover, though," Dirk said in a parting shot that Nick found unnecessarily hostile. "You're hot, but some in this business are decidedly racist. With *Manhole* it's always a pure white face."

Dirk left.

Nick was stunned by that remark. But he didn't doubt it was true. Well, if so, he thought, the laugh's on them. I get the money, and my secret is a little safer inside the magazine than it would be on the cover. They can do whatever they damn please with the photos.

Nick found £150 in the envelope. His eyes widened as he counted it up. That seemed like a fortune. On the other hand, he wondered how much *Manhole* magazine would be making off him.

Who cares? Nick didn't know a soul in England who would see it. Other than perhaps the art historian, Trevor Shannon, who would probably be waiting at the newsagent's for his copy, Nick thought lasciviously. Nick smiled.

He wondered if Trevor and his little group waited around to try and visit with him tonight.

No matter.

Nick left the club through a side door and felt the bracing cold of the night against his warm skin.

Instead of hopping on the Tube back to Peacehostel, he rounded the corner and purchased a pair of good leather shoes at his favorite trendy men's leather goods store, one that seemed to stay open round the clock. He ditched the worn "Sunday best" shoes he'd brought from America.

Nick jumped into a cab with a certain destination in mind.

Dressed in jeans, the bright and stylish new shoes, and his usual bland canvas coat and black scarf, Nick entered the recently opened Club View, a place close to the famous Abbey Road Studios. Club View was supposed to be, according to either *Time Out* or *NME* (Nick couldn't remember which), "tragically hip" and "probably not long for the world." But it also was said to be sort of gay and a hip stomping ground for the new wave of Brit rockers, guys who wore eyeliner and furs and played keyboards and synths, not guitars and drums.

"Drake invited me," Nick said. "Lost the invitation, sorry." He shrugged.

The doorman looked him up and down and smiled.

The shoes got Nick past the doorman and security. Or so he figured. But it was more, really, than just the shoes, though they mattered, sadly. Nick exuded confidence and youthful sensuality. With his spiky blond-tipped hairdo and cock-sure attitude, partly a pose and partly an actually relaxed sense of satisfaction, he impressed. He hadn't needed the invitation after all. He was raw, but he knew he had that diamond-in-the-rough quality that people were starting to notice and to wonder about, in places like this.

Who was Nick Davangere? An artist—well, a budding graphic artist and college newspaper cartoonist, but hadn't Andy Warhol himself started out in commercial art for advertising agencies? Or was he a poet? Hadn't he received an A in his poetry workshop? A journalist? A few things published in the *Punter*. Or was he an actor/singer?

The eyes scanning him up and down now might have been wondering about those general categories. The place had a decidedly gay vibe.

Was he a singer in a new band?

He swallowed hard, thinking about the stupid punk band he'd tried to join in college.

He'd never even worked up the nerve to sing and play his guitar at the college coffee shop on open mic night, but his college roommate, Casey, thought he was pretty good. He and Casey Zinder had played guitars together for hours, practicing together in their dorm room. Practicing for an occasion that never seemed to arrive.

He had warm feelings and complicated memories of Casey, who still occupied a large space in Nick's heart despite Nick's best efforts to move on. Nick checked that thought as the glittery scene of Club View shook him from his brief reverie. He had promised himself he wouldn't obsess on Casey anymore. He hadn't touched his guitar in many months before his January departure to London.

But he was thinking about the guitar now.

And an almost palpable sensation moved over his skin, an energy. The words *rock star* seemed to echo through his mind, and he felt transformed for a moment, like he really was acting the part of a star here in Club View. He wasn't the only young person posing like that in this glitzy, disco-beat-laden, purple strobe-light denizen of art and ambition.

But for all anyone really knew, maybe he was actually living this role.

Just a feeling, right? Just, he reminded himself with a tiny smile, a fantasy....

If he had only known his life was about to change forever.

FOR as much as he tried to play it cool, Nick knew he was just a stranger who had walked into Club View by accident. He wanted to belong here but was also afraid he'd be found out at any moment.

For now, Nick was trying to look *and be* cool. It was all about attitude.

He was succeeding.

Club View was by design dimly, atmospherically lit, flashing with strobe lights. A thumping electronic beat no one would deign to call "disco" (though it was) pounded out a tantalizing, enveloping dance rhythm—the English sound of the eighties still in its candy-coated infancy. Disco was dead, just like punk, so it was said almost everywhere. Of course, they would live on for decades, as Nick would find out to his happy surprise. The disco beat at Club View was crackling with life.

The club exuded something more than exclusivity and hip. It had a whiff of wealth, of silk and diamonds. Most of the people inside were white and young, but there were also a few blacks and Asians, some older people seated at the zinc-lined bar. Two exotic and chic Asian girls danced together at the center of the dance floor. A muscle-bound boy with a shaved head collected empty glasses, his bare chest gleaming.

"I hoped you'd come here tonight," said a gentleman with a deep, velvet-smooth voice. "Can I buy you a drink?" Nick turned to see a handsome stranger. A stranger, but one who looked familiar. And definitely a gentleman.

He was the guy who had tipped Nick at Sodom X, the one with the beautiful mane of silver hair and black close-cropped beard, soulful brown eyes, and a kind smile. He looked like a successful guitar player from the kind of progressive rock bands Nick had liked in the seventies in high school and disdained after punk and new wave emerged.

He looked like rock royalty.

He was a friend, or at least tablemate, of Trevor's. Was Trevor here tonight too? Would Trevor even be in a place like this?

Sodom X was, of course, much seedier. But it was secret, a barely public bar.

Club View was über-trendy, the kind of pansexual place that made news in the gossip columns, with paparazzi photos of glazed-eyed celebrities.

Or if Club View was still new and still under the radar, it felt to Nick like it was a mere five minutes away from that kind of notoriety. You could feel it crackling in the air. Nick could, anyway. Even if he was just a kid from Wisconsin and his main experience was apprentice-level writing and designing for a tiny college newspaper, he knew he'd crossed into a new land.

"I'm good," Nick said.

"Huh?" the guy said, holding out his hand. "I'm Rusty Maraba, and was that a yes or no on a drink?" He grinned.

Rusty had a warm English accent. Posh but not arrogant.

Across the room, Nick saw the guy who had given him the invitation. Drake.

Drake wore his shades even in this dark bar. He was talking with the muscular, shirtless boy. Pressing something into the boy's hand that didn't look like a coin or a bill.

"We seem to have some acquaintances in common," Nick said. "And yes, on second thought, I'll have a gin and tonic."

Rusty looked across the crowed room.

"Ah, you mean Drake. A music act promoter, quite successful. He gets around."

"So do you," Nick said.

"Only recently," Rusty said and smiled a little bit sadly. "I'm making up for some lost time." Nick, while about fourteen years younger than Rusty, could relate to that. He felt himself warming up to Rusty but only a little. It was so obvious Rusty was interested in him sexually. Well, he'd seen Nick's bare ass at Sodom X, and he'd already copped a feel.

"I know Trevor Shannon too," Nick said. "He's one of my teachers."

"And a dear friend of mine, I'm happy to say. He told me your name is Nick. May I call you Nick?"

Nick felt blood rushing to his face along with a wave of self-consciousness.

Nick nodded. "Everyone else does," he said and grinned.

"It must be tremendously liberating to go naked on that stage, as you did this evening," Rusty said. "Not to mention erotic." Rusty signaled the bartender and ordered cocktails.

"Glad you liked it," Nick said. "It's just something I'm trying out."

Rusty nodded, handing Nick his drink. "I'm trying out things too. Things I should have tried out long ago."

Nick took it Rusty, who seemed straight, was a married man. Perhaps he was slumming a bit in the gay world, taking that proverbial walk on the wild side. That didn't impress Nick.

"I'm not into older guys," Nick said flatly. Cruelly. He instantly wondered why he'd sought to wound Rusty, even if only slightly. What had Rusty done but express some interest in him? Nick wondered if Rusty thought he was available, a whore.

Nick had not tried hustling, but he was damn close to it. Wouldn't it add to his stock of experience to let Rusty suck him for a few pounds? Rusty was well-built and sexy. Would it be that bad? Moreover, it would be more cash. And in its own way, another sexual adventure. That was the journey he was taking this semester, wasn't it? Something he'd wanted to get out of his system.

"I apologize for being ancient," Rusty said. "I'm practically thirty-five."

Nick nodded. "I didn't mean it the way it came out."

"You might have, but I'm glad you changed your mind," Rusty said. "Because I genuinely like you."

How could he like Nick, Nick wondered. He didn't even know him.

But it felt real.

What was more, Nick liked Rusty. Something was happening between them, and it was happening fast.

Too fast.

"Thanks for the drink," Nick said, clinking his glass against Rusty's. "Maybe I'll see you around."

Rusty looked at him meaningfully.

"I'd like that," Rusty said.

Nick left Rusty's warm presence and engaging smile and walked around the crowded club by himself. He hadn't meant to be so rude. But Rusty was overwhelming. Nick needed to breathe. The drink was going to his head, and he felt the weight of the long day and longer night starting to drag him down.

He saw Drake from across the bar. He could feel Drake looking at him, even through those dark lenses. Nick looked in the opposite direction.

Nick avoided Drake. He went to the second level of the club and watched the dancers from a railing above the floor beside a massive DJ booth. There were three DJs at work, hot young guys, all of them wearing headphones. All cool as could be.

This was *the place*, Nick thought. Feeling kind of tired.

The place for... what?

He drank up and left.

THE next morning after his art history lecture, Nick waited to speak to Trevor Shannon as the rest of the class milled about. Roy and Candy and Jean had their backpacks stuffed and ready to travel (as did he), and they were eager to catch the bus for their weekend trip. They waited for him in the hall. It was cold and raining, but the Cornish coast beckoned, even if it was off-season.

"I'll only be a second," he told them.

"I met Rusty Maraba last night," Nick told Trevor when they were alone. "Is he one of your artist friends?"

"An appreciator," Trevor answered with a wry grin. He wore his frameless spectacles and paged through ragged papers handed in by his students. "Actually, he's a record producer."

"And Drake?"

"Him? A pop music promoter. He's ubiquitous. That means he's bloody everywhere."

"I know what it means," Nick said.

Trevor set the papers down hard on the oak table before him. He pulled off his spectacles.

"You have such a damn heavy chip on your shoulder, Nick," Trevor said testily. "So easily offended, so suspicious. It fascinates me, really. You want to literally expose yourself, but you think you're doing it anonymously, in private. Protected by some kind of impenetrable armor. You're secretive, Nick. What is it you're hiding?"

Nick felt stung by this rebuke.

"You think I'm a hustler?" he asked quietly. "Is that why you bring men like Rusty and Drake to see me?"

"Nothing of the sort," Trevor huffed. "It should be perfectly obvious why men wish to see you."

"He's married and in the closet?"

"Divorced and slowly emerging. Are you just a wee bit judgmental, Mr. Davangere? And no, I don't think you're a whore. I think you're experimenting, dangerously. But perhaps profitably. You're a risk-taker. I dare say I think you might be something even *more* interesting someday, maybe even a kind of artist in your own right. Well, haven't you expressed your desire or said as much in your introductory papers for this class?"

Nick was stumped on how to answer.

"Why do you care what happens to me?" Nick asked at last in a quiet, sad voice.

Trevor's face crumpled in sad exasperation.

"Why? Why indeed?" he said in a gravelly growl. "Can anyone ever really help the young on their way? I don't just mean with advice, warnings, money, and connections—vital as they are. What is that impulse to help a young person from blundering into the same pitfalls one has struggled with all his life? The road you're on has been traveled before, Nick! Some of us have the scars to prove it, but also the rewards... oh, what a lot of rot! Sorry!" Trevor threw his hands up and shrugged, his face turning crimson.

Nick felt ashamed.

"I don't mean to sound ungrateful for your interest," Nick said.

Trevor shook his head.

"I know that," Trevor answered. "Who the hell am I to play matchmaker?"

"Matchmaker?"

"I have no children, no son, Nick. No youth for whom I can provide a gentle guiding hand. But Rusty is my good, dear friend. And you... you're a bright young innocent drifting terribly close to the shoals I once foundered upon. I thought I'd find a friend for a friend. Seems I'm a silly old fool."

"Don't say that, Mr. Shannon. I'm coming off all wrong. I mean, I'm grateful you want to help me. I really am. I'm glad you brought Drake and Rusty to see me. I'm sorry I was suspicious of you and your friends. Honestly!"

"Drake is a cad, but he's a generous one," Trevor said. "A *user*, though. I should know. He was my lover."

Nick's eyes widened.

"Rusty is a sweet soul and a genuine talent," Trevor said. "He's the complete opposite of his business associate, Drake. And he likes you, Nick."

"I'd like to see Rusty again sometime," Nick said, feeling warm inside. "If only to apologize for being rude to him."

Trevor looked at Nick for a time.

"I think that can be arranged. And then? What will be will be," Trevor said and smiled. "Isn't that what Doris Day used to say?" He chuckled. "Your friends are out in the hall waiting. Don't be rude to them. Go off on your trip and have a wonderful time. Just promise me you will never stop being as alive as you are right now, in this bleak midwinter."

Nick didn't quite understand what Trevor meant, but he said, "I promise."

Chapter 5

THAT winter, Nick kept up his crazy double life of going to classes during the week and stripping for money and thrills on the weekends. Pretty soon he was skipping a lot of classes and hardly ever seeing his new friends at Peacehostel.

He was partying at places like Club View and spending a lot of money on flashy new clothes. His Peacehostel friends all warily noticed the change in him. Mostly they noticed his absence.

The weekend in Cornwall had been one of the last times he ever really spent with Peacehostel people. He spent freely and had a wonderful time. The short trip was not without a memorable incident.

It happened that first night.

Coming back to an otherwise empty, off-season bed and breakfast, Roy, Jean, and especially Candy had had a little too much to drink. Nick had sipped mead wine for the first time, then an expensive glass of champagne. He'd paid for every round of lager downed by his boisterous friends.

They seemed only too happy to oblige him and didn't ask how it was he came to have so much cash to blow.

The rain finally stopped as the four of them walked drunkenly on a moonlit trail along the seashore, heading back to the B and B. Candy, eyes half-open and hair damp, slipped her arm around Nick's waist and held him close as they walked. Jean, goofing off, took hold of him on the other side. She grinned, showing her child-like gappy white teeth. She wore lipstick in a shade of deep crimson. Before Nick knew it, Jean kissed him full on the mouth.

Nick tasted mint and tobacco and felt the warmth of her red lips. Then he looked behind him at Roy, who was glumly following along.

The look on Roy's face showed he wasn't at all pleased.

Nick was getting all the attention from the very girl Roy had set his sights on.

Without intending to, Nick had hurt Roy's feelings again.

Nick knew Roy liked Candy. But on this trip, Roy had told Nick in private that he would take his chances with Jean, assuming Candy didn't show any interest, as usual.

Like a lot of the kids at Peacehostel, Roy assumed something was going on between Nick and Candy.

In other circumstances, Nick might have found these misunderstandings humorous. But now they played into a sudden strategy that occurred to him.

Candy also had a sober expression on her face, placed there no doubt by Jean's kiss on Nick's lips.

Candy looked at Jean and Nick with an expression of bemusement. She struck a match and lit her umpteenth cigarette of the night.

Nick laughed, gamely slipping out of Jean's embrace.

"You're both pissed," he said to the girls, using the English slang. In America, getting pissed or pissed off meant you'd been angered. In Britain, getting pissed or pissed up meant you'd drunk yourself stupid.

For a moment, everyone stood stock-still in the moonlight, listening to the sound of the surf. There was a wistful feeling in the air. Nick attributed it to being a long, long way from home. Of being free, but lonesome, and desperate to experiment in ways they simply hadn't, for whatever reasons, in the confines of home and family.

These hungry travelers resumed their walk back to the bed and breakfast. The mood lightened.

The girls giggled as they walked, practically staggering, bumping into him and each other. They seemed to find it all very funny.

Poor Roy kept his somber face composed as he walked a slight distance behind them. Roy was such an inexperienced farm kid.

Nick recalled something odd Roy had said. Several weeks prior to this trip, Roy and Nick and Karl and some of the other guys were sitting around in Karl's room, shooting the shit. The ear-pricking subject of homosexuality had come up (how strange that this topic about something supposedly so hidden was so often on the tips of so many tongues!).

Nick affected paying no attention, but he listened keenly. Roy, the rural-raised high school wrestling champ said, "If you live on a farm, say, how would you ever figure out if you were gay?"

Karl had laughed. "What the hell, Roy?"

"I mean," Roy explained, "if you live in a city and there are gays around, that's one thing. You might identify with them if that's your thing. But what if you're just a farmer somewhere? How would you figure it out?"

Nick had turned a page in a book he was reading, the story of the Beatles by Phillip Norman. He kept his eyes on the print on the page.

"You can take the boy outta the farm, but you can't take the farm outta the boy," Karl said.

"Or the *farmer* out of the boy!" a curly-haired guy named Dean quipped.

Everyone laughed. Roy blushed.

Nick made a little mental note about this curiosity and naiveté of Roy's. Nick just assumed that if a guy knew he was turned on by girls, he would know he was straight. End of story. If it were boys that were on his mind, same deal.

Why wouldn't Roy know that?

Now the dejected Roy went to the room he would be sharing with Nick that night, saying he was going to take a shower and turn in. Candy and Jean urged Nick to come with them back to their room to smoke a joint. It was an English-style blunt, a hand-rolled cigarette with small chunks of hashish sprinkled in with the tobacco.

Nick went to the room with them, but he didn't smoke.

"What if the owner smells it?" Nick asked primly.

Jean shrugged. "It smells mostly like a plain, old, regular cigarette. But we'll be out of here in a day, so who cares?"

Candy was a bit more conservative. But tonight she didn't wish to seem so. She was in competition with Jean.

"It's too early to go to bed," Jean complained when Nick stood and stretched, yawning.

"You don't have to go to sleep just because I'm going to," he said.

She pouted. "Stay here, Nick," Jean said. "Don't be a party pooper."

"Yeah, stay," Candy said, also in a playful but childish whining tone.

In other circumstances, he might have stayed to see where this was leading, even if he had little interest sexually in either of these young women. But he really was tired.

And he wanted to check on Roy. Poor Roy would probably have given his right arm to be here with Jean and Candy and find out what kind of drunken playful games might be in store.

Roy just wasn't that lucky, Nick guessed. And Nick had other plans in mind than the possibility of bringing Roy back here for an orgy that might never actually happen.

Luck was playing its own ironic games on this moonlit night.

"C'mon, Nick," Candy said, grinning sexily.

"Not tonight," he said firmly.

NICK went back to the room he and Roy had settled into the previous morning, across the cold narrow hallway. The moon glowed through filmy curtains over a tall window. Nick felt a shiver of anticipation. He opened the door and saw, to his delight, Roy bent over his backpack perched on his single bed. He was digging for something inside. He was fresh from the shower and completely naked.

The thick, ruffled hair on Roy's head was towel-dried and sticking up all over. Roy smelled good, of soap and some kind of sporty-scented deodorant. Nick observed that Roy had a very good, solid body, muscular, compact just as a wrestler's body should be. All good wrestlers seemed to have that certain robust, raw quality, Nick observed. A low center of gravity, wide shoulders, narrow hips.

Nick's crotch flooded with warmth, and his dick stiffened with an ache that bordered on painful.

Nick had never really looked at Roy before. At least not like this. He'd concentrated his secret desires on Karl, who was a much more overtly attractive being. Roy was always dressed in boring blue jeans and baggy flannel shirts, unwittingly downplaying all that was covered up. But here was Roy revealed—all of him.

Nick quietly closed the door behind him but didn't take his eyes off of Roy.

Nick affected a yawn, and tried to think of something to say. But his mouth was watering, and he felt an ache of desire in his throat.

"Have your map in there?" Nick asked, gesturing to the backpack and trying to seem nonchalant. Even though Roy was giving him a very firm hard-on. "We'll need it tomorrow morning."

"I thought I put it in here," Roy said, glancing back. He moved around to the other side of the bed. He kept digging in the backpack. He gave up in frustration, grinned, then started looking again. "I can't keep track of anything, not even a map!" He didn't seem self-conscious, despite being completely nude. He seemed distracted, maybe a tiny bit pissed off. He might have been miffed about the girls and their lack of interest in him. And their obvious interest in Nick. Nick cleared his throat.

"Everything okay, Roy?"

Roy grunted.

"Here it is," Roy said at last, unfolding the map. "I think this is the place you wanted to see tomorrow, called Mousehole." Nick glanced at the map, then stripped down to his underpants and T-shirt and threw his clothes over a chair. He came over and stood beside Roy. He could feel the heat of Roy's body. He looked at the map.

"That should be easy to get to if we went this way," Nick said, tracing his finger along the map.

Roy turned the map. "Or we could take this route...." Then he looked at Nick and blushed with a grin. "Let me put something on."

Nick shrugged. He knew that wrestlers were weighed in stark naked in front of coaches and opposing team members; so maybe a casualness about nudity had been bred into them. The thought aroused Nick even more. He hoped his dick wouldn't be too noticeable. He pulled the bottom of his T-shirt down and over it. It would still be obvious, though, if Roy were to simply turn his head and look down.

"We can study the map in the morning," Nick said. "Don't get dressed on my account."

Roy laughed and Nick grinned at him.

Roy pulled on a pair of clean white underpants.

"I'm not a nudist," Roy said.

"I think I could be one," Nick said. "Or at least give it a try."

"I guess I'd try it," Roy said, "once."

The twin beds were close together in the small room. Roy pulled down the covers of his bed and slipped in, shivering.

Nick switched off the lamp and crawled into his bed in the darkness. Slowly, moonlight filtered in through the window as Nick's eyes adjusted to the dark. "Damn, it's cold in here," he said.

The window overlooked the rooftops of the little town, all the way down to the sea. The nearly full moon bathed the room in soft blue light.

Nick thought of the Greeks, who held Olympic wrestling events and other games in the nude. He thought of making a joke of it but then said nothing. He heard Roy cracking his knuckles and turning over in his bed. There was one good way to keep warm, Nick thought excitedly. But he was certain Roy was straight. Roy's crush on Candy was well known by everyone, it seemed, but Candy herself. Or maybe she had chosen to ignore it. Her focus was unfortunately on Nick.

"You're sore about the girls?" Nick asked.

"Just my luck," Roy said. "You have good luck with women, and I have *no* luck." He chuckled.

"I'm really not all that interested in either one of those two," Nick said.

"But you made it with Candy, didn't you?"

Nick cleared his throat. "It wouldn't be polite to say, would it, Roy?" Nick said cautiously. Not that it was very polite to allow assumptions to thrive.

"I s'pose not," Roy said.

"You've been with a girl, haven't you?" Nick asked.

"Of course," Roy said unconvincingly. It had just come out a little too fast and desperate. Still, it might have been true. "I mean, practically," Roy added, dispelling his own boast. Nick stifled a snort of laughter.

"You'll get laid on this trip, Roy," Nick said. "Just you wait and see."

"Well it better happen soon," Roy joked. "I'm so fucking horny I could...."

"Yeah?"

"I shoulda jerked off in the shower," Roy said and laughed. "Kidding!" he added boisterously.

After they stopped laughing, Nick said, "Everybody jerks off, Roy. It's nothing to be ashamed of." Nick decided to push his luck.

Roy exhaled slowly through his nose.

"You seem to be experienced, Nick. That's why none of this stuff seems like such a big deal to you. You're honest about sex stuff. Most people are fucked up about it."

"Think you're fucked up about it?" Nick asked, trying to sound like the man of experience Roy believed him to be.

"I think... I haven't touched a woman in a long, long time...," Roy said.

Nick thought, lyrically, *if forever is a long, long time....*

Nick leaned up in his bed. Daringly, he swung his legs to the floor. He hopped over and sat on Roy's bed.

"What're you doing?" Roy said, grinning widely but a little bit alarmed.

"I'm going to give you a back rub, Roy."

"Huh? In bed?"

"Why not? It's just a back rub."

"What makes you think I want a back rub?"

"Doesn't everybody want a back rub?" Nick laughed. "Roy, part of your problem is you're confusing sex with physical intimacy. You just haven't had anybody get close lately, not even to wrestle with. You need to loosen up. Why do you think girls are always hugging each other and guys are always punching each other? Just relax and enjoy it. Then you can rub my back, if you wouldn't mind. Help warm us up a little too."

Roy giggled. But he amazed Nick when he rolled over on his belly. "God, if anybody back home saw this, they'd say it was queer as a three dollar bill."

Nick slowly pulled the cover and sheet down from Roy's bare shoulders, down to the top of the waistband of Roy's white underpants.

ROY'S form was like sculpture in the moonlight.

Trying to breathe softly but trembling slightly, Nick placed his hands on Roy's warm shoulders.

Slowly, he began massaging the young wrestler's flesh.

"That doesn't feel so bad, does it?" Nick asked.

Roy groaned. He actually groaned.

"Not too queer?" Nick asked with a little laugh.

"I hope not!" Roy said and laughed nervously.

It emboldened Nick.

"Everybody's a little bit queer, Roy," Nick said softly, pushing it a bit further. "I mean, if we're being honest." Roy groaned again under the pressure of Nick's massaging hands.

"Have you ever…?" Roy asked.

"Have I ever screwed around with a guy?" Nick asked. "Well, not all that much, to be honest. But it's really not all that much different than being with a girl. Well, not that different to me, anyway."

Roy turned now, almost jumping away.

"You can't be serious," Roy said. Roy's eyes were wide.

"It's worth trying… once," Nick said. "Anyway, it doesn't turn you gay. You already fucked a girl, right? We know what we really want, don't we?"

"So why… I mean, what if we liked it?"

Nick felt his kindling desire begin to build toward a conflagration.

"It doesn't mean anything more than jacking off," Nick whispered daringly. "It's not something other people have any cause to know about. It can be private, I can promise you that. We're thousands of miles from home." Nick swallowed hard. He wanted this. He hoped Roy felt the same. "We should try it, Roy. Why jerk off alone when a buddy can help you with it?"

Roy turned all the way over and lay flat on his back. He exhaled, loudly, through his nose. He smiled sheepishly. "Can't believe I'm really gonna do this…," he said softly.

Then Roy pushed down the covers, and Nick could see Roy's hard-on straining against the front of his white briefs. For a moment, Nick wondered who was seducing whom here. Was it really possible Roy was opening up to him, like a rose in sunshine?

Nick pulled the blanket all the way down to the end of the bed. Then he swung a leg over and climbed onto Roy's trunk, straddling him, pressing his hard cock against Roy's. Roy moaned.

Nick put his hand over Roy's dick and softly caressed it through the fabric of Roy's underpants.

"Feels good, huh?" Nick whispered.

Roy closed his eyes and moaned softly in the affirmative.

Then Nick leaned forward and kissed Roy's warm belly and traced his tongue down to the waistband of Roy's underwear.

Roy seemed a bit startled and jumpy. But he did not protest. He was practically panting.

The belly kiss might have been going too far, but Roy responded with more passionate groans.

Nick pulled downward on Roy's underpants. Roy helped, lifting his legs. Nick tossed Roy's briefs to the chair across the room. Nick then quickly stripped off his own briefs. Then he lay down full over Roy, naked, skin to skin. Face to face. They embraced as if it were the most natural thing to them, something they'd done before, though they hadn't.

"Not so bad?" Nick whispered, his face close to Roy's.

Roy nodded.

Nick rubbed his hard dick against Roy's dick and belly. Roy closed his eyes and moaned, and thrust back.

Nick wanted to see Roy's ass and feel it. But he wasn't sure it was worth chancing. If Roy discovered just how into it Nick was, it might frighten him.

Before Nick could finish the thought, he felt warm spurts of come shooting against his belly. Roy moaned, almost crying out. Roy was climaxing already.

Nick rubbed himself against Roy, lightly cupping Roy's balls as his friend finished coming with a loud moan.

Nick rubbed his own dick harder into Roy's groin and belly, now slick with hot come.

Nick started shooting too, holding Roy as tight as he could, wanting to kiss him, to jam his tongue in Roy's mouth. But he didn't.

Bodies warm, skin hot, they were both spent. Nick rolled onto his back as Roy made room for him on the narrow bed.

They lay there, together, silently, side by side, still feeling each other.

After a time, Roy started to snore. Nick stood up and covered Roy.

Then, wiping himself off with a sock, he went back to his own bed.

Roy might have been more than a little drunk.

Nick figured Roy was not very experienced at all. And it was more than likely Roy had never been with a girl before.

But was Roy gay?

Not exactly.

But they screwed around again in the morning, jerking each other off to climax, and they would rendezvous several more times before Nick's semester ended abruptly that memorable winter.

NICK and Roy of course acted completely nonchalant the next morning when they hooked up with the rather hungover girls. But they practically glowed with good humor.

Roy was so relaxed and jolly, Jean started to take a real shine to him. Right there at the breakfast table. After a daytrip to Mousehole and some lagers at lunch, Candy watched as Roy and Jean made out at a little pub with an oxidized green mermaid over its door, and lots of rusting shipwreck debris decorating the warm interior. It was raining again. Nick played the jukebox, humming to himself. Wasting an afternoon in a pub at the seashore—okay. Why not? He ordered another round of lager.

Nick was feeling good. He liked Roy, and their encounter had been satisfying. But he was not in love with Roy. Yet, in a funny way, he did love Roy, just for being Roy. Nick was happy for Roy this afternoon. In a single night, Roy had seemed to blossom from his shell-like, closed bud. He was a lot more self-confident, relaxed, and happy.

Maybe it was Nick's special touch? Nick grinned, thinking these private thoughts.

Candy stayed sober as the afternoon grew darker and evening came on. Nick could tell she wanted some attention, but he remained aloof, drinking lager. He ordered sandwiches and potatoes and salads for the table, and his friends feasted. Nick paid the bill at the end of the night. He liked being able to cover everyone's expenses at a time like this. He knew his friends had to watch their meager funds.

"Where are you getting all this money?" Candy asked, taking him aside. "You told me your grandparents don't have a lot and that you're not depending on them for money, anyhow. So if you're just getting by on loans and grants, I don't get where the extra cash comes from."

"You sound suspicious," he said.

"You disappear a lot," she said accusingly. *Possessively.*

"So what, Candy?" Nick said.

"I would hate it if you were doing something like selling drugs. You saw *Midnight Express*, didn't you? That American guy, getting thrown into a Turkish prison? Think about it."

"Nothing like that, Candy," he said. "Besides, this is Cornwall, not Istanbul."

Nick walked back to the B and B by himself, singing. He sang "Baby Love," giving the Supremes' version his own sexy twist. Sometimes he liked the sound and feel of classic rhythm and blues, even if he fancied himself a rocker.

He wished there was someplace he could go and sing his heart out and strum a guitar.

He resolved to find a guitar and learn a few more numbers. Maybe Nick's next incarnation would be a busker, playing on Tube platforms for money.

Nick settled in for the evening, thumbing through a paperback biography of the late Jim Morrison. He dozed in bed.

Later, Roy came back to the room, explaining that Candy had insisted Jean accompany her to the room the girls shared—alone. Roy was a bit disappointed, Nick could tell. Roy was finally making time with Jean. This could have been a red-letter weekend for him. But it wasn't meant to be, at least not tonight.

A minor argument had ensued between the girls, Roy explained, with Candy angrily telling Jean she was definitely drunk. Jean had insisted she wasn't drunk, but left Roy and went with Candy anyway.

Since their room was just across the hall, Roy had heard the argument continuing in muffled voices. He'd had to duck into the room with Nick when one of the girls came rushing out into the hallway. Roy was fast enough to avoid a crash. He assumed it was Jean. The bathroom door slammed. The sound of retching could be heard.

It was Jean.

Roy locked the bedroom door and grinned at Nick.

"Guess tonight's not the night for me and Jean," he said.

"There's always tomorrow," Nick replied with a wink.

"I'm kinda trashed too."

Nick took in a deep slow breath. Roy had a twinkle in his eye and a strange half smile played on his lips. He was a bit high, Nick figured. Roy flicked the light switch off.

Roy was in Nick's bed almost as quickly as the light had gone out. The moon provided enough light in the room to see, and the emboldened Roy wanted to see everything this time. He was nude, and soon Nick was too. Roy apparently wanted to spend some time going over Nick thoroughly. He caressed and explored him with his lips and fingers. Roy had the potential to be a surprisingly gentle and playful lover. But he was in a rush, slowed down only by the amount of alcohol flowing through his bloodstream. He came hard over Nick.

When it was Nick's turn, he made the most of it.

ONCE back at Peacehostel, Roy pursued both Jean and Candy. In due course, he scored with both of them. It seemed he was well on his way to a life of sexual conquest. And pissing off women.

Not that those two best friends really fought over Roy. They shared him. After a time, they would all move on.

For a while, Roy kept asking Nick to take another weekend trip with him, didn't matter to where. Nick was generally busy—and getting busier—with his new friends. People Roy knew nothing about.

Still, Nick found his way into occasional clinches with Roy in the few private places Peacehostel had to offer. They even took a long bath together one early evening, using an upper-floor bathroom, the door locked of course. The few students at home on this evening were glued to the TV on the first floor. No one would disturb their bathtub party.

"Where do you go at night?" Roy asked, his soapy arms around Nick's middle. Nick leaned back comfortably against Roy.

"Exploring," Nick said cryptically.

"You have secrets, Nick," Roy said. "Why can't you let me in on them?"

"Because... just *because*, Roy," Nick said. "Don't make a big deal about it, okay?"

"Just tell me one thing," Roy said. "Is it girls?" He paused. "Or guys."

Nick exhaled through his nostrils. Annoyed.

"I told you, that doesn't make any difference to me," Nick said.

"I think it makes a difference to me," Roy said. "I know I like it with girls better... except...."

Uh-oh.

"Except," Roy stammered, "with you."

"Come on, Roy," Nick said. "You don't really believe that."

"Don't I?"

"We're just buddies," Nick said, trying to be gentle and sounding anything but.

"It's more than that," Roy said. "For me."

Nick exhaled slowly.

"Nick," Roy said, "I think I might be—"

"Don't, Roy," Nick said.

Nick could feel hot tears dripping onto the back of his neck.

"I think I'm in love with you, Nick," Roy whispered, choking back his tears.

Nick knew he'd made a very bad mistake. Because he didn't love Roy—not that way.

"And what about Jean?" Nick said, his voice grave. "And Candy?"

Roy was shaking. He was really upset.

"Oh, fuck," Roy said, and he sniffed. "I made a mess of my whole trip... one day I think I love Jean. The next day it's Candy."

"And today, it's me?" Nick asked, trying to make fun.

"Don't laugh at me," Roy said. But he laughed out loud now too, then followed it with a little sob that caught in his throat.

Nick hoisted himself dripping wet out of the bath, and helped Roy out after him. He dried off Roy's back.

Roy turned around quickly and threw his arms around Nick's waist. He kissed him hard on the mouth.

"I wish I understood you," Roy said. "Who you *really* are."

"I'm just what you see," Nick said.

Roy nodded and made a little grunt.

"It's what I don't see," Roy said. "That's what worries me about you."

Nick stepped gently back from Roy's embrace and finished drying himself.

Roy dressed and at last turned to leave the warm, misty bathroom.

"Hey, you gonna be all right?" Nick called.

Roy turned and smiled sadly.

"I'll be fine," Roy said. "I just hope you know what you're doing."

Roy opened the door slowly, and quietly peeped his nose out.

He looked both ways down the hall. Seeing it all clear, Roy slipped out and closed the door behind him.

Chapter 6

THE truth Nick didn't share with Roy that winter was that he was seeing a lot of a certain somebody.

Rusty.

And he was running around town with Rusty's crowd. Friends Nick considered at his age to be older guys. Friends who had money, position, and power—or who seemed to have those elusive, glittering qualities. Friends who were slick.

There was something interesting to do almost every night of the week with these guys. Nick was hitting nightclubs and parties, art openings and rock shows, restaurant openings and shop openings. It didn't matter what kind of opening it was, as long as it was hip and in London, Nick went there to party.

And the parties were fun. Even if Nick didn't recognize every singer or actor or musician, he understood these people were all successful artists of one sort or another. Or they were going to be successful, soon. If some of this feeling was based on the thinnest evidence or the most reckless sort of hope, that only added to the excitement.

At the center of this group were Rusty and Drake. Sometimes Trevor too. Though Trevor was much older than Rusty and Drake. He was hardly what you'd call a partier, in that he didn't drink much or partake in the endless drugging going on practically out in the open. Yet Trevor was a social butterfly with an eye for beauty in its many forms, and he hated to miss any of the amazing lot of happenings and to-dos lighting up London like a fireworks show. All of it tripped by on waves of new electronic synth-based music, vats of mascara, and oceans of shiny hair product.

Trevor mostly took Nick to cultural events of a higher order, such as to the symphony and the ballet. Sometimes Rusty came along, Drake joining them less often. Often the three or four of them would meet up late and go out to a posh good restaurant. Nick loved this kind of evening best, eating his fill, drinking champagne, and seeing beautiful, rich, and stylish people buzzing like bees around jungles of flowers, all bursting with nectar.

The ballet electrified Nick. The feeling was something that spoke to him innately. But the language of this form was something he grasped at desperately for understanding, like a foreigner struggling with an unknown tongue.

He used his library privileges to read as much as he could about classical music and ballet. In time, he became familiar with technical terms like *entrechat* and *glissade*.

If someone mentioned E.M. Forster, Nick would be entranced over the next few days reading *Maurice* and *Howards End*.

Trevor, seeing Nick's interest in such English literary legends, suggested he try Christopher Isherwood. Nick devoured *Christopher and His Kind*, *A Single Man*, and *My Guru and His Disciple*.

Every gay book (as Nick thought of them) he read led him to yet another author. He was already somewhat familiar with Gore Vidal and Tennessee Williams and Truman Capote. He read everything he could find by them or about them.

Nick spent his afternoons reading and drinking strong, sweet English tea, and his evenings hitting this new social scene. He barely went to class, feeling that *this* experience was his real education.

The pop music scene most of all dazzled Nick like fizz in his crystal champagne flute.

It was heady stuff for a Midwestern kid. The attention being lavished upon him felt good, like the buzz from his fifth or sixth glass of champagne. He was well dressed, smartly groomed, and he turned heads. He was playing a role, improvising, being for these people (mostly men, but also women) whatever they seemed to want him to be.

Rusty and Drake and Trevor were mentors, he the acolyte. They were teachers, he the willing student. They were cultured gay men. Nick was a ripening ingénue in their midst.

Sex always seemed to be on everyone's mind. But none of Nick's "mentors" and fast friends ever seemed to make a move on one another or on him.

Not yet anyway.

But Nick was very aware that Rusty liked him and had a special interest in him alone. Drake also expressed his interest. Drake was cruder about it, though. Drake was lust-filled, and it didn't seem to matter to him whom he was ogling.

Nick was enjoying the ride, though, and not about to take any of this seriously. His success with Roy had emboldened him even as it satisfied a basic need long denied. But Nick's relationship with Roy did not constitute an emotional attachment, as far as Nick was concerned. Roy was a sex buddy, and Nick wanted more such sex buddies.

He'd hated hurting Roy but doubted if Roy's feelings were much more than puppy love. Still, Nick knew too much about being on the rejected side of a love equation to not at least feel some sympathy for poor Roy. Even if he knew Roy would be banging more English and American girls or maybe even some other guy soon enough.

Nick was going places Roy and his fellow students could not go along with him. He was moving rapidly into a world he wanted to conquer and make his own—all his own.

It wasn't all about sex, despite sex's primacy in his youthful journey. It was about exploring a culture and finding his own place in it.

In the course of a single week, Nick attended a performance of the Vienna Boys' Choir, Mendelssohn's "A Midsummer Night's Dream," and the West End shows *Evita* and *Cats*, and (in Hammersmith) a rip-roaring comedy called *Noises Off*.

More dinners and more parties followed. Rusty was only too happy to show this world to Nick. And Rusty became Nick's primary guide.

At one party in a flat in the posh Marble Arch area, Nick had a bit too much champagne. A few people were seated on the carpeted floor before a large fireplace. Nick leaned back and closed his eyes, dangerously close to passing out.

Drake held out a small pocket mirror, placing it under Nick's nose. Nick saw a powdery thin white line of what could only have been cocaine. He'd smoked a little pot in school, like most of the kids at Ledgerock High. But he had never tried coke.

He'd seen Drake do it half a dozen times. Drake now proffered a shiny straw-like reed.

Pressing shut one nostril, Nick sniffed up the cool, burning substance through the hollow reed and felt an instant blast of bright energy pulse through his brain.

Rusty, who had arrived at the party late, coming directly from the recording studio, looked on with a slight air of disapproval.

Rusty sat next to Nick, and Nick smiled seductively at him.

Rusty moved in closer.

Nick was high, he was cheerful, and he was losing control.

Nick leaned in, getting his face up close to Rusty's. Rusty looked into Nick's eyes. Nick had never seen such soulful, handsome eyes in such a handsome face, the face of a lion. Nick kissed Rusty's lips, deeply. Rusty kissed him back and smiled but pulled gently away.

"I'm not sure I wanted our first kiss to be in such a public place, Nick," he said.

Nick was too high to really process this. But he felt protected, cared for—loved, even, by this wonderful new friend.

Nick looked around the room.

Drake, nearby and unsmiling, offered another line of cocaine to Nick, who quickly snuffled it up and then laughed. Now he was incredibly high but felt a sensation of pure clarity. It was the false clarity offered by the mischievous spirit of the coca leaf. But Nick didn't know that.

He turned back to Rusty and smiled knowingly.

"But you've been wanting to kiss me," Nick said to Rusty. "For weeks."

Rusty looked meaningfully into Nick's eyes.

"Yes," Rusty said softly. "I'm crazy about you, Nick."

EVERYTHING changed at that moment when Rusty expressed his feelings toward Nick.

It was simply amazing to Nick that someone as cool as Rusty could say something like that and mean it.

Rusty had a kind of warmth and look in his eyes that melted some barrier in Nick's heart. And it felt wonderful. And Nick understood that he was falling headlong in love too.

"We should do something about it," Nick said, feeling warm and bold.

"You have feelings for me, Nick?" Rusty asked.

"I have a crush on you, Rusty," Nick admitted. Saying it made it all seem to become clear. It was true Rusty was older than Nick. A man in his prime, very much in the mode of the fabulous rock stars in his orbit. Nick had halfheartedly tried to resist Rusty. But lately, Rusty was almost all he could think of.

It felt so right!

Nick figured, mistakenly, the coke had somehow aided in this revelation.

Rusty smiled, taking Nick's hand.

"I want to help you, Nick," Rusty said. "I want to give you a life many people can only dream of. For starters, I want you to move out of that terrible youth hostel and into my flat."

They had only been on about a dozen dates. They had barely even kissed.

Nick said with a grin, "I was going to propose we go out dancing."

They both laughed a little.

"Let's go," Rusty said at last.

Nick didn't look back to see Drake glowering.

THEY danced at a place called Zone Seven until the sun came up. Then they went to Rusty's spacious apartment on the top floor of a posh building in Kensington. The place was decorated in a spare, elegant style Nick found almost dowdy. The walls and high ceilings were white. The furniture was antique—heavy and substantial. The predominant colors were browns and blues.

Nick knew this look was probably considered classy. It felt rich but sort of uncomfortable. Like being in a museum.

Even Rusty's bedroom was conservatively appointed. Rooms spanned impressively from one to another, with many fireplaces and windows and elaborately tiled WCs. The paintings on the walls were mostly old baroque religious images in ornate frames. The bed was on a raised platform.

In one corner was a Roland keyboard. In another was an acoustic guitar. Rusty saw Nick looking at it. It had been months since Nick had touched a guitar.

"Go ahead," Rusty said. "Play something."

"Nahhh," Nick said. Trevor had told him Rusty's elder brother, a musician and recording engineer, had worked with the likes of the Beatles, and half a dozen other legends the names of whom had floored Nick. As a kid, Rusty had hung out in London's top studios, where he'd received his education with the giants of the music business.

Rusty lay down on the bed fully dressed.

"This is not an audition," Rusty said. "I saw you looking at the guitar. Don't be afraid."

Nick reluctantly picked it up. He was tired. Rusty was too. But Nick strummed a few chords in succession, then strummed a little tune.

"What's that?" Rusty said.

"Something I made up a while ago. Nothing really. Sort of a new-wave thing."

"Have any words?"

Nick felt blood rushing to his face. He cleared his throat and spoke-sang a couple of lines of lyrics from his unfinished song.

"It's been such a blank life / but you stepped into this void / and you replace it with a nothingness of your own / a nothingness I like."

Very downbeat and pessimistic, and nothing like the exuberant being that was Nick.

And as far as Nick was concerned, it wasn't singing at all. Even to Nick it sounded awfully affected. Like a bad Bowie impression with a little Talking Heads thrown in.

But that was what Nick had thought was hip, new, now.

Nick looked at Rusty, and Nick couldn't help but laugh.

"What's wrong?" Rusty asked.

"It's crap," Nick said.

"Oh, it's not," Rusty said. "I sometimes like that kind of angst in music right now."

Nick set the guitar back on its stand.

"You do?" Nick asked.

"I like all kinds of music, you know," Rusty said. "And I hear something in your voice that I like—and would like even if I didn't know you."

"Honest?"

Rusty nodded.

"I always say if you have a song, sing it," Rusty said.

"I love to sing," Nick said. "But just now… I couldn't. I mean… I was talking those lyrics, not singing them."

Nick came over and sat on the edge of Rusty's bed. Rusty slipped his arm around Nick's waist and gently drew him closer.

"I also loved the way you danced tonight," Rusty said. "You have charisma, a wild energy. I think you have star quality."

"If you say so," Nick said, flattered. He smiled, but his energy level was starting to fall.

For a time, they simply held one another.

Then, in the dim light of the room, they undressed completely and fell into bed together. Snuggling, they merely slept. Yet before Nick drifted off completely, warm in Rusty's strong embrace, Rusty asked him a question.

"Do you think you could try and sing for me sometime soon, for real?"

NICK told Monty by telephone he was through dancing at Sodom X. He had been dancing regularly and had been on the verge of making it a steady thing.

"That'll disappoint a few fans," Monty had said in a bitchy tone. "There's always another lad coming along, though."

"Great," Nick said. "So don't expect me tomorrow night. I'm through."

"No farewell performance?"

"No, I think I've worked this thing out of my system."

"There's one more thing you could do, though, Nick."

"Not more pictures," Nick said. "I'm already bracing myself for the shots in that magazine."

"It's not more pictures, and I'll be sure to get me own copy of *Manhole*. Time to lose that bottle-blond hair if you don't want to be recognized on the streets."

"I'm sure the audience that reads—if that's the word—*Manhole* isn't large enough to cause me any grief. *Manhole* isn't even sold in America."

"Word of those pictures did attract the attention of someone who would like to offer you an opportunity, though, Nick," Monty said tantalizingly.

Nick frowned. "I don't hustle."

"It's not a trick. It's something more along the lines of what I happen to know turns you on. It would turn on any exhibitionist."

"Like I said, Monty, I think I've worked through that particular kick. Thanks, I guess."

"This offer pays ten times what you received for those nude shots in *Manhole*," Monty said.

THE wood-paneled recording studio was intimate, clean, windowless, and bathed in warm light, exuding an air of glamor. And of history.

"Would you like a drink, Nick?" Rusty asked over the PA from the glassed-in booth. "A glass of wine or champagne?"

Nick stood on the sleek wooden floor of the paneled room where a black baby grand piano was spot-lit in a corner and electric guitars stood gleaming on stands. A variety of flat keyboards and synthesizers were arranged around a glittery drum kit.

"I'll have champagne," Nick said.

"Speak into the microphone, Nick," Rusty said with a smile, pointing at his headphones.

"Champagne," Nick said into the mike.

It was about three in the afternoon on a Sunday, and the regular work of recording an album had been completed for the day. A few people still milled about. One was a striking black woman with flowing black relaxed hair and hip-looking clothes and boots. She wore bracelets and rings with the air of a gypsy.

She handed Nick a glass of champagne and smiled.

"Do you work here?" Nick asked.

She mocked an expression of surprise and "clinked" her flute of champagne against his.

"I'm cutting a record here," she said in a voice that was mellifluous and warm. A singer's voice, and a black American accent. "So I guess you could say I'm working here. One of the hired hands." She chuckled and her pretty eyes twinkled under the lights.

"I'm sorry," Nick said. He grinned sheepishly. "I'm new around here."

"Nick, say hello to Marisa Tambov," Rusty said into the microphone behind the glass. Rusty smiled down at them.

That name sounded familiar to Nick. He looked up at Rusty.

"You remember 'Mighty My Tea, la da la da dee'...," Rusty said in a pleasant singsong voice.

"Oh, sing it," Marisa said, and they all laughed. Nick of course remembered the seventies disco hit "Mighty My Tea," by none other than the lovely Ms. Tambov.

She was radiant.

The thing was, Nick didn't recall ever seeing her face. The hit song was everywhere though. At least for that summer of 1976—or was it 1977? It was a tune almost everyone could hum.

"Wow, I'm pleased to meet you," Nick said, noticing the gold cross on a loose gold chain around her neck. She noticed him looking at her necklace.

Marisa touched the cross, giving Nick another warm smile that made him instantly like her.

"Rusty's producing your new record?" Nick asked.

"A whole album's worth of great songs," she said. "The Lord is good, and I believe in second chances, don't you?"

"I guess so."

The room filled with music, not disco music, but a kind of soulful pop. He recognized Marisa's voice.

"Like it?" she asked, sitting down in a leather club chair.

"It's different," Nick said.

"That could mean a lot of things," Marisa said and sipped her champagne. She was beautiful, and Nick judged her to be about forty years old. She was actually a little past fifty.

"I mean I like it," Nick said.

"Rusty says you know your way around the clubs and you dig the sound coming out of London these days. It's a new sound. Electronic, bouncy, danceable. Don't call it disco, though," she said with a snort. "Disco is dead. So they all say."

Nick nodded.

"I like harder music," he said. "Guitars, but simple. Punk, mainly."

Marisa made a face.

"What about Human League?" she asked.

"I think they're great."

"It's all keyboards… computers?"

"It's the new sound," Nick said. "Just wait till it hits the States."

Rusty had come down to the main floor and was clearing some cables out of the room.

"Marisa sings in nightclubs here in London, Nick," Rusty said. "She's been doing it for years. She's a cabaret singer now, singing jazz and standards in a smoky voice I've been in love with for years."

"It's what I love to sing," Marisa said. "The album, though, is going to be pop. Soulful rhythm and blues. But I need one good, solid dance song for the clubs. I need to connect to my gay audience."

Nick nodded, excited to be privy to such inside information.

"Rusty thinks you can help me," Marisa said.

Nick gulped down his mouthful of champagne.

"Me?" he asked, incredulous. "How?"

"We want you to help us write a song," Marisa said.

"Me?" Nick asked. "But I'm not a songwriter."

"That's not what I hear," Marisa said. "Rusty said you write pretty interesting lyrics and have a flair for melody. Pick up that guitar and freestyle something for me right now."

Nick was shocked. He'd been goofing around with the guitar for Rusty, but he'd thought that was just for fun.

"I'd much rather hear you sing," he said shyly.

"I'm on my break, honey."

They smiled.

"Go ahead," she said.

When Nick picked up the guitar, a tall man with thinning blond hair and a cowboy shirt placed a microphone stand in front of him. Rusty was back up in the booth, donning his headphones.

"You guys are serious, aren't you?" Nick asked.

Marisa stood before him now. She looked at him closely.

"Free association time," she said. "Let words and music flow out of you. Whatever comes into your head."

Nick started strumming, and though he felt very self-conscious, it wasn't long before he found a chord progression he liked. It was a rocking sort of beat. Then he sang.

He tried to sing his best, as he had sung in choirs back at Ledgerock, the Catholic high school his grandparents had sent him to near their home in Wisconsin. He had a clear, strong voice, but it was in imitation of a straight, white-bread singing voice better suited to the "Battle Hymn of the Republic" than to the sounds coming out of Britain in the morning of the eighties.

His lyric was sort of sexy. "*Wonder what it would be like,*" he sang. "*What you'd be like. How long will I wonder what you like? When am I gonna find out? I hope it's tonight.*" He let it grind to an abrupt stop, feeling the blood rush to his face.

He took a big sip of champagne.

Marisa leaned forward in her chair.

"That voice," she said. "That's not really you, Nick."

He grinned. "Then who is it?"

"Better question," she said. "Who is Nick Davangere?" She tussled his hair. "What is with this peroxide-blond stuff you got goin' on here? You tryin' to *pass*? Honey, I'm from Mississippi. I know a brother when I see one."

Nick felt his face getting warm.

"I'm mixed race," he said.

"I see. Raised by the white side of the family?"

"My grandparents," Nick said. Marisa liked to cut to the chase, it seemed. He liked that. But he didn't really like where the conversation was going.

"You came to the right country if you wanna stay out of the sun and pass as another pasty, pale punk." She winked.

"It's not something I ever really think about," Nick said softly.

"That's sad, because there's a *you* in there somewhere, and I bet he's just dyin' to come out."

Nick didn't reply.

"Let me hear you try something with a little more soul to it," Marisa said. "Something that gets inside that self that nobody but you knows about. Someplace in your heart you just know is there, even if you think sometimes you don't."

Nick set the guitar down.

"I'm not sure I know what you're talking about, Marisa," he said gently. "Anyway… I gotta go. Runnin' late." He looked at his watch. He stood up to leave.

Rusty came back into the big session room. He sat at a keyboard a short distance from where Nick and Marisa were. To Nick's amazement, Rusty played a very pretty and slow variation of the melody Nick had just sung.

"Wow," Nick said.

"Let's play with it," Rusty said, looking Nick in the eye. "Think about those records I had you listen to… about the construction of a pop song."

Nick blinked. Was this some kind of quiz? Nick had been listening to songs on headphones at Rusty's place and here at the studio. Songs Rusty said exemplified an "ethic" he was trying to achieve every time he came into the studio.

Nick had sort of laughed when Rusty had him listen to the sixties hit "It's My Party" by Leslie Gore. Those lyrics, "and I'll cry if I want to, cry if I want to," had made him laugh. But after a few listens, he started to understand what Rusty was saying about phrasing, about "deeper" singing—stronger but softer, from the diaphragm.

Singing a lyric as a character you could see, feel, and believe in.

Rusty had explained that the great producer Quincy Jones had created an example of the perfect pop recording with Leslie Gore. The "double vocal" tracks, the chorus, the horns—the song sounded bigger and bigger every time Nick listened to it. And he fell completely in love with it.

What, though, was Rusty up to?

And why did it have to be tonight of all nights? He had somewhere else he needed to be.

"That was fun, but I have an appointment," Nick said. "I'm already late." He looked at his watch again. He did not want to meet Rusty's eyes.

"Hell, I thought we were just getting started," Marisa said.

Nick was halfway to the door.

He turned around, stopped dead, and sang to them. Only this time the voice coming out of him was different.

It was a voice he'd used when he tried to imitate some of the soul sounds he'd listen to, way back when Grandpa wasn't around to catch him. Like when he used to like the Jackson Five, Gladys Knight and the Pips, and Stevie Wonder.

Rusty tipped the microphone toward Nick.

"*I wonder*," Nick sang, letting it run. "*I wonder....*"

"Good," Marisa whispered, gesturing, snapping her fingers. "Now give it some style, let the phrases move around you, up and down and through you."

Nick sang stronger. Rusty accompanied on the piano. It was pure improvisation based on the "song" he'd moments ago almost jokingly made up on the spot.

"From your soul," Marisa whispered to him fiercely. Nick sang into the microphone and improvised all over the place for about twelve minutes, and at points he seemed to find a groove that surprised even him. "Yeah, that's it," Marisa cried, clapping. "You found a strong backbeat." She clapped time against her hip and danced beside him.

She looked at Rusty, who glanced up at the guy in the booth with the thinning yellow hair. "Okay hold it," Rusty said. "Can we play that back?"

Nick bent, smiling, hands on his knees and almost out of breath.

In an instant, Nick's voice filled the recording studio. So did his guitar—crude, but built up with an echoing effect. Rusty's keyboard sound harmonized in. The result was rough, but big and—well, it was weirdly fantastic! Kind of new wave, sort of soul, definitely a dance groove in the rough. And very contemporary.

"Thanks," Marisa said, eyes closed and concentrating. "Oh, that sounds interesting. I like it. But I just don't know if it's for me," she said as the playback ended. She shrugged.

Nick was dumbstruck.

"It's a bloody good start," Rusty said with a grin. "Nick, how about another session tomorrow night? We can see where this song goes, and try to come up with a couple, maybe four or five more different pieces. We'll pull it out of you, Nick."

"Me?" he asked.

Marisa rolled her eyes and grinned.

"Don't you wanna work with me and your man?" she asked Nick, gesturing to Rusty. "He sure wants to work with you." She raised her hands up, waving them theatrically. "I just want a hit record. I don't care how we come up with it!"

She winked at Nick.

He gulped. They wanted *him* to help write a hit record? What the hell did he know?

It was crazy. But it sure sounded like fun.

"I'm late," Nick said. To Rusty he said, "I'll call you later."

To Marisa he said, "It was great to meet you, Miss Tambov."

She looked at him with a twinge of worry in her eyes. He didn't stay to let it linger. He was out the door.

"YOU'RE late," the filmmaker said. He wore dark round glasses and had a full black beard. English and plump, he affected a big-shot, movie-director look. As if he was trying to look like Francis Ford Coppola or Stanley Kubrick. He had some bread crumbs in his beard.

The hotel room was suitably squalid and smelled faintly of boiled cabbage. Old theatrical lights on rusting stands, dust-covered and battered, were aimed over the sad-looking little bed. An ogre-like, heavyset man, bald-headed but for some orange peach fuzz, was adjusting the lights as the filmmaker looked through the lens of his 16mm film camera. All of the equipment, while weirdly professional in a kind of dirty industrial way, was obviously quite decrepit. The room was hazy with cigarette smoke.

"Sorry," Nick said. No reason for him to tell them where he'd been or who he'd just been with. He thought how it would sound: I was just writing a song with Marisa Tambov—*the* Marisa Tambov. He could imagine the response: Sure you were. And I'm Princess Diana. Nick grinned.

"Wipe that smile away, kid," the director said in his gravelly English voice. "The look I want on your face is grim, American, hard, rough trade from the ghetto."

The ghetto?

Nick cocked his head.

"This one is a... he's *dark* too?" the fat guy asked, looking at Nick, then the "director." His tone was an insensitive stage whisper intended to offend.

The filmmaker shrugged.

"Not too," the director muttered. "Not my problem."

"I'm from Wisconsin farm country," Nick said coolly. "Not the ghetto."

"You'll have to do some acting then, friend," the director said. A door creaked open.

A young, very well-built black man emerged from the bathroom. Nick's heart thumped hard. The guy had close-cropped hair, a pleasant face, and was by no means conventionally handsome. He was very masculine. He wore jeans and a white shirt. And he was very dark-skinned. Nick felt something akin to panic, seeing this stranger. He silently forced this feeling back down to the pit of his stomach.

"This is Manny," the director said. "He's going to fuck you in the mouth for a while. Then he's going to rim your ass. You finish by fucking him in the ass, but pull out and be sure to shoot onto him *and* into the camera. Obviously we have a budget and very little film stock. Not much leeway for extra takes. It's going to be *cinema vérité*. No talking. Lots of grunts and groans and moans."

Manny stuck out his hand. Nick shook it. Manny was warm.

"You both walk in," the director continued. "Walk to the bed, backs to camera. You kiss. Then take off your shirts. Nick, you sit on the bed. Manny, you kneel in front of Nick. You take Nick's dick out of his shorts, and play with it. It's hard, Nick. Okay?"

Nick cleared his throat and nodded.

Nick felt a lot of strange emotions, one of which was a wish that this filmmaker, so humorless, would just shut up. Nick tuned him out. He felt himself getting hard. Despite his nerves, he was getting excited, and he knew he was going to enjoy this on some level. He wasn't at all sure he'd enjoy Manny, though. Manny frightened him.

Nick didn't even have any black friends, much less a black lover. He felt ashamed of his own prejudice, if that's what it was. He felt dirty and secretive.

And the strange thing was, this turned him on too.

"American?" Nick asked.

"No, from here," Manny said in a raspy, sexy English accent. "Where you from, New York?"

Nick wondered if Manny had ever heard of Wisconsin. Plenty of Brits he'd met had not. New York seemed to be what the Brits thought of as the States. That or California.

"Closer to Chicago."

Manny smiled. He had a nice, sexy smile.

"No fucking smiles," the director said. "And get that microphone out of the frame."

The fat guy, now in earphones, jerked upward on the fuzzy boom mic he held in his meaty, red hands.

"Let's fucking get this going," the director said. "Places."

Nick looked at Manny, who shrugged. They walked to the door, then turned to face the bed behind the camera.

"Action," the director said.

Chapter 7

The Present

"*CAN* you sing?"

At LAX, Nick smiled a little despite himself. Despite his grave worries. *Can you sing? If you try?*

He remembered that simple, yet mysteriously fateful, question, casually tossed out. And it took him back to another time. Back to his Wisconsin days, so many years ago.

The bright sunshine made him blink away a memory of snowy mornings and ice-covered roads.

Can I sing?

Sure, I can sing!

Nick smiled broadly now, looking at the haze over Los Angeles.

LA had its associations too, for other reasons.

Now he was in another limo, another time zone, another country, and on to yet another life. In many ways so very far from the Europe where he had lived for so many years.

It was warm here, almost oppressively hot. So unlike London or his home in Ireland, where the damp atmosphere always made him feel like buttoning himself up in cozy wool. Here the morning sunshine made the blue sky electric, and clothes felt heavy. He buzzed the window down. The heat felt good. The air had a tangy odor you never forget: city smells, traces of smog and baking tar and eucalyptus. Sea salt and lemon.

The smells of Los Angeles, of a sprawling Western city so spiced with its special flavor, greeted his nose. If Wisconsin summer air was redolent of pine and the manure of hayfields, and London smelled vaguely of piss and steaming curry, LA was a cotton candy carnival on the beach. Nick let the salty essences of the sea and humidity play upon his senses.

Los Angeles and the start of a new life. *Los Angeles and old trouble.*

St. Augustine, whose *Confessions* Nick had read earlier in the year, had said, "We are here to begin again."

Nick loved that. It gave him some solace now as his head cleared from sleep and the fitful dreams inspired by past events he was still ashamed of, to say nothing of the blackmail scheme with which he was apparently being threatened.

He closed his eyes tight, trying to pray away his worst feelings of dread. It was simply unbearable to think of Wolfy. *God watch over him and protect him*!

Nick believed in those second chances, that blessing that allows every soul *to begin again*. That was the story of his life.

And now his life was at another crossroads. A dangerous one. And he had no choice but to live through it.

He was anxious to get to the rental house—which was outrageously expensive but typical for the Coast—in the Hills, take a shower, and sit down and think all this through.

He had to keep his grinding fears at bay, he knew that. He was starting to feel so angry about the abduction of his innocent young dog he had to grasp the seat cushions of the limo and refrain from tearing them up with his straining muscles.

That kind of violence would solve nothing.

He simmered inside, not only about the blackmail scheme—the viciousness of someone trying to screw him over like this was bad enough. It was the outrageousness of taking an innocent animal that pushed his brain toward meltdown.

Those pictures of him, the younger him—Nick shook his head, snorting like a bull.

Fuck the pictures. Fuck all that! He knew he'd recover from that—wouldn't he? Wouldn't Tolanaro? Was it really Nick's fault Paul was in those compromising shots? Hadn't Paul acted of his own free will that night in 1984? *Why do I feel the need to protect him*?

Odd, perhaps, that Nick would consider the well-being of an animal more important than the reputation of a human being, one who had a long, long way to fall if these secrets got out.

Nick bristled, thinking of this, weighing it yet again in his over-tired mind.

He'd tear apart limb from limb anyone who harmed a hair on his dog!

Well, he was angry now, despite trying to stay cool.

The palm trees waved lazily in smoggy morning light. The limo approached the hills and canyons and enclaves of the talented and rich. How many damnations and tribulations lay behind those ivy-covered iron gates and stone walls?

A strategy was slowly coming together in his mind, at last. It was going to be difficult. It might very well put him in touch with the last person who ever wanted to hear from him, Paul Tolanaro.

Paul had been a featured speaker at the most recent national Republican convention. A "family values" advocate with his own lucrative line of baseball-inspired sportswear.

Paul Tolanaro had at least one secret, though.

He had been, in his golden youth, a lover—if only briefly—of a notorious bad-boy pop star named Nick Davanger, now "mostly forgotten" in the pop music world, though in the literary and theatrical worlds, people were taking notice. This forgotten pop idol was now on the verge of a comeback of sorts thanks to his newfound faith and a bestselling memoir and stage show.

LA was Paul's town.

He knew Paul Tolanaro would keep his distance, even if Nick was in his city again in a notable show. And Nick would keep his side of the bargain too, right? He'd never deliberately harm Paul. He had reluctantly erased something strong in his heart, in his past, and erased any and all connections between them.

He did that, right?

Nick closed his eyes and rubbed his throbbing temples. This ride to his temporary new home seemed interminable.

He'd made peace with Paul in his heart, that much he was sure of. But now that peace was about to be disturbed, big time.

Nick felt sweat in his armpits.

Paul's story had always been a compelling one for Nick, even if they had only been close for a very short time, a critical time.

But that's all past, man, Nick told himself now. *Don't dredge all that up again.*

Nick still loved him, he supposed, but at the greatest distance the heart could invent.

Nick's mood darkened for a few moments. Outside the window, expensive cars were parked in garden-groomed driveways.

He put on his sunglasses. He hadn't slept well on the flight, and his eyes burned, and his mouth felt dry.

His heart surged thinking again of Wolfy jumping in his lap to give his face a lick.

That couldn't happen now... Wolfy was in strange hands, malevolent hands. Evil hands.

Wolfy was a gift of pure love, a gift from the Lord.

Wolfy was his peace of mind.

But that bad feeling in the pit of his stomach wouldn't let up.

He checked his phone, which he'd turned off after the last message from the stranger who had Wolfy. It was filled with voice and text messages, several flashing *urgent*. All from Susie. He felt a bead of sweat roll down his forehead as he read, *"Call as soon as you get in, urgent. S."*

"Oh my God, Nick," was how Susie answered the phone.

He felt anger. He didn't like it when she or anyone started panicking or getting dramatic. It usually wasn't warranted.

This time, though....

"Susie, take a breath," Nick said calmly, masking his own sense of rising panic. "I already know that someone took Wolfy. I'm on my way."

"Hurry," she cried.

Chapter 8

1977

"CAN you sing?"

Young Nick Davangere stood on the wooden risers in the choral music room in the basement of Ledgerock High School of the Sacred Heart of Mary, in rural Appledale, Wisconsin.

The woman asking him that question was Sister Alphonzia. Most of the nuns at Ledgerock didn't wear habits anymore. They wore cheap pantsuits, stretchy slacks, and bland sweaters. Sister A, as the music teacher was known, was kind of hefty. She liked crew-knit sweaters from JCPenney. Students knew that she smoked cigarettes and loved Broadway musicals and used the occasional "damn" or "hell" in her speech.

Nick liked her, and so did most of the students at the private Catholic school at the edge of town overlooking an impressive pine-filled gorge. The "rock" in Ledgerock was one of the glacial boulders that poked out over the ridge of the gorge. Nuns had started a school there a century ago. At first it was a boarding school for girls. Decades before Nick attended, it had gone co-ed.

Tuition at Ledgerock was expensive for kids who bussed (or drove themselves) in from the best homes and neighborhoods in the area. But some local poor kids went there on special "need-based" scholarships, especially if their families were Catholic, as Nick's grandparents were.

Nick never felt more uncomfortable at Ledgerock than he did right now.

Sister A looked him up and down.

"Thank you for coming in here today," she said to him.

He nodded.

But was there any place at Ledgerock where Nick really fit in? It seemed like sports were the road to popularity and notoriety, at Ledgerock maybe even more so than at other American high schools.

But sports were not the road to Nick's self-acceptance or security, even if he was a good softball player.

He felt like a damn outsider in this rural white school.

And he looked like one.

Nick's tuition had been subsidized, in part thanks to an essay he wrote about his mother. "My Mother's Absence" had won a contest, but it had pissed off Grandfather and Grandmother. A constant theme through Nick's high school years was his grandfather's insistence on his athletic aptitude, based on Nick's strength and size, and Nick's contrasting far more artistic nature and tendency toward more solitary pursuits. Nick disliked high school in the years he was actually there. But he would eventually look back on those years with a kind of bittersweet smile.

Even this unnerving audition would be remembered by him as a sweet and possibly portentous rite of passage. But in the moment, it felt like an ordeal.

"Let's try some scales, Nick," Sister A said. She sat at the piano and ran her fingers over the keys. Nick cleared his throat.

What am I doing here? he wondered.

He was not one of the golden, wealthy kids. Nick actually had a job at school too. Nothing glamorous. He cleaned the varsity locker room and straightened out the athletic utility locker after games and practices.

For a while, some of the other kids didn't know he was a fellow student. But he found some ways to distinguish himself.

At Ledgerock, his cartoon-drawing talent had also landed him a so-called "arts scholarship," which further reduced his tuition—and didn't impress his grandfather one bit, despite the savings.

In some ways, Nick outshone many of his classmates in his first year at Ledgerock.

So why didn't he feel like a success?

He wanted success. He could even envision it.

Nick liked *MAD* magazine and dreamed about what it would be like to be a professional cartoonist like Mort Drucker or the wacky Don Martin. But his cartooning, while competent and even inspired at times, was not genius. He didn't place cartooning on a higher level than writing or singing or even reading. It was just something he did.

Like softball. He really preferred reading.

He read all the best sellers, like *Jaws* and *Coma*, and Howard Fast's *The Immigrant*. And he would imagine his own name on a glossy paperback novel.

Nick Davangere—writer. That sounded pretty good. Other days, it was Nick the artist, the contributor to *MAD*. Today, at this audition, the fantasy of Nick *the Singer* seemed absurd to him.

His daydreams were filled with all kinds of artistic pursuits and subsequent fame, fortune, and success. Of course he kept all that stuff secret.

Even more secret were his sex fantasies.

Wow, he thought, feeling suddenly naked on that choral room riser. Don't start thinking about that!

He thought sourly, *You stick out bad enough as it is, Nick Davangere.*

There was exactly one black boy and one black girl in the entire school: Rollo and Cynthia Birdswing. The whole idea of really celebrating school diversity at a place like Ledgerock was at least a couple of decades away, but the Civil Rights Movement and overall liberalism of the seventies somewhat eased the way for Rollo and Cynthia.

Somewhat.

Still, they were the only blacks, and they stuck out.

Stuck out in a way that Nick did not, or so Nick believed.

Rollo was very outgoing and popular. Cynthia, on the other hand, was withdrawn, hard, and had few real friends.

Nick was her friend. But he had to admit even then, it was because he wanted to get closer to Rollo.

Nick would not have described his fascination with Rollo as a crush. Not at the time. Though Rollo was good-looking, with mahogany fine skin, a perfect afro with a fro pick usually planted in it, and a bright, easy smile. He was funny, tough, profane, hip, and a bit dangerous. Or so he seemed in white-bread Appledale.

More than a few of the white boys in school seemed to not only befriend him, but to actually *be him*. The attempts at soul, swagger, and jive talk by some of these kids had to be seen and heard to be believed. Nick found it laughable. Especially since he believed that deep down most of the kids were prejudiced, based on their naïve opinions and occasionally thoughtless, hateful words.

For Nick, it was always complicated.

One afternoon, the school guidance counselor, Sister Beatrice, had asked Nick privately if he'd like to sit in on a special assembly panel with Rollo and Cynthia. It was "prejudice awareness week," she said, and it presented a perfect opportunity for "all the black kids" to tell the white ones how they felt about being minorities in an all-white school. To establish a dialogue and all that stuff.

Nick was stunned. Rollo and Cynthia—*and him*? All the black kids?

Well, was he black?

"I don't get it," he said to Sister Beatrice, who blushed from her hairline to her throat.

"I thought…," she stammered.

"I'm not black," Nick said.

He said it so convincingly he actually almost believed it. And, paradoxically, he knew he was discovering something quite definitively in what other people saw in him. It felt like some kind of truth, a potentially explosive one. Because it carried a freight of secrets and secret shames. The secret his family kept and made him complicit in.

Nick had a white mother, white grandparents, and—somewhere—he had a black father. Simple as that? *Simple nothin'.*

Nick's father, who was not referred to or mentioned around him—ever.

A man who obviously would have had some things in common with Rollo.

Nick's complicated feelings about black men were off and running. Even if he was too scared to see it.

Another teacher had once asked him if he was from Mexico originally. When he looked at her, she gulped and shyly and hopefully asked, "Puerto Rico?"

There was no one he could talk to about this stuff. Rollo was hard to talk to about any serious subject, and he made Nick nervous, besides. Any cute guy did but especially Rollo. Cynthia was too shy or maybe too polite to delve into Nick's personal stuff. Though her outspokenness at times belied that.

"You know, with those pretty green eyes of yours, you could get any chick in this school," Cynthia said in her typical joshing, tough style.

"Really?" Nick said with a grin. "Even you?"

"I know you ain't interested," Cynthia said. "A woman knows."

Nick just smiled.

"Ain't one boy in this school I'd mess with," Cynthia added forcefully.

Nick didn't know if it helped him or hurt him to have Cynthia in the room the day of his choral audition.

Cynthia and a few other girls and just one other boy sat in some folding chairs off to the side of the risers in the big empty choral rehearsal room. It was nearly four o'clock, after school, and the last tryouts for show choir were almost over.

The light was turning gloomy in a way that always made Nick feel kind of ill in the pit of his gut.

NOW Nick knew full well that the kids who got into show choir were usually the most socially successful and outgoing—and well-to-do—in the school. Most jocks had no interest in joining, but the few who did were immensely popular. There were a few nerds and (speculatively) gays also allowed in the show choir, based more on their sheer enthusiasm than on talent.

Nick didn't know where he fit in. He just liked to sing.

Correction: he *loved* to sing.

"I said, can you sing?" Sister A asked again, playfully. She sat at the piano and struck a chord. Why would he be here if he didn't think he could sing? It was late in the day. Maybe Sister A was fiending for a cigarette. Or maybe she was teasing him.

"I usually can," Nick stammered. He looked at Cynthia, who made a brave smile. "I guess I'm nervous."

"Nonsense," Sister A said. "You forgot the lyrics?"

He knew the lyrics to "This Land Is Your Land."

"I know 'em," he said.

"What?" Sister A asked, getting annoyed. "Speak up, Nick. I can't hear you speak, much less sing."

"I said I memorized the lyrics... I don't know... I don't feel too good."

Sister A frowned. She'd had enough.

"Thank you, Nick. You may sit down. Who's next?"

Nick felt as if he'd just received a cold slap in the face. His stage fright had just ruined his chances of getting into the show choir for the next year, which would be his senior year. There wouldn't be any more chances after this, he told himself.

"But... can I come back and try later?" he asked.

Sister A shot him a sympathetic glance.

"No," she said. "You're just not ready."

Nick stepped down off the risers. His face burned with shame. He was completely humiliated. Instead of joining the others sitting in their loose assembly, Nick left the room, closing the door behind him with a trembling hand.

It wasn't that he'd accepted defeat. Everything in him resisted it.

The problem was, he didn't fight for himself.

Why?

Nick wiped tears from his eyes and told himself it didn't matter. It was just a stupid choir.

At home that night he got the usual rough attitude from his grandfather, who was now retired and bored with his life. His grandmother too, had grown distant. It would be many years before he understood what Alzheimer's was or about the toll it took on the caretakers of people so afflicted.

Nick himself projected a taciturn and unloving manner at home.

Like a lot of teenagers, Nick was too wrapped up in his own dramas to notice what was happening in his own house to the couple whose hair had turned snowy white and whose struggle up an invisible hill grew steeper by the day.

"You skipped Mass again Sunday," Grandfather said, eyes narrowing behind his unstylish, clunky black frames. It was an accusation, not a question.

"I don't have time right now to talk to you, Gramps," Nick said, and he whistled for his dog, a Doberman-Lab mix named Lucky.

Nick knew that remark would draw a thunderous response from Grandfather. It did.

"As long as you live under this roof, you'll make time when I say so!" the old man bellowed, rocking violently in a creaking chair that seemed about to shatter apart.

Nick didn't explain about the humiliation at the show choir audition. Not that it would have done any good.

"Then I'll get out from under your damn roof," Nick retorted.

Grandmother just sat staring blankly ahead, her sewing materials, thread and scraps of colored cloth, strewn in her lap. Her bountiful head of hair had turned more silver than white, and she took to wearing it tied back and pulled up. She touched her hair gently with her fingertips as if that would keep it from standing straight up from all the electric tension in the air.

"What?" screamed the old man. "You know where the door is!"

"So did my Mama," Nick said acidly.

He knew they had been trying to find the whereabouts of his mother, despite the estrangement, for most of the past year. Nick felt he hated his mother at this stage of his life and that she deserved his hate. She ran out and dumped him with these two old coots. And left behind the mystery of his identity so taboo it amounted to little more than a lump in his throat for most of his adolescence.

"Don't you dare say that," Grandpa said.

"I'll say what I want," Nick said defiantly. "She was a bitch, how about that?" Nick grinned deviously. He found he took pleasure in riling Grandfather. He knew that was bad. But so what? Grandpa had arthritic knees from working, and he couldn't give chase. But he could still shout and holler. This comment seemed to up his volume level.

"You—get outta my sight!" Grandfather shouted.

"Sure will," Nick replied. "Then you'll be outta mine!"

He seemed to have no trouble improvising in front of an enraged old man. So why couldn't he utter a note in front of a generally encouraging nun, his good friend, and a few nerds?

He went out to play with Lucky, who was almost six, but still lively as a pup. Living just outside of Appledale on a farm (technically a "farmette," with just a few acres of barely tended garden), gave Nick a lot of space to run around and have his solitude. That's what he needed. The world inside that cramped little house was getting smaller and narrower.

By the time he came back later, he found his supper, cooked by Grandfather (Grandma was no longer allowed near the stove since she started a small grease fire by accident), in the fridge.

Poor Grandmother must have known she was losing her mind, little by little. Nick felt bad about that. Even though Grandmother had a harder time expressing herself and showing love and affection, he knew she loved him. Sometimes she was lucid, and at other times she seemed lost in her own world.

"I know you're special," she would say, when he was little. "I look into those green eyes that shine like jewels, and I just know God didn't make a mistake. He made a good boy, and he gave you to us. We'll never know why." And she would give him a warm, dry kiss on the cheek.

"What a life," Nick said to Lucky, giving her a few scraps of the meatloaf Gramps made three nights a week, when he wasn't boiling hotdogs or heating up a frozen pizza. Lucky snapped up the scrap, swallowed, and immediately turned her begging eyes on her next hopeful bite.

Her tail wagged and whipped. She raised her right front paw. Nick hugged her and buried his nose in her luxuriant coat, which smelled so good to him.

The best part of home was having Lucky. The worst, of course, was having to live with his grandparents.

A teenage boy, Nick didn't dwell on the sacrifices and trials of his grandparents. He resented them and wanted to be away from them. It would be years before he could see anybody else's side of the story and begin to forgive.

One day, Rollo and Cynthia stopped attending Ledgerock. They transferred to public school near Appledale.

Nick had never asked why because he didn't think he'd ever see them again.

But one day, he did see Rollo. Rollo was in a beat-up car, driving past Nick on a country road. Rollo almost didn't stop.

And Rollo wasn't in a friendly mood.

Nick shouted after the car. Rollo hit the brakes and came to a screeching stop.

"What are you doing way out here in the country?" Nick called, running alongside the vehicle. He leaned into the window of the rumbling, idling machine. The backseat was full of stuff—a suitcase, stereo, full plastic bags. "Where you going?"

"Far away from here," Rollo said. "Chicago, maybe. Or Florida or Mexico."

"You mean, you're going somewhere but don't know where?"

"Course I do," Rollo said, frowning angrily at Nick. "Away."

"Will you write me and tell me where you end up?" Nick asked impulsively. Lucky ran up and licked Nick's hand and pawed at him.

"That's something a girl would say," Rollo scoffed, and Nick felt deeply ashamed.

"I didn't mean it like that," Nick said.

"You don't know what you mean, Mr. *emerald eyes and high yella.*" Rollo laughed at his own mean joke. "This ain't no place for anybody who ain't a hundred percent lily white, and boy, you and me just ain't. Oh, you wanna be!" Rollo snorted a laugh. "But yuh ain't and never will be."

"Is that why you gotta go too?" Nick asked.

"I don't gotta do nothin' but stay black and die," Rollo snorted.

Nick said nothing.

"Get outta the door. You holdin' me up," Rollo said.

Nick stepped back. He felt burned. Rollo had no cause to be so angry with him. All he'd wanted was to be friends. And that's what seemed to anger Rollo.

"Please tell Cynthia I said hi," Nick said.

"See what I mean?" Rollo said shrilly. "You say *hi* when you oughta mean *bye*!"

"She's going too?" Nick asked weakly. But Rollo didn't hear him.

With that, Rollo roared away down the road, and Lucky barked until Nick pulled her close and softly whispered, "Shushhhh."

NICK did just okay in high school. But he managed to distinguish himself in some special ways at Ledgerock, a musty old school that smelled like chlorine and chalk-dust and moldering wood.

It would take years, but eventually Nick would look back on Ledgerock as a place of especially dedicated teachers, many of whom were nuns who struggled mightily to keep the school running and to provide a solid education to its generations of graduates.

But while he was there, Ledgerock felt like a prison. He was an outsider. He didn't know at the time that many if not most teenagers experienced feelings of alienation in school.

In some ways, Nick excelled.

In his drawing classes, he received As. His cartooning abilities stood out. Not only did his classmates appreciate this talent, some of his teachers also found it charming. Nick had an innate ability for storytelling too, and it showed in his writing. So he received As in his English classes and anything involving writing. He was seen as having imagination, creativity, a "certain flair"—even artistic aptitude perhaps rare at Ledgerock, or at least uncommon.

He took a photography course, for which he also received an A. In music, he only got Bs, in both junior chorus and in his guitar class. In chorus, he didn't "sing out," as Sister A had told him. He tried instead to simply blend in.

Blending in was apparently never going to work out well for him.

He got a B.

Same with physical education: Bs. He had gone out for freshman football but gave it up when time came for varsity tryouts. He played on the softball team his freshman, sophomore, and junior years but refused to go out for the sport in his senior year.

Nobody begged him to change his mind.

He was actually pretty good, though. But his heart wasn't in it. If anyone had asked him what he really loved among his budding talents, he'd have been stuck for an answer.

In math he'd gotten Cs and even a D until the comic-looking, plump, and gray-hued Sister Marie challenged him to study for his algebra exam. He liked her, so he did as she instructed, memorizing all the formulas and discovering that this trick could work in other classes too. Grandfather nearly fainted when he saw that Nick, who had always struggled with math, had an A on his report card in Sister Marie's class.

Nick was proud of that.

Nick studied in his biology class, too, despite disliking the old nun who taught it. Sister Frances resembled a frog, with brown-and-black warts on her rubbery face and hands. It didn't help that she was imperious, bullying, and dismissive. Once she'd called him to the front of the room to ask him why he'd spelled the same word two different ways on the same test.

The word was "entropy."

He didn't know why he'd done that. It was a mistake, not deliberate.

Sister Frances had a way of humiliating her students.

"Well?" she asked. "Why did you spell it correctly here"—she tapped the page with her pen—"and incorrectly here?"

Nick shook his head. All eyes in the classroom were on him.

"I don't know," he said. "Maybe I'm lazy?"

He grinned, deeply embarrassed. He supposed he'd hoped being self-deprecating would ease the sting.

"No," Sister Frances said, smiling. "You're stupid."

A few mouths dropped open among his classmates. Nick felt embarrassed as hell.

"I'm not stupid," Nick said, blood coming into his face. He stood very close to old Sister Frances. Up close he could see the nasty hairs on her chin and a tiny moustache.

"You're stupid," she taunted.

Any other student's parents, upon catching wind of this kind of bullying, would have marched over to the school and demanded a meeting with the principal, at the very least. Maybe Sister Frances knew Nick had no such parent.

Maybe that's why she called him stupid in front of everyone.

Nick never told his grandparents about the incident. But it made him wonder how a venerated nun at a school supposedly dedicated to the love of God, Christ, and the Virgin Mary could casually humiliate a student like that. To teach him how to spell "entropy?" She'd taught there for over forty years.

Nick received the highest score on the next biology exam. And though Sister Frances usually announced who made the highest grade each exam, she didn't bother to praise Nick. He saw the high score, and the A-plus. And he watched as Sister Frances wrote the high score on the blackboard and drew a graded curve.

So here was a chance for her to show him some praise. Perhaps contrast her assessment of him as "stupid."

She didn't do it.

She didn't like him.

The feeling was mutual.

Nick's Ledgerock years were eased somewhat by his movie theater job and the use of his grandfather's Ford Galaxy 500. He was able to save almost $3,000 for college. The movie theater, called the Squareplex, had two screens. He could see every film for free. Movies like *Smokey and the Bandit* played for months on end, but comedies also played there, like *Annie Hall* and a sexy, raucous Richard Pryor comedy called *Which Way is Up*.

It amused Nick to hear the redneck customers disparage Pryor for what was considered then outrageous sexual humor. These "critics" didn't always comment so much on Pryor's humor as on his race, in crudest terms.

In moments like this, Nick's ears pricked up and his face burned.

But he put on a good stoic, impassive attitude. And if strangers commented, as people would, upon his green eyes, his trademark, he would narrow them to slits. He went into a deep freeze. A cool that calmed the hot outrage and pain.

A kind of cool that threatened to ice over his whole heart.

AFTER work at the movie theater, after coming home late at night down ragged country roads in the Galaxy 500, Nick would find his meals wrapped in tinfoil on a plate in the fridge. Nick ate ravenously. By this late hour, after he helped shut down the movie theater after the last show, he was almost too tired to study and do his homework. But he made the best of it.

He also always tried to read a bit before bed. Stephen King's *The Shining* was his favorite novel of that year when he worked at the movie house.

Lucky slept on his bed, and Nick would bury his nose in her soft fur.

And that cold heart of his would melt a little.

Being calm, he could read, getting lost in a good story until he drifted off.

Nick almost always slept soundly, no matter what.

He hated getting up on those cold Wisconsin mornings in his threadbare underwear. It was cold, tramping to the bathroom down the hall. And some days, he just didn't want to face the world. High school just wasn't his scene, but it was something he knew he had to get through, get it over and done with.

If friends were hard to come by at a snooty Catholic school, adults weren't beating a path to his side either.

A red-goateed priest at Ledgerock seemed to have it in for Nick. One afternoon, Father Durg, who was pear-shaped and sadly had a hook where his right hand had been, told Nick to go to the principal's office and ask for a detention slip when he saw Nick eating a piece of red licorice at his locker.

"No eating in the halls," Durg had barked in his oddly soprano voice as he walked by.

It felt to Nick as if he was being singled out for this bitter man's attention and his wrath. Other kids chewed gum and ate candy in the halls between classes all the time. The same rules didn't seem to apply to everyone.

Still, Nick had broken a rule and been caught.

Nick obediently went to the small disciplinary office to get his detention slip. But just before he opened the door to walk in, he decided *to hell with that.*

If Father Durg had the nerve to follow up, Nick would probably get two detentions.

But if the priest didn't bother, he was free and clear. For now.

Nick left the office area without bothering to pick up his detention notice.

But Nick kept a wary eye out for the priest.

Nick noticed that Father Durg liked to joke and roughhouse with the most popular and good-looking male athletes at Ledgerock. And when Father Durg received an artificial hand (an event of school-wide curiosity), he sometimes teased certain of the male athletes with the hand's cold touch in a kind of game of tag. The removable hand was only worn on certain occasions, in place of the apparently more useful and dexterous hook. The peachy flesh-tone hand came to signify a jocular mood in the priest and an occasion for merriment and affection among his favorites. But he reserved nothing but scorn for Nick whenever he saw him. Nick detested the sound of the priest's metal hook tapping nervously upon the walls as he patrolled the hallways and restrooms. And he did not like the looks of that rubbery hand, even if it aroused sympathy for the priest's mysterious wound.

It was impossible to avoid the priest completely, though Nick tried. The school wasn't all that big.

Father Durg was not handsome, but he was not unattractive. Yet he was far from athletic and graceful, nor in any way cool or "with it." However, he affected to be so, and he exuded a kind of confidence or arrogance that was common at Ledgerock. It was bad enough when younger boys acted this way to curry favor among the top athletes. But a mature priest?

It was sickening. Almost as sickening as the way so many of the students sucked up to Father Durg, pretending to polish his bald head or fishing candy bars from the deep pockets of his voluminous robes.

One thing was certain, though. Father Durg did not like Nick, and he sneered whenever he saw him. He spoke roughly to him, with none of the affection he reserved for his favorites.

Nick didn't know what it was about Father Durg that made the old priest take a negative interest in him.

It might have been racism.

It might have been homophobia.

But these were not concepts Nick cared to analyze in depth.

It would be a long time before he started connecting the dots. At Ledgerock, if he didn't really care that much about fitting in perfectly, he at least wanted to lie low and remain unobtrusive.

That was of course impossible. He was different—a different color, acted in a different manner, and thought in different ways, in budding artistic ways. And he was growing up and growing into his striking good looks. His brilliant, flashing green eyes were getting noticed.

But not by the ones he'd hoped to attract.

Years later, Nick saw Father Durg by chance in of all places, a gay bar in Milwaukee. Thinner, no longer wearing a Roman collar, a reddish toupee on his head, Father Durg was nonetheless unmistakable. Nick was visiting some acquaintances at the University of Wisconsin at its Milwaukee campus, and he'd daringly snuck into the gay bar by himself, to see what it was like. There were no gay bars at UW-Stevens Falls.

The bar was called Sammy's Hideaway. It had no sign. Customers entered through a back door.

It was dark inside except for the lights coming from the dance floor.

Nick arrived relatively early that night, and the bar was not crowded. Nick felt fairly anxious being there, but his curiosity gave him just enough confidence to keep his cool. He looked around hopefully at the smattering of other guys in the bar.

And there was none other than Father Durg, in blue jeans, leaning against the bar, looking out at the small dance floor at Sammy's Hideaway. He still had that red goatee. Gloria Gaynor's "I Will Survive" was pumping away over the big speakers.

Nick could hardly believe his eyes. He stared across the room at his old tormentor. When Father Durg saw that he was being noticed, he gave a big smile to Nick, apparently not yet recognizing a former Ledgerock student down here in the city famous for its breweries and endless corner bars.

Nick deliberately and slowly produced a very knowing sly smile on his face. A look that simmered with seductiveness but also with catlike satisfaction. Father Durg looked intently back at him. And then all of a sudden, his smile went flat. It kept falling. His eyes widened with fear.

He recognized Nick.

Nick chuckled and sipped his drink, looking at the DJ booth, the spinning mirror ball. Checking out the other guys. What on earth would he say to Father Durg if he came over to talk? This thought added to the strange electricity of being in such an illicit place. God, if his friends at Stevens Falls saw him in a *disco*, they'd be aghast. And if they knew what kind of disco, they'd probably shit themselves!

When Nick looked over again, Father Durg was no longer at the bar. He was gone, having made a very hasty exit.

A few years later Nick learned from a gay waiter he knew that Father Durg had left the priesthood and moved to San Francisco. But during the time he was still teaching biology at Ledgerock, he'd snuck into gay bars and blew gay waiters. But only after getting stinking drunk.

Nick would come to think of this as a typical Ledgerock story. Hypocrisy through and through. It would be a long time before he felt sympathy and forgiveness for those people.

Though from time to time, he thought of poor Father Durg with his false hand and his false hair, and the one and only time he had ever smiled at Nick or showed him any positive interest.

Why couldn't he have been a help to Nick at school, instead of just another bully? A powerful one at that.

High school was tough on everyone but was tougher on those seen as outsiders, he thought, even at his tender age.

Despite Nick's disappointment about the show choir, he was asked by Sister A to join the much larger, far less prestigious mixed chorus, which performed more traditional choral music every year at Christmas and Easter.

Nick was even given a solo to sing at Christmas, in Latin, from the "Requiem" by Verde. He imitated the singing style of a popular jock, which seemed sort of clear and straight, if not something right out of the Lawrence Welk TV program.

Nick's voice was clear and strong, and he went over well.

He found out he loved the sound of the applause.

IN HIS senior year of high school Nick learned how to smoke pot, drink beer, and occasionally fight with his fists. He hung out with a couple of somewhat motley guys who also lived outside of town. Jonny and Buzz had long hair, loved Led Zeppelin, and talked ceaselessly about girls, usually in pretty crude terms.

Not surprisingly, both were unlucky when it came to attracting female companionship.

Jonny was a bug-eyed blond with bandy legs.

Buzz was a reddish brunet with a handsome Roman nose and a pudgy face rife with acne and pockmarks. Jonny was skinny as a beanpole. Buzz was muscular, and he wore tight, dirty white T-shirts that showed off smooth biceps.

Nick was considered a much better-looking boy, but he had little status among the cold cliques at Ledgerock.

That situation worsened one afternoon in the school commons when a bullying, towheaded, oversize jock named Stirvus called Nick a fag.

Nick had turned around slowly to face the bully. Buzz and Jonny had kept moving. In high school, being called "fag" didn't necessarily mean you were gay. But if you were even slightly afraid you might be, and this was your deep dark secret, it carried a special sting. In fact, it left a scar.

"Come on," Buzz called after Nick.

"You say something to me?" Nick said to Stirvus. He said it coolly. His stomach was doing flips and dangerous swan dives. He surprised himself with his daring. Was he actually going to stand up for himself? The scared little boy inside him was making a dangerous play to meet that newfound height and athleticism with which his body had filled out over the past winter.

Nick stood up to his full height. He thrust his chest out and held his head high, elongating his neck. He stuck out his chin and narrowed his eyes, the way he'd seen actors do on TV. Clint Eastwood came to mind.

Maybe he was only acting, striking a pose. But didn't animals do that when asserting dominance?

Stirvus got in Nick's face. He towered over Nick.

"What if I did, *spook*," he said.

Spook? That was a new one to Nick. Of course he knew it was no compliment.

This Stirvus character was (and this could only happen at a smarmy school like Ledgerock) a school leader. Popular, mean, considered a real amusing guy. Not only did the other popular kids like him, the faculty, priests, and nuns also admired him.

Nick thought Stirvus was a pig-face. They were not quite evenly matched in size, but Nick wasn't going to back down. Not this time.

Nick gave a derisive snort, then turned to follow his friends. Stirvus blocked him, causing Nick to walk right into him. Stirvus felt hard, unyielding. Like a wall of fat.

"Whoa, watch where you're going, cocksucker," Stirvus snarled.

Nick surprised Stirvus. He surprised himself too. He made a fist. No sooner had he closed his fingers than he shot his arm out like a lion's paw. He brought his powerful fist up and around lightning fast and smacked Stirvus in the side of his head.

Stirvus took two steps backward before his eyes rolled up in his head.

A couple of Stirvus's friends started toward Nick.

Nick held up his fists.

The friends of Stirvus backed down. They helped the stumbling Stirvus away.

"You'll regret that," said a girl with red hair and freckles on a bland donut of a face. Despite her lack of charm, this girl, called Paulette, was powerful in select Ledgerock circles.

"You can kiss my ass too," Nick said, pumped up.

But Nick knew his remaining days at Ledgerock were going to get worse.

Before this incident, he didn't think that was possible.

But he also knew that no one was ever going to mess with him again and not get a fight in return.

SOMETIMES Nick had feelings for Buzz, feelings he couldn't quite name.

"You lookin' for something?" Buzz asked Nick once. Nick realized he'd been dreamily staring at Buzz, who was lounging in the springtime grass in his white T-shirt and filthy jeans.

"No," Nick answered, sounding sort of offended. Nick tore up a handful of grass and let the blades sift through his fingers.

But he was looking for something.

Every once in a while, for many years to come, he would think about Buzz's question and all the things it really implied. Sometimes, it was an admonishment, or an invitation, or just an innocent question. Yet he never forgot it.

Romance of a sort had come to Nick in a way he'd not expected, earlier in his senior year.

A girl named Caroline in Nick's photography class took an interest in him. She had long, flowing brown hair and a kind of hip style that Nick found easygoing.

Nick took Caroline to the homecoming dance, and they kissed on the dance floor as a mirror ball glittered over the festively decorated student commons. The other students and faculty saw this kiss. That had upped Nick's status some. But what about his true feelings for Caroline?

One cool fall afternoon, before the sun set over the pretty farm where Caroline lived with her prosperous parents, Nick and Caroline walked along a marshy path and shot pictures of the landscape and of one another with their 35mm cameras.

They stopped and sat beside one another against a big glacial boulder. They started to kiss and make out, like they usually did out here.

Nick didn't really enjoy French kissing with Caroline. He liked her well enough. But it was obvious she liked him a whole lot more than he did her.

"Everything okay?" she asked.

"I guess so," he answered.

She smiled sadly. Her eyes were big doe's eyes, and her hair was radiant in the fading sunlight.

She was sweet, innocent, and a kind of rebel white girl willing to risk the nasty glances and gossip small-town, small-minded people made when they saw a white girl with a not-so-white boy.

Holding hands, their solidarity felt like a power against this provincial scorn. In a way, he loved her for it.

But after a time, he stopped calling her. They never had a break-up scene. She never asked what had happened between them that caused them to drift apart.

Nick would not have been able to provide an answer if she'd asked.

On graduation night, at a party at someone's house—the well-to-do family of a popular girl named Twigs—Nick ended up in a bedroom on top of a pile of coats with a boy who had never spoken a single word to him through four years of high school.

Bern was midlevel popular, an athlete, dark blond, and cute in a rugged, rough way. His skin was still spotty, and his smile mildly gap-toothed. Not someone Nick would have pegged as gay or bi-curious.

Or whatever Bern was at that particular moment on that high-spirited night.

They were both pretty drunk. Bern had chatted up Nick all night long. It actually thrilled Nick to have Bern's attention.

Late that evening, they slipped away from the party, going into the bedroom where the coats were stacked to smoke a joint together. That intimate act between young men, in which saliva is swapped on the damp end of the joint without a second thought, seemed to spark a magnetic attraction. Then, mildly shaking with the first rush of the high, they rested side by side on a bed covered with coats. Staring up at the ceiling, they laughed convulsively then looked deep into each other's bright eyes.

They were alone with the door closed, having committed this secret, forbidden act of smoking. The air was foggy with the familiar burnt-leaf odor. A small, low-wattage bulb burned in a lamp beside the bed.

Smiling, Bern leaned against Nick, and the next thing Nick knew Bern's warm, moist lips were pressed against Nick's. With a light scrape of beard stubble, they kissed deeply.

Now this kiss was different! Very different than Caroline's kiss. It was electrifying, and it sent Nick's heart soaring to the moon and set his blood boiling and his loins afire with desire.

They kissed in the semidarkness for a while, moving their hands smoothly over chests and arms and legs. And they kissed some more. Forbidden, completely tantalizing kisses.

Every part of Nick's body felt like a magnet attracted to Bern's body. Needless to say, his penis throbbed with heat and splendid sensations.

The bedroom door opened just then, and two giggling girls rushed in. Nick and Bern had time to jarringly separate their lips and hands before the girls saw them. The girls jumped on the bed and soon Nick had one of them in his arms, and so did Bern. Molly Smithson and Gail Thomlin. Best buddies. Snobs too, at least until this night.

Whatever was in the air this night, Nick loved it. It was, he thought in a rush, not only the last celebratory night of high school, but a night of childhood's ending. Of adulthood's beginning. *Of freedom.*

Now these giggling girls wanted in on the party. One was a redhead and the other was a brunette with a bowl cut.

"Smells like good weed," Molly exclaimed.

"Don't keep it all to yourselves," Gail chimed, leaning against Nick. "Share and share alike."

Molly found the joint on the night table and flicked it to life with a red plastic lighter. She and Gail toked and giggled some more.

Pretty soon all four of them were rolling around together on the bed, laughing riotously at first. But then there was silence as they kissed and began to explore.

Nick was charged up enough to perform with Gail, he figured. Molly pulled her top off and placed Bern's hand on her breast. She straddled his trunk with her long legs and ground against him. Bern watched as Gail played with Nick's erect cock through his pants, which she slowly unzipped. Bern struggled to get his own pants and shorts down, and was soon pumping away on top of Molly as she moaned with pleasure.

Gail stripped most of her clothes off, and Nick closed his eyes. He felt his pants being tugged down by Gail.

Nick sucked on Gail's tits as she jerked him off.

Before he knew it, she climbed on top of him, and she guided him into her. He felt his hard-on sliding into her tight, slick, hot vagina. He was fucking her! Bern looked over at him with a wide grin. He sort of collapsed on top of Molly, exhausted.

Gail cried out, coming. Or at least that's what it sounded like. She climbed off of Nick and took his dick in her hand.

Nick came in Gail's hand in an explosion that seemed to make the room spin.

After that, everyone passed out except for Nick. No one in the house seemed to notice or mind what had just happened in this room. Nick would find out the next morning that some people had spied through the partially cracked door. He laughed when he heard that. And when he heard that most of the other party-goers had all passed out hours earlier.

Nick dressed and switched off the lamp beside the bed. His head was starting to spin a bit. He sat, then he lay his head down on the pile of coats. Just as he was about to fall asleep, a hand sought his.

He grasped back.

Bern's hand. Buried beneath the covers. Nick held his hand tightly. Sleep came quickly.

In the morning, the four of them had pancakes at the Ihop in Appledale and smoked cigarettes and drank black coffee. They all looked a bit worse for wear but were in good humor, laughing and joking. Bern, Molly, Nick, and Gail, who had never really bothered to get to know one another at their little high school. All of them promising to be friends forever, no matter where the four winds scattered them.

But that was the last Nick ever saw of them.

Chapter 9

IN 1978 Nick got into the university at Stevens Falls thanks to his creative writing skills and his art abilities. His essay and a couple of poems impressed an English professor on the admissions and scholarships committee. Nick was even granted a work-study scholarship on the staff of the school paper.

At the *Punter,* he was supposed to draw cartoons and write the occasional piece on assignment, which he did with relish. The general layout of the weekly paper was also his responsibility, and he found he loved graphic design. For eight hours a week, he also worked in the graphics arts laboratory beneath the library where the newspaper was published, learning to set type, shoot PMT images, and design other print graphics in black and white. For a kid growing up loving *MAD* magazine and being crazy about the print medium, the job was a dream come true.

Being on campus in the golden Wisconsin autumn felt like a wonderful fantasy. Romance was in the clear, bracing air. Colorful leaves crunched underfoot as Nick walked past venerable old campus buildings where bells rang out and youth was in full blossom.

It was generally agreed at Barrows Hall on campus that Nick had the best work-study job imaginable, and he did feel lucky his freshman year. Blowing up images of pop stars into posters he hand-colored (never giving a thought to copyright violations) also gave him cachet with his new group of college friends.

His greatest stroke of luck, though, was meeting Casey Zinder, who became his best friend. After the first semester, Casey and Nick became roommates and shared a dorm room for the next year and a half.

It was a blessing and a curse.

If high school had been a time of confusing if somewhat loosely explored sexuality for Nick, college didn't seem to be presenting the answers he was looking for. He was technically an adult with a lot more freedom. But he'd yet to really taste the sexual freedom that would be a lasting legacy of the late seventies. Everyone else seemed to be deep into sex, drugs, and rock and roll. Nick felt like he was merely watching from the sidelines.

He turned heads on campus. Both genders! Even though male homosexuality was very on the down low, it was obviously going on more than anyone admitted. This was the end of a really closeted era and the flowering of gay rights and coming out gay consciousness. If New York and San Francisco were exploding with gay pride and gay power, towns like Stevens Falls in the Midwest seemed mighty far away from all that. Though all college towns had gay people, budding gay activists, murmurs of incipient revolution.

Nick kept his feelings to himself. Even though his feelings grew more powerful as the weeks went by.

Nick fell headlong in love with Casey, an olive-skinned, muscular guy from a remote northern Wisconsin town. Casey, despite his name, claimed Italian and American Indian heritage for himself. Into his dark eyes, Nick could fall endlessly, the way he did for Marlon Brando when he watched his old movies on TV.

Casey became Nick's hero. He could do no wrong.

Casey played a steel string guitar. Like Nick, he was not a serious musician, yet he had natural ability. Many a night they played songs together on guitar, trying out their own versions of the music of Neil Young, the Beatles, Bruce Springsteen, and James Taylor.

This was the year that Nick started getting into The Cars and Devo and Talking Heads. "New wave" music many others on campus found strange. Casey got into it too, and together these inseparable roommates wrote gag songs with a punk edge. Nick always found the Sex Pistols music just a little too out there and unmelodic to boot. But he liked Blondie, The Pretenders, and a group out of Los Angeles called X.

One night Nick and Casey brought their guitars to the coffee house in the student union on open mic night. But neither of them could work up the nerve to get on stage and sing.

It wasn't like the kids getting up on stage were much better than Nick and Casey. But they believed in themselves. Nick and Casey didn't have the self-confidence to face the criticism they imagined awaited them if they were to sing on an obscure stage in a town barely on the map.

"Let's go," Casey said. "I'm not ready for this."

"I guess I'm not either," Nick said, trying to hide his disappointment. The night wind was cold. They walked close side by side, their cased guitars in tow.

Instead of making their stage debut, they went to a local honky-tonk and got drunk on beer. But the night was more memorable to Nick than any stage appearance could have been. That was the first night they'd kissed.

Back in their dorm room, alone, in the dark, Nick tasted love in his first sweet swoon.

To Nick's everlasting frustration, nothing happened with Casey beyond those kisses. Wonderful as they were, they were not enough.

At night, in their respective beds, Nick on the bottom bunk and Casey on the top one, Nick would dream of holding Casey close.

"Are you awake?" he whispered.

Casey grunted a reply.

"Don't you feel like... doing something?" Nick asked, his mouth dry, his throat aching.

"Doing something?" Casey asked. "What?"

"I thought maybe... well, maybe you'd know," Nick said.

When Nick tried to express how he felt to Casey, however inarticulately, Casey shrugged it off.

"Uh... hmm," Casey said sleepily. Not finishing whatever it was he was saying. And soon he was sleeping, the rhythm of his breathing slow and deep and steady.

On the night of those experimental kisses, back in their dorm room after many rounds of drinks, Nick urged Casey to join him in his bed on the bottom bunk.

"I'm not queer," Casey said, laughing. He undressed down to his white briefs and climbed up into his own squeaking bunk, on top. There were more squeaks of bedsprings as Casey settled in above Nick's head.

"I'm not either," Nick replied. "But... I'd like to... you know... uh...."

"Hm," Casey replied in that thick sleepy voice, a grunt of a response that meant... nothing. The matter was dropped in the darkness. Forgotten, and yet not really forgotten, by morning.

Life went on unremarkably, falling into a routine that included classes, studies, and those trips to the gym together, exercise and running, and then the shower.

Nick always took secret furtive glances at Casey's beautiful body in the shower. The whiteness and tan-lines marking his jutting ass. The powerful poetry of his thighs. The way his sparse chest hair flattened out under the shower spray. The poignant beauty in his sex.

Casey haunted Nick's waking hours, and his dreams.

Whenever Nick again brought up the prospect of actual lovemaking as a possibility between them Casey made a joke of it.

"Come on, Casey. Let's just try it out, once," Nick proposed daringly.

"You're kidding, right?" Casey asked roughly with a half grin.

"Maybe," Nick mumbled in reply.

Casey would verbally wrestle him down. He'd find a way to stop the conversation from happening. Then they'd go to the gym, yet again walking over the icy black trails of a Wisconsin winter night. They would run sweaty laps around the gymnasium balcony, lift a few barbells and dumbbells (neither of them were very serious about weightlifting), and come back and shower together.

And that was it.

Nick eventually tried to keep himself from the sweet torture of seeing Casey's naked body, but sometimes he couldn't. Casey often went around naked in the dorm room they shared and took to sleeping in the nude.

It didn't occur to Nick at the time that Casey would consciously tease him—or torture him. Yet how could Casey not know that showing himself naked in front of Nick was provocative in the extreme?

Nick was so distracted and disturbed and aroused by these seemingly innocent displays. When Casey would leave for class, Nick would strip completely and jack off, all the while fanaticizing about Casey, and come to a powerful climax. His semen would blast out, one time shooting over his head when he was lying flat on his bunk.

Despite all this, Nick still didn't think he was 100 percent gay. Instead, he conjured up an idea that maybe all guys felt this way toward each other under certain circumstances, depending on the person or object of their interest. In this scenario, all "normal" guys (like Casey and like Nick) could have these kinds of healthy attractions. In the manner of the Greeks Nick was reading about in the works of Plato and Aristotle.

Casey obviously cared about Nick. Maybe loved him, in a buddy kind of way.

Nick felt that love, and so much more.

And he literally prayed Casey would eventually feel the same way toward him.

But as time went by, it became more and more obvious that Casey didn't seem to feel, or couldn't feel, that way about Nick.

Or if he did, he just wouldn't bring himself to act on it. Nick held out hope for this modicum as his crush deepened and worsened.

Meanwhile, he tried to divert himself to what was ostensibly his reason for being at Stevens Falls. His studies.

Nick took a drawing class and was thunderstruck to learn that in a more advanced art class, next door in the modern, concrete-and-glass fine arts building, a male athlete posed twice a week completely nude.

The thought simply haunted Nick. It was one thing to see naked guys in the shower. It was quite another to know one was posing as others gazed at him intently.

Nick would go as far as to walk back and forth by the door to the classroom, hoping to catch a glimpse. The idea a guy was exposed like that continued to play into Nick's fantasies. He all but burned up with passion thinking about it, this unseen, naked male stranger, though he had never so much as laid eyes on the model.

But he was unlucky and never did see the naked student. He was beginning to feel that all of his luck had run out and he was never going to fulfill himself.

Near the end of the semester, three things happened that would have long-lasting implications in Nick's life.

And then a fourth thing that would shake him to his core.

A SHORT story Nick wrote entitled "The Ghost of a Mississippi Slave" was published the following spring in the campus literary magazine, called the *Horn of Plenty*. Just as Nick had excelled (by UW-SF standards, which were not too shabby) in his essay writing, the story won him some special attention. A prize letter was signed by the governor. The shock came when the citation called him "one of Wisconsin's young and gifted black artists of the 1980s."

Black artist? Me?

Black, that was one thing.

Artist? Now that was something, too, and he liked the sound of it.

Nick did not think of himself as black. He thought of himself as basically white, no matter how nonsensical that suspect sentiment was, even to him.

At this point in his life, he also did not think of himself as gay. He thought of himself as straight.

A belief was a belief, no matter how the ground shifted or quaked beneath it.

Now there was a crack in the firmament. His journey was not at all what he'd planned when he set out. But was anybody's? Nick's heart was already searching where his mind refused to go.

On an afternoon of clear blue skies, but murky and misty interior thoughts, an English teacher had assigned Nick's class the reading of

"Sonny's Blues" by James Baldwin. The story, while powerful, did not affect Nick in any special way. His ears pricked up, though, when the teacher, buxom Mrs. Hanson, told of how Baldwin had become a controversial writer when he wrote a groundbreaking "homosexual love story" set in Paris called *Giovanni's Room*.

The novel was decades old, but even its name carried a whiff of forbidden—and tantalizing—mystery. Nick had all but run to the college library that night to find it and begin reading it.

He read the novel over the course of a few clear, cold, starry nights.

His mind was on fire each night as he left the library. He let his other studies go while he absorbed this amazing tale.

And that book changed his life. He felt it as he neared the end. The shock of recognition. The perspiration on his hands and armpits as he turned the final pages.

He read everything he could by James Baldwin. It struck him as only slightly strange that Baldwin, a black artist, had written in *Giovanni's Room* about white people. The main character, who was white, was a guy Nick identified with. The guy didn't especially want to be a homosexual. But he was deeply in love with the tragic and beautiful Italian, Giovanni. The denial of that love had led to tragedy.

Nick rewrote his tale with James Baldwin in mind. It was only ten pages long. The ghost, who had only been an observer in the original version, now avenged himself against an old family that had oppressed *his* ancestors and their descendants for years.

It wasn't a great story, Nick knew. But it struck a nerve in him, and he hoped it would do the same for others.

Nick sent it in to a statewide competition, just slipping it in before the deadline.

In the fall, a check for $500 from the state Arts and Humanities Board would help Nick secure his place on the semester abroad program in England. A trip he looked forward to with sleepless, eager anticipation.

He'd made up his mind to take the trip and get as far away from his home and college as he could. England seemed plenty far.

Nick met with his advisor in the cramped office in the Main Hall on a bright autumn day.

Mr. Jin reviewed Nick's application to study abroad, as well his financial statement. "You can barely afford this program, but that's not unusual among our students," said the graying Korean professor. "A loan will cover your basic needs, and a lack of spending money might keep you out of trouble and a little closer to your studies."

Nick nodded.

"I want to talk about something more serious," Mr. Jin said, setting Nick's heart racing.

"Okay," Nick said.

"It's your academic record. Here you are collecting honors, and you are barely cutting a three-point GPA, Nick. Why is that?"

Nick felt shame warming his face.

"Is that so bad?" he asked.

"No, it isn't bad at all, but you obviously have the talent to do better. Looking at your transcripts here and your personal records, you seem to dabble in many areas. Music, painting, and now writing. But without real mastery in any of them."

Nick was stunned, but listened carefully.

"You need to focus on one thing, not be a jack of all trades," Mr. Jin said. He was a kindly and conservative Asian gentleman who was never to be seen out of crisp blazer and tie. "I've seen your drawings, and in your personal essay you say that you can sing 'above average', play the guitar, design graphic images, write fiction and critical reviews... but where do you see this taking you ultimately?"

"I think I could write a book, maybe short stories," Nick said hopefully. He didn't dare say that perhaps he'd be a coffee house singer, like Neil Young or Chuck Mitchell or Bob Dylan had been. Everyone started somewhere. But somehow, saying he might be a writer sounded, to Nick, like something a little more solid.

"Write a book on supernatural lines, like your ghost story?" Mr. Jin asked.

"It works pretty well for Stephen King," Nick said and grinned.

"Yes, and he is one in a million. The rest of the authors barely get by, and some starve. That's a hard row to hoe, you must know that."

"It doesn't mean it isn't worth trying," Nick said. "Same with painting. Same with singing."

"All noble pursuits, but unless you can make a living, they are hobbies. Journalism. Reporting. That is a paying job. Same with graphic design. For a newspaper or a magazine, maybe an advertising agency. Have you considered marketing your skills in that direction?"

Nick nodded vaguely. He had only this semester left to complete before he was off to London, if he was accepted into the study abroad program for his final semester before graduation. He wasn't looking too much further ahead.

And yet he wanted success. Not modest success, not just finding himself a simple job somewhere on a newspaper or in an ad agency or a public relations firm.

He felt emboldened, having that modest award and check.

"I think I'm going to make it, but I don't know how," Nick said. "I'm going to be somebody important. I don't know where or when, exactly... but I have this feeling."

"Ambition," Jin said softly.

"Don't you have ambition? Or didn't you, when you were my age?"

The conversation had grown uncomfortable. The room felt too warm.

"Realistic goals," Jin replied dryly. "Maps and plans. In my day, it was getting a job on a daily newspaper that was the thing. Not much money, but a steady paycheck and a sense of adventure. I furthered my education and became a teacher of communication arts. My life is, if quiet, a prosperous and satisfying one."

"And you don't write any more, do you?" Nick asked.

Mr. Jin made a small smile.

"You make a hard observation," the older man said. "Like many in my profession, I have deferred that great book I'm going to write to that semi-mythical day when I have the time to do so, when I'm comfortably retired."

"And old!" Nick said.

They both grinned, though Nick knew he was not showing proper respect to his esteemed advisor, someone who kept a certain distance, but who also cared about Nick and his future.

"I want my glory and fame now, while I'm young, when I can really enjoy it," Nick said.

"That's what worries me," Mr. Jin said. "I've seen talent pour through this institution. I've seen heartbreak. I have to tell you that students with twice your abilities have ended up bitterly disappointed, not because they aimed so high, but because they refused to accept the huge likelihood of failure in such ambition."

"I'm not afraid of that," Nick said.

"You've never tasted it," Mr. Jin said darkly. "Not real failure." He closed the folder on his desk. "I'm recommending you for the semester abroad program."

"Thank you, Mr. Jin," Nick said, excitedly jumping up and pumping Jin's dry hand.

Mr. Jin smiled a little sadly.

"Each must find his own way," the older man said softly. "You have made a good start. Now, keep your feet on the ground no matter how fast they carry you, or how far."

The meeting was over.

MR. JIN'S words stuck in Nick's mind, where he turned them over and over. Nick didn't want a "safe" career. He wanted to make it big. But doing what? Music seemed like the toughest career path in the arts. But that didn't stop him from having rock star fantasies.

A fellow editor on the newspaper was deep into punk and new wave music. What was more, Andy Severn was a musician and had professional equipment and amplifiers. And a real rock band, of sorts. He played lead guitar. Nick didn't know his drummer or his bass player, but the guys welcomed him to Andy's cruddy basement rehearsal space on a cold November day.

"If you're going to play rhythm guitar for the Andy Severn Group, you're going to need an electric guitar," Andy said. "Your acoustic guitar just isn't going to work. You can use mine until you get your own."

Nick was not invited to join the band, but he was welcome to play with them. He had the feeling he was being "tried out" or auditioned.

For a few weeks, the guys jammed almost every night. They played covers but also dabbling with their own "stuff," song fragments, rarely a complete song. They wore eyeliner and skinny black ties. The costume and image, crude as they may have been, seemed as important to these guys as the music itself, which Nick thought of as merely okay. Rehearsals were as much about smoking marijuana and bullshitting as they were about "finding their sound," as Andy put it.

It began to feel serious, though, to Nick. He was relieved they didn't ask him to sing.

The nightly rehearsals/hanging-out sessions also had a side benefit of making Casey jealous. Casey saw that Nick seemed to be falling in with "real" musicians, away from him. For a short period of time, things got frosty between the roommates.

Casey seemed to spend all his time studying at the library. The gym didn't seem so important to him anymore. He had other friends but no steady girlfriend.

It bothered Nick a lot that he and Casey seemed to be drifting apart. But the band made up for some of it. It occupied his time. It gave him something to daydream about, in a way that felt concrete and constructive.

And there was the semester in London to think about. Nick's hopes and spirits remained high.

Then one day Nick received a terrible blow.

"We had a discussion, me and the other guys," Andy told Nick outside the dilapidated house where they rehearsed in the basement. It was twilight, late afternoon close to the Thanksgiving weekend.

Nick felt a lump form in his throat and a feeling of dread.

"We feel it's not really working out with you, Nick," Andy said.

Nick felt tears prick the back of his eyes.

"But I thought we were all starting to sound really good together," Nick said weakly. "Finding our sound."

"It's still pretty raw, actually," Andy said, cocky as ever. His spiky hair was purple this week. His heavy eyeliner did indeed give him the appearance of a real rock musician. A punk rock musician. Nick still looked like a college jock from Wisconsin in blue jeans, with three days of sexy beard stubble on his handsome face.

"I don't get it," Nick said. "I'm working as hard as you are. Maybe harder," Nick added.

"It's not your skill," Andy said, frowning. "Hell, you're better than most of us. Or at least as good."

Nick sighed. He knew they were all equally terrible. But what was real was the fantasy. So what if they had inflated a few weeks of stoned "rehearsals" into personal myth.

"Then what is it?" Nick asked warily.

"It's an image thing," Andy said, casting his gaze from Nick, not looking him in the eye. "The look of the band."

"I can change my hair," Nick said. "If that's what you mean."

"You still wouldn't have the look, Nick. The punks I've seen are all English, you know what I mean…."

Nick had a sick feeling he did, but said, "No… what do you mean?"

"I mean, they're…."

"White?" Nick asked.

A cool silence enveloped them. Nick felt himself turning to ice.

"It's more… like a cultural thing about hard rock and roll and punk," Andy said in his supercilious way.

"And I'm not white enough," Nick said bitterly. "Is that it?"

"You have a different look, a different style. It's not what works in our kind of band, that's all." Andy squared his shoulders.

Nick narrowed his eyes.

"Your racist band is shit, Andy," Nick said. "You need me."

Andy winced.

"You don't need to say that, Nick."

"Fuck you, Andy!" Nick shouted. "You just ruined everything."

Now Andy was angry.

"It didn't work out, okay?" Andy shouted. "That doesn't mean you can't make it somewhere else. Just not with us. Not with me."

"What makes you so sure you're going to make it, Andy?"

Andy could not have looked more cocksure.

"I'm sorry, okay?" Andy said.

Nick turned and walked away. Despite what he had just said, he felt sure that the band was going to make it big, and that someone like Andy couldn't miss. And they had just dumped him on his ass.

Of all people to console Nick that night, Casey was the right one. And also the wrong one.

"Fuck those idiots," Casey said, showing his true loyalty, as if he had come riding into the fray like a knight. Nick had been so blue he'd shed a few tears, and it affected Casey, who noticed right off, despite Nick's attempt to hide it from him when Casey returned to the dorm room.

Casey listened to Nick's story with purest empathy, but also maybe a little bit of jealous satisfaction.

Casey didn't want to see his best buddy hurt this way. He got some beer, and they sat up together in their room listening to albums that night, mostly Simon and Garfunkel, Springsteen, the Beatles. Older stuff they both liked best. Casey even lit candles and burned some incense they used to cover up the smell of marijuana. The room sure looked and felt like the setting of a romantic situation. Despite that this could never be what Nick wanted it to be, *because they were two guys.*

And yet Nick's love for Casey, and his desire for him, was as powerful as ever. Hope rekindled anew in Nick's heart.

Casey suggested they practice just one number on their guitars and then really give it a go at the next open mic coffee house. But Nick couldn't face the guitar.

At last Nick said, "Casey… I have to tell you something."

Casey smiled.

"You don't have to say anything."

"No, Casey... I do."

Casey, sitting on one side of the bed with Nick on the other, cleared his throat.

"It's better if we just... let it be," Casey said.

Nick shook his head.

"You must know how I feel about you," Nick said.

Casey nodded.

Nick was shaking.

"Casey... I'm in love with you. For real." He looked into Casey's eyes.

Casey did not reply for a long time.

Then he said, "I suppose I knew that. At least, I believe you think you feel that way."

"Then what's the difference between feeling that way and only thinking you feel that way?"

Casey sighed.

"I could never... do that," Casey said.

"I could," Nick quickly replied.

"I think it's unnatural," Casey said.

"It isn't unnatural for me," Nick said softly.

Casey stood, his back to Nick for a long silence. Then he blew out the candles one by one. He switched the lamp on at his desk, where his books were piled up, waiting for him. The harsh lamplight hurt Nick's eyes.

Casey took his toothbrush and soap and towel and went out the door, padding down the hall to the bathroom as Nick lay flat on his back on his bunk.

Then Nick rolled onto his belly and hid his face in his arms.

NICK pretended to be asleep when Casey came back to the darkened room from the bathroom. Casey undressed and turned out the light. He climbed up to his bunk. The bed squeaked and creaked and settled.

They were quiet for a time. Nick could hear Casey breathing.

"I'm sorry if I hurt you," Casey whispered.

Nick cleared his throat. Casey rolled over and reached down his arm, and Nick reached up and took his friend's hand in his.

They held hands like this. Quiet for a time.

"I didn't mean to embarrass you or put you on the spot," Nick said, still holding Casey's warm hand in his. "The only thing that matters is that we remain best friends. Because you're the best damn friend I could ever have."

After a few moments, Casey withdrew his hand, and rolled over to a settled position on his upper bunk. His breathing grew steady. Casey fell asleep.

Things would never be the same again between them. The weeks that remained in the semester were filled with intensive studying, and Nick and Casey didn't really socialize together, except for an occasional meal in which few words were exchanged. In the room, the only time they were together was when they slept, in their separate bunks of course. Finals ended, and Casey went home a day earlier than planned.

Nick came back to the room to find him gone.

He left Nick a book. It was a copy of *The Stand* by Stephen King, a dog-eared paperback. It was Casey's favorite book.

There was a note attached.

The note said, *I hope you enjoy this as much as I have. It's time for me to let it go, and I can't think of it falling into better hands than yours, a writer's. With love from your friend always, Casey.*

A writer.

That was a nice thing for Casey to say, Nick thought tenderly.

Over the Christmas break, Nick worked back home in the movie theater almost every night, saving up his money for his semester in London, which would begin (incredibly soon, it seemed to Nick) on January 5, 1982. A couple of weeks away.

He wrote to Casey, just filling him in on news, stuff about movies to see and about music, new records.

The letters he hoped to receive from Casey never came.

Nick would find out, much later, that Casey did not return to school for the spring semester. Instead, he surprised everyone and joined the Army. He didn't tell anyone about his plans. Nick found out when he called Casey's mother, looking for him, almost a year later. She was not forthcoming or friendly on the phone the way she had been to him in the past.

Nick's final days at his grandparents' house in Appledale just seemed like one long waiting game, something to get through, in many ways alone and on his own. His upcoming last semester of college, in London, to begin with a flight from Chicago to Amsterdam, was all he focused on, night and day.

And something else had changed.

At last he said to himself, *I'm gay, whether I like it or not. Better get used to it. Better do something about it!*

In London, so far away from home, he'd find what he wanted and *lusted* for, in every way, in *everything*, and he would be free. Or so he believed.

Nothing else mattered.

Chapter 10

1982

MARISA TAMBOV ended her vocal with a long, sweet high note. She closed her eyes, composed her face, and lightly touched her manicured nails to the headphones she wore. She looked radiant, utterly serene. Nick watched and listened closely.

"And that's a wrap," Rusty said over the PA. He was up in the booth with Drake Atka and some other studio tech people. On the session floor, a drummer thumped a final-sounding beat to mark the end of the session, and followed up with a light cymbal crash.

Other musicians laughed and there was a general feeling of completion, a satisfied vibe. Nick felt it and couldn't help but smile. He understood himself to be in a privileged place, a witness to history. The most important tracks had been laid down. The heavy lifting part was over, at least for the musicians. It was time to party.

Some of the record company brass were in the studio tonight too. Nick saw expensive tailored suits, Italian shoes, sunglasses worn despite the windowless warren of wood-paneled recording session rooms.

Marisa, sitting on a tall stool before the microphone, removed her headphones. She rubbed her earlobe and smiled at Nick, who handed her a cool glass of water.

Marisa often came to the studio with her hair tied back in a colorful scarf. Usually she wore a leather jacket, jeans, and boots. But tonight she had her luxurious black hair styled elegantly, and it flowed over her pretty, glittering midnight-blue blouse. She wore expensive creased slacks the color of soft silver, buttery soft, over open-toe black shoes, also stylish and expensive. She looked rich, warm, every inch the recording star.

The gold necklace with the cross on it dangled at her neck, against her smooth skin. And in her earlobes were two small emerald earrings, a gift from Nick. He'd used a good portion of his first paycheck from Rusty, for his studio "gopher" work, to buy them.

Emeralds were fast becoming his signature emblem, and "emerald eyes" was a nickname Marisa gave him. The earrings were his gift to Marisa to celebrate the completion of her studio sessions, here at last.

"Thank you," Marisa said, handing the empty glass back to Nick after a quenching drink. "I have a surprise for you."

Nick brightened, smiling.

"I want you to sing a background part on that number."

Nick grinned. "Really?"

"Yes, really. You are gonna lay down the backing tracks with me, in harmony."

Nick's grin went from ear to ear.

"I thought this was your last night in the studio," he said.

"The main vocal tracks and arrangements are done, sure. Now it's time for the details, the sweetening, orchestrating and mixing," Marisa said.

Nick smiled. He loved everything about studio recording. He was soaking it up like a sea sponge in champagne.

She whispered, "It's just the beginning."

Rusty came into the session room as a few musicians packed up their instruments. Everyone was boisterous, making plans, heading out to party and celebrate.

"Tell him the bad news?" Rusty asked. Rusty was smiling, so Nick knew it couldn't be all that bad.

"It's mixed news," Marisa corrected. "I already told him about backing vocals. But not the other part. Let's go have a glass of wine and something to eat. We can discuss it later."

Nick shrugged and pretended he wasn't dying to hear the "news," whatever it was—good, bad, or ugly. How bad could it be? He was staying at Rusty's flat most nights, for free, made money helping out in the studio, and his goofing off at the recording console had even resulted in a song called "No One Can Ever Replace Your Love" that Marisa had recorded for her album.

If it became a hit, Nick would be entitled to a share of the royalties. That could lead to more songwriting opportunities. As Marisa said, "Everything can be a new beginning if you look at it this way."

"When do we lay down the backing vocal tracks and all the other mixed-in sounds?" Nick asked, donning his new leather coat, a gift from Rusty. He wanted to stay on the upbeat side of this conversation. It was a night of gifts and accomplishments to celebrate. No gift was greater than the chance to make music and play with sound in the recording studio.

Now Rusty cleared his throat.

"Can't be soon enough for me," Marisa said brightly.

Rusty said, "Nick, I think you know that everything we do in this business, or art, or whatever you want to call it, is a gamble, and there aren't any guarantees, anywhere down the line. But there's always the next thing, and the next thing, and the thing after that. That's the place where an artist lives. Understand what I mean?"

Nick smiled sheepishly. "Yeah, I think so, but somehow I don't like the sound of what's coming."

The room grew quiet. Marisa looked at Rusty, then at Nick.

"Nick," Marisa said, "'No One Can Ever Replace Your Love' is not going on the album after all. I'm very sorry. It's a great song but not a Marisa Tambov song."

Nick simply froze himself inside. He didn't even let a beat pass.

"Oh, is that all?" Nick said. "I actually kind of agree with you."

Rusty said, laughing, "Now wait a minute, I'm also one of the mothers of that sweet little tune. I happen to think it's a winner."

"Just not my winner," Marisa said and winked. "Not that it isn't, as I said, a wonderful song—for someone."

"I'd love a gin and tonic," Rusty said, deflecting. But he smiled at Marisa. "You just recorded my favorite record of all time, so I am not going quibble about it."

Nick tried to smile.

They went out into the blustery night. Snowflakes were darting through the air. Drake, who had been in the studio, perhaps listening to this conversation, quietly followed along behind. Evidently he would be joining them.

In the bar of a very posh hotel restaurant, they met Trevor. Drake and Trevor sat down to their scotches at the long mahogany bar as Nick, Marisa, and Rusty were escorted by a beaming maître d' to a cozy white-cloth table in a room that glittered with fairy lights, gold, and glamor.

Really fancy restaurants intimidated Nick, but he loved them. He took all his cues about what to order from Rusty and Marisa, who couldn't have been more at home in such surroundings. Rusty waved at a well-known record producer at a nearby table, and three stylish young Englishmen Nick would soon learn were members of Duran Duran.

It had been rumored that Princess Diana, heavy with the royal fetus, had popped into this place a few nights before with her brother.

"So what's the *good* news?" Nick asked. "Didn't you say it was mixed, so you must have some more good news for me."

"You tell him, Rusty," Marisa said, and sipped champagne.

"How would you feel about doing your own recording of 'No One Can Ever Replace Your Love'?"

Nick's mouth fell open. He smiled broadly. He could barely believe his ears.

It was like a gong had gone off in his mind, echoing the word *Wowwwwwwwww....*

He dared not hope for such a proposal, but in a way, he felt he was prepared for it.

He'd been listening at Rusty's flat to all those Dusty Springfield recordings and the sounds of such great soul singers as Marvin Gaye and Smokey Robinson, Luther Vandross and Teddy Pendergast. A good mimic, he had perfected the sound Marisa had coached him to produce for her background vocals. Soulful, edgy, hip, masculine— uniquely Nick.

That soulful yet pop-bright edginess was the sound of "No One Can Ever Replace Your Love."

The trouble was, it wasn't Nick's sound.

Nick felt he was a rocker at heart. He loved the rough, raspy vocal styling of Clash. He even liked that sort of stunned sound of new wavers like David Byrne of Talking Heads, and even the goofiness of Devo.

Nick liked hard guitar sounds with a punk rock edge. The stuff he and Casey went for. What he thought of as real rock and roll.

Yet when he listened to a singer like Marisa Tambov, and sang along with her, it all came so naturally, so easily. He was growing to like it, despite himself.

Once again, Nick was at a crossroads.

He was speechless, though, with joy. He took a gulp of champagne. Make his own record? *Pinch me! I'm having a wonderful dream!*

"Think I can do it?" Nick asked at last, trying to contain his excitement, and failing.

Rusty nodded enthusiastically.

"Why don't we give it a try, and if it sounds half as good as Marisa's version, we could see if a couple club DJs I know would give it a spin? Try out a London radio station or two. Maybe develop enough interest to sell a forty-five single throughout Britain. How would you like that Nick?"

"I think I'd be out of my mind if I didn't like it," Nick said.

Marisa smiled and said, "And if it's a hit, I promise I won't be jealous. Long as I get one good solid hit record off my album, that is."

"And if we had crystal balls we could gaze into," Rusty said raising his glass, "would we dare to? I suppose half the fun of this game is in the unpredictability. Nobody really knows what makes a hit. Or we'd all do it every time."

"Crystal balls ain't in the collection of my family jewels, either," Marisa said. She looked at Nick. "Rusty is right. No one knows what's gonna take off. It happens once in many thousands of tries. Takes a lotta hard work and a little bit of magic."

"Here's to doing our part," Rusty said.

They touched glasses and drank with gusto.

Nick raised his glass too. It was all he could do to keep himself from jumping up and touching the ceiling.

NICK went home with Rusty again and got ready for bed. He was getting used to the sprawling apartment, to the clothes Rusty bought him, and to a comfortable life. That night, as he changed into his silk pajamas, he heard Rusty having a heated conversation on the phone in the next room, which was his study and library.

Rusty Maraba was obviously a smart business man. Still, he came off as a very mellow cat, one whose sensibilities were still very much of the freedom-loving sixties and hedonistic seventies. Nick had never heard Rusty speaking to anyone with such vehemence before, and it surprised him.

He looked into the study and saw that Rusty was pacing back and forth. His genteel English manners were giving way to something else, maybe English rage.

"Damn it, Jill, how can you pit our own child between us?" Rusty fumed. "Janette still thinks we're going to somehow make this all turn into a fairy tale and get back together again. *I'm telling you this is not going to happen!* And calling me vile names, especially in front of our daughter, isn't helping."

Rusty nervously stroked his well-groomed beard. On Rusty's large oak desk was a framed photo of Janette, his teenage daughter. She was a pretty girl, with her father's dark almond eyes. She had her mother's pert mouth. The photo of Jill, Janette, and Rusty on holiday in Spain was one of the smallest amid Rusty's framed menagerie.

Rusty looked up then and saw Nick. Rusty's eyes were red. He held the phone receiver away from his face for a second and made a mock-exasperated face for Nick's benefit.

"Look, I have to go. You've taken up enough of my time this evening," Rusty said into the phone. "What? Jill, it's none of your business who I'm with, so don't ask rude questions. And for the last time, I am not going to play policeman with our daughter. You might not approve of Clive Gardner any more than I do, but Janette isn't going to give a damn what either of us says to her at this point about him. She's obviously enjoying making you squirm."

Rusty held the receiver away from his ear. Nick could hear Jill's shrill voice.

Rusty said into the phone. "Yes, well, good, then, good-bye." He hung the phone up.

He came over and embraced Nick.

"My past has come back to haunt me," Rusty joked. "Actually, it never left."

"Who is Clive Gardner?" Nick asked.

"He's a budding con man, a little teenage thug, and much too old for Janette." Rusty caught himself and blushed. "Old being a relative term."

Nick smiled.

Rusty ran his hand through Nick's wavy hair, which still had traces of peroxide blond in it. "You ought to grow your hair out a little longer like these new romantics are doing it. I think you'd look like a proper pop sensation. Not to mention the most handsome man in London."

Nick liked the sound of that.

They went to bed but as usual didn't get naked.

Nick was growing very fond of Rusty, but he wasn't sure if it was love he was feeling. Love, in the tortured way of his crush on Casey, which still lingered in his heart.

As they spooned, Rusty said, "I promised I wouldn't rush you, and you promised me you'd give me time to prove myself to you… but I do wonder where all that sexual energy of yours is going these days. Where's the boy who couldn't wait to be naked, exhibiting his bits for any bloke walking in off the street?"

Nick snuggled against Rusty in the dark, in the comfort of a wonderful bed, so luxurious compared to any bed he'd ever slept in before.

He was going through another kind of change, he knew. The rush of sex that had come so wild and rough in Soho, and on his trips with Roy, had given way to a sweeter desire for something more innocent and maybe longer-lasting. Nick had somehow satiated himself for the time being. Or so he thought.

As for his stripping, he didn't know if he considered these sexual acts after all. Acts of foolishness, perhaps, or transgression, or simple youthful wildness and risk-taking.

He didn't know what to call them. All he knew was, the beautiful black model he'd been with making the porn film had impressed him somehow. It wasn't that Nick was in love with the guy. It was more like he was haunted by him.

In a strange way, that "hit and run" sort of encounter had been the most satisfying of his life.

Nick wished he could forget about that. He wanted to recede into innocence, or something like it. Marisa Tambov had picked up on Nick's ambivalence and general sense of being unsettled. She even asked him how he felt about Rusty—whom she clearly loved as the dearest of friends—about his own life, and about an all-important subject to Marisa, spirituality. Nick had merely shrugged. "If you want, let's talk sometime, when you're comfortable about it."

It.

He didn't know if she meant about God or sex or love or what. But he knew Marisa was a wise spiritual woman. But also a very sensual one. She was no prude, and nothing like the white Catholic nuns he'd known back in Wisconsin.

Rusty sat up now and reached to his night table.

"I want to take you somewhere, Nick," Rusty said, lighting the pipe of blond hashish and passing it to him. "Somewhere where we can be really free."

"Where?" Nick inhaled deeply. Then returned the pipe to Rusty. He exhaled, then snuggled up close to Rusty again.

"Somewhere warm, a beach where I can indulge in some of my own fantasies. How does Spain sound? Mallorca, Ibiza. Maybe North Africa."

"Is it warm there this time of year?"

"It will be in a month or so when we've completed Marisa's project. Lots more work to be done on that, and you can help me, Nick.

We'll then both be due for a good vacation. We can use the break, believe me. There will be a whole lot more work when we get back. The whole marketing and promotional side."

"I want to do more," Nick said. "I'd like to design art for the album cover, take some photographs, work on the typography."

Rusty smiled. "It doesn't hurt to try, and if we can't get the record label—notoriously controlling types—to use your design, you can always put it in your portfolio."

"And we're going to make my single too, remember."

"It's practically done. A couple goes at the lead vocal, and we're in business. We'll use that other thing you did, that little experimental song, as a B-side. Freshen it up using electronic instruments. Come up with any more lyrics?"

"Oh, that's easy," Nick said. He let his head sink luxuriously into the soft pillow, his mind racing pleasantly with thoughts of success and much to dream on.

Rusty smiled and kissed Nick, and they both settled down to sleep.

AT PEACEHOSTEL, a small storm was brewing behind frosty windows. Nick had come home after a long weekend hanging out with Rusty and his new friends. Roy looked at him haughtily.

"Well, well," Roy said. "Looks like Jack the Ripper didn't get you after all."

Karl looked up from his yellow highlighter-marked history book. Candy, watching TV with Jean, also took notice of Nick's return. They remained silent, though.

"Mr. boss man has been looking all over for you," Karl said.

"Mr. boss man?" Nick asked.

"Our esteemed chaperon, Mr. Collins."

Nick started up the stairs. None other than the gray-skinned and slightly bent Mr. Collins barked at him from the landing. He must have heard Nick's arrival or had been eavesdropping.

"Davangere!" he called in an unfriendly, nervous tone.

Nick looked over his shoulder at the balding professor who seemed to have aged since the start of this trip.

"Yeah," Nick answered tonelessly.

"Nick!" the old professor shouted.

Nick turned and faced the angry inquisitor. Nick's expression was passive.

"Are you just going to look at me like you haven't got a clue in the world what's wrong?" the professor growled. He was really angry. His authority had been breached. He was also afraid, Nick knew. He was responsible for all these green American students. Naturally he would have been worried about Nick's absences and mysterious whereabouts.

Nick decided to pull back from the attitude of reactionary defiance that seemed to be his default mode around any authority figure. He would instead take a calm and decisive action.

"I'm quitting this program," Nick said.

"What?" the professor shrilled. "You can't quit!"

"I'm moving out of Peacehostel," Nick said.

"Have you lost your mind? What about your classes? You'll lose the credits you need to graduate."

Nick shrugged.

"Oh, so it's all a game," Collins said accusingly. "Is that it?"

"Well, isn't it?" Nick said, knowing he was being a smartass. He also had an ace up his sleeve. Rusty, in offering Nick a job, had helped him get a work permit. A new visa, allowing him to stay in the UK if he chose to do so, was in the works.

But that smartass attitude was one Nick would come to regret. Yet right there, on the old threadbare carpeted Victorian stairs at Peacehostel, he just wanted to move on—and move *out*.

This place was square, he decided. It was homophobic. It was filled with Americans from the heartland who hadn't any idea what it meant to be *different*.

It was also drab and boring to him.

The professor sputtered, "I can send you back home just like this"—he snapped his dry fingers. "I have the authority to do so."

"And I'm twenty-one, an adult, and I'm done with this mess," Nick said, gesturing. "I know it's a headache for you. Some paperwork. I'm sorry. But you're not gonna stand in my way."

Nick turned and climbed the stairs. He realized he felt tired. Maybe he'd acted hastily. On the other hand, there was no way he was taking back his decision, and he'd be damned if some teacher was going to talk to him like that.

Nick went into the room he shared and started taking his clothes out of the dresser drawer assigned to him. Karl and Roy and Candy were soon gathered in the doorway, watching him. He packed his few belongings in his over-size backpack.

"Mind if I ask what the fuck is going on?" said Karl.

Nick saw a look of concern on Roy's face too. And Candy just looked pissed-off, color in her cheeks, her arms crossed over her chest. But she was damn interested! It was suppertime at Peacehostel, when the student residents usually lined up outside the dining room. Instead these three were up here, and they wanted a scene with Nick. Curiosity trumped their college-kid bottomless hunger.

Nick couldn't let the theatricality of the moment go by without expressing himself somehow. He wanted to grin. But he didn't. He'd shaken this place to the core without even really trying. They couldn't believe he had the balls to just up and leave, move on to the next adventure in his excitement-filled life. That's how they must have seen him just then, he thought, gloating selfishly.

Yet in a way, he already knew he would miss these guys, Candy included, and even Jean who apparently couldn't be bothered to come up here with her friends. Maybe he'd see them someday, the kids with whom he discovered a little slice of London, so far away from their snowbound Wisconsin homes.

He'd made an impression on them. A far larger one than he'd figured on.

"I found the world I was looking for when I came here," he said. "Didn't you?"

"What's that supposed to mean?" Candy said. She was *really* angry.

"He thinks he's found the end of the rainbow," Karl said. "Your own pot of gold?"

"Maybe," Nick answered.

"Nobody finds everything they're looking for on one trip abroad, Nick," Candy said, sneering.

"I didn't say it was everything," Nick replied. "But this is my new beginning. And for me, well, it's good-bye. At least for now."

"Can we at least ask where you're going? Get a phone number?" Roy said. "Is that too much to ask for?"

"I don't want his phone number," Candy said. "If he wants to be Mr. Mysterious, let him. I'm done." She raised her hand. Then she turned and left the doorway, heading for the stairs with an angry stride.

"See, knowing how to walk away isn't just my gig," Nick taunted.

She turned back, her eyes brimming with tears.

"We're worried about you, you asshole!" she screamed, furious. "Oh, fuck you, Nick! What the fuck do I care!" She ran and bounded down the stairs.

Nick knew she was still in earshot when he said, "Well, don't these little white girls know how to cuss?" He said it in self-defense, he supposed. Inside, he felt bad.

"What's this white girl shit?" Karl said. "What are you now, some kind of soul brother?"

Once again, Nick was caught off guard. But he just had to play it cool.

"Thanks for noticing me, bro," Nick said.

Roy shook his head.

"So that's what this is all about?" Roy asked. "You think we're racists?"

"Nope," Nick answered. "This is about Nick. Me, not you."

"God, how egotistical can you be?" Karl grumbled.

"Oh, very," Nick replied haughtily. "This is really just a little appetizer for me, not the main course I have coming."

He chuckled at his own coldness.

Then Nick turned and zipped up his backpack. He was all packed and ready to go.

He shouldered past Roy and Karl.

"Don't you even want your mail?" Roy asked. There was a strong trace of real sadness in his voice. That chord struck somewhere in Nick's bold heart. For a split second, he felt his cool armor melt in a place over his breast.

Roy looked as vulnerable as he sounded. He held out two envelopes. Of all the kids at Peacehostel, Nick received the least amount of mail from home. No care packages, no checks. He hadn't even bothered to check the mantelpiece in weeks, the place where the daily mail was collected each morning for pick-up.

Nick accepted the envelopes from Roy, glancing at them. One was from Stevens Falls. It looked like an official form of some kind. The other letter was from home, and that really surprised him. He recognized Grandfather's scrawl.

Nick looked into Roy's eyes.

"S'long, mate," Nick said with a grin, joshing like a cool Englishman.

At the front door, Professor Collins, now joined by the other chaperon, round Mrs. Frederick, whose bust heaved with upset, cried, "You are placing us in a very awkward position, Davangere! The police might well have to be involved. The US embassy! You can't just walk away from this program!"

"But I can walk anywhere I damn please, fool," Nick said, barely looking at her. "Watch and see if you really don't believe me."

"You are a selfish young man, Nick!" she cried, enraged at his cheek.

Nick spun around. "You want me to sign a release form?" Nick said with anger in his voice. "You need witnesses?" Roy and a few other students were observing. "I am leaving of my own free will, y'all hear that! I'm responsible for me, not you!"

"You have a return ticket back to the States," the professor sobbed. "It's paid for."

"Cash it in," Nick said. "Buy yourself some damn pork chops! The food here is some kinda shitty."

IT WOULD be a long time before Nick thought about Roy again, and the possibility that he might have hurt him along with his friends. His abrupt departure was filled with extra attitude.

Why had he been so rude to his Peacehostel friends? And what about the trip advisors? It was true they were bossy and were seemingly standing between him and what he really wanted. But wasn't it their job to keep an eye on him? Wasn't he, at least in part, their responsibility?

The bolder new Nick didn't give it much more thought.

Nick was in a hurry to break from his past. In a hurry to cut himself loose from anything and anyone in his way. Especially anyone asserting authority.

Nick was not a naturally cruel person. He was generally an exceptionally kind and thoughtful one. But now he was in a hurry. In a hurry to times he just knew were ahead of him. Times to make up for lost ones. Times to find his own meaning of the concept called freedom. For now, he was on his way to the next party, to music, to flash and glitter, and of course on to the next sex thrill, wherever and whatever and *whoever* that might be with.

The last thing Nick thought was that there would be a price for his pleasures. Or that he didn't know the value of friends and loved ones with their feet firmly on the ground. If the Peacehostel crowd was not quite living up to that ideal, well then Nick had now assured they wouldn't have a chance—nor he a chance to grow closer to them.

Nick was blasting off into the stratosphere, he believed. He didn't care for the ground or its bothersome gravity.

Nick tossed the unopened letter from his university into the trash in the Tube station. He ripped open the letter from Grandfather. His heart started to race and his hands trembled as he read. His cool started to fizzle.

Dear Nick,

Wish I had good news to share, but the only news this winter is bad news. Still, I am proud of you and enclose ten dollars I hope will buy you a decent meal or a beer, and some good cheer. I think you will need it.

Grandmother is very bad off with her senile dementia, and I don't know how much longer I will be able to keep her at home. That will be pretty much the end for both of us, I'm afraid. It's no use coming back in a rush to see her, though. You'll see us both in June. She won't know the difference, and she doesn't know either of us. It should go without saying we have not heard from nor received any help from your mother, who is another sad case, I am so sorry to have to say. You are a man now and must know that your mother is sick in her own way too. A drug addict, alcoholic, and worse things. As much as we pray, well, it hasn't done any good. She has disappeared and seems as good as dead to us.

Guess these difficult things are easier to say in writing, in a letter, than in person, though it hurts me terribly to read these words I've just put down here for you. As I said, you are a man, and it is time for the truth, even sad truths.

Please keep these women who loved you in their own way in your prayers, Nick, and keep me there too. I do think about you, and often. I do apologize for how rough I've been on you. None of it was your fault, after all. Just life, I guess. As I said, I'm proud you are a college boy.

Now another very hard piece of news to tell you. I am so sorry that your beloved dog Lucky died this past week. She took sick one afternoon and was violently ill all that night. I stayed with her every second. She loved you with all her heart. We all miss you.

Grandpa

Nick swallowed hard just once and tried to calm his thumping heart. He was getting too good at stuffing his feelings inside, though. As bad as he missed Lucky, and now would never see her again, never touch her warm coat nor feel her lick his hand, he told himself he would think about it some other day. He wasn't going to bust out crying on the damn Tube.

Today, he was going to have fun, he resolved. Today, he was going to drink cold champagne and move about in a world of art and celebrity, beautiful people, beautiful things.

He closed his eyes and felt the vibration of the train, blocking out everything else around him, and a lot of what was in him.

At the studio, he didn't tell Rusty and he didn't tell Marisa about any of this.

He didn't say anything about his grandmother's condition or anything about the scene at Peacehostel when he left.

He didn't talk about losing Lucky.

Didn't say he'd lost his parents, because he had never had them.

Instead, he took a series of black-and-white photographs of Marisa as she listened at the console to the master tapes of her recording session. He sat with Drake behind the control panel, watching Drake smoke cigarettes languidly as he assessed his big marketing schemes on page after page of scrawled notes, and drew up big promotional plans.

The late afternoon turned into evening in the cozy windowless warrens of the recording studio.

The drinks began to flow as the evening sessions began, tinkering with mixes, copywriting, more photography, and endless phone calls to the coasts of America.

This was the pattern of creativity that Nick felt he was born for, and he was kept busy with a multitude of tasks.

The nights of work flowed into late mornings in bed with Rusty, strong coffee and newspapers in posh cafes, and limousine rides to corporate media offices, radio stations, and the famed BBC.

Without ever quite telling Rusty his plan, Nick moved his clothes into an empty chest of drawers in a small room in the flat. He hung new coats, caps, and scarves in a corner closet, and piled his new shoes beneath them on the closet floor of the room he more or less took over with his own sketch pads, notebooks, records, mags, and photos.

Nick and Rusty were usually the last ones to leave the studio, often staying to tinker with Nick's personal project, his own 45 rpm record.

He and Rusty played around with electronic beats on a loop, recording late one night in the studio when everyone else had gone home. Nick figured out synthesized sounds not unlike those being used by the ultra-hot Human League. Rusty recorded some tracks of this, mixing them as sort of throw-away fragments he'd maybe use someday. Rusty was clearly delighted by Nick's enthusiasm and boundless creativity. It was a trait they shared. They amused each other this way, high on champagne, hash, endless Silk Cut cigarettes, and creative bursts of sexy energy. During the day, Nick cut and pasted together a prototype album cover for Marisa.

She liked it. The record company corporate office had their own ideas, though.

Nick kept his design, with many others he was creating, in a smart brown leather portfolio case Marisa gave him as a gift.

She also started bringing him to the jazz club where she still sang three nights a week, keeping her voice strong and supple. Nick got to know and like the musicians in the little combo that backed her up. All of them had recorded with her on the new album, performing a very different kind of music than they played on the tiny club stage.

The club was intimate and its style was purist, a forum for jazz standards and freestyle improvisation. Sometimes there were barely ten people in the audience, but they were ten cool people. People whom Marisa said would hate with a passion her new pop album, people whose tastes were fine and rigid, not eclectic and soulful like hers, like Nick's.

One night, Marisa asked Nick to sing with her, some backup and some harmony, right next to her on this cozy, purple-lit stage. At first he was nervous.

"It's all attitude," Marisa told him. "You know you can sing."

"Not like you," he answered.

"Well, of course not," she joked. "But a whole lot better than you think. And a whole damn lot better than a lot of those cats you watch on Top of the Pops."

"What's the secret?" Nick asked.

"Billions of secrets, but no single one. You dig breath control, phrasing, reading a lyric like a character in a story, acting it, *feelin'* it! But it comes down to what I said, honey and that's *attitude*. Impact. Emotion. It's what you believe. You believe you belong right where you are, in that spotlight, on that mic. And you believe what you're giving... well, it's not just you, it's something moving through you. You're giving it not just to those folks out there, but offering it back on up to the Lord, where it came from in the first place, see?"

"Yeah!" Nick exclaimed, though he wasn't at all sure.

"Give the best of what's in your heart, Nick, and I promise you what you have to give is gonna be sweet."

"Truth is, I just don't know about all that," Nick said, feeling a shiver when he thought of being on stage *singing*.

She chuckled, her shoulders shaking with her good-spirited mirth.

"Lot's you don't know, child," she said. "When I was your age, I sang in Memphis, New Orleans, rough places, good places, bad places... I just wanted to sing."

"And now you got a great new album," Nick said.

She grimaced, but then smiled broadly.

"I think so too, but I am so nervous as hell about that, Nick."

"Sorry," Nick said.

She placed a warm hand over his.

"It's okay, because I know it's all going to be all right. Do you believe that?"

"About what? The album?"

"Not just that," she said. She touched the gold cross she always wore around her neck. "I mean with me, with you, with Rusty... all of us. *All will be well*," she said. "And all will be well, and all manner of things will be well. With *Him*." She cast her gaze upward, then looked at him and smiled warmly.

Nick smiled back. He didn't know exactly how it was someone could be as optimistic, and so faithful, as Marisa seemed to be. Of course, she was older and wiser. But she must have known her share of pain and discrimination. Bitter just wasn't a word in her vocabulary. Nick knew that bitterness was a feeling plenty of people much younger and much better off than Marisa liked to cultivate in themselves.

He sure wished he could walk in the same light Marisa walked in.

But, he wondered, how do you do that? Was wishing enough?

SOME days Nick would spend his time with Marisa at her little flat in Knightsbridge.

If Rusty was the person with whom Nick wanted to spend all his nights, Marisa was easily the person with whom he wanted to spend his days. She was a best friend and a teacher and a guardian angel all rolled into one. He helped her with everything from grocery shopping to set lists and promotional copywriting.

"Long ways from my Southern home," she would say, looking around at her modest room. "But not all that far," she would add with a rich laugh.

Marisa always cooked up something good for them to eat, for Nick was always hungry. He'd grown tired of fish and chips, so he relished Marisa's pork chops, pastas, and fried potatoes. After a good meal with wine, she'd sit down at her electric piano and sing songs old and new.

One day she took Nick shopping at Harrods.

"I just got part of my advance, and I want to treat you," she said.

"You don't have to do that," Nick replied, feeling that she had already lavished so much upon him. "I'm getting a regular paycheck from Rusty's production company. I can afford my own clothes."

"Hmph, coulda fooled me," she said and elbowed him good-naturedly. She laughed. "You're still kinda a kid. And you dress like one. I'm gonna get you a nice wool jacket. That's your first piece of clothing as a grown-ass man."

It was no use arguing with Marisa. Nick knew she'd been given a tidy sum by the American record company set to release her album on both sides of the Atlantic. He also knew she had a daughter she never spoke of. He figured it would not be kind to ask about her. So, in the end, it wasn't hard to let her mother him a bit. And the charcoal-black blazer she picked out for him was drop-dead elegant. He loved it.

Marisa was also after him to read.

"I read plenty," Nick said. "I'm a writer, you know."

She did not seem impressed. "Yes, you're a renaissance man: painter, artist, poet, singer. Try acting yet?"

"Just with you, Marisa," Nick joshed. "And I have never tried painting for real, just drawing."

"Lord knows you could do a whole lot better than some of the weird stuff Trevor is going on and on about over at the gallery."

She went to a tall bookshelf and selected a volume.

"You know who Maya Angelou is?" Marisa asked.

Nick shrugged.

"Well, it's time you learned," she said, handing him a book. He looked at the cover.

"*I Know Why the Caged Bird Sings*," Nick said aloud. "Hmm, that's some title."

"It's some book," Marisa said. "Nick, I think it'll do you good to read it."

Nick knew Marisa was getting into some potentially dangerous personal territory. But the book felt positively electric in his hands.

"I promise to read it, every night until I'm done," Nick said and grinned.

"Be serious now for a moment," she said. "Do you know what the term *displaced person* means?"

Nick shook his head. It was a little lie, though. He had never really heard the term before. But he knew, somehow, what a displaced person was. Not every displaced person was a refugee of war. He was, in his way, a kind of displaced person. Marisa had as usual hit a bull's-eye. This one was in the center of his heart.

"You're living a beautiful young life right now, Nick," she said solemnly. "But it can be a dangerous life at times. I already know you've taken some crazy risks. But it's okay, because you were never alone, not once, the whole time, not ever. Do you know what I'm talking about?"

Nick felt a heavy lump in is throat.

"The Lord?" Nick answered.

Marisa nodded, looking deeply into his shining green eyes.

"He doesn't make mistakes, and He made you," she said. "Believe that. No matter what mistakes you think you have made or ever will make, God made you just as you are, and He loves you for it, every bit of it. That's why He sent Jesus here to die for you, for every single one of us."

Nick looked at the book in his hands.

"This book is about the integrity that's in us, even when we think we've been laid real low," Marisa continued. "See if you can see a little bit of yourself in this strong woman's story."

Nick nodded.

"I'll try, Marisa," he said with conviction that constricted his throat to the point of real pain.

Chapter 11

SEVERAL weeks later, on a cool spring morning, the first copies of Marisa's new album were delivered to Rusty's flat. Rusty and Nick were packed and ready to catch a flight to Barcelona, with a connection to Mallorca.

"I'd better call Marisa before we take off," Rusty said.

A young woman barely out of school named Susie, who had recently signed on as one of Rusty's personal assistants at the studio, would be house-sitting the flat.

"You'll be late," she warned, shaking auburn bangs from where they always hung over her pretty, kohl-rimmed, violet eyes.

"I wanted to be with her when she held it in her hands for the first time," Rusty said, looking at the LP in its shrink-wrapped package. "Nothing in this business happens the way you'd expect it to, on any kind of convenient schedule." He tore off the plastic. The front cover featured a photo of Marisa in a black dress, low cut, showing cleavage. It was a beautiful portrait.

The album title, *This Is Marisa Tambov*, was done in a retro, eye-popping yellow font.

On the back was typeface that looked simply staid to Nick. Not what he would have selected. But neither he nor Rusty made those decisions independently of the record company. Rusty was "just" the producer. Powerful, yes, but not all-powerful. He had creative input on packaging, but the record company executives had final say on almost all matters. Rusty expertly slipped the album out of the sleeve. The inner sleeve was glossy purple, with lyrics and production credits on one side. Rusty turned the inner sleeve over, and handed it to Nick.

"Surprise," Rusty said.

The photo was a black-and-white portrait Nick had shot of Marisa, a candid, slightly hazy image of her smiling.

It was a sensationally beautiful image. Warm and sexy, it captured something of Marisa's buoyant soul. Below it was Nick's photo credit.

Nick felt a rush of exultation and pride seeing his name, despite being a little under the weather today. The previous night, they had seen Depeche Mode in performance. The party after the show had left Nick feeling, this morning, a bit hungover. He had smoked too much hashish and sniffed a lot of lines of cocaine, Drake egging him on. He couldn't remember how many glasses of champagne he'd downed.

It didn't matter to him now. He was proud of his work.

"Susie, can you drop about ten copies at Marisa's on your way back from the airport?" Rusty asked. He scrawled a note on his special linen stationary, then handed it to her. "Pick up a dozen white roses, too, and a bottle of Cristal for your delivery."

"Should we put it on the turn table and give it a listen?" Nick asked, though he was being a bit disingenuous. He'd already heard every song so many times he was almost growing weary of them. "Faded Blues," "Time Is Of The Essence," "When You Call"—he knew them by heart and then some. Only one song seemed to him to be truly contemporary, a bouncy danceable number being marketed as the first single: "Faded Blues." The rest of the vocal-rich album had a sultry R&B vibe to it. He knew Rusty was eager to get going on their holiday.

"We'll be back by Tuesday when the single is released," Rusty said.

"And what about *my* single?" Nick asked teasingly. He'd worked his tail off on it, and it now felt like months had passed with no news whatsoever.

"I think we might have an offer," Rusty said. "I didn't want to say anything until something firm came in."

Nick brightened.

"It's a very small label, but... well, who knows with these things?" Rusty added.

"American?"

"No, English."

"Like you always say, start small."

"Well, we haven't started yet," Rusty said and gave Nick a peck on the cheek. "Let's not miss our flight."

Nick felt that now they had something to celebrate. Marisa's advance copies and a nibble from a record company for his own potential single. He tried to keep his cool. Not get his hopes up.

Of course he knew there was no way to avoid that. He was aching with great expectations.

THE Spanish beach, redolent of suntan lotion and steaming paella and calamari sold at little roadside stands, was not entirely private, as Nick had hoped. He'd wanted to sunbathe and swim in the nude. There were other people scattered about, though everyone seemed to be minding his or her own business.

Some of the women were topless, he saw. Some of the men were entirely naked in the dazzling sunlight.

Rusty parked their large beach bag in the warm sand near the shade of a palm tree. He undressed completely. Even though they had been living and sleeping together for a few months, Nick had not really seen Rusty so naked before. Not in the clear light of day, anyway. Rusty had a nicely muscled body. He was a picture of good health, vitality, and strength. He also had a very cute butt, Nick noted. He wondered if others in the vicinity were as appreciative.

"Come on now, Nick, get undressed," Rusty said. "The code here is nudity and complete freedom. Join the club."

Nick hesitated.

"Come now, you've shown off in worse places," Rusty said.

Nick sighed.

"Sorry," Rusty said.

"I can't explain it," Nick said. "It's different here. I was different back there, in London. This is out in public."

Rusty bent down beside Nick and kissed his face.

"This is a beautiful beach, warm sun, blue ocean," Rusty said. "The people here are free, or at least they're trying to be. Those places where you were naked were secret places, where sex is considered naughty or dirty and shameful—and I suppose rather hot. This is another side of life, just relaxed."

Nick nodded and stripped down to his underpants. He looked around nervously, excitement rising happily in his breast.

Then Nick pulled off his underpants and stood naked beside Rusty. Rusty took him into his arms. They kissed deeply.

Nick hoped this place was as free as Rusty claimed.

"I want you to know something," Rusty said, very serious now. Nick saw that Rusty's eyes brimmed with tears. "I am falling in love with you, Nick." He closed his eyes. "That's not it…. I mean, I *am* deeply, deeply in love with you."

Rusty looked into Nick's eyes.

They kissed. Nick felt his dick getting hard.

"Rusty…," Nick said in a hoarse voice. His throat was dry.

"You don't have to say it back to me," Rusty said. "I don't want to pressure you in any way. I only want you to be happy."

"I am happy, Rusty," Nick said. "Because I'm with you."

Rusty smiled widely.

The sky was aqua blue, the sea a deeper shade of aquamarine, the light buoyant with thousands of miles of sun-reflected Sahara sand. Mallorca had once been an ancient outpost in the Mediterranean Sea visited by Romans and Greeks. It was eternal. "Paradise, if you can stand it," Gertrude Stein had called it (Nick had read the guidebooks), a home to poets and artists, a hideaway between Spain and Africa.

Like gods, Nick and Rusty walked arm in arm to the water.

"This is our world too," Rusty whispered. "To taste, to savor, where we can be completely free."

Nick grinned. It felt wonderful. He noticed other lovers at a distance. No one paid them any mind, or if they were watching, they were too polite to let on.

"It's bringing out the poet in you," Nick said.

"You bring out the best in me, Nick. I want to give you the very best the world has to offer. You deserve it."

Nick did indeed feel he'd stepped barefoot into a life he'd always dreamed of, and Rusty was offering it to him.

They ran along the beach, letting the waves break over their feet and legs.

The water was cold, but their skin was so hot it didn't matter. It felt bracing and good.

Together they swam out into the deep waters of the Mediterranean, quite far from the sandy beach. Nick was a strong swimmer. His newfound confidence surprised him. Maybe some of it was rubbing off from Rusty. Rusty was strong without having to show ego. He was naturally relaxed. Artists trusted his decision-making because he exuded confidence and talent.

Nick wanted to be like Rusty.

And he didn't want to share him, even if Rusty seemed to preach the gospel of free love among men.

Nick knew he was really falling in love.

Back on the beach, in the shade of palms and ancient olive trees, they made love for the first time. They were partially secluded and a fair distance away from others (some of whom were doing exactly the same things). Yet Nick was quite aware that their ecstatic and athletic embraces were happening in broad daylight. Nick was on fire, covered in Rusty's hot kisses.

It felt to Nick like the world was, as Rusty had claimed, theirs too.

For a long time after making love and having profoundly powerful climaxes, they lay on their beach towel in each other's arms. Nick almost fell asleep, he was so relaxed, and loved the feeling of sinking into the soft sand as he held tight to his lover.

Later they dressed and walked back to the luxurious but casual and relaxed hotel (a restored medieval villa festooned with colorful flags and umbrellas), showered, and went to the hotel patio bar for a glass of wine. The warm sun of Spain felt so good after the cold damp of England.

Nick must have looked like he was daydreaming (he was, as usual) because Rusty smiled and said, "Penny for your thoughts, Nick?"

"I'm just thinking about how lucky I am," Nick said. "Like I'm on the right track for once."

Rusty clinked his glass against Nick's.

"And hopefully with the man you were looking for," Rusty said and winked.

"I think so, Rusty…," Nick said.

"But…." Rusty raised an eyebrow.

"Well, nothing. I know you want to have a serious and lasting relationship."

"Don't you?" Rusty asked.

"Yeah… eventually," Nick said. Nick grinned and shook his head. "I mean, I want what we have now…."

"Well, we're not married," Rusty offered, hopefully. "I want to be your partner in life, Nick, but I don't want to take away your freedom, in any way. I'd never want to do that."

"I do want to be with you, Rusty. I've decided. I mean to live with you. Permanently."

Rusty smiled and his face glowed with happiness.

"I'm delighted, Nick," Rusty said. "Consider yourself home, with me, wherever we are. And I mean what I say. I don't want you to ever think that I own you or something silly like that. I want you to sow your wild oats. To explore everything, as much as you like. With whomever you like. As Whitman envisioned it, an adhesiveness of comrades, all of us."

"I don't know," Nick said. "I might like monogamy."

"If you so choose," Rusty said. "But I really do mean I'm fine with you playing with whomever you choose, and I will not ever stand in your way. Love is something else, though. What I want is your love for myself. That's the one thing I can't share."

Nick took a sip of wine.

It was a strange moment he would long remember. AIDS was just a whisper on the horizon. The era of sex, drugs, and rock 'n' roll was—

it seemed—alive and well. But maybe it was actually sliding away with the sunset, forever.

"You're really something, Rusty," Nick said softly. He wanted to say, *something like an angel.* But he simply smiled and saw the radiant love in Rusty's soulful eyes.

In a life of many happy, glittering moments, rising above the flats of confusion and occasional swamps of real despair, this moment was to be one of Nick's heartfelt treasures.

Take a mental picture, he told himself. *Remember what the light is like, so golden, the color of Rusty's shirt, his tanned skin, the smell of sea salt, the warmth of Rusty's body so near.*

Nothing of this earth is meant to last, Nick reckoned, and even as Nick took stock of the golden moment, he could almost sense it passing upon a silent river of time.

THAT night Rusty and Nick went out to some gay bars in Palma, the lively tourist-thronged capital city of Mallorca.

Nick enjoyed the dark smokiness of the clubs and the pulsating, hypnotic disco beats. He even imagined what it would be like to hear the songs he'd recorded at Rusty's studio blaring over the bass-heavy speakers. That was a distinct possibility, and it almost made him swoon. Fantasy was becoming reality.

ONE morning, several weeks ago, Nick had come into the studio back in London to find Rusty weary from an all-nighter, tinkering with the Marisa Tambov project. Or so Nick thought. Rusty grinned.

"Listen to this," he said, flicking a switch. A sweeping melodic sound blew through the room, heavy on the bass notes and backbeat, and rich with synthesizer tweets and burps and sounds that were as cutting-edge as anything by Human League or Soft Cell.

But the music was happier, brighter, somehow *gayer.* At least to Nick's way of thinking.

It was one of the songs Nick had recorded. A throwaway thing, as Nick thought of it. Currently known as "untitled," its lyrics some rhyming nonsense sung in a large buoyant style. Somehow, Rusty had mixed it into a luscious, big, bouncy, danceable record. If the top English synth groups had made music with a lot of minor-key angst, this little ditty was the opposite of that: a sunny, candy-coated, featherweight number that was infectious if (to Nick's critical ear) a tad daft.

Still, it amazed Nick to hear what Rusty had achieved. It was pure fun. And Nick's voice was at its soulful, sultry, sexy, electrifying best.

They danced around the room together, laughing. Even Nick's vocal sounded sweeter, richer, bigger. He could hardly believe it was him.

"I can't promise you a hit record, Nick," Rusty had said, "but we'll damn well try."

Nick had grinned and shouted, "Yes!"

"Oh, Nick, don't jinx it," Rusty said. "Actually, forget you ever heard it." Rusty suddenly seemed frightfully concerned. He cut off the music. Maybe it was the all-nighter. Maybe it was a few too many lines of coke to keep him working all night.

"What's wrong, Rusty?" Nick asked.

"What's wrong is it's an impossible business, and I'm a bloody bullshitter to fill your head with dreams of success. Too many people in this business pull this shit, and it's mainly just to get into somebody's pants."

Nick grinned.

"People like Drake," Nick said.

"Exactly people like Drake! Just promise you won't take this business seriously. I knew you'd love this sound, but now I'm filled with regrets making you think we've got it made. Your value as a human being has nothing to do with the tawdry pop-music business."

Nick embraced Rusty.

"Listen, I'll be happy to just design covers or sing backup or, or… sweep up the studio! For now, I mean," Nick said. "It's a blast working with you. And if I really want to be a singer someday, I'll be like Marisa and sing for the joy of it."

Rusty frowned.

"She makes it look like a joy," he said. "That's because she's a pro. But some nights it's just a living, and a tough one."

"All she needs is one hit single," Nick said.

Rusty widened his eyes.

"Yep," he said jokingly. "That's all." He snapped his fingers. He affected a mad laugh and kissed Nick.

Nick laughed too.

With that, they locked up the studio and went for coffees at the little shop down the street.

Nick was feeling a bunch of conflicting emotions. Sure, the new mix by Rusty was fun, but it wasn't really what Nick wanted to do, musically. And even though Nick had seemed to agree with Rusty that he wouldn't take the music business seriously, owing to its near impossible odds, he had hidden his true ambitions from the person he loved most in the world.

Coffee and pastries arrived, and Rusty tucked into his breakfast with gusto. And that's when Nick admitted to Rusty that no matter how foolish it may have sounded, he wanted to be a success. A huge success.

Well, didn't many if not most young people fantasize about such things? And yet, most young people were not sitting on a launch pad with a legendary pop-music producer, who also happened to be his lover.

"I know it's idiotic...," Nick said. "But I want to be an artist... a wealthy one, brilliantly successful, and totally free. And really, really loved. I want to be a star."

NOW, in the disco in Palma, Nick would have been a liar to himself if he didn't equate this pulsing DJ scene with his own desire for stardom and success. It was his own record he wanted this room rocked with, his own voice penetrating every surface, every smile, every brain and nervous system. The flashing lights, the throbbing beats—he knew it was egotistical to want to somehow be the focal point of it. But someone's voice was being listened to with rapt attention; someone's face was glowing and shimmering on the huge video screen. Why not his?

Nick was not only a singer, as he saw it. He was also a songwriter and producer. Being a real, honest to goodness record producer partnered with the likes of Rusty Maraba was Nick's idea of a pretty posh career, and an incredibly bright future. Maybe they'd branch into films. Have a bloody media empire!

Dream big, Nick—that's what he told himself. The big fruity cocktails he'd been sipping fueled him up.

In a bathroom stall, Nick and Rusty did a couple of lines. The cocaine seemed to fire his ambitious dreams, making everything larger than life, and also made him horny.

"Let's see about the back room in this place," Rusty said.

"Back room?"

"Yes, I did a little research. This place has a naughty back room where naughty boys do naughty things."

"What are we waiting for?" Nick asked.

The dark back room was crowded, shoulder to shoulder. The air was rife with the pungent odor of marijuana.

A film projector flickered away, and on-screen a nose and moustache and lips in close-up were pushing between bare buttocks, lapping at hairy balls. The wet pink tongue went slicking upward into the crack. Disco music pounded.

Rusty handed Nick a cold beer. The film ended with come shooting all over a handsome bearded face.

Behind the bar, two muscular Spanish guys wore studded black jockstraps and nothing else.

Rusty led Nick toward some stairs traced in purple neon. The room behind it was sunken down a few steps, and darker. Torches burned as in a dungeon. Men in street clothes like Rusty's and Nick's stood watching an exhibition.

A young black-haired man was secured naked in a kind of sling, his legs spread, everything showing, everything as if "up for grabs." His head was tilted back, and, upside down, he sucked on the dick of a pale, naked redhead hovering over him, who reached out and stroked the young man's hard cock. Another young man, also stark naked, knelt at the suspended ass of the black-haired man, and rimmed him as if delving into a honey-pot of the most delicious pleasures.

Nick's head was practically spinning.

After a time, the rimmer stood up and started to fuck the black-haired young man.

Several guys watching had taken their dicks out of their pants to jerk off. Every now and then you'd hear a groan and spurts of semen would shoot up or down to the floor.

Rusty held Nick close.

The scene turned Nick on, he had to admit. But he was far from wanting to try public masturbation himself, or even to expose his rock-hard penis. Yet he had the idea that if he'd gone for it, Rusty would have sucked him off right then and there. Just for the thrill of it.

"Let's go to the bar area and get another beer," Nick said.

Rusty nodded.

"Of course. This doesn't upset you, does it?"

Nick shook his head.

"It's sure a lot wilder than the nudie show I used to do," Nick said.

They walked to the bar, and Nick admired the bartender's bare butt and straining strap. Rusty ordered the drinks, and Nick turned to look at the porn film flickering on the white screen in the corner. And he nearly choked.

There on screen was the crude 16mm porn film he'd "made" with the young black guy, back in Soho.

There, for all to see, was Nick.

HOW the hell did Nick's porn film get here, to Spain? Of course there would be copies all over the place, Nick told himself. But this coincidence was enough to sober Nick up fast.

Slowly he turned and saw that Rusty, his expression hard, was looking intently at the film screen. Nick gulped.

Nick could barely look at himself on screen. This was definitely not the "dream" of notoriety he'd been playing with at the back of his mind all evening. He thought he looked spotty. And silly too, what with those peroxide-blond bits in his hair. And of course there he was, completely naked on screen with a hard-on. The black guy, also nude, gently pushed Nick down on the bed, on his back. Then started sucking him.

Nick's heart pounded furiously as he watched the film.

The memory of that guy, his smooth skin, his fresh bubble-gum smell, it all came back to Nick in a weird rush. The look of discomfort on Nick's face in the film embarrassed him. It was mixed with winces of pleasure.

Rusty looked at the screen.

Nick could see his own distinctive green eyes on the screen. He was obviously identifiable as Nick. Clearly Rusty knew it was him.

Well, this would certainly put Rusty's "free love" policies to the test, Nick thought nervously.

And then some. Undoubtedly Nick should have warned Rusty. And now he knew he must say something. But what?

A bearded young German beside Nick looked at him, then at the screen, and then back at Nick.

"Looks like you," the man said in heavily accented English. He grinned. He had thick dark eyebrows and a masculine jaw. "Is it?"

Rusty was looking at the guy now too.

Nick said, "Maybe it is."

"No way," the German said. "It isn't really? Is it?"

Rusty stepped forward.

"No, and would you excuse us?" Rusty said calmly. Nick could hear the anger, though.

"And who are you?" the German said playfully, giving Rusty the once over. "You're somebody, aren't you. But who?"

"Everybody is somebody," Rusty said. He gently guided Nick forward, and they shouldered past the German.

The German guy lightly cupped Nick's ass as he passed. Gave him a pat.

"Actually, you're much cuter than the guy in the film," the guy whispered flirtatiously.

BACK in the hotel room, Rusty was so horny he was beside himself.

"I thought you'd be upset," Nick said, undressing.

"Why should I be?" Rusty said, pulling Nick to his naked chest and enveloping him in his strong, warm arms. "I love that you're this free, wild creature. I was so repressed for years, Nick. Married and in the closet. I loved seeing your sexuality playing out, and I always will. No matter where or when."

Nick shook his head with disbelief—and also relief.

"I'm not really that guy in the film, you know, that wild man," Nick said. "It was just a game I played."

"I love that too. Why shouldn't you play? You're young. You're free. And you're beautiful, Nick. You should no more be covered up than Michelangelo's David."

"But I'm not sure I should have done that stupid porn flick," Nick said. "Can't quite see David doing that."

"Don't be silly. You'll never regret what will, in all likelihood, soon be forgotten. It's an experience. That's all. Trust me."

Nick wasn't so sure.

Rusty saw Nick's remorse.

"It's done," Rusty said softly. "Let's just say you've now crossed it off your to do list."

Nick grinned and Rusty kissed his smiling face. Soon they were all smiles, and wearing nothing else.

The sex with Rusty was getting better and better. Rusty liked to do simply everything, and Nick did too.

Much later, a sleepy-eyed Rusty poured out some lines of cocaine on a mirror tray. Nick watched with trepidation. The hedonist was making up for lost time. And yet just as Rusty was nonjudgmental,

Nick cleared his thoughts of guilt over this indulgence. Or at least Nick tried to do so.

"I want to get a copy of that film," Rusty said, smiling, "for my own personal collection."

He offered Nick a line, which Nick snorted through a rolled-up pound note.

"If you don't mind, I'd rather not see that film ever again," Nick said, sniffing.

Rusty looked confused, but then he said, "Okay, Nick. We won't watch it. But you can tell me; is it something about your lover in the film?"

"He's not my lover," Nick shot back. "He never was. I'd never met him before. Never saw after. And I'll never see him again."

"But that encounter, too, was nothing you should be ashamed of," Rusty said.

Nick did not agree. The shame of it, the *dirtiness*, as Nick thought of it, had been one of the attractions of doing it. It had felt wrong, bad, outlaw.

That's why he'd done it. Or so he reckoned.

After doing the lines, they showered together, dressed, and went back out into the night to find another hot club Rusty had read about.

It was four in the morning. They were wired and on holiday. And in the throes of sexual passion, bonding them ever closer.

They spent the rest of the wee black hours of morning in a deafeningly loud club, dancing, shirts off, surrounded by men similarly undressed and gyrating, all in the rhythmic, ecstatic, and unwitting last throes of an era about to come crashing hard into its epic, operatic finale.

Chapter 12

IT TOOK Nick almost two days to recover from his hangover, back in London. He came straggling into the recording studio at about six o'clock in the evening, puffing on a Silk Cut cigarette. Outside, a soft London rain was falling.

Nick was dressed in his latest guise. Ray-Ban aviators, some scruffy sexy beard growth, a Burberry scarf, gangster-style leather jacket, and Italian leather boots.

He doffed his coat and scarf in the entryway. Marisa and Rusty were arguing grouchily if not too sincerely, mostly over the management services Drake was supposed to be arranging for her.

"If he's really going to manage a tour of the Continent, I need a decent place to sleep at night, don't I?" Marisa asked, pacing the studio. "He hasn't confirmed a single hotel room. Am I supposed to sleep on the tour bus?"

Rusty handed Marisa a cup of tea. They sat down at the pine conference table in the business office, outside the open studio door. Nick sat in the elevated sound booth. He slipped on a pair of headphones. He listened to the B-52s and played along on electric guitar. But he decided after a few minutes that he'd rather pay attention to whatever fires Rusty and Marisa were trying to put out. Lately, he'd become something of a diplomat and broker between them. He surprised himself, as well as Marisa and Rusty, with his acumen. After a while, he joined Rusty and Marisa. Sitting down, he popped open and sipped from a cold can of Foster's.

"Drake's waiting to see if you have a hit record," Rusty said to Marisa. "That's really the difference between a first-class hotel and, well, the bus."

She affected a cold shiver.

"Don't scare me, Rusty," she said softly. "I need you on my side."

"It'll all be just fine," Rusty said. "You know I'll never leave you or stop fighting for you."

She didn't look convinced. The single would come out in a matter of days, just a few weeks before the album was to be released worldwide. The record company in the States, one of the biggest, would have an ear tuned to Britain and all eyes trained to the bottom line. Marisa, usually so calm and cool, was having a bad case of nerves.

Rusty, who had appeared calm, suddenly glanced up with an expression of alarm.

Nick looked across the room, and there stood a well-dressed, attractive woman about Rusty's age. The frosty look on her rich, made-up face was one of barely suppressed anger. She gave Nick a once-over glance that seemed to strip him bare. Behind the woman was a young couple, teenagers. There was not a smile among them.

"Jill," Rusty said, standing, "what an unexpected... displeasure." He grinned at his joke.

Rusty's ex-wife, in a long, expensive wool coat and cashmere scarf, opened her bag and curtly withdrew papers. Nick recognized the young woman. He could tell by her good looks and the few pictures he'd seen of her that she was Rusty's teenage daughter Janette. They eyed one another suspiciously.

"I need you to sign this," Jill said in a commanding tone. She thrust out the papers forcefully with a grip like an iron claw.

"Oh more papers, what fun," Rusty said. He stood beside Nick, letting his hand lightly touch Nick's shoulder. To his daughter and her companion, Rusty said, "Hello, Janette. Clive."

Marisa retreated to the hallway beyond the business office, not looking back.

Janette didn't reply to her father. Her hair was slick with styling gel, and her eyes rimmed with kohl, giving her a rocker look. Nick supposed she wanted to look tough, but the baby fat-plumpness in her pleasant face showed something of the child she had been and in some ways still was. Clive was thick of neck, with short, cropped black hair and a brutish, pimply face. He wore a leather jacket, torn jeans, and black boots.

"And who might that be?" Jill said, gesturing to Nick.

"Oh, don't be jealous, Jill, darling," Rusty said. "He's a friend, and he won't bite you."

"You're barmy," she said to him. "And I can just imagine what sort of friend too."

"No, you can't," Rusty said. "Your imagination is too limited, unless you're thinking really nasty thoughts, which no doubt you are. In which case, you're wrong."

"You shouldn't speak to her like that," Clive said roughly.

"Down Clive," Rusty said. "Don't get excited." Rusty looked at Nick. "Clive Gardner here is all bark, no bite."

"You wouldn't want to find out," Clive snarled.

Rusty ignored him. He moved aside an electric guitar that had been between himself and his ex.

"What's this you want signed?" Rusty said, taking the document. "Oh, you want more money. I'm shocked."

"It's not for me. It's for your daughter," Jill protested.

"Thought she didn't want any help from me," Rusty said, giving a quick glance at Janette, then narrowing his eyes at Jill. "Isn't that what you said last time we spoke—erm, screamed?"

Janette rolled her eyes.

"I knew you'd give Mummy a lot of shit about this, Dad," Janette hissed. "That's why I came along here today with Clive."

"Oh, some extra muscle in case I don't pay up?" Rusty asked. "For God's sake, Janette, I offered you much more than the court decreed, and you took it freely, all but spitting in my face when you walked away. You know damn well all you have to do is ask for anything from me and you'll have it. Why play games with your mother and me over this?"

"She wants more money," Janette said. "So do I." She looked at Nick. "Maybe we're not the only ones staking a claim."

Nick was feeling very self-conscious, and also protective of Rusty. It didn't surprise Nick that Jill would be hostile, but Janette and her rough-looking boyfriend were something else again.

"I don't mean to butt in," Nick said, standing, "but we happen to be in the middle of our work and you seem to be here to pick a fight.

You're getting in *my* space too, and I don't know you well enough to engage in a family fight."

Jill's look of surprise was quickly adjusted to a sneer.

"You *are* butting in," Jill said coldly.

"Better back down, mate," Clive added, taking a step toward Nick.

"No, you'd better back down," Nick growled.

Rusty raised his hand.

"Okay, everyone, let's all take a deep breath," he said. "This drama has gone far enough."

Jill tapped the papers in Rusty's hand.

"Good," she said. "Sign this and we'll leave."

Now Drake approached. Drake, while capable of the campiest of moves, was still an imposing and large figure, with an air of the underworld about him. His face was grim, his jaw set hard. He took the papers from Rusty.

"I handle business and legal matters under this roof," Drake snarled at Jill, with obvious loathing. He shot Clive a look that withered the younger tough for a moment.

"This is personal business, not studio business," Jill replied.

"Since you've chosen to conduct business in this studio, you've made this mine as well," Drake said. "The request will be reviewed by the appropriate legal representatives, and you can expect an appropriate response in a reasonable amount of time. Now get the hell out before I throw you out on your skinny arse."

"You bastard," Jill muttered. She turned and walked toward the door. Janette stepped toward Drake.

"Drake, we only wanted to—" Janette's protest was cut short.

"Don't try to get sympathy from me, Janette," Drake said, swooping in on her, his voice deep and cool. "I was on that bridge you burned between you and your father, remember? My arse is still sore from the flames and the fall."

"But Uncle Drake," she cooed.

"I'm not your uncle, you daft little bitch." Drake looked at Clive. "And I'm not *your* uncle, either."

Janette spun around furiously and stormed out the door after her mother. She had tears running down her face. Rusty closed his eyes. Clive, following after, turned at the door and looked back at Rusty.

"You'll all regret this," Clive said menacingly.

Drake picked up the empty teacup Marisa had been drinking from and fired it at Clive. Clive ducked out the door, and as it closed the porcelain shattered loudly against it.

"Uh-oh," Marisa said, peering in from the doorway at the dimmed hall.

"Christ," Rusty muttered. "I need a belt of something, preferably scotch."

Drake started laughing. Nick felt his heart in his throat.

"I'll tear this up," Drake said, holding the documents Jill had brought in.

Rusty held out his hand for the papers.

"Thanks, I'll deal with it," he said.

Drake's eyes widened.

"They've already bled you nearly dry, Rusty," he protested.

"Janette is still my daughter, and kids are allowed to go through these kinds of stages," Rusty replied. "And we'll make the money back. I never worry about that."

"Maybe you should," Drake said.

"Now don't you get started," Rusty said and smiled wearily. "I think we've all had enough of this shite for one day. Let's take Marisa out for a good, relaxing dinner somewhere special."

He reached for her hand, and she clasped him tightly.

"I'm awfully sorry," Rusty said sadly.

"Me too," Marisa said sympathetically. "I know it's not easy with them."

"Nothing is going to be very easy for any of us, with all we have to do around here, especially you," Rusty replied evenly. He smiled warmly. "As you damn well know, it's going to be more hard work—"

"And hard partying!" Drake interjected with a grin.

"At any rate, we don't need our Diva's nerves worked over due to my past mistakes," Rusty said. He winked at Marisa, and she smiled.

"I can hardly wait to thank you when I make my Grammy acceptance speech," she said and laughed. "The producer's producer!"

Drake snorted slightly. Despite Drake's wide-gapped grin, he was in a foul mood. Nick could see this in his narrowed eyes and fidgeting hands, despite Drake's jocular comments. Something was bothering him. He'd been touchy for several days, if not weeks.

Drake crossed the room and picked up the artwork Nick had mocked up for his own potential single. It was a pattern of color bars. The photo was a high-contrast black-and-white image, with Nick's hair spiky-stiff. The title was emblazoned in red, "No One Can Ever Replace Your Love."

"This is shite," Drake said. "Where am I supposed to shop this?"

"Not your problem, because I'm doing all Nick's business," Rusty said.

Nick saw Drake's eyes widen.

"That's news," Drake said. "Not good news."

"It's non-news," Rusty said. "This is our little in-house project, Nick's and mine. I'm going to see if a couple DJs will give it some air… get a small label release for the 45. Start small with room to grow, low overhead, and let this trial balloon be our market study."

"What's the b-side?" Drake asked.

"Thought we'd try 'Wonder What', that little so-called throwaway of Nick's I happen to be rather fond of," Rusty said, referring to the somewhat tawdry electronic "disco" mash-up Nick had devised on the wing.

"That crap?" Drake asked.

Nick felt stung, even if he agreed the song was too disco, too skimpy—but fine for a b-side of a 45 if he was lucky to get a deal. "No one Can Ever Replace Your Love" was a pop classic, in Nick's mind. Marisa's version, anyway, certainly was. He liked his own version quite a bit too.

"It's Nick's sound, and I mixed it up bright," Rusty said defensively. "You'll be surprised."

"Well, this artwork isn't going to do," Drake said.

"It's just a prototype. It's Nick's artwork too, so be sure to place your foot a little further into your mouth, Drake."

"No small no-budget company is going to let you do this. It's too much expensive color production," Drake complained. "You're an unproven talent, Nick," Drake said. "Sorry, but red-carpet production values only come with proven success—money, profit." Drake rubbed his fingers together in a greedy gesture.

Nick grinned.

"Thanks for saying *talent*, at least," Nick said.

"You need a photo with your shirt off or at least open, and those green eyes twinkling," Drake said. "If you don't sell your best assets, you're wasting your time and everyone else's. And frankly, that's what sells you."

"That'll do," Rusty said. "Let's go get a bite."

Drake put his coat on. "You're taking on all the business details for this project, eh?" he asked. "It's just a vanity project."

Rusty nodded. "And if we had crystal balls…."

"We'd walk funny," Drake mused. "Well, perhaps we have crystal balls, after all, judging by the swishing!" He laughed at his own joke. Then added, "You're both daft if you don't show some tits and skin on Nick's record cover!"

MARISA'S single came out the following Tuesday. It didn't chart immediately. It didn't chart after a week and a half. Three weeks later, "Faded Blues," a great song, was considered dead in the water. The album, *This is Marisa Tambov*, was set for release with no hit song to support it.

Nick sent flowers and champagne to Marisa and called her on the phone several times a day, but she usually said in a friendly way that she didn't have time to talk. She was rehearsing for her tour every day at a warehouse in Ealing. The mini-tour of the Continent was only a couple of weeks away. She kept herself completely focused on her work.

A kind of tension about the album seemed to turn from expectation to near-resignation. Rusty gave Nick a bunch of brochures about Greece, suggesting another trip.

Nick wanted to do something for Marisa, anything. But Marisa seemed to want to keep him at arm's length while she worked day and night. The studio sat empty but for the small business office where Rusty and Drake worked into the nights. Nick contented himself with drawing in the evenings. It seemed that the wheels that had been spinning so fast around the prospects of his own single release had stopped now, too, at least for the time being. The stagnant sensation attending poor Marisa's album release seemed to poison the air.

Was this what the record business was all about? Boom and bust?

It seemed like a prescription for ulcers, hypertension, and heartache.

One evening Rusty got a phone call at the flat. Nick, drawing a still life of a guitar and other household bric-a-brac on his sketch pad, could hear the somber tones in Rusty's voice. Rusty hung up the phone and walked into the living room. Twilight glowed blue through the windows. A spring rain had been falling all week on London.

Nick held up his sketch pad. Rusty smiled sadly at the rather well-done little drawing.

"Marisa's mini-tour of the Continent is off, for now," he said softly.

"But the album is out," Nick said.

"This is a very ruthless business," Rusty said.

"We need to see Marisa," Nick said.

Rusty shook his head. He set down his leather attaché case, then sat down beside Nick. He embraced Nick.

"She wants to be alone tonight," Rusty said. "But you're a good and true friend. She knows that." Rusty kissed Nick.

"I hope she doesn't get too down...," Nick said vaguely. Of course she'd be "down." Yet even so, Nick didn't know anybody stronger. Still, this was going to take time to heal. But Marisa would bounce back. She had to.

Nick's optimism was hard to sustain, so badly did he feel for his friend. It all seemed so unfair. All those hours of rehearsal for the tour, the musicians who had been counting on a paying gig, not to mention all the work and talent that had gone into the album—an album that just like that, no one was going to hear?

Nick slumped on the sofa.

"I almost hesitate to tell you that the day's news was not all bad," Rusty said.

Nick sat up.

"A tiny little start-up label called M-Politik is going to release your single, Nick," Rusty said. Nick's mouth fell open, and he hugged Rusty tightly. Rusty kissed Nick and went to his leather carryall bag. "I didn't want to tell you any of this until I was absolutely sure it is going to happen." He pulled out a 45 record in a glossy little paper sleeve.

Nick gasped. It was real! He came to Rusty with his hand out, his heart thumping.

"Because M-Politik is small, they can move quickly," Rusty said. "They've already done a first pressing. Their marketing people are pushing this at every radio station, newspaper, record store, and media market in the British Isles."

What? No Way! Really? Nick couldn't believe his ears. He was utterly and completely elated.

He let out a hoot and felt tears of gladness stinging his eyes.

Nick took the record into his hands. It felt amazing. His first record! The first thing he noticed, after seeing that the artwork was a simple graphic, green and black on white, was that his name was misspelled. "Nick Davanger," it said.

"They left the E off my name," he said.

"That can be corrected in future pressings," Rusty said. "It happens."

Nick looked at the "face" on the cover. It was a close-cropped portion of his face in high contrast black and white, and a portion of his muscular bare chest. A slightly out-of-focus nipple was visible. The only other color was the lime-green of his eyes. They had inked that in. Nick laughed.

The name of the song was inked in the same bright green: "No One Can Ever Replace Your Love."

"I look like a cartoon character," Nick said. "But I like it."

Rusty turned it over.

There was a small proper black-and-white photo of Nick, one Rusty had taken. Nick wore a vest, open, with no shirt beneath. It showed off his muscular chest and arms. His fists were clenched.

Nick barely recognized the brooding, spike-haired, "new waver" with his black hair gelled slick at the sides, eyes outlined in black.

In small print on the back were the words, "Side 2: "Wonder What."

Nick slipped the black vinyl 45 from the sleeve and smelled it.

"Wow," he said, getting a whiff of the plastic chemical odor of a new record.

M-Politik had a purple label and typescript that looked oddly Eastern European, with some backward letters. Nick liked it.

And there was his name again, *Nick Davanger*.

Nick got song-writing credit too, along with Rusty and Marisa. Rusty was listed as producer.

"I'm glad you like it," Rusty said.

"Like it?" Nick dissolved in mirth.

Rusty embraced Nick and they kissed.

"Thank you, Rusty," Nick said.

"You might not thank me after all the press interviews and photo sessions and signings in shopping malls," Rusty said. "But of course if that all happens, it means we have a hit, we're successful."

They looked at one another for a moment, keeping their smiles on like banners, not allowing the prospect of failure, so palpable, to exert its gloomy presence in this room yet again on this night.

"Know what I love most of all? I love that we're a team, you and me," Nick said.

Rusty beamed.

"Our M-Politik finalized contract is in my carryall, ready to be signed, Nick. But as we know too well, today, most debut records do fail commercially. Think of this as a good beginning, and you won't go wrong. Might even get a little money and some fun along the way. Certainly some experience. And I'm transitioning from studio wizard into an actual businessman on this one. Hope you enjoy being my pilot project."

"As long as I have a special place on your roster of stars, I'll be content."

Rusty smiled.

"First things first. We have to plan a release party," Rusty said.

Nick sighed.

"I think we should hold off on that," Nick said. "I know Marisa is hurting. Maybe this isn't the time to celebrate."

Rusty sighed and looked at Nick.

"This is the only time we've got, Nick."

As it turned out, Marisa had a surprise in store for them—and for herself, and for the whole world.

Her album debuted in America the following week in the Billboard top twenty, catching everyone completely off guard. And taking the music world by storm.

With no single to back it up, Rusty attributed this lightning bolt to a combination of gay word of mouth among club DJs and just plain old-fashioned luck.

Who knew America was, it seemed, just waiting for a Marisa Tambov record?

Suddenly, the tour was back on track, only instead of a mini-tour of small rooms in Continental Europe, the musicians were all rehired to back up Marisa at theatrical venues in North America.

On the night before Nick's single was to have its market debut (only a few friends were told), Drake and Rusty threw a huge party for Marisa at Club Cheri in the West End, and hoards of celebrities descended with the media in their wake. It seemed every Fleet Street reporter wanted to be the writer who "re-discovered" Marisa on the eve of her worldwide smash hit tour.

Drake had just hired five more musicians for Marisa's tour and five extra personnel to join them in America. The trip would begin in New York with a performance and appearance on a hot new TV show called *Late Night With David Letterman* on NBC.

The party rocked on until the next morning. Nick danced and partied and consumed his share of alcohol and cannabis. He was so happy for Marisa. And he was pumping rocket-fuel through his veins in anticipation of his own career launch. He knew not to have great expectations. Even a tiny success would be enough, he told himself. He just wanted to hear his song on the radio. And then see what came next.

"Will you call me every day?" Marisa asked him, speaking into his ear as they danced. "Will you take good care of Rusty while I'm away?"

"Yes, yes, and I wish I was going with you," Nick said.

Nick was not among the crew chosen to sing backup for Marisa's tour. He hadn't even tried out for the spot. It wasn't really discussed. Maybe he should have pushed for that. For something. Something to take the edge off a sensation that wasn't exactly stage fright, but a kind of anxiety attending a potentially colossal unknown.

In the weeks that followed that giddy party, he began to feel he'd made a grave mistake.

MARISA called Nick every day. Not only was her tour a smash, she'd begun an affair with a salt-of-the-earth guy who worked on her crew, Deshawn. She was in love. Nick was thrilled to learn that she had been booked to play the Hollywood Bowl. What was more, she was looking at a new home in one of LA's most exclusive canyons. As she said, her ship had come in.

It delighted Nick to hear the little details of Marisa's triumph, and that she was able to really savor her success, buying gifts for family and friends. And buying herself things she never could have afforded during those London club years. Things like Hermes scarves, good shoes, fine clothes for Deshawn. She told Nick that when she offered to promote Deshawn to a less back-breaking job on the tour, he refused, preferring to remain where he felt he could do her the most good. He then surprised her with a simple band of platinum she wore on her ring finger.

Everything seemed to be going great for Marisa, except for one thing. One person, to be exact. Nick was not all that surprised Drake was causing some concerns on the tour. He'd gone on some epic binges. Money was missing in the wake of these. He'd been accused of sexually harassing some of the members of the tour entourage. He'd even gotten violent with Deshawn. Marisa was on the verge of firing him.

Still, that problem couldn't blight the main event in Marisa's life. Lightning had struck. Gold seemed to pour in.

As for Nick? Nick's own record seemed to come and go in silence.

It didn't break into the top two hundred, much less the top forty. Nick never heard it on the radio, not even once.

"There's still time," Rusty said, arranging for Nick to sing to a back-up tape at two London discos and a gay bar in Manchester.

Time... time to promote, time to hope, time to hustle.

No guarantee but hard work. Hard work that would, odds being what they were, come to little or even nothing.

Nothing but experience.

Nick was hungry for experience, and he plucked up his spirits and told himself, this is being in the business. This is part of it. Just be patient and soak it up. *Take it all in. Learn.*

He psyched himself up for the prospect of a not-too-glamorous round of small-time appearances. He would be expected to sing just one number, his single, maybe standing on a stage, maybe even on a bar top, to a roomful of disco dancers or a crowd of one or two at the bar. Then he'd sign records if any could be sold. Oh yeah, he was also the salesman, roadie, and record schlepper.

That was part of the biz too.

He put together a costume made of glittery jeans, black boots, and a brown leather vest to be worn over bare skin. Luckily he was working out almost daily. Good thing, because he was partying hard at night. He had grown his hair out, it was now relaxed and wavy, thick with gel product. He once again "tipped" the ends, blond and flame orange. He looked the part of an eighties new waver, eyes rimmed in mascara in the way of the new romantics stomping all over London.

Nick's music had the electronic thunder of Depeche Mode and Human League. But rather than a deadpan vocal style favored by Human League and others, Nick sang with a rich soul voice that could swing deep and rise to a powerful tenor. He was in good form for his "tour," such as it was. He was ready.

Then he learned that even these meager gigs were being put on hold.

Who the hell had ever heard of Nick Davanger? There were hotter disco divas in competition for the gay dance-bar circuit. So Nick was out, for the time being.

He packed away his costume and took to sleeping until noon.

On a break from her wildly successful tour, Marisa came to London to clean out her little apartment and finalize some business. She was moving herself and all operations to Los Angeles. The tour would continue for at least the remainder of the year.

It was snowing when Marisa came to dinner at Rusty and (now) Nick's flat. She was radiant, a bit slimmer, relaxed. She came alone.

Dinner was a simple Irish stew, prepared by Rusty. The wine flowed. Talk was easy and free. Nick observed Marisa's concerned glances in his direction. He knew she could see that he was frustrated. She knew all about the "flop" of his single.

She held Nick's hand. The firelight reflected in her warm eyes.

"You never know what's going to happen in this business," she said. "That's why you can't give up hope, and you can't really have expectations, either." Rusty sat on the sofa, on the other side of Marisa, and took her other hand.

"Your hand is cold, Marisa," Rusty said.

"I'm still a little scared," she said. She turned and looked at Nick. "That never really ends... it keeps you humble. But it never defeats us."

Nick sighed.

"Marisa, I miss you so much," he said.

They had a lovely reunion, and Nick felt much better about everything. It was good to see Marisa so happy, speaking warmly of her fella, Deshawn.

At the door, Rusty kissed Marisa and said, "I'd tell you to break a leg, but you've apparently already broken both of them along with all the box office records."

She smiled.

"Come and see me in Dublin at Christmas?" she asked.

"Of course," he answered.

"And bring me a new song," she said with a wide grin.

"Nick and I will get to work on that," he said.

"I'm only partly serious," she said. "I know how busy you are starting the new production company. When do you sleep?"

"Nick makes it all possible," Rusty said. "And he's also busy building his career as a pop star, on top of it."

Nick's face felt flush. He'd had a bit too much wine. Rusty was being kind about those pop star possibilities, Nick thought. He'd never felt like less of one.

"I'll have the business to fall back on," Nick said, a little too fervently. He was far from giving up on fame, though. He just didn't have a clue what his next move would be. Or if there would be a next move. It scared him and humbled him, but hopefully in the good way Marisa had described.

"Thank you, Rusty," Marisa said. She winked at Nick. "You have a hell of a producer, you know that?"

Nick nodded.

That night a foot of snow fell. Time seemed to stand still. Rusty and Nick held each other in their warm bed.

For the first time in what seemed like months, Nick felt secure. As if in letting go of those big hopes for his record he could move on and face whatever happened.

He also knew he'd need all the courage he could muster.

NICK read the trade papers. The group he liked best, U2, was recognized as the best of the "new wave" of bands coming out of Europe. He loved that rocking, rhythmic guitar sound they made. Wham UK, Haircut 100, and even Adam Ant were climbing up the charts that season. And still, no one had ever heard of this Nick Davanger guy.

Rusty didn't seem too concerned about the situation as he started a recording session with two young sisters from Leeds, classically trained musicians trying their hands at pop. The youngest sister, Abigail, was only fifteen. She played violin, and her older sister played piano, and they sang harmonies in a style that seemed to combine folky rock with Celtic fairy tales set to music. Nick had no idea to whom this music would appeal. Rusty had a hunch, though. He was putting his money on it—and his time and talent.

That left Nick with even more time on his hands.

Nick wrote news releases, took publicity shots, and wrote up a treatment for a video for the sisters. He considered asking Rusty about directing it himself but thought better of it. They would need a pro. But Nick could learn from the pro, so he made sure to sign on as an assistant.

And while thoughts of video art direction excited him, he still had nagging anxiety about his own single. It was said to be in limbo, but would it be there forever? Had Rusty moved on already? And what about the record company? Small as they were, wasn't there more they could do to get Nick's record played on radio?

"Should I talk to someone at M-Politik?" Nick asked Rusty one evening when they were tidying up the studio (to save money they had temporarily let their janitor go).

"No, best leave them alone," Rusty said. "Think about what you'd like to do next."

"You mean, give up on the single?"

Rusty shook his head. He was tired. The sessions with the sisters and their domineering mother were taking a toll. A lot was invested in this new enterprise.

"I mean that this part of the business is out of our control, and you're an artist, not a businessman."

"I think I'd better be both," Nick said. "Aren't you reinventing yourself as an entrepreneur? Taking on the business side?"

"Yes, well, to pay the bills I'm on the production side, and that's really all I have time to think of." He smiled sadly. "I'm sorry, Nick. I know you're disappointed."

Nick smiled too, and held up his chin.

"I never liked the record that much anyway," Nick said. He hadn't meant to sound petulant. But wasn't he at heart a rocker, not a disco bunny, no matter how tricked up his record was with computerized synth beats?

"Oh come, never put down your own work," Rusty said. "There are plenty of bloody arseholes out there to do that for you, you'll find."

"And if I don't?" Nick said.

"Well, you'll have missed a bit of pain. Meanwhile, you're here to begin again, isn't that what Marisa is always saying, quoting Saint Augustine and that Christian stuff?"

Nick grinned.

"It seems to have made an impression on you too," Nick said hopefully.

Rusty lit a cigarette.

"I wish," he said. "I wish I could really believe that about myself all day long. Right now, I seem to be spending a lot of time looking back at the wreckage." He placed his arm around Nick's shoulder, and Nick caught Rusty's gaze on a small painting of his daughter Janette. "Come on, let's go get a well-deserved drink," Rusty said, blinking, rubbing his eyes and showing a brave grin.

On the table, amid a bunch of trade journals, was a folded-over newspaper. It was open to a story about something called AIDS, which had barely been given its new name, and was only slowly emerging as a crisis of some kind on the other side of the Atlantic.

Though the news was scarce, this new disease would change everything, forever.

The Falklands War had also arrived.

Unexpected events had begun to dominate headlines, and pop music seemed a bit trifling. Nick was training himself to think in pop terms, though. So the times were changing, a bad moon seemed to rise, even as the glittery nights of glamor, booze, and drugs dulled a country's pain and kept the party going.

Another revolution, though, would have a greater impact on the life of Nick Davanger. That newest "British invasion" of pop that was so well underway on both sides of the Atlantic was about to sweep him up into the glare of history.

And he would never be the same.

Chapter 13

IT WAS spring when Nick heard, for the first time, his own voice coming out of the radio at a little newsagent convenience store near the recording studio.

He had to stop and think for a minute. *I recognize that. Who is it?*

A strange shiver moved over the surface of his skin. Nick looked past the rows of tabloid newspapers, shiny magazines, and chocolates to the tiny black speaker mounted on the wall above the wireless.

"That was Nick Davanger, 'Wonder What', by request," the English DJ said in a cool, deep voice coming from the speaker. "And if you're not dancing, you must be either in a coma or perhaps you're already deceased."

The young female clerk behind the counter grinned at Nick. "I love that new tune," she said. Squat and solidly built, she had a punkish streak of purple in her dark hair and a pleasing comic face. She could not have been more than seventeen. Nick could have kissed her.

"That song," Nick said, paying for his bag of crisps and a cola. "You've heard it before?"

"That's my *favorite* new song, love," she said in a throaty, sultry voice. "Of course I've heard it. Haven't you?"

Nick said, mischievously, "Yeah… somewhere."

"Well, it's a big new hit," she said authoritatively.

The really curious thing was that it was the b-side of his supposed first single. It was supposed to be a throwaway number, a fairly trashy disco beat, done just for fun. For laughs really. The lyrics and the middle eight were among the first things he'd ever put on tape.

Yet surprise of surprises, in a completely different context, it was an undeniably infectious song. It was bright and fun, and it flew like a beam of sunshine against the atmosphere of glum news coming out of a particularly long winter.

Nick also paid the friendly young woman for some gum and walked out to the street. The air tasted sweeter, the sunlight seemed more brilliant, even diffused through English clouds. The cars and busses passing by shone with a new luster. A young Pakistani family walked by him, and the small children's faces seemed more beautiful, more innocent than any human faces he had ever seen before. Had he not been looking? Not really feeling?

Had everything in life been "on hold" as if for this little moment? His breakthrough? His moment of creative success?

World, meet Nick Davanger.

Nick, say hello to the world.

He closed his eyes and smiled, letting a warm feeling simply envelop him. He giggled with mirth. It was just so incredible!

Nick knew, somehow, as he had not known before (would not have dared venture even a guess) that his little song was going to be nothing less than a smash hit.

Walking around North London, where he'd gone to pick up some printed promotional posters, he heard the song three more times. Once, it was blasting in the doorway of a hip clothing store. Another time, some kids walked by with a large radio, and it boomed out.

Nick's feelings of euphoria were mixed with a surreal sensation that this was almost like a dream.

At a red pay phone booth Nick dialed Rusty. He was practically hyperventilating.

"Nick, you sound completely breathless," Rusty said. "I have an inkling as to why! M-Politik has been trying to reach us the past two days."

It turned out Rusty caught wind of the news of this surprise hit at just about the same time Nick had. His phone had been ringing off the hook all morning. In the days before cell phones, he couldn't reach Nick fast enough to tell him. It was wonderful that Nick found out for himself.

Nick was happy for himself, for Rusty, and for the little record company that had taken a chance on him.

At last, Rusty and the tiny team over at M-Politik Records had something positive to discuss—a major hit on their hands.

"How did it happen?" Nick asked.

"M-Politik put out the single in the States about two weeks ago," Rusty said. "Did it on their own. They had no license to do so in America. Completely illegal. But their mistake is our advantage."

"How is that?" Nick asked.

"How fast can you get home?" Rusty asked.

NICK met Rusty at a pub near Pimlico instead of at home. It was time to celebrate. He downed a lager at one go and quickly ordered another. The lager and the whole thing were going to his head, fast.

"Nick, you've got a hit record on both sides of the Atlantic. Some DJ in New York loved the b-side, and it was pirated all over the East Coast. Not to be outdone, M-Politik pressed out tens of thousands of copies on the West Coast."

"They weren't supposed to do that," Nick said.

Rusty nodded sagely. "Theft has always been a marketing tool in this business."

"But the record isn't even for sale in the Midwest, where I'm from."

"And still, it's in the top twenty in every market. It will be so in the Midwest as well, I assure you. The wildfire is spreading. It will be a hit in Europe, Japan, all of Asia. As for Britain, well, any radio station or club DJ worth his salt has fished your record out of his files, hopefully not his rubbish bin—ha-ha—and simply turned it over to discover gold. Those silly enough to discard the first printing have been calling M-Politik since midnight last night. They're going back to the factory at day's end and ordering—are you ready—500,000 more copies."

Nick shook his head in happy disbelief.

"Wow," Nick said. "It's like it took forever, but now it's all happening so fast...."

"Everything is about to change, Nick. M-Politik wants to offer us a rather tidy share. It's a fraction of what we'll get in the long run."

"How? Or why?" Nick said.

"Leave that to me. I know what a hit record means. Marisa's album has brought the studio back into the black. But this record is our baby. Hope you're ready, Nick. You've got your work cut out for you."

Nick smiled. "I do?"

"I want you in the studio playing with the tape machine and your guitar. Songs, Nick. We need songs. In the vein of 'Wonder What'."

Nick just couldn't believe it. Rusty was going to drop everything and rush Nick into production.

They were going to produce an album. *A Nick Davanger album.* That was almost too much to believe.

What came next, though, was like an earthquake.

SEVEN days later, Nick was completely exhausted from his all-nighters at the studio. He and Rusty had spent every waking moment working, composing, laying down basic tracks, inventing out of thin air.

Nick imagined that being in this windowless recording studio would focus him and blot up his mounting anxiety. Instead, he began to worry about the quality of the songs. What if he couldn't simply snap his fingers again and produce a whole album of sparkling pop tunes on demand? Who on earth could? But these initial sessions were all about producing essences and raw material—stuff to tinker with and massage and build in the studio into potential songs. Then those productions would be enhanced with more singing, more recording. The goal was to create a bushel of music, and then pick out the eight or nine brightest gems.

Running out for junk food just added to his mood swings. His hit song was playing everywhere he went. His photo was in the newspapers. His name was being spoken in the streets, on TV, and of course over the radio.

An image was forming in the public's collective consciousness. The reality would have alarmed everyone. Nick was barely sleeping. Washing down greasy fish and chips with champagne and keeping himself fired up with lines of cocaine were taking their toll.

Nick wanted to party, to celebrate, but the party was in the studio and the musicians dropping by were not just well-wishers. They were offering inspiration, ready to get in on a good thing. Yet everyone knew they were gambling.

Members of the press were calling too. Among his million and one other duties, Rusty was preparing some basic remarks for Nick, a sort of blueprint to help him communicate. Photographers would be coming around next.

Day ran into night and into day.

These were weeks of work, exhilaration, high happiness, and crashing lows of frustration. It helped to have Rusty beside him, but Rusty too was running toward this main chance with afterburners smoking in his wake. The line dissolved between the party and the press conference, the vocal track recording at four in the morning, the record-store signing, the half hour of sleep in a hard chair.

After vomiting in the toilet, Nick picked himself up and rinsed his mouth with Listerine. He looked in the mirror at the dark circles under his eyes. His hair was greasy and nappy. He looked strung out.

He closed his stinging, burning eyes hard, alone in the studio toilet. What on earth had he done to himself?

He thought about what Marisa had always told him about finding his inner light. All you need is one little candle. One tiny spark. That's what you needed to light your way.

"Help me, Lord," he prayed. "Don't let me blow it. This is the beginning of the best time in my life… let me be strong, enjoy it, help others with what small gifts I have to share…."

He steadied himself. Took long slow breaths. People were waiting for him.

He washed up and returned to a room full of studio musicians all standing by. He met their grim, tired faces with a proud smile. Rusty nodded from behind the glass up in the control booth.

And it was back to work for another ten hours.

Late one evening, he dozed on an office sofa, his feet clad in new trainers dangling over the edge. Sleep was usually elusive. Joints helped a little. But he knew he'd reached a wall. After a long day's session, all he wanted to do was go home and get some rest. Yet he couldn't sleep through the night.

Rusty sent him home in a taxi.

At home, Nick showered and changed into silk pajamas, a gift from M-Politik, along with a potted lemon tree and a case of Spanish wine.

Rusty had called and told him to wait up for him. Rusty kept Nick waiting at home for him half the night. Nick calmed himself with a glass of scotch, and then another.

When Rusty arrived, he was jubilant.

"News, Nick," he sang. "Very good news indeed."

Nick rushed over to him.

"Tell me," Nick said.

"The record just went to number one in England." Nick sat down slowly. "We've worked out a deal with M-Politik to distribute the single and one more single, worldwide." Nick sank back in the sofa. "They've already shipped to the remaining North American markets, Japan, Continental Europe, and Australia."

"How can they do that? They operate out of a matchbox."

"They just made a deal with IBI International to back them up," Rusty said. Nick had heard of the corporate media giant. They had some of the biggest recording artists, going back to the fifties. It didn't sound possible.

"*The* IBI…?" Nick said.

"Yes, the IBI… they just signed Nick Davanger to a two-album deal, with an option for five, and they had competition, believe me. M-Politik will release the first single off your new album in a joint venture. Then we're done with them."

"Just like that?" Nick asked. "I don't get it."

"You made their name, Nick. It works out well. You're now an IBI artist."

"Two albums?" Nick stood up. His knees felt weak. "We can barely get one together...."

"I have the contract for your signature right here in my bag. Nick, they've paid you an amazing sum. You've already sold platinum with your first single." Rusty shrugged and they both laughed.

"What does it all mean?" Nick asked.

"It means you've beaten some incredible odds, Nick. You've won the lottery. It's extremely rare for a single to explode this large. It just builds on itself. All the big players wanted a piece, Nick, and they played somewhat recklessly, to our great advantage. We set up an auction, you see. IBI was not to be outdone once they got in. They brought a very big checkbook. And they won."

"How much are they paying me?" Nick asked. He leaned against Rusty.

"In pound or in dollars?" Rusty asked.

Nick's heart raced.

"Dollars," Nick answered.

"An advance of one million dollars," Rusty said. "Nick... You're a millionaire pop star with a number one hit record."

"WHO is Nick Davanger?" asked the jowly man in spectacles.

"If you don't know," said the stylist in spandex tights, "you must live under a rock." She pointed her thumb at Nick, who was getting his forelock tinted blazing orange. He wore a silver cape and a cool expression.

The old man's jowls quivered.

"I don't mean that literally," he huffed. "I mean who is he in his *soul*."

The old guy had an air of theatricality and a face and physique like Winston Churchill's.

The lady shrugged.

"I want the soul," the old guy said devilishly and grinned. The grin warmed him up considerably. He held up his elaborate camera and looked at Nick through a long lens.

"Don't shoot me in the hair and makeup chair," Nick said with a laugh.

He was in a soundstage in Ealing, ready to shoot the dance sequence of his new video. Dancers in futuristic, shiny costumes were doing stretching exercises on the stage. Outside, it was snowing, and the week between Christmas and New Year's Eve, 1983, was drawing to its climactic conclusion. And a heady holiday it had been, indeed.

"Why shouldn't I shoot you just like this, as you are?" asked the man, who was not only a photographer but a very important one. "You don't want the world to know that Nick Davanger is polished bright and wrapped up like a shiny package, ready to be sold to a hungry public via a whorish media?" The man laughed.

"And who might you be?" Nick said, standing and taking off the silver cape. Nick wore a body-tight green suit fit for a superhero or an aquatic god. It left most of his chest exposed.

"Hey, I'm not done," said the stylist.

"I'm Lord Plover," the man said, extending a beefy hand. "I'm about to make you immortal."

"I've heard of you," Nick said. Plover was famous for taking portraits of everyone from the Rolling Stones to Charles and Diana to Ronald and Nancy Reagan. Years before that, he'd taken prize-winning pictures of men at war, many prints of which were hanging in museums all over the world.

The video director, a small hairy man, was pissed off when Nick went outside with Plover, where a series of street-corner shots were taken with snow blowing around Nick's strikingly beautiful face.

"My best work is in black and white," Plover said, sounding out of breath. "But I brought along some color stock. I'm glad I did. Those green eyes of yours and that cinnamon skin are too good to waste." He laughed again. "I sound like a damn poofter. No offense."

"Oh, so word is out about me?" Nick said, grinning. He said it in such a way that it might have been taken as a joke.

"Oh, word is out about just about everybody in this business, Nick," the old man said. "I just need a couple more angry smiles from you to please an editor paying me a small fortune. Then let's duck in that convenient pub over there and have a warming and reviving glass of gin."

Nick obliged with the pose, and Plover shot. No one had dared to say a word when they exited the set and then the film studio, but all eyes were on them. They drew a small crowd on the street. Now they entered a cozy pub exclusive enough to have a large doorman in crimson costume "welcome" them with a barely approving sneer.

In a comfortable booth near a roaring fire, Plover toasted Nick.

"I get a good feeling about you," he said in his gruff voice. "You're not as pompous as many of the preening pop royalty I've dealt with."

"Am I royalty?" Nick asked.

"As long as you sell hit records and sell tabloids, you're a prince among men. But I happen to know this sort of thing doesn't last for many of your kind."

"My kind?"

"I meant nothing about your race or color. I meant ambitious, stage-struck, star-spangled young men who get a taste of life most people can only fantasize about. Sex, drugs, inflated egos, inflated importance. And a fickle little thing called talent. Save your gold, Nick. For the day when all of this fades."

"It's barely begun," Nick said quietly.

Plover raised his glass.

"Then be wise," Plover said, touching crystal to Nick's glass pint of lager. "Enjoy it for what it is, a grand illusion."

Nick and Lord Plover downed several more drinks before Nick decided he'd better get back to the video set. Plover shared his wisdom and skepticism with tantalizing stories about stars he'd photographed and gotten to know well—stars like Sophia Loren, Grace Kelly, the Beatles, the Stones, Andy Warhol, and on and on.

Nick would have liked to have stayed and listened for hours, but at last they settled their bill (Plover treated) and left the pub.

Out on the cold street, the old man faltered and dropped his large bag of equipment.

"Let me help you," Nick said.

"I'll be fine," Lord Plover said in a pinched voice. His face reddened. All at once the great man appeared frail and every year of his advanced age. "My car will be here any second."

"Let's go back inside and sit down a moment, Lord Plover," Nick said.

It was too late. Lord Plover collapsed to the pavement. Several people on the street rushed over. Nick knelt beside Plover.

"Can you hear me?" he shouted to the old photographer. Nick looked up. People had gathered, their faces bright with alarm. "Call for help, hurry," he cried.

Plover's face was turning blue.

Nick knew enough from watching TV programs, or maybe just some instinctual sensibility, to calmly clear the old man's airway with his fingers and listen for his breathing.

He gently pinched Plover's nostrils together and blew into his mouth. The lungs filled. Nick pressed his ear to the massive chest and listened for a heartbeat. He pressed down several times on Plover's chest. Then provided resuscitation again.

This time, the older man stirred. Nick pulled Plover up to a sitting position as the red-faced old man coughed and gasped for breath.

By now a crowd had gathered. A few photos were taken, flashbulbs going off. Then Nick heard his name being whispered. Nick couldn't quite believe he was being recognized. He had thought for a moment that maybe it was the famous and revered Lord Plover the shutterbugs were after. But no, it was Nick himself. Soon the ambulance arrived.

By that time, much of the pink color had returned to Lord Plover's ruddy face.

He gently took Nick's hand.

"You saved my life, Nick," the old man rasped.

Nick smiled. "Save your energy," he said calmly. The medics moved in.

Plover was checked out by the emergency rescue team, placed on a stretcher, and loaded up in the ambulance. Nick remained at his side. Now Lord Plover was smiling at him.

"Nick, when you speak of this, be kind," Plover joked. "Auf Wiedersehen." He waved limply, and Nick felt cheered and completely sobered by the experience.

Someone tugged on Nick's arm.

"I'm from the *Sun*," a man said. "That was Lord Plover, wasn't it? You just saved his life. You're a hero! What's your name?"

Nick smiled shyly. So he wasn't world famous—yet. What he was, he thought ruefully, was very, very late about getting back to the video set. He hoped they would understand but knew they'd be furious, even if he told them the truth of what caused him further delay.

"Let's just say I'm a good Samaritan," Nick said to the reporter.

"Hey!" shouted a teenage girl. "I know you! You're Nick Davanger!"

The reporter called, "You *are* Davanger, aren't you! Say, this is quite a story."

"It's not a story," Nick said. "It's just something that... happened."

"It's a great story because it happened to you, don't you think I know my own business?" the reporter said with a wide grin. "The publicity you'll get won't hurt your business, either, mate!"

"But....," Nick said. Cameras were flashing in his eyes, more and more of them.

But I didn't want this attention, he thought. This wasn't some kind of publicity stunt.

He turned and ran toward the studio doors.

Nick, stunned, at last returned to the set. The director seemed to have chewed off a bit of his own beard. He was somewhere between the age of forty and sixty and was in a state of apoplexy.

"I'm sorry," Nick said.

"We're hours behind schedule!" the director wailed.

Nick then affected a breezy indifference.

"So let's get moving," he said, slipping off his coat. He was not going to let this director intimidate him, even if Nick acknowledged he'd inconvenienced everyone. He'd kept them all waiting.

Well, wasn't that what stars did?

The director spat loudly upon the ground.

Nick was untroubled. Hadn't he kept Stanley Kubrick, the great American director who now lived near London, waiting for a month now about a meeting for a part in some new movie? Nick just didn't have time for filmmakers, big or small.

Everyone took their places as the director barked and cursed and complained. A young female choreographer kept close by Nick, her eyes fastened to his feet.

Nick barely had the energy to dance and lip-sync into the camera, a device he'd been trained in a few short weeks to seduce, to love, to imagine the greatest crush upon.

He'd barely read the script.

In the final scene, he was to ride a motorcycle on wires up into a bank of tear-inducing artificial fog. He didn't know where he would find the energy, until the director's cute assistant, a muscled, Indian-featured youth, offered a line of cocaine in the makeshift dressing room between takes.

Just another day in the life and whirlwind career of Nick Davanger, pop star.

LORD PLOVER survived his heart attack. So did his shots of Nick, one of which would grace the cover of *Tattler*, a superslick and influential English magazine. The photo was stunning, Nick's emerald eyes sparkling like magic jewels in a sunlit crystal brook.

The tabloids ran the story of his "heroics." He never thought of the quick-thinking that may have saved the life of a national treasure as exactly "heroic." He genuinely felt that what he'd done—rendered aid—was what anyone in the circumstances would have done. That too was straight out of the hero playbook, of course.

Rusty was especially proud of Nick. But he was having some serious problems of his own, about which he never complained.

Nick was too busy getting a huge celebrity makeover and pushing himself into an ever-greater creative mindset to see that Rusty was battling on several fronts.

Rusty made it all look easy. He had perfected his laid-back English style of cool. To Nick, Rusty seemed to observe the world passing by with those warm, sympathetic eyes of his, and no matter what crisis popped up, nothing furrowed his handsome brow. His healthy mane of silver hair gave him the appearance of a Celtic prince, strong, brave, and unflappable against any dragon or enemy.

Despite the hedonistic lifestyle Rusty both practiced and preached, his body was in excellent condition, thanks to his discipline at the gym and pool. That discipline was also applied to his work ethic. He was ever the creative producer in the studio, an artistic partner more sought after than ever. And now he was maneuvering the corporate landscape as he created a dynamic business structure the centerpiece of which was none other than Nick Davanger, overnight superstar, heart-throb of both sexes, owner of a monster hit still riding a crest around the galaxy and beyond.

But every soaring golden arrow has its arc. A small critical backlash against Nick (inevitable, Rusty knew) had already begun. And Rusty was also Nick's first line of defense.

Some of the rock press dismissed Nick as fluff. A few envious fellow artists "slagged" him in print. Fans came to Nick's defense in droves, but some "important" (self-important) rock journalists were fashioning a small box for Nick Davanger. It was decidedly coffin-shaped.

Still, Rusty had plenty of resources and a lot of experience maneuvering in this game.

Strong, too, was the business structure Rusty had put in place years ago. Changes were bringing growing pains, though.

As a business partner, Drake was becoming more and more aggressive, even as he spiraled into a cocaine habit that was costing him—and the company—thousands of pounds per day.

Rusty himself was drinking too much scotch and smoking too many joints, so he could hardly fault Drake—at first. Coke kept Rusty up at night working in the studio, meeting deadlines, grinding out business. His first pot of black coffee in the morning kept the new business of Nick Davanger and company running, but not as smoothly as anyone would have liked. Especially Rusty himself.

The night after Nick made his first appearance lip-syncing on "Top of the Pops," the English hit records music program, Rusty and Drake had a huge fight and were asked to leave a posh restaurant.

The item made the papers.

Rusty responded with an epic bout of drinking, and for the first time since Nick had known him, the mentor-lover-Svengali who could do no wrong seemed to Nick to be spinning out of control.

It scared the hell out of Nick to see his "rock" in this condition; it scared him more than any stage fright or momentary lapse of self-confidence.

As the year went on, it got worse.

Chapter 14

NICK wandered down the street, thinking he'd dash into a quiet pub, grab a drink, and call a taxi home to the flat. The thought of the flat made him cringe. It was doubling as Rusty's overflow office as the little studio received its own special upgrade from exclusive boutique production outpost to this year's center-of-the-pop-universe.

The home that had once felt like a sanctuary was not only littered with monolithic towers of papers, contact sheets, videotape recordings, and other business-related detritus, it was heaped with ashtrays overflowing with roaches, with empty champagne bottles, trays of half-eaten meals, and endless piles of discarded clothing, junk food wrappers, and unopened mail.

The place was a total mess, and reflected in a distorted mirror the chaos of Nick and Rusty's life together over the past six months. Rusty refused to let a housekeeper near the flat for fear of any important papers being tossed out. He promised an epic cleanup, but like most of his recent promises, it was contingent on the completion of a treadmill-like array of business details with no end in sight.

Somehow they had managed to "crash" out the Nick Davanger debut album and deliver it on time for a rush into an awaiting world market.

The album wasn't up to snuff, according to Rusty and Drake. According to Nick, it was rubbish. He practically hated every song on it, especially the hot song that made him a small fortune, almost every penny of which was now tied up in this new precarious business venture.

All the songs that made the final cut of the album sounded to Nick like knockoffs of "Wonder What," a song he had grown mightily weary of hearing everywhere. It seemed as if it popped to the top of the charts in a new country each week. That precipitated a whole new round of press interviews, satellite TV links, visiting photographers, nosy reporters looking for a weak link somewhere to exploit. Nick almost found that funny. There were so many to choose from. And yet no one wrote that Nick was "queer" or that Nick lived with his producer or any such thing. The sale of millions of magazines and other merchandise depended on the boyfriend fantasy figure Nick presented to girls all over the world (as well as, to a lesser extent, certain boys).

The machine rolled on.

It wasn't as if Nick was having a bad time. It was that his good time was so mixed up with the confusion of sudden success in a fickle business. He knew it was like walking on the edge of a dazzlingly high ledge, steps from a deadly fall.

He didn't know what was down there at the bottom, only that it felt like something a long way away from the lofty place where, by tiny threads of safety, he clung to Rusty's precarious side. Down there it was dark and cold and lonely. Up here... it was hard to hang on.

So the party and good times kept rolling on, numbing the pain, and putting an exclamation point at the ends of words like Hit! Success! Millionaire! Rich! Phenomenon!

But fate had a strange game of its own, it seemed to Nick. He felt like a kind of observer even in the eye of the storm, even as he *was* both eye and storm.

The album, called simply *Nick*, spawned not a single follow-up hit, despite three launch events in the UK, Europe, and the States. It went gold quickly, though, and was inching toward platinum.

Amazingly (to Nick, anyway), IBI said that wasn't good enough to fulfill expectations. It wasn't going to sell enough copies to cover Nick's personal advance and the even more colossally expensive PR machine created to promote it.

With no single hit song, the fine-suited executive brass threw their hands up and started charting a way to cut losses.

The US launch was downgraded, sensing expectations were not going to be fulfilled.

Who, ultimately, made these decisions, in which hundreds of people were fired from paying jobs and a million connections severed? On the basis of what? Phrases like "good money after bad," came in telex messages. Publicity shots on TV shows on three continents were hastily scheduled, cancelled, rescheduled, and reshuffled.

In the meantime, perhaps as bitter fruit out of some of these frustrations, Rusty had made a startling deal to purchase M-Politik in a somewhat hostile takeover. The two original owners had invested poorly, and were rumored to have devastating drug problems. Seeing no better alternative, they made a tidy sum and signed over the business to Nick and Rusty. M-Politik Communication (communication singular, not plural) would be housed in the old studio space, with three floors above purchased in the deal to serve as worldwide headquarters for multiple media production—video, television, and (it was hoped, as Rome burned) feature films.

The pace of it all was insane, and possibly unsustainable.

Whether a dream or nightmare, drugs and drink made it all a bit surreal.

Nick, sober, walked past a newsagent stand, seeing his face on the cover of a familiar daily tabloid. It was the same old story about saving the life of Lord Plover, retold for the umpteenth time. Curious about what, if any, new angle could possibly be exploited in this aging "news" story, Nick (partially disguised in Ray-Ban sunglasses and a knit cap) reached for a copy. Behind it, he saw an unfamiliar men's magazine. The kind that are usually hidden from public view.

Nick smiled cynically, thinking of the poor, closeted poofter who must have been browsing it, and then been too embarrassed to return it to its proper slightly hidden place on the stand, much less actually purchase it.

The magazine was called *Manhole*.

Nick picked it up with a trembling hand.

The out-of-focus profile on the cover was of a rather debauched-looking youth, his hand and naked crotch "blanked" out by a splash of red print announcing, "Cuddly Randy Sandy." It was a very cheap, bad photograph that flattered neither the model nor the photographer, but which by its very tawdriness telegraphed a dirty and cheap thrill.

Cuddly Randy Sandy, eyes closed, face spotty and hair ridiculously streaked with blonde highlights, was none other than Nick himself.

Nick swallowed hard. He was certain he wasn't really recognizable in this bad, out-of-focus shot. He was not only a little older now and more mature, more manly and handsome, but he'd had a complete makeover. His light-coffee-and-milk tone skin had been all but sandblasted smooth, his hair styled and colored (his own dark shade with subtle highlights), his muscles toned through diet and workout, and his hands and feet manicured to perfection.

He now looked every inch a star athlete or actor. Add a few shakes of glitter, and Nick was an instantly recognizable, dazzlingly sexy pop star.

The kid on the cover of the pulp porn mag looked—while damn cute—poor and maybe even a little bit mean and tough.

This "kid" of barely a year or more ago bore only a little (but obviously some) resemblance to the rugged man now staring at him.

Nick purchased both the tabloid and the skin mag from a disinterested Pakistani clerk. He used a public phone to call a taxi home.

In the back of the taxi, he hid the dirty magazine behind the tabloid and looked at the photos.

The photoreproduction was as cheap as could be. The grainy shots of a naked Nick were explicit in the extreme. Luckily most of them were somewhat out of focus.

Would anyone be able to make the connection?

One photo in particular caused him some worry. His green eyes shone sleepily as he half smiled into the camera, semen on his bare belly, slicked into his black pubic hair, dripping from his big balls.

He closed the magazine and decided he'd burn it as soon as he could.

Or, on second thought, keep it under lock and key.

The thought of simply destroying the images, crude as they were, and of that face burning up, was to Nick simply sad.

He did not ask why, but instead thought of the drink he would pour to calm his racing heart, just as soon as he was alone in the bedroom he shared with Rusty.

NICK had hoped to surprise Rusty by picking him up at the studio in his new car, a sporty red Jaguar. He'd hidden the car up the street. But it was Nick who got the surprise. He stood hidden in the night shadows and listened to a heated discussion between Rusty and Drake.

"AIDS," Drake whispered. "Don't fucking pretend you aren't shitting yourself with worry!"

Somehow Rusty and Drake had drunkenly made their way on foot back to the partial-construction site above the old studio that would become M-Politik Communication. They were both ripped, Nick observed. The moon was obscured by clouds, but hints of it glinted in the shards of a broken green beer bottle in the gutter.

"It's an American... conspiracy," Rusty said, and he laughed hoarsely.

Nick was ready to clear his throat and announce himself. Instead, he hesitated.

"Then what's this?" Drake asked. He bent and pulled his pants-leg upward. He made a half turn. The maroon-colored spots on his calf looked like nasty little bruises.

Rusty's eyes widened and Drake's trembled with tears. Showing fear was not a trait Nick had ever seen in the tough bloke.

"Have you seen a doctor?" Rusty asked.

"There's no bloody cure!" Drake hissed, letting his pants-leg slide back down, covering up the strange marks. "It's a death sentence!"

"Lower your voice, please," Rusty implored. "You'll draw a crowd!"

"I'll not lower my voice," Drake said in a deep, lordly baritone. He shook his head, his face crumpling. "I've got nothing to lose anymore!"

"You don't know if it's AIDS, much less if it's going to kill you," Rusty said to Drake.

He rustled his keys from his coat, opened the door, and gestured for Drake to follow him inside. But Drake was apparently not finished with his rant.

"It's a curse," Drake wailed. "It's damnation for all this." He held up a small bag of white powder and tossed it onto the ground. "And this!" He spilled a pocketful of pills to the sidewalk, which was white with construction dust. "But most of all it's for being filthy perverts," Drake whispered.

"That's rot and you know it," Rusty said.

"We fucked against nature, and now nature is fucking us!"

Rusty frowned. "You need to get your head together, Drake," Rusty said. "Remember your pride."

"Fuck my pride!" Drake thundered. "I want my *life*!"

Drake slid on some rubble, caught his balance, and leaned over a bicycle rack at the curb. He braced himself, holding on hard, his back to Rusty. He heaved a heavy sigh.

Nick knew he was eavesdropping on a volatile scene, but he wasn't sure what to do or what he would say if he came forward now. Before he could give it another thought, Rusty spoke.

"Drake, I have something to say—"

"You!" Drake hissed, pointing a finger at Rusty and jabbing at the air. "You have something to say! Ha! There's nothing you can say to me! You of all people! *Fucking two-faced traitor*!" he hissed. "Dirty sod!"

Rusty came closer to Drake and sat gingerly on the curb. Then he clapped his hands together and rubbed them slowly.

"Drake, you've made this very difficult, but I have to tell you something," Rusty said. "I think it's ultimately going to be for your own good… but it's going to hurt."

Drake turned his head abruptly and looked even more alarmed, if that were possible.

"Oh?" he asked cockily. "You think you can hurt me?"

"I'm going to help you, Drake," Rusty said. "With your career and with whatever it is you may be suffering from. Even AIDS, or whatever it is. But the partnership we've had is being dissolved, and we will no longer be in business together."

A long silence ensued, and street noises of the wee morning hours drifted in. A car door slammed. A dog barked in the distance. Nick was riveted to his spot in the shadows.

Drake let out a sigh, followed by a gasp of air.

"Nick's North American tour...," Drake said, as if just remembering it. "The venue at the bloody... *Olympics*... no less!"

"That's a brilliant engagement and we're both grateful for the strings you've pulled, but it's not working out between you and me anymore, Drake," Rusty said. "The business has changed, and we've all changed."

"Nick said so? That little shite!"

"Don't blame Nick. This is my call."

"But he agrees, doesn't he? And Marisa Tambov? She wanted to fire me, and instead I made her a star in America! And you think you can discard me like... like fucking toilet paper?"

Rusty shook his head.

"Drake... we're both a bit ill... not only in the way you seem to think, with the virus. But the excess. The dope. The good times are ruining us both. Catching up to us at last. And I'm not going to drag Nick down in it. I'm going to steer us both out of it."

"You bloody hypocrite!"

"You've got a brilliant track record, Drake. And a future. If you get off dope."

"You're one to talk, *yer bastard*!"

Rusty produced a sad smile.

"I'm dealing with mine," Rusty said. "I hope like hell you can deal with yours. But the fact is, you've done damage."

Drake looked at his business partner and old friend, his face turning another shade of red. Tears trembled in his eyes.

Drake stood up, his knees creaking. He took a deep breath and a vestige of a strange smile began to form on his lips as his eyes narrowed.

"It's nothing compared to the damage I'm *going* to do to you—and to that no-talent punk-fuck Nick, who you call a lover," Drake whispered menacingly. "He doesn't love you!"

Nick's heart pounded. Pity was turning to anger inside of him.

Rusty smiled calmly.

"Threats aren't cool, Drake. And as exits go, this is just a bit too dramatic, even for an old diva like you. Now go home and be warned I will call the authorities and lawyers and whoever I need to keep you out of my life if you so much as dare try anything stupid."

Not for the first time, Drake's face showed actual human pain.

"How dare you?" he stuttered softly.

"It's my life. Mine and Nick's... and this discussion is long overdue."

"How *can* you just toss me aside? We built this thing together."

"You've prospered," Rusty said evenly. "You've taken far more than you've given, and far more than your share. You know that."

Drake turned as if to walk in the direction where Nick was hidden. Then he jerked his head around, looking hard at Rusty.

"I'll take a damn sight more too," he thundered, "before we're all dead!"

Drake stalked off, weaving along the sidewalk. Nick remained unseen.

Rusty leaned forward. He sighed and held his head in his hands.

As Nick was about to step out of the shadows, he saw Rusty withdraw a silver flask from his jacket pocket. Rusty drank deeply.

Nick was standing before Rusty as Rusty looked up at him with baleful eyes.

"You heard all that?" Rusty asked, his voice thick with hurt.

Nick gently offered his hand.

NICK'S single "Wonder What" stayed a great big hit in America that spring, becoming a club fave, especially in gay discos. It was confounding, then, to be told that an album that was bound to go platinum eventually was considered a failure. It did not produce a follow-up hit song. It did not meet its projections.

"Wonder What" was all Nick had. It wasn't enough.

Bookings were not great either. He didn't have enough material or enough of a reputation to fill a medium-size theater, much less an arena.

A group tour was proposed and scrapped. Then he was considered as a possible opening act for some big-name bands setting out on tours, but the "disco" stigma attached to him torpedoed that idea quickly.

Nick didn't consider his song "disco." It was new wave, like Human League and Soft Cell and Culture Club. But some people said that was just disco music too.

It was decided by IBI brass that Nick needed both experience and exposure in the UK. Unfortunately, the song was reaching the over-saturation point in the UK. The bookings were all for small, lower-end venues.

After a dismal tour of discos and gay bars around urban England, singing to a back-up tape, and occasionally being doused with lager, Nick was deemed ready to make a mini-tour of the States.

He had dates set with a real, live backup band in New York, Boston, DC, Chicago, Dallas, Las Vegas, and San Francisco.

Nick was too busy and too overwhelmed to think about what a trip home to the United States would mean on a personal or family level. On a business level, he was coming home a star with a white-hot song on the charts.

There would be no time to visit his grandfather and ailing grandma in Wisconsin. Thoughts of his mother were met with his own haughty indifference. He couldn't help imagining her seeking him out, maybe backstage somewhere. And then he'd stand her up and pay her back for years of rejection.

That was one scenario he occasionally toyed with.

Another was infinitely more painful to contemplate. A tearful reunion that was not going to happen. Because in his heart of hearts, he believed his mother neither cared for him nor loved him enough.

It was work to keep that bitter little lozenge stuffed deep down and out of sight.

He was determined to have fun, and the American tour was bound to be a lot more fun than the rough bar tour of the UK.

Nick was in top physical shape, so the speed and the alcohol he was consuming seemed far from catching up with him. He looked great, he felt confident but also a little bit angry, ready to conquer, to fight the backlash, to battle it out in a business that had already partly written him off.

Nick had something to prove, and he didn't have time to consider that his million-dollar payday might have made anyone else feel pretty damn fulfilled. Aside from some clothes and a few toys he'd purchased, he just didn't have time to enjoy the money.

Rusty drove Nick to Heathrow. Rusty wasn't accompanying Nick on this tour; he was up to his eyeballs in business details here at home in England. An American promoter who had worked with Marisa Tambov was taking care of all the stateside details, publicity, TV, newspaper and radio interviews, and autograph signings. And of course the gigs themselves, in those medium-size theaters the IBI men had only a few weeks earlier claimed Nick wasn't big enough to fill.

One had already sold out, in San Francisco. Nick was super excited about meeting his hired-gun band.

Rusty looked exhausted behind the wheel of the car. He drank a Coke and downed some pills.

Nick looked at his lover with concern and a small measure of disapproval.

"What you need is a vacation," Nick told him. "Let's go to the West Indies when I get back. Did you look at the brochures I put on your desk?"

Rusty laughed a little too derisively.

"I've got a business to run. We have albums to produce, including another one for you. Songs to write."

"I've already decided I want to record in LA," Nick said. "I want a rock producer, this guy who's worked with some of the LA punk bands."

"So I'm fired as producer?"

"You're executive producer, Rusty. But I want to do a guitar-based album. I'm sick of this synth-based disco pop."

"You need to make a Nick Davanger album, not a hard rock album. You have a fan base, a market. A wonderful, soulful, upbeat style, whether you know it or appreciate it or not. It isn't time for a Sergeant Pepper-style reinvention. You're the fun, sexy boy with the slightly funky electronic beats."

"It isn't me," Nick said sullenly. "I can't believe I'm going to sing this shit every night with a fake smile plastered on my face."

"If it's fake, they'll all know it. You'd better find a way to make it real, Nick. And you need to think carefully about where you're taking this career. You've been incredibly fortunate. And it sounds like you're hell-bent to blow it."

Nick angrily blurted out his reply.

"And what about you, Rusty? The partying, the endless work, fueled by drugs? You're ruining yourself. You're ruining...."

"Us?" Rusty said sadly.

Rusty pulled the car up to the gate where a porter instantly opened the door and started removing bags.

"That's not how I want it," Nick said. "I love you, Rusty." Nick felt the weight of his words. His eyes welled with tears.

They embraced.

"Nick, we'll make this work, I promise you," Rusty said.

A car honked behind Rusty's car as Nick stood bent at the window, holding Rusty's hand. Rusty winked and placed his hands on the wheel. He drove off, leaving Nick at the curb.

Nick felt the cold mist of the morning on his face. He took what would be his last breaths of damp English air, for a while. He could hardly believe it, but he was going back to the United States at last, and he was a very changed man.

Inside, the heat and warmth of the big airport felt cloying, leaving him feeling hollow, empty, and cold. He pulled his hat down and adjusted his sunglasses.

"Right this way, Mr. Davanger," said the porter. "We'd better get into the VIP lounge before the fans catch wind you're here. If you get mobbed for autographs, you'll miss your flight."

Nick swallowed hard. With a calming breath, he willed his steely strength forward through his strong limbs to the ends of his fingers and toes. He nodded, but he couldn't speak. He coughed, and found his voice.

"So let's get moving," he said in a strong, authoritative voice. He smiled, and when he looked up, a group of girls near the entryway screamed with excitement.

"It *is* him!" one of them cried. "It's the Emerald Idol!"

"Nick! Nick!" they cried. And in their desperate, excited voices, he could hear a wail of agonized wanting that echoed something in him, something he'd known all his young life.

Chapter 15

1984

NICK loved Marisa Tambov's opulent hardwood-and-glass house perched on the lush side of a Los Angeles canyon. And while he lived at the Beverly Hills Hotel most of the winter and spring, Marisa's home was his true shelter.

It had been his sanctuary the previous year too, when he'd made his first visit to Los Angeles during his precarious mini-tour of the States. Hard to believe more than a year had passed.

The house was built on a steep slope and was surrounded by dozens of tall trees, conifers and palms, and succulent plants, giant ferns, and tons of flowers. Lemon and orange trees were everywhere, even inside, in dramatic wooden baskets and terra-cotta pots. Marisa loved orchids, and there were more colors and kinds than he could count. It was like the cozy but expansive cottage of a fairy princess of the earth, and a very rich one at that.

Marisa's Grammys were displayed in a lighted cabinet in a corridor next to her wall-mounted, framed gold and platinum records. In the few years since Nick had known her, she'd gone from singing in a tiny London jazz club and living in a modest bedsit, to performing in stadium-size venues all over the world and living in this modern, state-of-the-art pocket palace.

She handed Nick a glass of red wine, and they curled up on either ends of the comfortable sofa beside the warm glow of the big flagstone fireplace.

She was polished and elegant, even in her comfortable "at home" silk slacks and blouse, a cashmere sweater draped over her shoulders. Marisa was always a picture of elegance. And now she was also, for Nick, like the calm center of a storm. The storm was Hollywood, show biz, and pop music.

Nick had changed a little too. He'd cut his hair short. He was through with color highlights and the gelled look of the early eighties. He was also sick of the disco space cadet outfits of a flamboyant rock star. He wore a simple black cashmere sweater, white cotton slacks, and soft Italian moccasins without socks. The watch on his wrist was a ten-thousand-dollar Rolex. The delicate gold chain around his neck was worth a small fortune. The diamond stud in his ear had cost about thirty thousand dollars.

If Marisa was a pop royalty queen, Nick looked like nothing short of a prince that season.

And he had never appeared more handsome and together. It was a studied look, to be sure. If Nick was suddenly a storm-tossed veteran of the biz, somewhat blinded by the glaring lights of fame, he was also getting used to it all. He was a pro, and he carried himself like one.

They touched their glasses together.

"As they say, 'I been poor and I been rich,' and, honey, rich is better," Marisa said with a laugh.

Nick nodded.

"Now the trick is staying on top," he said with a wink. "Wanna share that one with me?"

She laughed and gave him a nudge, touching her manicured fingers to his shoulder.

They both knew what he meant. Nick Davanger had never sailed on a wave this high, and he was definitely on a professional decline, the so-called "sophomore slump." They both knew most recording artists never recovered from it.

But they were happy tonight, and Nick felt like anything but a victim of misfortune.

"If I knew that secret, I'd bottle it," Marisa said with a guffaw. "Anyhow, you look better than ever, and you're rich with a thing called youth. That don't last either, by the way, honey. You know, you look almost like a real brother," she said, teasing him. "I like it."

"I'm liking it too," he said. "Everyone thinks I'm an Englishman, a disco bunny. Nobody gets my rock thing."

She shrugged.

She knew as well as he did that his hard-fought, guitar-based, punkish album, with songs more like those of U2 and Clash—hard-edged, angry, loud—had not charted, despite its release the previous month with a lot of corporate-supported hype and media fanfare.

The album was called *Next Millennium,* and it featured a fair amount of dark, gloom, and doom-laden disaffection. And screaming guitars. Nick loved the melodies, but they were decidedly challenging to pop fans who had an idea what a Nick Davanger record was—and what it wasn't.

The review in *Rolling Stone* was short, sharp, and brutal. "Just when Davanger's ubiquitous if infectious bubblegum hit has been thoroughly embedded in our brains ad nauseum, he follows up with an out-of-his-depth, unrecognizable attempt at rock relevance and fails miserably."

"'Wonder What' he was going to do for an encore?" mocked a Boston Globe writer. "Wonder at your own risk."

A London critic wrote, tartly, "Davanger seems to want to be a punk Jimi Hendrix, but actually manages to get further lost in what now seems like a public identity crisis."

A *Village Voice* writer went as far as to say, "Nick Davanger is a space-age Uncle Tom, and his latest attempt at 'passing' doesn't pass go. He seems hopelessly lost in a closet with see-through walls."

That one had made Nick wince. Of course he hadn't "come out of the closet" as gay, and the barely interested suits at IBI had been working hard to construct a straight persona for the teenage girls to whom they marketed Nick. Their backing of the album was minimal, but they still exerted control. There was just enough innuendo in the *Voice* review to stoke the rumor mill.

Was handsome, single Nick Davanger keeping a secret?

That sort of thing.

The video had been rejected from the programming method MTV called "steady rotation." The first single release bombed. The songs were written by Nick, with a little help from a highly skeptical Rusty, and recorded in Los Angeles with two producers who simply couldn't get a handle on him.

Rusty wanted Nick to try a somewhat raunchy song, and they composed "Backseat Driver"—*You know she never can stop / When she backs up on top / She's a backseat driver / She's callin' all the shots.* Rusty believed it had a chance to break out as a single. IBI barely wanted it on the album, and no further consideration was given to its potential as a 45.

Despite their rock chops, the LA producing team kept pointing to the more poppy Michael Jackson and Prince as the future. As if Nick could somehow imitate these black-identified artists. As if he was somehow possibly one of them.

The album became a mishmash, a compromise that pleased no one.

"Old Green Eyes Ain't Back," blared one headline. "And he's barely black!"

Nick had been offended by that headline since he didn't really understand what it meant. He was also perplexed by it.

Marisa came to his rescue.

Now, in the comfort of Marisa's home, Nick tried to come to grips with a problem Marisa had spotted the moment she'd met him.

"I read those books you gave me," Nick said to Marisa, referring to Ralph Ellison's *Invisible Man* and *The Soul of Black Folks*.

"Good. I think it's high time you made a habit of reading up on the side of your family you been hiding."

"I haven't been hiding anything," Nick said. "You know how I was raised. With a white family that was ashamed of me."

"You need to make peace with that too, brother. And with the man upstairs. You think about coming to my church with me?"

Nick rolled his eyes. "I have to rehearse."

Nick would be performing for the athletes and gargantuan crowds at the Olympic Stadium the very next night. The gig had been booked for over a year. He was more than excited. The trouble was, he was contracted to sing—what else? His one hit song of almost two years ago, "Wonder What." The stuff on his new album wasn't going to cut it. That one song was all they wanted, and he had agreed to deliver it with a smile. Being on that stage would be incredible. But knowing his career felt stalled would make it a pretty tough acting job. Now he had two dud albums under his belt. And that damn song around his neck.

"You'll be great, and the athletes from all over the world will be singing right along with you," Marisa said.

"Everybody knows the words, the melody… just like a bunch of trained zombies."

"Just have fun with it, baby," she said. "This is not a hardship, you know. Let's be perfectly serious a moment. You read what I sent you, that story about a boy named Emmett Till."

Nick nodded soberly.

"Emmett Till and countless others never had a chance like you had," Marisa said gravely, referring to the infamous case in which a black boy was murdered after being accused of whistling at a white woman. "You read the book I sent you about Jackie Robinson breaking the color line in 1947 and integrating baseball?"

Nick nodded.

"I read it, but what do I really know about pro baseball? I never made it out of my high school league." He grinned.

She laughed.

"And here you are, going up to the Olympics," she said and refilled his wine glass.

"You know, I read James Baldwin in college," Nick said. "I related to gay stuff. But *Giovanni's Room* is about white guys."

"Let's go to my library," Marisa said. "You need to study James and everything he ever wrote. And Maya, and Alice Walker, Toni Morrison."

"You sound like a teacher," Nick laughed.

Marisa gave Nick a tour of the new additions to the house, which included a light and plant filled painting studio. Marisa dabbled in wild colors, using acrylic paint to explore figurative images on big canvases. Nick wanted a studio like this someday. He wanted to explore all these areas of his creative impulses—painting, writing, sculpting, just as Marisa was doing.

Not just music.

Music was food for his soul but not the only food. Marisa was a total artist, and Nick wanted to be nothing less. If he teased her about being a teacher, he was actually only too happy to be her student.

Later Nick looked out the window at Deshawn, who was clipping his prize roses. "Must be nice to be able to afford help around the house," Nick joked.

"Deshawn turned out to be the best kind of help I ever found," Marisa said.

"Husband material?"

Marisa shrugged. "Might be," she sang. "For now, he's everything I need and then some."

They went back to Marisa's pretty sitting room.

They joked and joshed for a while, and then Marisa grew serious again. Nick knew she was going to ask about Rusty.

"IT'S just that I worry," Marisa said. "I worry about him being alone."

"It's just for a time," Nick said softly.

"I understand," she said. "And then again, I start to wonder and worry…"

Nick had been thinking a lot about Rusty, more even than he usually did. It was around this time that Rusty made a big change in his life. Under a doctor's orders, Rusty took leave of London and his business, and was staying at a rustic cottage on the stunning west coast of Ireland, where he finally began coping with his demons. He was supposed to be writing songs too, working his way through and out of his dark places, brought on by too much hard work, too much hard partying, and the exhaustion exacerbated by his divorce and Nick's absence. Songs were to be his therapy. Songs for an album to be recorded at M-Politik by the youngest and arguably most gifted—and difficult—of the Abeche sisters, Abigail. Whether that project would come to fruition or not was up in the mist-shrouded and bracing air.

Nick knew as well as Rusty did that the place where Rusty really needed to be was in alcohol and drug treatment, not necessarily at Lord Plover's "secret hideaway" on the rugged coast of the most beautiful country Nick had ever seen. Plover had lent the cottage to Rusty and Nick, saying it was at their disposal whenever they wanted it. They'd only visited it a couple of times, falling completely in love with its breathtaking blue ocean views, quaint country lanes and farms, and pastoral green hills scented with laurel and pine.

Despite that it was drafty and lived up to the word "rustic," both Rusty and Nick were especially mad about the house, too, with its fresh sea-salt air, windows opening to the roar of the rocky surf, and those winding country roads leading to pleasant rural towns and cozy pubs.

The cottage was ivy-covered, and its storybook stone chimney and hearth, like something out of a fairy tale, exuded warmth and magic in winter and summer.

It was a special place for them.

And yet, Nick was not there. It seemed that Rusty needed time on his own, and Nick too was finding his way, alone for now.

From far-away California, Nick called Rusty every day, his voice warm with affection, concern and genuine love. And occasionally worry. M-Politik was a success, over its critical hump as a new company expertly run by Rusty and (usually from a distance) Nick, and now capable staff hired to manage day-to-day operations. But making M-Politik a success had cost Rusty his peace of mind and threatened his health.

Thus this respite in Ireland, to help restore Rusty's energy. The creative process was Rusty's real passion, not making deals and crunching numbers. That he'd learned. Though he was adept at it, and took pride in his accomplishment. Nick took less and less interest in the business, which he had in some ways come to resent.

Nick had the big gig at the Summer Olympics in Los Angeles, but his plate was suddenly free of many other responsibilities. The Nick Davanger "show," as he thought of it, was all but over. And that was setting in slowly.

Still, there was one more performance to do. And it was a big one.

NOW, in LA, Nick sat beside his spiritual and artistic advisor, Marisa, and he pined for and missed Rusty. Missed him like hell. And he was worried about him too.

Rusty wasn't talking to anyone these days but Nick. He was unplugged from the world, even from his dearest friends.

Marisa sighed. She went to the kitchen to get them a snack.

He fiddled with the phone, then started to touch-tone dial Rusty's number, but he ended up setting the receiver down. He just had to keep himself from disturbing Rusty several times a day with long distance calls made impulsively. Rusty needed to rest, to restore his creative juices, to enjoy the creative solitude alone with his guitar or at the keys of his piano.

Songwriting was now Rusty's favorite occupation. The cottage was an artistic haven.

Thousands of miles away from Rusty, on California's West Coast, Nick swallowed hard, picturing Rusty there. Wishing he was there beside him. Missing him.

Marisa padded into the room with a tray of tea and biscuits. Sunshine washed over the expansive new porch constructed of bleached pink brick and designed by Deshawn. Flowers and thick cacti animated the low table between soft chairs and a loveseat draped with an Indian blanket in startling blues and reds. A dozing orange tabby flicked an ear at the sound of pouring water.

"Rusty always sends you his love," Nick said to Marisa. "I spoke to him on the phone last night for a long time."

She smiled, but he could see a trace of sadness in her eyes.

"I miss him so much too," she said.

Nick felt his heart grow heavy.

"Now don't let your throat clench up," she said. "Keep it supple. Drink this tea with lemon."

Nick nodded. His throat felt fine. But Marisa was one who believed in preserving the "instrument" on a day of performance. She barely permitted him to speak. Instead, she served hot tea and sat with him in silent prayer and meditation, channeling the spiritual forces that she knew helped the gifted present their gifts.

Nick drank down his tea.

"I'd better get over to the Coliseum," he said.

THE Games of the XXIII Olympiad, otherwise known as the 1984 Los Angeles Summer Olympics, provided a venue not only for the world's greatest young athletes. It was a mind-boggling stage for American entertainers. Hollywood and the music industry were right in the backyard. Nick knew from the moment he arrived at the Coliseum by limousine that he would never forget his experience there.

Not only was the place packed, the VIP areas were crammed with superstars rubbing shoulders with international athletes. Brilliant sunshine poured from a hard, blue sky over majestic palms and Southern California opulence. Electricity was in the air.

Nick took part in a guided tour before the music festivities began. The smell of chlorine at the sun-bright, dazzling pools and the pristine tracks and gymnasiums all made a strong impression on him. The event was simply colossal, and he marveled at what an experience this was going to be for all of the young athletes of the world. It was true the Soviets and Cubans and others in the socialist world were boycotting the games, just as the US had boycotted the games in Moscow in 1980. But a feeling of goodwill and camaraderie prevailed.

When asked by a TV reporter what he thought of the political controversy, Nick smiled. "It's sad, but you can't put a dent in the enormous good that this gathering really means," he said. "In the end, that goodness still triumphs over politics."

The reporter's eyebrows rose slightly. If he'd been expecting an airhead pop star, he was mistaken. Nick had become a lot worldlier in his travels of the past year. At a time when show-biz folk rarely touched the topic, he'd expressed himself forthrightly. Nick knew he might have said a whole lot more. He might have criticized President Ronald Reagan for speaking not a word about AIDS, a topic that was on everyone's minds. He might have done and said a whole lot more himself on that topic. But in 1984, he was deep in the closet, and AIDS was associated with gays and a harsh stigma. Nick didn't think he was important enough to be truly political, as if that privilege belonged to other more "relevant" people, and not "mere" citizens.

So instead of being critical, he kept it positive. And when the cameras snapped his image, he smiled. He was by no means the biggest star on this stage, which he felt belonged to the athletes not the entertainers. But he was greeted warmly everywhere he went. His hit pop tune was known the world over. He and it were inseparable, as far as fame went.

The opening ceremony was incredibly moving, and Nick found himself riveted by the parade of nations, the flags, the pomp and circumstance.

The music of "Bugler's Dream," forever associated with the Olympics, stirred Nick's heart as he passed by TV monitors when he made his way to the dressing rooms.

Backstage, Nick shook hands with some of the American competitors before the concert started. The handsome champion diver Greg Louganis smiled and shook his hand. The gold-medal speed skater and cyclist Eric Heiden said hello.

At last it was time for Nick to perform with several other American acts brought together to entertain the athletes and mega-audience gathered from all over the world.

Of course he sang "Wonder What," in an abbreviated version, and it was well received. The night sky was filled with fireworks exploding in vibrant colors, and the Olympic torch blazed over a backdrop of stars.

The performance of a lifetime ended with a bang, and Nick, drenched in sweat, exited with what felt like a cast of thousands to deafening cheers.

The games were underway, and it felt incredible to be a part of it.

Nick felt very revived by the experience, and he couldn't wait to call Rusty when he got home. He showered, changed out of his costume, and prepared for a night of fun.

A meet and greet with some of the athletes and officials left him almost speechless, so intense was the energy and sheer physical beauty and strength all around him. The flashbulbs popped and the cameras rolled. Everywhere he went, foreign athletes asked for his autograph, and he graciously signed and asked them for their signatures on his official program in return.

After the hubbub and the main ceremonies, the parties began in the vicinity of the Olympic village. Of course, many athletes were competing the next day and as they were in training would hardly be out partying. But the entertainers, journalists, and spectators were energized to make the most of this night. A jam session started up in a large lounge in a famous hotel where Nick found himself amid a glittering array of stars and gorgeous young people. Nick had a couple of glasses of champagne, and when he was called to the stage, he surprised himself by standing up and striding confidently to the mic stand.

He'd been received very warmly by the immense stadium crowd earlier when he'd sung his familiar old hit song. Now, the smaller crowd was polite but less enthusiastic.

Nick whispered something to the pianist. Then he turned and smiled to the audience of international athletes and a few pop singers and film stars, all crammed into the big lounge. The alcohol was really flowing, and the party was getting wilder.

"This is an old standard," Nick said to the crowd. "A Johnny Mercer number."

It was a song Marisa had taught him.

Nick sang "Accentuate the Positive," and nearly brought the house down. He sang in a jazz style, letting his voice run smoothly over the melody in a deep soulful style that surprised him.

"Bless you all," he said at the end of the number, to wild applause.

"That was amazing," someone said, behind him. "Can I buy you a drink?"

Nick turned around and looked into the chocolate, sweet eyes of a drop-dead handsome young athlete.

"Sure," Nick said. "I'm Nick Davanger," he added, holding out his hand.

"Duh, I know who you are," the guy said, grinning. He was about Nick's age, twenty-four. Maybe a little younger. He had a somewhat darker café con leche color than Nick did, and thicker curls.

"What's your name?" Nick said. "You an American, right?"

"I'm Paul Tolanaro," he said, grasping Nick's hand. The grip was tight, the body solid. He had just the tiniest trace of a Spanish accent.

"I should know who you are," Nick said. "An athlete, but from what country?"

"I'm on the American baseball team," Paul said, laughing.

"Baseball," Nick said. "Wow!"

"Can't believe I'm actually talking to you," Paul said shyly. "You're the biggest star I've met since I got here to LA."

Nick smiled. "Well, you're the brightest star I've met. Baseball is my favorite sport by far."

"It runs in my family," Paul said. "My father is Cuban-born, but I was born here, in Miami. He played ball in Cuba and then in the Majors for a while. My Mom is Anglo."

"So's mine," Nick blurted.

"And your father?"

"Just an American guy like me," Nick said. He let it drop.

Paul nodded, maybe not sure what to say. Nick smiled. He liked Paul's face, and Paul's body was amazing. He was very powerfully attracted to him. In fact, he could feel himself developing a crush, and they'd only just met. Was there a connection sparking between them? Nick doubted a super masculine athlete like Paul would be gay. But then, wasn't that thought just playing into a silly stereotype?

"How about that drink?" Paul asked.

Paul purchased two beers, and Nick followed him through the bar.

"I'd like to get away from my team for a little bit," Paul said. "Most of them are milling around here. If they see us together, they'll all just want something silly, a photo or your autograph, then we won't be able to talk."

"You don't want my autograph?" Nick laughed.

"Of course, but I'm meeting so many celebrities. I've been told it's not cool to ask for an autograph. For some autographs, anyway. Not everyone is as friendly as you."

"You'll be the one being asked for signatures and photos," Nick said. "Who do you play for when you're not competing in the Olympics?"

"I'm in Triple A right now," Paul said. "In the minors. But I'm headed for Chicago or maybe even New York or Boston."

"Wow," Nick said. "Where's home?"

"Miami is still my home," Paul answered. "That's where I have about a million relatives. My Dad brought his whole family here right after the revolution. I've never set foot in Cuba, even though it's all I hear about down there."

"That's a shame you can't visit there," Nick said. "Why won't our government let us travel to Cuba if we feel like it?"

Paul rolled his eyes. He had found them a quiet booth in the lounge, near the back of the big room. It was angled so no one else could see them. The place was starting to empty out.

"It's a long story," Paul said. "But I'll never set foot on the island as long as the communists control it."

"I wouldn't let that stop me," Nick said.

"You're not Cuban," Paul said.

"Do all Cubans think like you?"

"Conservative ones do," Paul said.

Nick wondered just how conservative Paul was. He had to have been breaking some training rule, staying up late and having a drink. Nick got the feeling Paul made his own rules.

Paul looked serious and sad for a few moments, perhaps thinking about Cuba. Then he brightened up.

"So, what's it like to be a famous pop star?" Paul said, grinning now. Nick could tell Paul was star-struck. Nick knew the look. He'd seen it too many times before. But he didn't mind seeing it in Paul's eyes. He liked Paul more and more by the second. It was not that unusual for a straight guy to be so star-struck he'd break a rule or two.

"You'll find out about fame," Nick said. "It gets you a lot of stuff, more than your fair share. But it has drawbacks."

Paul touched a cross on a chain around his neck. He kissed the cross.

"I know how to keep things in perspective," Paul said. "This is what matters." He held the gold cross between his fingers. "You Christian?"

Nick shrugged.

"I have faith," Nick said. "But I don't go to church."

"My family would be so disappointed if I stopped going to Mass," Paul said. "Our community church is like my second home."

Just then a thin man with a bony face and faint moustache lurched in next to the table, holding up an elaborate camera. He shot several pictures, flashes momentarily blinding both Nick and Paul.

"Hey, do you mind," Nick said, holding up his hand. "We're having a private conversation."

"Just give me one more, Nick," the photographer, a total stranger, taunted.

"You got your shot, dude," Nick said. "Why don't you beat it?"

That pissed off the photographer.

"Get over yourself, Nick," the man said. "Better yet, hold up your fist like you're angry. I might even be able to sell a shot like that somewhere." The photographer seemed to be drunk.

"What is your problem?" Nick asked.

"You're a has-been and these pictures probably won't even fetch me fifty bucks," the guy said, obviously trying to taunt Nick into causing a scene. A dramatic conflict kind of shot would be a lot more saleable than one of two guys sitting at a table having a beer. Nick remained calm.

"You're funny," Nick said, smiling. Coolly, he added, "And now that you've got your worthless shots, why don't you get lost before I break that camera over your head."

"Who's he," the photographer asked, ignoring Nick and gesturing to Paul.

"I'm the guy who's going to kick your ass after Nick breaks your camera," Paul said with a smile.

Paul leaned forward, and the guy jumped back.

"You think you're so special," the photographer hissed at Nick. "You'd be nothing without the press, guys like me putting your face in magazines."

"I'll take my chances," Nick said.

"Haven't you heard? Your chances were already taken and lost."

The guy stormed off.

"What an asshole," Paul said.

Nick shrugged, draining his glass.

"Just part of the business," Nick said.

"I don't like that part," Paul said.

Nick said, "Let's get out of here."

"Sure," Paul said. "Where you wanna go?"

Nick thought for a second. An idea came to him.

"Think we can get a car to the beach? It's a beautiful night."

"I have a rental car," Paul said. "We have more than a few days of down time, and I want to check out this city. Let's see what the Pacific Ocean looks like in the moonlight."

PAUL drove the black Corvette convertible out of the hotel parking lot and toward the freeway. The scene sprawled before them like a vast network of ribbons, bleeding red and white lights. Nick rubbed his eyes and took in the warm night air.

Nick figured Paul knew what he was doing, even if that was breaking some team rules about leaving the Olympic village for a beach drive.

Nick scanned a map Paul handed him. He knew LA pretty well but not perfectly. They drove past the Santa Monica Pier, festooned with lights like a carnival. It was a perfect summer night.

"How about we find a place to park and take a walk on the beach?" Nick asked. "Maybe even take a swim. Don't get an opportunity to hit the beach living in London, where I'm based, and out here all I seem to do is work in dark, windowless recording studios."

Paul smiled, and Nick pointed to a spot on the map off the Pacific Coast Highway.

"I grew up at the beach," Paul said. "I love swimming at night." He shook his head and grinned. "God, if my family knew I was hanging out with you… a rock star… wow."

Nick liked that "rock star" comment.

"They must be pretty impressed with their ballplayer son," Nick said. "I would be."

Paul shot Nick a look.

"It was expected of me… but it does help in the girls department."

Nick smiled. "Yeah, I'll bet."

"I'm sure you get plenty of girls throwing themselves at you."

"Mm-hm, and you'll find out, if you haven't already, that it can be a lot of fun sometimes, and other times more trouble than it's worth."

Paul looked thoughtful.

"You're right," he said.

It didn't matter to Nick at this moment if Paul was straight or gay or something in-between. It felt good to be with him, and the feeling seemed to be mutual. Far away from Rusty, Nick had acted on a few impulses here in LA and on the road. Not that he and Rusty had taken up a vow of monogamy. Just a "safe sex" vow. Nick tried not to take advantage of it, because he felt like a hypocrite whenever he felt jealous about Rusty. He knew Rusty was probably celibate when Nick was away.

For one thing, Rusty had a tremendous amount of work to do. For another, Rusty was rethinking things in light of AIDS. If that wasn't a dark enough thought to ponder, Nick also knew that Rusty was usually in no shape to have sex in his recreational hours, few as they were. Rusty's drinking and drugging had taken on a solitary dimension. Nick had his doubts about Rusty's self-cure strategy in Ireland. A rehab facility seemed a better bet. It was the sort of problem that would call for a serious conversation. But in this new age of anxiety, Nick didn't want to show disapproval or nannying toward Rusty, who was after all making a good effort to get healthy. And what if Rusty were entertaining some red-haired, red-chested Irish buck this very night? Who was Nick to begrudge Rusty his comforts, even as they both knew there could be consequences.

Tonight, on the beach, Nick felt as wild and free as he ever had in his life. It was a paradox of sorts, and he knew it. His career as pop star was at its nadir. The album was in oblivion, on a one-way ticket to nowhere. The concert at the Olympics was a high. But it was also an ending, and he couldn't dismiss this persisting feeling.

Unless he replaced it with the hot new thrill sharing body heat beside him.

Nick knew he looked good, and he caught Paul checking him out more than once.

Nick felt his own rude good health and surging blood. And with his stronger, more mature body, he felt more comfortable with himself. It showed on the handsome features of his face. It showed in his masculine stride. With his black hair cut and styled short, and his gym body straining against the fabric of his expensive sports clothes, he could have passed for a young movie star.

Could have *passed*....

Nick felt his "passing" days were going to be behind him, forever. The punky-pop kid with the dyed-blond hairdo was gone for good. And Nick liked the guy who'd replaced him. A guy with soul, comfortable in his skin. Or at least appearing to be with young brother Paul's hand grazing his.

It didn't hurt Nick's confidence that he still had most of his advance money intact, a business to work in with Rusty, no need to struggle with the ordinary day-to-day stuff most young people his age were dealing with as they entered the job market and embarked on careers.

Of course it also helped that now Nick had the seeds of new plans in his heart. Artistic plans, business plans, *life* plans. He'd be going home to Rusty soon.

He'd be leaving pop-stardom-Hollywood land. He'd soon be entering a new phase of his life, and he was still so young.

But before that happened, one more conquest seemed imminent.

They had parked on the road, left their shoes behind, and in the moonlit darkness walked to the edge of the water.

Both guys were still a little buzzed from their drinks. Nick could see lights from the houses on the cliffs, and a ways off down the beach, he could see a small bonfire. Otherwise, they seemed to have perfect privacy here.

"Let's take a dip," Nick said.

"Sure," Paul answered, as if he was being dared.

"Not afraid of sharks, are you?" Nick said with a grin that shone in the moonlight.

"Hell no," Paul answered. "Told you I've been swimming my whole life."

Nick wasted no time stripping off every stitch of his clothes.

Paul hesitated.

"It's okay," Nick said. "No one can see us."

Nick could see that Paul was shy. But he was also so clearly enamored of his famous new friend. It was so clear to Nick that Paul would have done anything for that friendship.

Anything.

It was startling how much the young of America esteemed its stars, the guys on TV whom they emulated, the actors and athletes and musicians whose mere glance sent endorphins soaring.

Nick, staying aloof, watched Paul undress. Nude, Paul piled his clothes on top of Nick's. In the moonlight, his naked body seemed outlined in silver. He was beautiful. Nick felt his passion rise. The surf rolled in and fell hard upon the sand.

They smiled at one another, but there was an awkwardness about this that soon made them both laugh.

Nick said, "Come on, race you," and he ran toward the surf, very aware that Paul would be looking at him, at his nakedness.

Paul came running after, arms outstretched, diving below a wave.

They swam for a while, laughing and wrestling in the surf. Nick's heart swelled with the joy of newfound friendship, and he could see that Paul felt this bond too. A kind of rare seduction was playing out quite naturally.

Nick wanted to take it all the way. Wanted it more than anything.

Just as Nick hoped, it soon seemed impossible they would be able to keep their hands off of one another. Wrestling clinches turned to lingering embraces, skin sliding and pressing together, closer and closer. Paul seemed to want this intimacy too.

Nick was head over heels in lust. But he truthfully couldn't really tell how Paul was feeling. Nick was hard, but Paul, half-submerged, was impossible to gauge below the waist. Nick didn't dare touch him intimately and break the spell.

At last Nick trudged through the surf back to the beach and lay down on a pile of his clothes. Paul followed, and sat down next to him upon his own shirt. Nick noted that Paul did not cover himself up. It felt wonderful and free to remain naked.

Nick sat up cross-legged beside Paul, who was now leaning on his side. Now Nick could see Paul much better. Paul had such a beautiful athletic body, a little bit of black hair on his chest, and long powerful legs. Moonlight reflected in the beads of water on them.

Nick looked on brazenly, and Paul met his gaze.

Both breathed deeply. For a time, they were quiet, close together, as if waiting to cross a chasm. At last Paul spoke softly.

"I'm not gay," Paul said softly.

"Neither am I," Nick lied.

"I have a girlfriend, and we're gonna get married."

Nick nodded.

"She came out here for the Olympics?" he asked.

Paul shook his head. Nick wondered how it was possible a potential fiancée would not have accompanied him for the event of his life. Unless, of course, there was no such girlfriend.

"Paul, I don't know if it's right, but I like you," Nick said. "And… I want to…."

Paul seemed to be breathing hard.

"Yeah?" he said in a hoarse voice.

"I want to kiss you."

Paul didn't reply for a few moments. But then he surprised Nick and said, "Go ahead."

Nick moved his naked body closer to Paul's. Nick's heart pounded fiercely.

He kissed Paul deeply on the mouth, and Paul responded, kissing back gently and warmly. Nick's dick was hard and so, in an instant, was Paul's.

"It's okay," Nick whispered. "You don't have to do anything you don't want."

"I'm already past that part," Paul said, and grinned sheepishly. "But, God, you know I wouldn't even think of doing anything like this... except...."

"Yeah?"

"Well, you're Nick Davanger. This is really blowing my mind."

Nick moved his hand up Paul's inner thigh. He cupped Paul's balls as Paul sighed.

"Hold me like this too," Nick said.

Paul leaned forward and took Nick's hard dick in his hand.

"Ah," Nick said. "Yeah... just like that... good."

Seconds later, Nick bent down over Paul's smooth masculine torso and began to caress him with his lips, his open mouth and tongue. Paul responded, his nipples hardening and his dick getting even harder, throbbing hot. Paul then bent forward and repaid Nick the favor being lavished upon him. Nick was lost in perfect ecstasy, and it amazed him that Paul was so responsive, so into it too, following his every move, measure for measure.

AFTER their experience on the beach together, which Nick found more than perfectly satisfying, Paul came back with Nick to a famous hotel Nick often stayed in. Nick got them a nice room. Paul stayed the night.

They drank up most of the minibar, ordered a lot of food from room service, and watched old movies. They both then more or less passed out in the same bed.

When Paul woke up before Nick the next morning, he was in a foul mood.

"Shit," he said. "I gotta call my manager. I'm supposed to practice today."

"You have plenty of time," Nick said groggily. His head throbbed. His feelings were a jumble. He stole a glance at Paul's bare back and felt a deep throb in his crotch. Paul was just so damn sexy.

Paul brooded.

"You okay?" Nick asked.

Paul shook his head.

"I feel... kinda guilty," Paul said. "Like I told you, I'm gonna get married! This ain't my scene, this shit. It was just a one-time shot."

Nick nodded. Inside he felt conflicted, and he tried not to let it show on his face. He more than liked Paul. Just looking at him made Nick's heart thump hard. Then thoughts of Rusty colored his desire with shame. Sex on the beach was one thing, actually falling in love quite another. Nick sighed. He let his head sink back onto the luxurious pillow, and he rubbed his eyes. He knew he mustn't confuse a sudden infatuation with actual love.

Yet Nick had no doubt in his mind. Paul was the greatest lover he'd ever had. Not that Paul was some kind of sexual expert. Paul was in fact a complete novice, but that only added to his charm. Paul was Nick's physical ideal. His skin color, his muscles, his hair, his sex—he was a god.

Nick was in agony.

Paul said emphatically, "Nick, I like you... I want us to be friends...."

"Seems like we are," Nick grinned.

"Not like that, I mean. Nick, you're gonna be married someday too, have kids, like me. Wouldn't that be cool if we were still good friends, without... messing it up any more than we already did."

Nick tried to look thoughtful.

"That may be, but we're here right now," Nick said. Nick reached out his hand to Paul's warm shoulder. "And... I think you're beautiful."

"Shhhhit," Paul said, taking a hard step away from Nick's reach. "Guys don't say that kinda stuff to one another! Hell, I'm a Christian."

"And so am I," Nick said forcefully. In his headlong fall for Paul, and in this utterance, something inside of him felt like it had just been jarred loose. Something that had been frozen in him for a long, long time.

Nick had been trying to shrug off his personal shame for ages, never quite escaping the reach of its shadows. Now, a kind of light felt so close to him it actually warmed him and emboldened him.

Paul had made this so.

Marisa had helped too, of course. She'd seen who the real Nick was all along. Nick Davanger was a spiritual man. He was a black man. And he was a gay man. And those were good things. Because they were a goodness of soul. Nick thought this was something Paul could be and sense and feel too, couldn't he? Tenderly, as a comrade. Paul just had to see this, he simply had to!

Nick felt electrifying energy coursing through him, feeling these things.

Paul pulled a sheet from the bed and covered his nakedness.

"Maybe we better... not see each other anymore," Paul said.

Nick was not exactly hearing this.

"Why?" Nick demanded.

Paul pointed at the door.

"What the hell do you think people would think if they knew?" Paul said with anger in his voice.

Nick pulled the sheet from Paul's hand, uncovering him.

"Why?" Nick said again forcefully. "Because we had some joy together that they, *those people* out there, say we shouldn't have? Well who are they? What do they really know? God made this body. God made my body. He made your body. He made us beautiful, Paul! And he gave us feelings, feelings called love. Feelings called friendship. Tell me one good reason we shouldn't express these feelings?"

"It's... unnatural," Paul stuttered. "It's wrong!"

"How can something wrong feel so right?" Nick said and caught himself. He laughed despite himself, recalling the lyric of a song. Paul smiled despite himself.

"It's just an old song," Nick said, "but damn if it isn't the truth!"

Paul shook his head stubbornly.

Paul made a grab for the sheet, and Nick deftly reeled him in close to him with it, right back onto the bed.

Suddenly they were both laughing as they fought over the bedsheet.

Nick leaned forward and pulled Paul close, kissing Paul's lips.

Paul shook his head no, even as he folded his beautiful legs around Nick's naked waist.

"Come on," Nick whispered.

Nick rolled onto his back, pulling Paul on top of him. Paul sat up, his hard dick looming over Nick's belly.

"You're crazy," Paul said, half-smiling, eyes closed. Nick stroked Paul's dick, and Paul started moaning and grinding his naked ass over Nick's throbbing groin.

They fucked around like this until Paul blasted off several hot spurts of come onto Nick's belly and neck.

In the shower, Nick came, rubbing up against Paul's slick belly, fingering his voluptuous ass.

Back in the bedroom, Nick lounged between Paul's legs, satisfying him again with sweet intimacies, kisses, and caresses with his probing tongue that went on for hours.

Nick held on to Paul like he'd never let him go, like a drowning man afraid of losing everything. Passion put his mind in a fever that was close to despair. He didn't want to give up Paul. Ever.

Later that morning, Paul dressed quietly. At the door, he turned back and said, "Nick, don't say anything... just let me leave."

Nick leaned forward, as if to reach out his hand.

Then Paul left. He went off to practice in preparation for his Olympic competition.

Nick fell onto the bed, crushing his tearful face into his pillow. He tried not to think about Paul but failed completely.

NICK cancelled his next several days' worth of meetings with agents and directors. What was the point, he thought. He already knew the video production schedule had been postponed. Probably forever. In fact, there would be no videos, except perhaps much lower-budgeted affairs targeted at certain foreign markets where Nick Davanger might still sell a few records.

Even that was considered a long shot.

It was hard for Nick to consider business when all he thought about was Paul. That's all he *could* think about.

And yet he had no choice but to face his prospects in the music industry.

The money guys who analyzed every angle of market projection saw Nick in the red side of the ledger, a money-loser, and ultimately a bad investment. Had his career been built up slowly over time, a failure like his current album might have been viewed as a bump in the road. A bad bump, but not a dead loss.

Rusty understood it. Nick was a victim of instant success and its subsequent expectations. He simply flared brilliantly, and there was no way that smashing success was going to be repeated, he was told. He could reinvent himself on a much smaller circuit, but not with the big-time players who had been banking on him. They had already moved on.

Nick had moved on too. He had no regrets at all about doing the new album his way. The way he looked at it, he had proven himself as a commercial success, even if it was all but accidental. Hustling for scraps just didn't make much sense to him.

Now he wanted to be an artist. His kind of artist. He had the freedom now to do that. And quite a bit of money.

So in a way it was a luxury that business was fast becoming the last thing on his mind.

He worried about Rusty, but he thought about Paul constantly. He planned to attend the baseball competition at the Olympics, then thought better of it.

He knew he'd never feel farther away from Paul than he would as a member of a huge crowd of spectators.

He called Paul, tried to reach him, but received no word in reply. His worst fears were coming true. Paul did not want to see him again. Paul was living up to his words.

Nick watched Paul on TV, competing in the Olympics. Saw him at play. Saw that steely concentration in his eyes and observed that coiled power concentrated in his body.

It only inflamed Nick's desires further. And he allowed himself to sink into a depression that belied his newfound confidence in himself. What good was spiritual knowledge and self-discovery if your heart was breaking? Would he have to keep climbing back up this mountain again and again, all his life?

He spent the next few days in the darkness of his room, drinking whisky.

Slowly, he worked himself back into a routine: late breakfasts, exercise at the private gym at his hotel, swimming, taking fast pleasure drives around the hills and along the coast, listening to music, having lunches and dinners with Marisa, and writing journal entries and scraps of ideas, cartoons, little drawings.

Nick divided his time almost equally between Marisa's house and his hotel room. He called Rusty, but the conversations were brief and sometimes edgy and guilt-ridden.

"Yes, I'm working, and there's a bloody lot of work to be done," Rusty said late one afternoon, his voice gravelly. It was already very early morning in Ireland. Yet Rusty had not been awakened by the call.

"Is everything okay?" Nick asked. He simmered over Rusty's workaholic nature, his seeming inability to really relax and take the reflective break everyone had been led to believe he was taking.

"Of course it's okay," Rusty snapped. "You get to play pop star in la-la land while I sit in a rainy, leaky cottage in the middle of nowhere, in the wet wilds of Ireland."

Nick smiled. The place was hardly a leaky cottage in the middle of nowhere. It was something close to paradise.

"That cozy cottage is what I'm dreaming of, every night," Nick said, and he meant it, with real longing.

"And is that all you're doing at night? Dreaming?"

Nick paused before answering.

"No, Rusty."

"I didn't expect so."

Nick felt his face getting hot.

"Weren't you the one, Rusty, who told me to come out here to experience my life at its fullest, to kick down those repressive boundaries you thought were holding me down... wasn't that your advice?"

Nick heard Rusty sigh on the other end of the line.

"Everything has changed now... it's too dangerous, Nick. I was wrong. Nick, I want you to come home."

"Rusty... are you crying?"

"What if I am?" Rusty shouted.

"Rusty, you sound drunk!"

Nick immediately regretted calling Rusty out.

"Don't you dare speak to me like that," Rusty said in his raspy voice.

Nick laughed derisively, regretting it before he'd finished. "Come off it, Rusty, you're not my mother."

"Come home," Rusty cried. "Just come home!"

Nick cleared his throat.

"I have some business to finish here," Nick said. "I don't see how I can get back to Ireland or London for at least a week or more. And the Olympic Games... I want to be there for the closing festivities. I wish you were here, honest. But maybe it's better that you're not over here right now...."

"Who is he?" Rusty asked.

It was so uncharacteristic of Rusty to be jealous. A part of Nick felt almost relieved. Yet it also hurt to know Rusty was suffering for any reason.

"Rusty, you need to take care of yourself, do you understand me. You're the only one who can do that."

"Are you in love?" Rusty asked bitterly. "Or are you just getting fucked?"

Nick was angry now.

"You sound like a jealous wife," Nick said. "Well, then maybe you deserve to be treated like one. You should know I'm a free man, and no one, not even you, is ever going to make me feel beholden again. I hope you can get your head clear enough to think that over carefully, no matter how long it takes you. But don't wait forever!"

Nick hung up the phone with trembling hands.

ON HIS last night in LA, Nick met up with Paul again in his hotel room.

Getting Paul to agree to a meeting was a hard-won battle in the extreme. The only reason Paul finally took one of Nick's calls was to plead with him to stop phoning, once and for all.

Nick agreed but only if they could talk, just talk, one last time, face to face.

Paul arrived at Nick's hotel suite freshly showered, shaved, dressed in a crisp white Polo shirt, pressed slacks, new shoes. He was also wearing dark sunglasses and a plain white baseball cap with the bill pulled low.

"I'm not like you," Paul said, sitting in a big leather wing chair by the window.

He accepted a glass of ice water from Nick. A huge TV with the sound turned off showed the electric-blue pools of the Olympic Games, where the competition was going strong a few miles from the hotel.

"You mean you can't accept yourself as you are," Nick said. "The way I accept myself, as gay."

"I'm not gay," Paul said. "I like women."

"Yeah, but if you also like me, that means you're at least bi."

Nick poured himself a glass of water from the heavy crystal pitcher beaded with condensation. Nick wore white linen shorts, Nike running shoes, and a loose silk shirt in a shade of pale blue. They both looked like two pretty well put-together guys, dressed to impress one another, cleaned up and ready to hit the town on a date. But that was the last thing that was going to happen.

"I gave it a try, with you… that's it, and I'm done," Paul said. "I can see now that was a mistake. I think it's unnatural for men to have sex together."

"You mean for all men or just you?"

"I mean all men," Paul said. "It's wrong… it's sinful."

Nick knew there wasn't any way to convince Paul to change his mind. But Paul's body was another matter.

"Man, you need to relax," Nick said.

"This is not a relaxing place for me," he said.

"Too many haunting memories?"

"Very funny," Paul said.

"Maybe you're thinking too much about this stuff," Nick said, biding his time. Right or wrong, he wanted Paul. Needed Paul. Needed to feel his touch, hold him, have him. Not even his obsession with his college roommate Casey came close to this desire. If it was wrong to pressure Paul into doing something he was so damn conflicted about, then he wouldn't pressure him. He'd comfort him.

Paul drank down his cold water. "I need to go," he said.

Nick came over close to him and extended his hand.

"You wanted my friendship," Nick said. "I'm offering it, wholeheartedly."

Paul looked at Nick's hand.

"I didn't know you… wanted more than that," Paul said.

Nick checked his anger. Hadn't Paul wanted more? Paul was not queer in his estimation. All the blame, shame, and guilt resided with Nick, then, as Paul would have it.

Nick kept his hand held out to Paul. Paul at last took it and clasped it.

The heat of this handclasp, and all the drama stirring in the hearts of these two young men, seemed to fuse them together for a long moment. Nick's heartbeat was nearly audible in the quiet room.

They ended up in bed again, despite Paul's words.

Nick had simply gone from holding Paul's hand to rubbing his tense shoulders and back. Paul took over from there. Paul may have thought sex with Nick was wrong, but Paul's body couldn't seem to resist it.

They made love slowly, the curtains pulled against the bright California sunshine, the light diffused. Nick studied Paul's naked body as he skillfully played his hands and lips over skin hot with passion. Knowing it was the last time.

Later, after Paul came in a scalding climax, he became sullen again.

They lay in one another's arms in a kind of twilit silence, at last broken by Paul's thick voice.

"So I'm human… a sinner," he muttered. "You know how to take advantage of a weak spot… you can't be proud of that."

Nick frowned.

"I need you, Paul," he said. "It's not a matter of pride."

"I told you I'm going to be married," Paul said. "My fiancée is pregnant," Paul said and stood, looking at Nick still naked on the bed. "That's why she's not here."

It sounded true, even though Nick wanted to call Paul a liar.

"And you should get married too," Paul admonished Nick and started getting dressed. "This is no life."

The luxurious hotel suite, bathed in shadows, seemed suddenly creepy, cold, sealed off from the summer sunshine.

Nick shook his head.

He let his head sink into the pillow. Paul was fully dressed now and at the door. He was about to leave again.

"This is goodbye, Nick," Paul said. "I'm going off to the big leagues," he said with a grin, meaning Major League Baseball. A long-term contract was ready for him to sign. "That's a world where *this kind of thing* doesn't happen. Get it? I mean it *can't* happen."

"I kind of doubt that, Paul."

"None of *this*," Paul said, gesturing in an exaggerated way. "None of this ever happened between us, get it? You would ruin me if you even tried to contact me. As it is, people saw us together. I can't afford rumors or loose talk."

Paul hesitated for a moment but then came over and held out his hand for Nick to shake.

Nick grasped Paul's hand. Then Nick tenderly kissed Paul's hand.

"No!" Paul said violently, pulling his hand away. "I don't want to be like that, don't you understand? I don't want you to be like that!"

"But I'm like that," Nick said. He didn't say, "and so are you," because as satisfyingly cruel as that would have been, he really didn't know for sure. Paul was a star-struck young guy from a very insulated world, going into the holy realm of American sports. Nick, not much older, was far more sophisticated. Paul might have been experimenting, or he might have been deeply in the closet with plans to remain there.

Nick knew he'd lost. But he cared about Paul. He thought he loved him. He sat up on the bed.

"I promise I will never do anything to hurt you, Paul."

"Don't write, don't call, don't try to see me somewhere—ever. Don't ever contact me! Ever. Forget me. Do you understand?"

Nick nodded.

"Yeah," he said.

Paul picked up the bag he'd brought with him and walked out of the room, and closed the door behind him. Nick let his head fall back on his pillow and tears streamed down his face.

He knew it was crazy. Rusty was his lover and life partner, not Paul. Paul was mixed up at best and very cruel at worst. Maybe both.

Nick loved Rusty, really loved Rusty, and he knew Rusty loved him. Rusty was in trouble and needed him. But Paul represented a kind of love too, an aching ideal love, deeply erotic. Unattainable. A fantasy come true but only for a short time.

And so what had barely begun, ended. And Nick intended to keep his promise to Paul—forever.

No matter how much it hurt.

Chapter 16

The Present

LOS ANGELES—sprawling, glittering, smoggy, sexy. Nick drank it in and tried not to let a rising tide of panic engulf him.

When he'd left here, two decades before, he didn't know if he'd ever come back. The freeways and streets had a familiar scent, baked asphalt and sea salt, the jasmine perfume of blossoms in the canyons of the wealthy and ultra-successful.

He exited the freeway and made his way up to an enclave of green, palm-lined, lavish homes.

Susie was shaking and crying when she greeted him at the door of his rented villa.

He tried to calm her. She was inconsolable, and dark circles ringed her pale watery eyes.

"They took Wolfy from me," she sobbed. "I turned my back for just a few seconds, and he was gone. I could hear him whimpering and barking frantically. There was nothing I could do…."

Nick winced. He steadied himself.

"I know, I understand," he said, embracing her. "We'll get him back, I promise, and everything will be okay."

But he had no idea if everything would be okay. He said that to Susie in part to console her and to console himself. To try to will calm into his mind so he could make decisions about what he needed to do.

It was bad enough that the photos would probably ruin Paul Tolanaro's career, and maybe even his life. It was bad enough that Nick would be forever linked to that damage. But the cruelty of taking his canine companion was… it was *twisted* and unnecessary, and it hurt Nick so much to think of how scared Wolfy must have been that Nick was afraid he would start picking up fragile things in this stylish house and smashing them.

To anyone who might possibly say *"It's only a dog..."* Only a dog! Nick would have been utterly appalled.

His love of that dog was special, and all love is special! Nick set his bag down and steadied himself with a hand on the back of a big, stuffed chair. The room spanned out with pools of dappled sunlight, pots of pretty blue hydrangeas, and colorful mosaic art on the wheat-colored walls. He vowed he'd get Wolfy back and make whoever had done this crime *pay*, and pay dearly! There was no reason to endanger the animal! Nick would have paid the ransom money if that's what it took. He would have accepted the personal embarrassment of the photos of himself, if it came to that, if there was some way he could keep the ones of Paul secret. But what if he couldn't? What if the explicit sex pictures of Paul and him were released to the public anyway?

He would help Paul in whatever way he could. Though there would be no help on earth to repair that damage, he knew.

Still, there was time to prevent anything terrible from really happening—wasn't there? If he kept his head, kept his cool. The blind rage at this injustice—*how could someone do this to me?*—was as destructive as any drug, any poison. He knew that. Now was not the time for a crisis of confidence, of a fall back into a darkness from which the grace of God alone had rescued him.

Hang on, Nick! Just hang on!

Nick felt a sense of unreality. Everything was violently breaking apart in him. The past rushing into the present, the ghosts of yesterday threatening his very soul.

He was jet-lagged, anxious about the rehearsal schedule and all that was riding on it, and beyond worried for the sake of his kidnapped dog.

LA had always represented a kind of hell in paradise for him. Every creature comfort tainted with his mixed-up youth, his sudden success, and the way he had seemed to crash and burn, including the lowest ebb in his relationship with Rusty. The passion and rejection that Paul represented still hurt.

Even though he had grown up long ago and found more than a measure of peace in a rich and fulfilling artistic life.

A life that, like all things, passes away, leading to new chapters, new chances, and of course new challenges.

No longer that cocky kid who had burned so brightly on the first immersion into LA, Nick tried to remind himself now that he was a cool and comported man of the world, whose elegance and style belied the storms within.

He prayed to the Lord he would have the strength to endure the next few days and whatever they brought him.

The Hollywood Hills house he was leasing was elegant, a Spanish design, open and airy. He carried his bag up the curving staircase to his new bedroom, all spruced up by Susie with flowers and crisp bedding and masculine furnishings. He stepped out through French doors onto the tiled balcony overlooking the pool below, beyond which were lemon trees and a wall of dense green cedar.

Nick's eyes filled with tears. This was supposed to be his new beginning. He had already lost so much. But Nick couldn't allow himself to fall apart. He felt a warm hand on his back. It startled him.

Nick turned. The woman's hair was streaked with silver, her face older, wiser, yet more beautiful than ever.

"Marisa," Nick whispered.

"Baby," she said, embracing him hard. "Susie let me in. Baby, I've missed you. Let me look at you."

He took a step back.

"Honey, you're better than ever," Marisa beamed. "But you better tell me what's wrong. I could see it on Susie's face, and now I see it on yours. She told me only you could explain."

Nick looked past her at Susie, who stood in the doorway with a crystal vase filled with more fresh flowers. Her nose was red, and her eyes were wet, showing extreme stress.

Nick shook his head. "I'm in trouble, Marisa," he said. "I don't even know how to tell you... or if I should."

She took his hand in both of hers.

"Come and sit with me," she said.

At last Nick told Marisa the whole story. It took a whole bottle of good California white wine, which they split, but he managed to get it all out. They sat in the foyer overlooking the gardens and pool.

Nick and Marisa prayed. Susie had taken a strong sleeping pill and gone to her bed, leaving them alone.

Marisa said little, but she prayed, holding Nick's hand in her surprisingly strong grasp.

At last she stood up. He watched her.

Marisa paced back and forth for a while. Despite being rich beyond her wildest dreams, she had the same down-to-earth quality he had loved in her from the first time they met.

"Susie is not involved in this scheme," Marisa said. "I wondered for a moment, but I'm a good judge of character, and this kind of evil is not in her. And I don't use a word like evil lightly."

"Unfortunately, I do have some enemies," Nick said.

"Who doesn't in show biz?" Marisa said, trying to make light for a moment. She frowned then. "We have to call the police."

Nick shook his head.

"They said not to," he said. "I can't stand the thought of what they might do to Wolfy."

Nick felt sick just saying those words.

"I never would have guessed it about that big ex-baseball player, Paul Tolanaro," she said. "He's a big right-winger out here now, a very important man in certain conservative Christian circles. See him on Fox News a lot. I mean, you just can't tell who's into what, and of course people do things in their youth… experiment, I mean."

"Don't I know it," Nick said, producing a half smile. His green eyes twinkled. He sighed deeply. "I can't contact Paul. I promised. And what would I say, where would I begin? He'd panic. The pictures are either going to come out or they're not. If I called to warn him, he'd only worry, maybe needlessly. Who knows what he'd do if he thought his whole life and career were gonna be blown to kingdom come."

"He has a lot to worry about," she replied. "He's a big man in this town, like I said. His sportscasting career is about as big as it gets in that world. Why, he's even been mentioned as a possible candidate for office."

"No way."

"I'm sure I read that in *People Magazine*. Just imagine what everyone would think if they saw him, a big conservative Republican, all nasty in those photos. Actually, I'd like to see that!" She laughed and covered her mouth.

"Marisa!"

She rolled her eyes.

"I'm sorry… too much wine… honey, if this wasn't such a horror for you, I really wouldn't care about that guy, though. He hurt you."

"It was a hundred years ago… everybody gets hurt. I sure wouldn't want to hurt Paul, though. I promised him he'd never hear from me again. He's married and has kids and everything. What a mess."

She came to his side.

"Let's think this out proper," she said. "You've had a long journey, and you've been worried sick."

"It's not just the money," Nick said.

"How much?"

He told her. She whistled.

"The weird thing is," he said, "this happened to me once before. Blackmail. Rusty and I paid."

She did not conceal her surprise.

"How much?" she asked.

"Nearly twenty-five thousand pounds."

"Never told the police?"

"We just paid it," Nick said.

"Any ideas who might have been behind it?"

Nick looked away. He'd never wanted to think about that horrible incident again.

But now he didn't have a choice.

Chapter 17

1990

SIX years after he left LA, Nick had his first brush with blackmail. It had been six years since he'd had his fling with Paul, and six years since he'd ended the brief phase of his life in which he'd been a *near* top-of-the-heap pop star.

Life in London and Ireland with Rusty had settled into a routine that was mostly good, even when it was frantically busy. Long periods of separation were still a given, but as the 1980s came to their close, Nick held on to a special kind of hope.

He'd thought 1990 would be a good year, a new beginning. The beginning of a new decade always held promise, he believed. But 1990 was starting on a chilling note. It came in with a terrible shock.

Nick arrived home in London after a long international flight, and he was tired. Tired but not weary or disappointed. Arriving home after business trips usually felt really good. This one felt better than ever. He figured he'd settle back in this posh house in this jolly old town for good, and to hell with all this travel. It had taken some time to get to this comfortable place in his life.

For six years, after his time in LA, Nick simply picked up the pieces of his life and tried to forget about Paul, who was, after all, "just" a brief fling. It was easier, in a way, because he was so busy working.

Life with Rusty was never dull. After his months in Ireland, sorting through his demons, Rusty threw himself more deeply than ever into the work of making M-Politik a major player in the pop music business. His obsessive patterns were probably an ingredient in his success. Nick accepted it, and simply started taking on more and more responsibilities, which often took him thousands of miles from London, from home.

It helped him find his new role in a tough industry and also aided him in figuring out what he wanted ultimately to do with his talents and unique experiences. No question, whatever he did, it would be with Rusty.

In that first year of this new life, and into 1985, Nick still played a few gigs in Japan and other far-flung places, but his main project now was M-Politik. The pop appearances were mainly curiosities, shows put together on the fly. The press had zero interest in him on these trips, and that was fine with Nick. He played his songs, usually with a pick-up band, and sometimes even with just an audio tape. He collected his check and moved on, sometimes making valuable connections along the way. Those kinds of jobs fell fewer and farther between, and eventually died out altogether. Other aspects of business filled the breach.

At home, he learned the business of running a media machine, from top to bottom, dividing time between London and the Plover cottage in a state of refurbishment on the west coast of Ireland.

Rusty was the ultimate workaholic in those years. He brimmed with ideas as always, and he sharpened his keen sense of deal-making, just as he signed on young new artists and shepherded their careers with a growing list of freelance producers, talent agents, and, now, film people. A whole new challenge that promised even more creativity—and hard work.

If Nick had thought he'd spend his time as a gentleman poet or painter, he was mistaken. While Rusty developed talent and made gigantic deals, Nick became the public face in many foreign markets where his one-time star power still generated some energy and interest, at least among the bottom-line-watching business types known as suits. It was true his albums had failed, but the success of M-Politik drew attention. It didn't hurt that everyone could hum the opening notes of "Wonder What." Hardly anyone would refuse a meeting with him. He closed deals in Canada, the Philippines, Japan, Israel, Turkey, Poland, and Iceland.

Next he conquered the Netherlands and Scandinavia.

Rusty was his mentor, lover, confessor, and fellow merry-maker. And if the wine (exceptionally good stuff) was still flowing, so was the cash. Or so it seemed.

Nick now sported two-hundred-dollar haircuts, and styles from Savile Row and the best of Bond Street. Making deals with filmmakers, real estate corporations, and news media moguls required a certain look, style, and confidence. Nick simply imitated Rusty at first. But soon he developed his own style: athletic, suave, exuding confidence.

No one really knew that his home life, with the person he loved more than any other, Rusty, had begun to amount to little more than late-night long-distance phone calls, hasty dinners in private rooms at luxury hotels, and all too rarely brief rendezvous on a private beach or yacht of some billionaire they were doing business with. Hardly the vacations together that they really needed and Nick craved.

One particularly vexing reunion took place on the grounds of a Swiss sanatorium, where Rusty had been sent by his doctor after collapsing from exhaustion. Fatigue was a factor, Nick knew. Drug and alcohol addiction was another.

Rusty had tried mightily to keep his addictions at bay. But like so many who refused the help of others, relapse was a constant possibility.

But Nick couldn't discuss that touchy topic with Rusty in those years. Aside from doing battle with his ex-wife, Rusty had other demons lashing him toward his success with M-Politik.

"You've both been tested for HIV, right?" Marisa asked, over five thousand miles of transatlantic telephone cable.

"The connection on this line is crackly," Nick quipped. "We'd better say our 'I love you' now before we're disconnected."

"Very funny."

"We've had this conversation before, and I think you know how we feel about that topic," Nick said. He tried to picture Marisa in the presidential suite of some five-star hotel, sipping champagne after another sold-out concert. Nick was in a so-so hotel room in Frankfurt, his flight delayed by the weather. He was sipping expensive cognac and living out of his carry-on bag for at least the next twelve hours.

"And your head is still deep in the sand?" she admonished.

The conversation was identical each time. It went nowhere. Nick would say it's no good knowing the truth about HIV status, because there was no cure at that time. But in actuality, he knew that both he and Rusty feared the truth for far more complicated reasons. They simply would not be able to face bad news about one another. Bad news they feared, even as they practiced safe sex.

"I love you, Marisa," Nick said and rang off.

Nick knew he had Rusty's love. What he wasn't always certain of was whether he had Rusty's respect. He wanted Rusty to really listen to him and trust him, about everything.

Rusty was, for some unknowable reason, living as if in fear of failure, on a treadmill of sorts. How could Nick or anyone help make him confront the implications of that problem? The way it built walls up between lovers and other people. He wanted to save Rusty and save the business that had become, for both of them, a lucrative but dangerous obsession.

One of Nick's greatest lessons in business was that one could take nothing for granted. Just a few minor reversals could send a business trending in the wrong direction.

They both knew what nobody else suspected: the business empire that glittered too brilliantly in the public sphere actually hung by a thread. In its quantum phase of growth, it was at its most vulnerable, in a shark-filled, murky sea of competitors. M-Politik was dangerously overextended, overcommitted and run by a team that seemed to be living and spending as if there was no tomorrow.

The goal or finish line of secure profitability seemed to be close, but something always made it slip a few more inches beyond their pounding footfalls.

Flying first-class overnight from airport to airport, Nick dreamed and daydreamed of a pair of soft, comfortable blue jeans and a T-shirt, no shoes… and a stack of books, paints, and canvases in his rarely used little study at the Irish cottage they thought of as their escape, their sanctuary.

If he couldn't be there in reality, he dreamed of it, and the dream was a sweet one.

Ireland was where Nick would be able to write and Rusty would build on his newfound interest in painting and make music for the sake of music alone. And the phones would be switched off, and the world could be kept far, far at bay. Nothing would come between them, though they could surround themselves with the warm friendly neighbors they'd gotten to know in the small villages nearby, and they could care for animals and tend gardens... and live as simply as country people have for centuries.

It was such a nice fantasy.

But when could it possibly come true? That's what Nick wondered, even as he swiped his black plastic card at yet another exclusive airport club where glamorous models and talented young musicians hid from the light of day and fame's glare. Amused, he didn't envy them. He barely had time to think about his next series of connections as he nursed a lager and scrolled through phone messages.

It was after a return to London from a business trip to Australia that Nick found the dirty manila envelope delivered by post, stacked with other mail in a large orange art-glass bowl in the foyer of the comfortable yet neglected London home he had shared with Rusty for so long now.

And that was the beginning of Nick's first brush with blackmail, a crime that carried an acrid whiff of Victorian England.

Nick dropped the manila envelope on the burnished wood tabletop and turned, very surprised to find Rusty holding two glasses of red wine and with a smile on his weary, handsome face. A fire crackled in the grate behind him. Mozart played on the stereo.

They embraced for a long time.

"What's in that ugly envelope you were looking at?" Rusty asked.

"I'm almost afraid to open it," Nick said. "But I guess I'd better."

He ripped open the envelope and read the words scrawled in thick black marker... *your ruin... your money... your time is running out...*

"What?" Nick whispered to himself, reading and rereading the dirty blackmail note. He looked with concern at Rusty, who looked instantly alarmed. A quiet evening at home was dissolving in the tense electrical charge now suddenly in the air.

Rusty took the note and sat down heavily in his favorite comfortable chair.

"This can't be," Rusty whispered. But then he looked at the accompanying documents. The photos.

Being blackmailed like this, with such outrageous photos, was an event that might have sent Nick over an emotional edge, but he stayed strong. At least on the surface. For Rusty.

"A spot of bother," Nick said in the English, stiff-upper-lip manner. He grinned and took a sip of the delightful claret. Inside, he was whirling, his heart slamming hard in his ribcage.

Why this, why now?

In business terms, things were once again relatively stable. M-Politik continued to impress as wildly successful, at least on paper, at least in media articles. So much so, Nick and Rusty had been able to purchase this stunning house in the posh Marble Arch section of London. And Rusty had agreed to go through an in-patient rehab facility for substance addiction. The stress had taken a toll on him to the point at which he had agreed to this course of action. Nick was not going to let this latest "spot of bother" harm Rusty at such a vulnerable point in his life. He would make himself look and sound strong, and hope that the act would convince not only Rusty, but himself as well.

But the blackmail threat dredged up his own buried feelings of insecurity.

Nick felt as if he'd left a trail of failure behind him in the US. The cottage Lord Plover had left him in his will was the one place Nick felt he wanted to be that autumn. Not in London, not around the fickle music business. And nowhere and in no place that reminded him of Los Angeles, the place he most fought to forget. Even if Marisa was there, he'd had enough of it.

And now, blackmail, a threat from an unknown anonymous source.

Their first reaction was to fight back. These were simply the erotic pictures of Nick anyone could have seen, had they been a devotee of the long since defunct *Manhole* magazine.

There were none of the beach photos Nick would be threatened with years later.

The immediate threat, in 1990, was of the kind of exposure that could threaten M-Politik, though. Nick's singing career was over, true, but not his career as the public face of the business. What foreign business people (a generally conservative breed, even in music) would want to meet with him after a scandal if the picture became widely known?

Perhaps none.

And if Nick's image existed at all in the public consciousness at large, it was as something wholesome, something nostalgic. This could be ruined for good by the photos Nick had thought had simply faded away over time.

How dare some creep try to control Nick's destiny in this way? How dare they screw around with the reputation of M-Politik, so carefully built, brick by brick, with Nick and Rusty's sweat and toil!

Nick tried hard to suppress his fury, to not show Rusty how upset he really was.

The blackmailers had included photos of Nick in certain trademark clothing he'd worn that long ago winter of 1982: his weathered denim jacket, his American-style Adidas sneakers. Even if Nick were to claim that the younger guy in the picture, while resembling him, was not him (a lie or a hoax), the blackmailer or blackmailers, if there were more than one, had carefully constructed a valid, credible case. Who knew what other connections they would be able to make? This package of goods would instantly make a juicy, embarrassing news story in one of the English tabs, no question. Outed and exposed in one fell swoop. Fleet Street editors would lick their chops over it.

The note instructed them to wait for a phone call. They didn't have to wait long.

The phone rang that night as Nick and Rusty finished their dinner of squab by candlelight.

Nick had an eerie feeling as the phone rang, almost as if the house were being watched, and the blackmailer knew that Nick had arrived home.

RUSTY looked at Nick with a flash of wariness in his eyes. The gentle blaze crackled in the fireplace. The phone rang again.

"I'd better answer it," Nick said. He took a big gulp of wine.

"Okay," Rusty said.

It was the blackmailer. Nick listened carefully. The voice on the other end of the line was muffled and low, probably male. But that was hard to determine, for the voice was so deliberately distorted. Nick thought some kind of electronic filter was used.

"We have a drop location and a bag man ready to accept the money," said the voice. Nick had less than twenty-four hours to make his decision, the voice continued. The money had to be delivered or the photos were going straight to the *Daily Mail*.

"No police," the voice rasped. "No car, with a cop or anyone else hiding in the boot!"

"Of course," Nick whispered.

THAT night, Nick and Rusty compiled a list of possible suspects. They decided, regretfully, it must have been someone close to them, or else how could they have nabbed the nonporn pictures of Nick in his identifiable clothes, photos that were the personal property of Nick or Rusty, and had obviously been stolen. The crude photocopies proved possession of the originals by the crooks.

Nick eliminated the people he'd known in his stripper days. They would not have access to personal photographs, though they certainly would be able to confirm Nick's past to the press if a scandal broke out.

Could they have been working in concert with someone close to Nick and Rusty?

The list included Drake Atka and an old college schoolmate of Nick's, Andy Severn. Severn had stalked Nick in LA, hoping Nick could help him with his rock band and "career." Nick had ruefully declined, remembering Severn's rejection of him during their school days.

Nick felt a bit guilty about this petty payback, if that's what it was. In truth, Nick didn't want to waste his time determining whether

Severn had the chops to be legitimately referred to one or two of the few LA music insiders Nick knew who might have made a difference. Lining him up with M-Politik was simply out of the question, as that roster was already full to the bursting point.

Nick had told Severn that the agents and producers were just as available to Severn's rock band as they would be to anybody; that the industry was in fact looking for new talent in local clubs. A demo tape would be listened to.

"Yeah," Severn had complained bitterly. "Competing with thousands of others that come in every year."

Nick wasn't having any of Severn's petulance.

Severn was already bitter, distinctly lacking in charm, too cynical to believe that success was possible without that critical "connection" the envious always seemed to believe in.

"It's who you know," Severn groused, his face showing alcoholic bloat, eyes bleary from the partying lifestyle he had the gall to call a "career."

"That shows what you don't know, Severn," Nick said, casually dismissing his old schoolmate's guilt-tripping ways.

"And in my case, who I know is a real asshole," Severn shot back. "Thanks for nothing! I look forward to returning the favor!"

"That sounds like a threat," Nick had said.

"It's a promise!" Severn had said.

Nick hoped he'd never see him again.

Was this blackmail attempt Severn's revenge? Or Drake's.

Drake had not been seen or heard from since his nasty argument and business split with Rusty.

Rusty was reluctant, naturally, to consider his ex-wife Jill, who was having her own battles with alcohol, and of course with him, despite ample payouts. Or (even worse to ponder) Rusty's estranged young daughter, Janette.

"It just isn't possible Jill or Janette could be up to this," Rusty said. "I'd give Janette twice this amount if they really needed it. She knows that. She wouldn't risk jail. And neither would Jill."

"And what about Clive Gardner?"

Rusty had to consider that. Gardner, Janette's tough-guy boyfriend, was a far likelier candidate for a stunt like this. Clive had also made ugly threats and enemies of Nick and Rusty.

With those terrible thoughts racing through their minds, they climbed the oak stairs of their warmly appointed house and prepared for bed.

The master bedroom was all burnished wood, like a room in a baronial men's club. The big bed was soft and sumptuous. Naked, Rusty pulled Nick close.

In the soft light of the moon coming in the window, Nick marveled at his lover's form. Rusty had taken care to stay fit, despite the abuse he had put his body and soul through over the years. His body was still sexy and hard, but his genes and constitution must have been even stronger. He was made of good stuff.

Rusty gently caressed Nick's face and smiled tenderly.

"We're going to survive this, Nick," he said. "I promise."

Skillfully, they made joyful love as if they had no problems or cares in the world. In the morning, they decided to sleep in, holding one another in a strong embrace.

Eventually, though, they got up, showered, dressed, and had a late breakfast. They spoke little. Rusty was not going into his office, he decided. He spent some time in his home study, but for the most part, they did not leave one another's presence all day.

In the end, Nick and Rusty didn't have enough time to sort through the details or suspicions of the blackmail scheme and work up a Sherlock Holmes-style solution, somehow foiling the bad guys. Late in the afternoon, they went to the bank (Barclays) and got the money in cash, and Nick prepared to make the drop as directed.

It left a bitter taste in their mouths, but they decided to leave the police out of it. For several reasons. But mostly because they were afraid of the unknown tormentor and the threats they had received. Maybe if they followed orders, the matter would be resolved. Then they could slowly begin to consider all the clues, if they wished to. Or they could simply write off the expense with a sigh of relief.

They really didn't have much choice on this day of inclement weather.

Night fell and the appointed hour quickly approached.

"I'm coming with you," Rusty said at the door.

"I'm going alone," Nick said. He wore a leather jacket and cap pulled low, heavy Italian boots, a gray cashmere scarf. "That's how they want it, and it's me this is aimed at." Rusty's eyes showed real pain. He was Nick's hero, and that's what he wanted to be now. Nick loved him dearly and couldn't allow him to take a single step into this mess. It was too dangerous.

The past few years had been hard for Rusty, and now it showed in the weariness in his big dark eyes and in a few character lines that had formed in his brow. Even his hair was now a bit whiter than the dazzling silver of his prime. He seemed a bit fragile. Nick knew Rusty was not through dealing with his own demons.

Neither was Nick through with demons of his own. He was about to face them on their terms, and it scared him.

"They might be watching the house," Nick said. "I have to leave here alone."

"Nick, I can't let you go through with this," Rusty said.

"This is nothing compared to what these *motherfuckers* will put us both through if I don't. All they want is money. That's all they'll get, I promise."

"I changed my mind, Nick. I think we should call the police after all."

"We agreed not to, and we were warned not to, and we're not going to risk it."

"Nick—"

"Please don't say anything more, Rusty... I'll be back home before you know it."

"But Nick!"

"I'm handling it, and don't you dare try and follow me, Rusty. You could get us both killed, do you understand? Once the blackmailer has his money, it'll be over. I'm sure of it."

He wasn't really sure of anything but that he had no choice but to follow the instructions and stand firm.

They kissed and embraced at the door. It was hard for Rusty. Nick knew Rusty didn't want to let him go. Nick secured beneath his arm the cloth bag with the money.

He went out into the night.

LONDON, that night, was living up to its atmospheric reputation. Thick banks of fog rolled along cobblestone streets up to the turreted rooftops, dense as proverbial pea soup. Lamplight glowed yellow upon the slick pavements.

The Whitechapel area was the chosen place for the drop off. *No cops.* No one accompanying Nick. Just Nick and the bag of cash. He took the Tube there. On foot, he was able to duck down a few back alleys, assuring himself he was not being followed, as he might have been more easily had he taken the car. He simply felt he had more options this way, whether he was correct about this or not. But at least no one would be able to suspect he had someone hidden with him. He was demonstrably alone.

A shudder passed through his body. He'd left the house holding his body tall, showing he was feeling brave and confident, looking forward to simply getting this matter over with.

Now he wondered if an even worse trap awaited him than this cowardly form of thievery. Well, at least Rusty would be safe.

The night air smelled cold and bracing. Soon he could barely see even a few feet ahead of him. The streetlamps glowed eerily through the scrim of foggy gloom.

Nick knew, of course, that this was the area where Jack the Ripper had committed his horrific crimes in the nineteenth century. The stabbings and dismemberment of several prostitutes. Theories abounded about the Ripper's identity, but the crime was never solved.

Nick felt his heart beating fast. His feelings of anger were replaced with cold trepidation. What, indeed, if there *was* something more to this caper than blackmail? What if they were out to kidnap Nick Davanger, one-time pop idol?

He grinned despite himself.

Nick was practically an ex-idol, if he were being truthful with himself. His ride was over. But he wasn't even thirty yet, and he had a whole life ahead of him.

Didn't he?

Steady, Nick, he told himself silently.

The street was lonely. The weather must have kept people indoors, Nick figured. He walked past unfamiliar structures. The buildings here were, of course, very old. He imagined that perhaps not much had changed since the days of Jack the Ripper.

It occurred to Nick that an old fan might see him out here and cause a commotion. That was still conceivable. He had his collar up and the snug cap on, against the chill night air. He'd changed, matured, grown more manly, filled out. He wasn't that easily recognizable new wave kid with the blond spikes any more.

Even a die-hard old fan would be hard-pressed to peg him as the pop idol he'd been. Those green eyes, though; they would be unmistakable to anyone who had ever really looked at Nick, in person or on TV. Or, unfortunately, in a magazine.

Or on a dark gloomy street in the Ripper's territory....

"Got the money?" someone said behind him, startling the hell out of him. Nick froze, a jangle of wild electricity racking his body and frazzling his nerves.

Nick stood stock still.

"Don't turn around," the person said. A male voice. Deep. Unfamiliar, slightly cockney. It sounded to Nick's trained ear like an imitation, like an actor putting on an affected voice to disguise himself. Just a guess, but Nick was convinced of it. He could not be sure, though, if it was the same disguised voice he had heard on the phone.

Nick didn't move a muscle.

This person behind him was someone who believed Nick would recognize his voice, Nick surmised. And therefore, someone he knew.

Who?

"I have it all," Nick said softly. "It's in this bag." He lifted the bag slightly.

"Good. Set the bag down on the ground."

"How do I know you won't send the pictures to the press anyway?" Nick asked.

"You'll just have to trust me," the man sneered.

"Trust a blackmailer?" Nick should not have challenged the guy. But he couldn't help himself. He received a hard blow to the back of his head that sent him crashing forward to the ground. His face hit the pavement. That would leave a nasty black eye and a bump.

"If one penny is missing, you'll hear from me again," the blackmailer said angrily. "And you'll pay a higher price than money."

Nick touched his bloody lip.

"It's all there," Nick said, not looking back.

"Get up and start walking fast. Straight on, no funny business. And don't look back."

Nick got up, unsteadily. He started to walk, limping. He walked briskly in the same direction he had been heading in, past a certain pharmacy—"chemist's," as they were called in London—past dark doorways and corners empty of people and streets empty of cars. Nick was heading farther and deeper into Whitechapel.

He walked half a block, wondering if he was being followed or watched. He didn't dare look behind him to check. Not yet.

He walked another block. Then another, on streets that were desolate and empty of all life. Not even a dog or a mangy cat out on this dreary, damp night.

He was lost, and the sensation was frighteningly nightmarish. The great masses of fog moved in low, slow dense drifts, making it impossible to see more than a few feet in front of him. He felt disoriented. He was not sure which way would lead back to the Tube station. He lost his sense of direction.

He hadn't meant to go much farther in this strange direction. His face hurt, and he could taste blood in his mouth from his nasty fall. He slowed, but didn't stop. He prayed he'd see a taxi but still he saw not a single car on the streets. And if he attempted to turn around, what if he ran into the blackmailer again?

Blackmail. Such a funny term.

Oscar Wilde had been blackmailed, he remembered from his reading, thinking suddenly of the great writer. He'd read that gay men of the Victorian age were constantly under such a threat. Wilde suffered a graver fate, though, than mere blackmail and scandal. In the end, he was ruined by a society that would not abide so talented an artist given to sodomy and to biting social criticisms that still made people laugh a century later.

Nick wished like hell he was home in Marble Arch, reading Wilde by the fire, with Rusty beside him. He tried to keep his mind on that comforting scene. And on his favorite books, his beloved poets, Whitman, Cavafy, Rimbaud, all waiting for him in his warm, safe home.

Thoughts of Wilde made him think again of the Victorian section of town in which he now wandered, lost, hurt. So very, very far from home, it seemed.

He thought of those prostitutes, the victims of the Ripper. Did their souls somehow haunt these streets?

The idea scared him and excited him. Ghosts really could be scary, whether they existed or not.

He promised himself that if—he corrected himself quickly to when—he got home, he'd sketch out a ghost story or two. He'd take his writing seriously. All art would be his real life's work, and business would be a secondary necessity.

He'd already made up his mind upon returning to the British Isles that he would visit the Irish country cottage of Lord Plover and set up his own painting studio beside Rusty's, and a place where he could write and read poetry and great books to his heart's content.

These pleasant, dreamy plans, set in the sunny Irish coast, helped quicken his pace through grimy, dark streets of abject horror.

He would draw some of these gruesome old buildings by day, he told himself. He knew his drawing and sense of composition had vastly improved over the past year. In addition to successfully taking over art direction responsibilities for M-Politik, he had once again dabbled at drawing and planned to paint, if only for his own pleasure. Sort of a fantasy, but why not? Wouldn't the west coast of Ireland be a fine place to paint and spin some magical tales?

He had plans all right. Maybe not grand ones, for they had nothing to do with business or commercial success. Just art for art's sake, and then, who knew? He felt very content with such plans.

Nick knew that dreams could come true out of such fantasizing. There was so much he still dreamed of doing.

But if dreams came true, so did nightmares. This night had been bad enough. And it wasn't over.

If only he could find an open pub, duck in, call a taxi.

He suddenly felt weak, the blood rushing to his brain. Maybe the fall to the ground had been worse than he'd thought at first. This panicky thought would do him no good, he decided. He took a deep breath and made up his mind to turn down another street, any street, and see if it led to a sign of life.

That's when he heard footsteps behind him.

Chapter 18

The Present

DETECTIVE Anson Bay looked younger than Nick would have expected. He was also well over six feet tall, black, and devastatingly handsome.

Nick was speechless.

"I told you you'd like each other," Marisa whispered, an aside into Nick's ear. She snickered. Anson heard every word.

"Come on, Marisa," Anson said in his deep mellifluous voice. "You call me up here at this hour, and now you gonna tease me? You said this was serious."

She nodded, leading them to the plant-filled living room with its stunning view of the grid of Los Angeles lights far below Nick's rental house. "It is serious, Anson—I mean Detective Bay. But you said you were off the clock."

"And you said this matter involved a serious crime," Anson said, all business. "I need to know if I'm going back on the clock. It's pretty late." He glanced at his watch.

"We'll get to that," Marisa said. "Anybody see you come in?"

"As a matter of fact, there was someone parked on the street in a Toyota, alone, when I pulled up. Whoever it was started the motor and took off."

"A man?"

"I couldn't tell. But they were in a hurry to leave."

"But they saw you, right?"

"I'm sure of it."

Nick sighed. "Someone was watching the house."

Marisa said, "They don't know who Anson is, or that he's a police detective. He came in an unmarked car. For all they know, he's here on a date. If they saw me come here earlier, maybe they think he's *my* date." She snorted. "They don't know what team Anson plays on."

Anson shot a look at Marisa. Nick thought this was an odd time to play matchmaker. But she sure knew his match, if looks meant anything. Nick was almost embarrassed at his own thoughts. He was in trouble badly, and he was wondering if the cop here to help him had a boyfriend back home.

I wonder if you're lonely, like me....

A pretty lyric went through his mind. Then he thought again about little Wolfy, and the levity and flirtation was over, as far as he was concerned. Did the crook have his frightened young dog in the Toyota with him just now, yards away from the front door? Nick felt sick at the thought.

"Let me get you a glass of wine," Marisa said to Anson. "Nick, you look like you need to sit down."

Despite his trepidation about involving the police, Nick sat with Anson in the spacious living room and told him everything.

"Forgive me for not recognizing you at first, Nick," Anson said. "I don't go for much pop music, so I'm pretty ignorant about who's who in that world."

"But you like music, don't you?' Nick asked.

"I like jazz and classical."

Nick figured Anson was thirty at most. Maybe too young to remember Nick's one-hit record, in its day. But naturally he knew the song, as an "oldie." "Wonder What" had made a kind of funny comeback recently, on a movie soundtrack with a lot of other eighties songs. Then the chorus had been used for a while in a popular TV commercial. So it was back on the cultural radar. Nick himself was, of course, long out of the spotlight. And now he'd just told Anson things he wouldn't tell a priest. He couldn't help but wonder if it bothered Anson to know that Nick had performed in a porn film, among other things.

Nick had described Paul Tolanaro as simply "a famous athlete" without using his name, which Anson, like nearly everyone, would instantly recognize.

Anson cut right to the chase. "Do you think this athlete is being blackmailed too?"

Nick hadn't considered that. He settled back on the soft comfortable sofa and looked at Anson seated in a leather club chair beside a table with framed photos of Rusty and Wolfy, and a crystal vase full of purple and yellow tulips.

"I haven't talked to him in over twenty-five years," Nick said. "As a matter of fact, he made it clear he never wanted to hear from me again."

"He's part of the case now, I'm afraid," Anson said. "Who is he?"

"I can't say," Nick said.

Anson frowned. "Shit, man, I'm not asking for idle gossip from you. Whoever is blackmailing you and dog-napped your pet is committing a serious crime. You want my help or not?"

"I just don't know," Nick said. "That's the truth."

"The right thing to do is tell me the whole truth and trust me."

Nick looked into Anson's sexy eyes. He wanted to trust him.

"It feels like a betrayal to say this," Nick said slowly. "But it's Paul Tolanaro, the former Major League pitcher."

Anson's eyes registered just the smallest flash of surprise.

"What about that assistant, Susie?" Anson asked, quickly moving the conversation forward. "She was the last person in possession of Wolfy."

"She had nothing to do with it, I would swear to it," Nick said. "She was one of the best friends my late partner Rusty ever had. She's been like a rock to me. She's my right hand."

"I'm sorry you lost your partner," Anson said. "I'd like to talk to Susie, though."

The world stopped for Nick, for just a moment, and a lump caught in his throat. *My late partner Rusty.* He'd never quite get used to that phrase, that reality.

Rusty was looking down from Heaven, though... Nick could *feel* him, right then and there, stronger than ever, giving Nick the strength to get through this catastrophe. Nick gulped, guiltily. Nick's faith was strong, but how could you ever more than just *hope* a lost loved one was somehow making their Heavenly presence felt? How could you truly *believe*?

Nobody really knew. That's what faith was about, Nick reminded himself, as he cleared his throat and refocused his thoughts. Nick took a deep breath and exhaled slowly. *Rusty, meet Anson*, he thought.

Marisa came in and refilled Anson's wine glass.

"Susie is sleeping," Marisa said. "It's been a bad day for her. She's in the guest room."

"I'll want to interview her first thing tomorrow, then," Anson said.

Anson didn't touch his second glass of wine. He took down a list of possible suspects, the same names Rusty and Nick had compiled all those years ago in London. And a few others. Anyone who could have gotten close enough to Nick to want to hurt him. Because financial gain did not seem to Anson to be the only motive.

Nick said that he had lost touch with most of the people on his suspect list. Drake had seemed to simply disappear. It was possible, old friends like Trevor Shannon had said, that Drake had committed suicide. Drake had talked about drowning himself in the sea or in the River Thames.

He'd left owing money.

Anyway, it was also very possible that Drake had died of AIDS. Back in the time when Drake told people he was infected, there was no cocktail of life-saving medicines.

Then there was Jill. Rusty's ex-wife had eventually asked for more money and received a tidy sum. A gift from Rusty and Nick, not a matter of legal settlement. She'd kept her distance from then on.

But had she suffered a reversal of fortune, and now needed money she might have thought of, dementedly, as somehow rightfully hers, and not Nick's? She'd made no secret of her anger toward Nick, an extension of her inability to forgive Rusty. But anger nonetheless.

Rusty's daughter Janette had not bothered to attend her father's funeral. It was well known to Rusty that Janette and her erstwhile boyfriend, the abusive Clive, had gotten deep into drugs. Rusty blamed that propensity upon himself, and it tortured him to the end.

Like Drake, Janette and Clive had seemed to disappear from Rusty and Nick's lives, years ago. An estrangement that became permanent. Jill said they'd gone to America. But she didn't say much else. She too was estranged from the troubled daughter she'd had with Rusty. There was more than enough bitterness to go around in that little family, and it was the source of the sadness Rusty never really recovered from.

Anson took all of this in without a trace of judgment or admonishment on his face. He was a consummate professional.

At the door, Anson said to Nick, "Try not to blame yourself for what's happening, Nick. Just because those pictures left you vulnerable to this kind of thing. Everybody makes mistakes in their youth. You just happened to be in a tough business."

"Wise words from such a young man," Nick said.

"This young man is going to help you," Anson said. "Anyway, I'm not much younger than you. And I made detective before age thirty for a reason."

Nick nodded. He liked Anson and admired his self-confidence. He did feel a little better now.

"Thank you, Anson," Nick said.

But the warm feelings didn't last. That night, he barely slept.

Chapter 19

1990

"NICK... Nick Davanger?"

The startling voice sounded familiar.

But who would be crazy enough to be walking around Whitechapel at this hour, in this damp foggy weather? Nick's excuse was paying off the blackmailers, and he'd already taken a nasty fall when his assailant gave him a dirty hit from behind. Bleeding and lost, he'd been wandering for the better part of an hour.

"Who's there?" Nick asked, stopping dead, turning his head warily, just enough to see. At first, no one appeared to be near. Then the slowly rolling fog parted slightly and a dark form approached.

An old man in a fine overcoat and bowler hat came closer to him. He carried a furled umbrella. His twinkling eyes were familiar. The hair below his hat was whiter. The body somewhat smaller, a bit shrunken with age. But Nick recognized him. It was Trevor Shannon, his old professor of art history. The friend who had introduced him to Rusty. It had been years since Trevor had retired, and Rusty said he spent most of his time in Italy these days.

"Trevor, what on earth are you doing out here?" Nick said.

"Let's just say I was visiting a friend," Trevor said. He gestured toward an ornate old building with a wrought iron gate. "A model, shall we say. And let's leave it at that."

Was it possible the area, known for prostitution in the nineteenth century, was now the home of a hustler or two? Of course it was possible. Nick said nothing in deference to Trevor's discretion. He simply smiled, almost overwhelmed.

"You can't imagine how happy I am to see you," Nick said, giving Trevor a manly hug. "I'm a bit lost."

Trevor's eyes widened with alarm, seeing that Nick was hurt. But he didn't say anything.

"My car is right around the corner. I'll give you a lift. Where are you living these days? How is Rusty? I miss him. Miss you both."

Nick and Trevor caught up on the ride to Marble Arch. Trevor had temporarily lost touch with Rusty and a lot of his London friends. And like everyone else, he had not seen or heard from Drake in years, he claimed. It was an incredible stroke of luck to run into Trevor this way, Nick thought. But was it really a coincidence? On the way home, Nick hated to admit an unpleasant thought nagged him slightly. Was it possible Trevor was somehow involved? But if so, why would he show himself? The thought made Nick feel guilty.

Despite his advanced age, Trevor looked fit. His car was nothing special, though. Nick tried to dismiss the notion Trevor was in want of money.

"Anyway, it's a shame about Drake Atka," Nick said, bringing the conversation back round. "You know Rusty and I fell out with him quite badly, a long time ago."

Trevor nodded. "Who didn't, with Drake, I mean," Trevor answered. "Poor man. So many problems. And now… this plague it seems."

Nick believed Trevor was telling the truth about not seeing Drake. Yet Trevor declined to come into the house for a drink when they pulled up before the grand leafy entrance in Marble Arch. Trevor's eyes widened, seeing the façade and its classical features and planters overflowing with flowers. Even at night, the place appeared positively regal.

"Come in and say hello to Rusty," Nick urged.

"I'm expected somewhere," Trevor said in an oddly testy tone. "Just wanted to see you home safe and be off."

"Sorry you aren't able to come in. Rusty will be terribly disappointed. We have to get together sometime soon," Nick said.

"Yes, we mustn't wait too long to get in touch," Trevor said. He reached out and placed his hand firmly on Nick's muscular arm. "Nick, you look wonderful. You've really turned into a splendid man. I do hope everything works out for you. If it's a comeback in music, or whatever it is, be happy, Nick. Never lose that joy I saw in that free-spirited youth I once knew."

Trevor smiled but his eyes belied a kind of sadness. Nick nodded and shook the old man's hand. Trevor's grasp was cool and dry and a bit frail.

Inside the house, Nick found Rusty incoherently drunk, already in bed. He'd left an empty bottle outside the bedroom door on a small table beside a spray of white roses. After kissing Rusty and embracing him, assuring him they were both safe as houses, Nick took the bottle down to the lower floor where the kitchen was, and gently set it in the dustbin.

Rusty's nerves had gotten the better of him, it seemed. Nick was disappointed. He walked up the stairs, taking in the features of their home together.

The house was elegant beyond compare. And the couple who lived here, Rusty and Nick, seemingly rich beyond their dreams.

And yet, tonight, they were wretched. One a victim of blackmail, the other a victim of his addictions. Nick didn't want to think of them that way, but the hour of the morning seemed to be pressing down on the house, from the chimney pots to the foundation, and down upon his soul. This was success?

Nick's jaw and eye hurt. His hand was scraped raw where he'd tried to block his fall.

Nick undressed in the master bathroom and cleaned his cuts and scrapes.

Beneath the medicine cabinet, a note was scrawled in Rusty's hand on a small silver tray beside a low crystal vase filled with lavender and thyme.

Call your grandfather. Urgent. No matter what time.

Nick's heart sank further.

A few years before, he had moved his grandparents into a nice condominium in suburban Chicago. A place close to shopping malls and grocery stores. The farm had been sold, but it didn't raise much money. Nick paid for the condo and its maintenance and all the living expenses of his grandparents. Yet he saw them so seldom, almost never. Still, he made sure they would be comfortable.

The greatest expense was the care provided by a visiting nurse, who made it possible for his grandmother to live at home with Grandpa. Her Alzheimer's was severely advanced. She didn't know anyone anymore. She was completely lost in her own world. He had more or less expected she would die soon.

Nick assumed the phone call to Grandpa would bring bad news. He took a deep breath, holding those guilty feelings at bay, as much as he was able to, anyway. What he'd provided the grandparents who had raised him amounted to a comfortable abandonment, he admonished himself. He justified it by telling himself Grandma didn't know him anymore, and Grandpa... well, that had never been a comfortable relationship.

He dialed the international number. After a time, the phone began to ring in the Chicago condominium. Nick braced himself.

Grandpa sounded very old when he answered. His voice higher, thin, and frail.

"I'm sorry, Nick... so sorry to bother you."

The sound was so tiny, and so very far away, like a voice out of another time, a time long past.

"No, it's okay... Grandpa... is it Grandma you called about?"

There was a long pause, in which Nick felt the room starting to whirl around him. "No," the old man answered in a choked voice. "It's your mother. I'm so sorry, Nick. So, so sorry. But... she's dead."

Chapter 20

The Present

THE sunny LA morning felt like a beautiful lie.

The drive from Marisa's house in the elite and fashionable side of a canyon, though, helped Nick clear his head enough to get through at least the next few hours.

Like he had a choice.

He decided he and Susie would stay at Marisa's for at least the next couple of days. Anson, somewhat disguised in sunglasses and a baseball cap, would check in and out of Nick's rental house. But only once the sun went down. If anyone was watching, they would probably think it was Nick.

Anson, meanwhile, would be on-call and in constant communication with Nick and Marisa as he continued his investigation.

They were all waiting for the other shoe to drop, as the saying went. The dog-napping blackmailers could be expected to make a move soon for their money. They would be in contact with Nick via telephone.

Marisa's BMW was sleek and powerful, and Nick enjoyed speeding down the highway. When you've been left to feel powerless over situations beyond your control, even the horsepower of a hot car could give you a little lift.

Nick knew he had to stay calm, centered, and most of all confident. The self-confidence of a mature man who held the reins of power, creativity, wealth, and fame.

Nick was a long way from being that confused kid who tried to find himself in London. Exploring his sexuality and an exhibitionist impulse had been liberating, and it had oddly led to stardom. A twisted path if ever there was one. But it was his path. His life.

Now these years and experiences had become the wellspring of his new creative life.

The one-man stage production was called simply *Memoirs*. The director, Cory, was a pro, and the rehearsals and tryouts in London had been a resounding success. Acting was not Nick's favorite art. He'd done far too much acting of a sort in his real life. Acting white. Acting straight. Acting too brave when he was scared, alone, and abandoned.

In writing the story of his life, in the book version of *Memoirs*, he'd found out how to be real, first and foremost to himself.

Business and even most social interactions required some acting. Nick knew that. But that flashpoint between the true self and the theatrical "mask" was the reason behind his one-man stage production. It was almost funny. The book reviewers had gushed over his disarming honesty. If only they'd known how much he'd left out.

That was another lesson for Nick. How to be true, but keep a vast reserve of privacy. That cliché about someone's life being an open book just didn't resonate with him, though people undoubtedly thought this must be the case of memoirists, of poets and artists who seem to strip themselves bare and expose their souls.

And yet, Nick knew there was a part of the soul that was reserved for only one. Him. The Lord.

Nick's eyes were stinging as he drove toward Hollywood.

Dear Jesus, please protect the innocent and take me instead if you will it, he prayed.

Nick knew too much about love to disregard the love of any being in this world. Wolfy was a beloved companion, a vulnerable innocent. And love was infinite.

Love was the biggest part of Nick's salvation.

No amount of money was worth love. Nothing material, nothing in this world, could replace love—or defeat it.

Nick prayed as he roared down the freeway. He thanked the Lord God for the blessings of Marisa, of Rusty, of all those good people who had tried in their way to give love back to him. Grandpa and Grandma, rest their souls. And Mama....

Those who raised him had made their mistakes with him, and he loved them anyway. He was not their judge. He had been their child. If their love had come up short, by some estimations, he now refused to see them at their weakest. He was grateful for their love and sympathetic to their plight. As he was forgiven, he forgave.

Mama had passed from years of abusing drugs and her body. She suffered the fate of an alcoholic who ends up on the streets. She probably heard his hit record in cars that passed her as she begged for food and money. Nick just never knew exactly what had become of her, and for her own reasons, she had never reached out to him.

Nick told himself he would have helped her, if he could have. But for her own desperate reasons, she had preferred to remain a stranger to her family, her parents, and to her own son.

Back around the time she died, he simply froze up. How very long ago he had learned to protect himself about Mama by willing a stone wall around his heart, built as if in tribute to her distances, her loss. Or so he had thought.

He had flown home on the Concorde. With very little emotion, he made all the funeral arrangements. He and Grandpa picked out the casket, the plot, near their old farm up in Wisconsin, and a small white tombstone upon which was etched a single rose above her name and the dates of her life.

After her burial, Nick stayed at the graveyard alone for a time. The light began to fade from the country sky. He must have looked an odd figure there alone beneath a big maple tree, sitting on a little wrought iron bench beside his mother's final resting place.

He tried to play pictures of her in his memory. Long lost little snapshots of those times when they were together, he a tiny toddler, she a lovely woman, young and very confused.

He knew that somewhere inside of him, feelings of overpowering love must have been locked up and hidden away. For years and years, as if millions of eons had passed. Because he could not truly remember. And he could not really feel.

The tears he shed were tears of regret, because he had closed off a part of himself for so long. On his knees he prayed to God to give him back that part of himself that had been vulnerable and open to love, and even the hurt of love.

The clouds did not part in the skies above. No ray of sunshine illuminated the mystery. All he had to go on was his growing faith, and hope that someday this lost love would come back in some form, somehow, from his loving Father. In the meantime, Nick prayed that despite his own lack of conviction and feeling, that this faith would always continue to grow, and, so important to him, that Mama would be at peace with God for eternity.

And that one day they would meet, in the light of God's grace.

With that, he left his mother's grave.

He needed to fly out that very night. But before he left, he held his grandmother's hand and kissed it. He looked into her uncomprehending face. She didn't know him, it seemed. But then, a glimmer of light appeared in her old eyes, and she smiled just a little.

That felt like something to go on. He kissed her warm cheek.

Saying goodbye to Grandpa was harder. He could see the old man looking him over, seeing the big strong man he had become, but also probably not being able to ever quite get over Nick's brown skin, his race. The expression on Grandpa's face was inscrutable.

"Goodbye, Grampa," Nick said. He held out his hand.

His grandfather nervously grasped it, and they shook. For a few seconds, the old man did not let go of Nick's hand. The weight of a mountain of hurts and misunderstandings seemed to list in the balance of space above and between them.

Another kind of sign? A sense of peace there for the taking?

Grandfather was a man of few words, and these days, he seemed all talked out. The old rages had cooled down. He couldn't speak when he opened his mouth.

Whatever it was he tried to say simply didn't come out.

Just because an old man could not say I love you, or I'm sorry, or I care about you—that didn't mean he didn't want to. It didn't mean he didn't feel it.

Nick couldn't say it to him either.

Nick went home to England.

Nick had paid for the care of his grandparents, whose old age was at least physically comfortable, and all their health care needs met.

First Grandma passed, and it was a blessing. She'd been a stranger to herself, and to her everyone was a stranger. Now she was with Jesus.

In less than a year's time, Grandpa died too.

Nick had them buried side by side, husband, wife, beside their daughter. In that little cemetery on a hill outside of Appledale, in the shade of that big tree.

And then Nick resumed the process, which seemed never ending, of trying to make peace with himself, with the help of God.

Chapter 21

2007

THE cottage on the west coast of Ireland, left to Nick by Lord Plover, was truly home now. Nick and Rusty traded their luxe Marble Arch house for the lives of country gentlemen. Trips to London and America became less and less frequent. The business had stabilized a few years before, just before the music downloading "crisis" seriously hit the record industry. As the boys stepped back, off the brightly lit stage, younger producers stepped in and the list of new artists at M-Politik, never huge, was brought down to a manageable level. Manageable by others. New artists, especially hip-hop artists, were still filling the recording studio schedule. Finally, Nick and Rusty sold the business for a decent, but underwhelming sum, as the actual marketing and sales of the recordings went into another state of flux. The digital media age was reaching a point of critical mass.

Rusty and Nick had paid off their debts and had done very well for themselves indeed. The new owners of the record company actually got themselves a deal at bargain prices. Always a tough business, the young Turks would sink or swim based on their own talents, shored up with the lasting pedigree and gloss of Rusty's sterling professional reputation.

That summer in Ireland, Rusty and Nick seemed to have everything they needed, at last. But one of life's surprises awaited them on a perfect day, and would take them unawares.

RUSTY was painting in the garden. His almost completely white hair was trimmed short now but remained full as a wolf's pelt, and his neat beard still gave him the look of an aging rock star. Few of their country neighbors knew (or would care) about his legendary rock producer past. Those things didn't impress these country folks.

The cottage had a comfortable buffer of seven woodsy acres, as well as an ocean, between the couple and the outside world. The building dated from the nineteenth century. It was modernized, with several skylights, a dazzling new kitchen, bathrooms with marble tubs, and rooms paneled in handsome wood. A huge stone fireplace anchored the living room, which spanned to Rusty's music room. His painter's studio stood just beyond, in an attached impressive greenhouse. Upstairs, beyond the sprawling master bedroom, Nick built a book-lined study. A modest antique desk, wooden with a marble top, stood before a great bay window and a view of the sea.

Nick came out onto the mossy flagstone terrace carrying a pitcher of iced tea slushing with ice cubes and lemon slices.

It was warm, high summer. The garden was in full bloom, flowers exploding in every color along winding pea-gravel paths. Clever statues and arching bowers of blooms created an atmosphere of abundance, of almost storybook fantasy. Beyond the garden, a grassy, rocky cliff overlooked the sea.

The sale of the business and the Marble Arch house had made them rich, but not staggeringly rich. It had taken quite a bit of their money to restore the cottage, but they wouldn't have had it any other way. They were together in a setting that was for them unparalleled in its comforts and beauty. This was a blessing beyond their fondest prayers.

The two green Jaguars, side by side in the driveway next to a huge red Ford truck, had become their neighborhood signature. People minded their business here and guarded their privacy. Yet everyone knew when Rusty or Nick was about by those vehicles.

A few miles down the road was a small village with a top-notch restaurant and a couple of pubs where the couple occasionally dined. Rusty hadn't touched a drop of alcohol in years, after a final lengthy stint in a rehab in the Caribbean. Nick would have the occasional Guinness or glass of wine, but nothing like the old days. Recreational chemicals were a thing of the past. Meditation, contemplation, and not taking themselves—or anything else—too seriously made for peaceful days and blissful nights.

For now, their drink was an herbal iced tea sweetened with honey. Nick poured and surveyed Rusty's flower-filled landscape on canvas.

"What d'yer think of it?" Rusty asked, making a funny voice in imitation of the local dialect.

"I love it," Nick said truthfully.

"Well, you have to say that, don't you?" Rusty joked and kissed Nick. "Because you love me."

"I think I'd love it anyway," Nick said, sitting in a cushioned wicker chair. They were both wearing comfortable baggy shorts and Polos, and leather sandals. Nick had on sunglasses and a Chicago Cubs cap. "Just a couple more paintings, and you'll be ready for a show."

He never took for granted that in addition to this view, these Eden-esque grounds, and this cottage, each man had his own studio for painting and writing, song-writing or just meditating, if they felt like it. Nick knew how good this time of his life was, and he took stock of it almost daily. He'd had a small chapel built out of one of the sheds on the grounds, next to the one Rusty sometimes painted in during the winter months. Nick prayed in his chapel almost every day.

It was a small place, but the stained glasswork windows were stunning. A great wood cross stood against one wall. Copies of Renaissance paintings of Jesus, Mary, Joseph, the Apostles, and various other images of Christ adorned the interior walls. Nick liked Bible scenes, whether medieval and haunting or contemporary and even a little kitschy.

Anyone who wished was welcome to come into the chapel. In the fall, a local young couple would be married there. Already, a baby had been christened in a tiny ceremony with neighbors crowded inside along with a priest from the village.

He planned to leave the little chapel to the community someday, and he wanted it to be not only a peaceful place, but a beautiful one. He would stipulate it be available to anyone of any faith who wished to pray. While Nick grounded his faith in his own Christian tradition, on his own terms, he was interested in all religions. He felt at least marginally Eastern in his expanding philosophy, and including the meditative consciousness of Buddhism and Hinduism didn't conflict in his mind or heart at all. He wished to learn as much as he could about such things. And if some elements within the worldly body of Christianity rejected Nick and his kind, his answer was not rejection in return but expansion and inclusion.

Nick, after all, tried to remember he was merely a humble and imperfect man, as prone to sin as anyone, but redeemed as a child of the Holy Spirit.

To Nick, chanting "Hare Krishna" was another joyful way of saying "Hallelujah" and "Praise be to God."

Being a philosopher-artist was a full-time job, but he discovered to his lasting joy that it was the only job he ever really wanted. The local charitable works he and Rusty founded and toiled in would be, Nick believed, their greatest legacy. A halfway house for recovering drug addicts was one such effort. A homeless shelter in a church basement, stocked with good food and staffed with enthusiastic young counselors, was another. Whether it be with money or their time or hard labor, Rusty and Nick were generous.

Rusty had already had a couple of small exhibitions of his paintings. The paintings were good, but Rusty didn't kid himself that they were great. He didn't care. He might have taken more pride in them than he let on, though. It was because of who he was that they always sold, he said, not because he was the next Picasso. The money he earned on his work all went into the local charities.

Nick had made good on his promise to himself to write. In his small book-lined study on the second floor, overlooking the sea, he had written several of what he called Irish ghost stories, after steeping himself in the genre. Some were based on legends he'd heard from his neighbors. Others were pure inventions. The best of the seven he produced were published by a respected London house.

The book sold well in England, where it eventually became a modest best seller. It did okay in America.

Nick decided he would try his hand on a novel, and always seemed to be tinkering on this or a story or some other of his ongoing writing projects. Like Rusty, he only worked for pleasure and when he felt like it. Which was most days. When Rusty asked if any of the novels were done yet and ready to be seen, Nick would just shrug and smile. "Maybe someday…."

Lately, Nick had preferred drawing, an old love of his from childhood on.

It was in this study that he would write his *Memoirs*, the very successful autobiographical story of his search for identity that would become a one-man play, starring none other than Nick himself, in London, and then Los Angeles.

But that was all still years away.

It was on this very morning Nick had jotted down a few notes in his journal, planting a few tiny seeds for this eventual project.

Nick had before had little thought of talking about his experience in the way that writers like Maya Angelou or May Sarton had done. Spinning personal pain and joy into poetry. He didn't know if he could do it.

He set his journal aside and watched Rusty mixing colors that grew brilliant in the sunshine.

"I should drive into the village and pick up the week's groceries," Nick said, setting down his empty glass of sweet tea. They had no servants, but a couple who lived down the road, the MacMurphys, took care of many of the daily chores, coming in about three times a week. Rusty's gal Friday, Susie, had yet to join them. She had remained in London, promoted to a good position at M-Politik. But reportedly she didn't like it. Word had it she missed them as much as they missed her.

"Let Barry do that," Rusty said, referring to Mr. MacMurphy. "He's probably bored stiff."

"I would, but I want to stop into that new bookstore," Nick answered. "I want to help support them. Besides, I need something new to read."

"But there are crates of books in the house you haven't looked at."

It was true. Nick was hoarding books he truly intended to read. It was just that he couldn't resist buying them whenever he came upon books for sale. It was in a way, his last extravagance.

"I'll get to those books someday," he said. "But I also need to keep up with what's new too."

"Get me something good too, then," Rusty said. He stood up to return to his easel and paints. "I'd like something sexy this time. Nothing staid."

"You're referring to a novel, right?"

Rusty smiled.

"Yes, get me something you know I'd like."

Nick drove off down the gravel path and up country lane in his shining green Jaguar.

Later, Barry MacMurphy told Nick what must have happened.

He said that Rusty had stood suddenly in the sunlight before his new painting. Rusty had squinted, as if his vision had grown a bit fuzzy, not quite coming into focus. He blinked a few times.

"It was just as you were driving off," Barry told Nick. "I'd walked over along the garden path. I could see right off something was the matter with him.

"I heard Rusty say, 'That's strange' very softly," Barry said. "Then he shrugged and reached for his paintbrush."

Barry said that Rusty then bent in pain, holding his arm.

"I rushed over, calling out to him," Barry said.

Nick nodded, swallowing hard.

Rusty told Barry that he felt dizzy, that he'd had a slight headache all morning. Rusty hadn't told Nick, probably not wanting to worry him. After all, what was a mild headache? Nothing to get alarmed about.

But then Rusty's knees buckled right before Barry, and Rusty started to lose his footing.

Barry helped him down to his cushioned pine chair, which teetered under him slightly. He managed to knock over the easel and the paints. Rusty had then cursed under his breath, looking to be nauseous and on the verge of passing out.

Barry remembered an odd detail. An orange cat, Rusty's favorite, rubbed up against Rusty's ankle.

The cat Benjy looked up and mewed at Rusty. And Rusty smiled just then, according to Barry. Barry said for a moment he was sure that

Rusty could hear Nick's Jaguar receding in the far distance, the sound of the motor fading down the lane.

"He was looking after you," Barry said.

Then Rusty looked out to the sea.

Barry said he tried to keep Rusty from falling from his chair, but Rusty just slid away. Barry told Nick the fall could not have hurt him, though. Rusty was already unconscious before he touched the soft grassy earth.

Chapter 22

The Present

THE money was secretly marked this time, and the police, directed by Anson, were integral to what they hoped would be a successful sting. Yet placing the stacks of banded bills into the brown duffel bag reminded Nick of his previous brush with blackmail.

These were American dollars, not English pounds. And it was a lot more money this time too.

It was his money, of course, not the police's money. Nick looked up nervously at Anson. Anson projected pure confidence in his calm countenance and steady gaze. He nodded silently, as if to say all would be well. Nick trusted that Anson knew what he was doing.

The rental house in the Hollywood Hills, not too far from Marisa's home, felt strangely cold and empty, more so than usual on this fateful day. Nick decided if he stayed in LA, it would not be here, despite the lovely Spanish detail of the place, the black wrought iron gates, the statuary and all the huge terra-cotta pots overflowing with bougainvillea.

"Gonna be hot today," Anson said, standing in front of the French doors, looking out over the pool.

Nick placed the last of the stacks of cash in the bag and stood up and stretched. Nick looked at the pristine blue pool surrounded by boxwood hedges, beyond which grew a grove of thick pines. This was a very private place in an elite enclave. But were they being watched by blackmailers?

Would the blackmailers figure Anson for a cop? Not in those shorts and Tommy Bahama shirt, Nick mused.

Anson was more than just a damn good-looking young man. He was also a brave one. Nick hadn't felt attracted to anybody else in a long, long time. Anson was growing on him, and he knew that was possibly inappropriate under the circumstances. Anson, after all, was a cop and here to help Nick, not get down with him. But Nick grinned thinking that "rescue me" was an apt lyrical phrase indeed.

"Feel free to take a swim, the lecherous man said to the nice police officer," Nick joked.

Anson chuckled, flashing a dazzling white smile he'd kept in check behind that sober mask of professionalism.

"I'd sure like to… maybe when all this is over," Anson said.

"Amen to it being over," Nick said. "But you know I was just kidding a little. You must get hit on all the time."

"My share," Anson said. "It's usually the mature ladies who make a move on me these days. But I play it cool with most people."

"And why is that?" Nick asked. "As if I need to ask. You're married, aren't you?"

Anson narrowed his eyes.

"You know we can't marry," he said. "Not till the Supreme Court knocks down Prop Eight."

"It's a figure of speech," Nick said.

"It's also a right denied," Anson said. "Paul Tolanaro, that asshole baseball big-shot you're protecting, happens to be one of the most vocal opponents of gay marriage in this state. He's making it part of his platform in a run for public office. Believe me, if I wasn't a sworn officer of the law, I'd be very tempted to stand back and laugh if some of those pictures of him got leaked to the media. In fact, you could make an argument for it."

"Yeah, well, my ass is in those pictures too," Nick said.

"With any luck, I'll get a look for myself," Anson said. He didn't smile. "I mean of the pictures in the perpetrator's possession." He didn't sound convincing. The look on his face showed he hadn't meant to be.

Nick exhaled slowly.

"You really think I should throw Paul Tolanaro under the bus? 'Cause he's a right-wing family guy?"

"Not my family," Anson said. "You still have feelings for him?"

Nick felt his face getting hot. "Now, that's not the most professional question I've heard out of you, Anson."

"Yes, but it crossed my mind. I know you fell hard for him, because you told me everything, right? The publicity from explicit pictures probably wouldn't hurt you all that much. Maybe a little embarrassment. But it would guarantee that one-man show of yours is a great big hit. Maybe even carry you to Broadway."

"I don't really need a hit," Nick said.

"Then why are you doing it?"

Nick took a deep breath.

"To tell my story," Nick answered. "To tell a story some young person might get something out of... and because, well... if there's one thing I learned, it's that if you got a song, *sing it*."

Anson put on his sunglasses and a Dodgers baseball cap.

"There's more to your story than you're telling," Anson said. "I guess I'll have to wait for the sequel, huh?"

He started for the door.

"Anson, you're a young man," Nick said. "There is more to everyone's story. And there are parts of everyone's story that are not strictly one's own."

Anson didn't smile as he continued for the door. He was back to business.

"The drop is set for tonight," he said. "We better focus. I want you to understand that I'll be armed. This could be dangerous, you know."

Nick looked into Anson's eyes through those dark sunglasses.

"I'm ready," Nick said.

AFTER Anson left, Nick decided he would take a swim to settle his nerves. He had a few hours before he needed to drive into the city for rehearsal. That left enough time to grab a bite on the way back to the house, in time to rendezvous with Anson.

And prepare to make the drop.

Anson had unsettled him a bit just now. Almost as much as the drop itself was making him start to sweat. But he also realized that despite a dangerous situation, he would get through it.

He believed it. He had to believe it. Even if this time, there would be guns and who knew what else?

Was it worth it? He wondered if he should have just handled it all alone, as he'd done back in London the first time he was blackmailed.

And if anything happened to Wolfy—well, he couldn't let himself imagine that.

But now he had someone else to worry about. What if something happened to Anson?

He decided that no matter what, he wouldn't let that happen.

Nick stripped down completely. He grabbed a towel from the closet by the French doors and padded outside to the pool. He could smell the lemon trees warmed by the sun.

If he was being spied on, it didn't really matter to him now. In fact, maybe it would be a good thing if he were seen here alone by the blackmailer. It was risky having Anson come by, even in an unmarked car. But anyone watching would make their own assumptions. They would probably know there was at least some risk that Nick would have decided to involve the police. But they would have no proof that Anson was an undercover detective. For all anybody observing might have known, Anson could have been a friend. Nick smiled; that assessment would have been true, as well.

Nick dove into the water, enjoying the feeling of submersion pleasantly shocking him with bracing cold, refreshing him, and clearing his head.

He swam several laps until his muscles were tired and he had all but exhausted himself. It felt good.

Nick climbed out of the pool and dried off. He pulled his shorts on and decided to read his script for about a half hour before he had to change and drive to rehearsal.

He hadn't realized how tired he was. Relaxed on his chaise lounge beside a lemon tree, he started to doze off.

He had only just closed his eyes when he heard the sound of a dog whimpering. He sat bolt upright. The sound had come from the pine grove about twenty feet away.

Or had he dreamed it?

He listened intently, every fiber of his being bristling with expectation.

Then he again heard the familiar heartrending sound of the animal's whine, followed by a frantic little bark.

He'd have known Wolfy's bark anywhere.

It was a distressed, excited bark.

Nick was on his feet in a split second. He ran to the edge of the pines, searching for the source of the dog's cries.

"Wolfy!" he shouted.

The little dog barked frantically, still hidden somewhere in the thick greenery that bordered the property. Nick knew now that Wolfy could hear his voice. Nick's heart hammered hard as he searched through branches that scratched his arms and snapped and swatted at the air. He ran deeper into the pine grove, dodging and ducking the sharp limbs, his bare feet grinding painfully into needles and pine cones. He desperately fought through the shadows in the direction of the frantic, frightened barking.

He couldn't find him! He jumped back out of the grove onto his manicured lawn, feet pounding the grass. He ran along calling out his dog's name.

It was then that the strange, haggard-faced woman stepped out of the wooded hedge in front of Nick, startling him. Nick stopped dead.

She looked like a witch! Her face was ugly with scratches and bruises. Her hair was stringy, and her clothes were filthy rags. In her bony and scarred arms, she held Wolfy tight, grasping him with dirty fingers. Seeing Nick, the young dog struggled to free himself. The whites of Wolfy's deep brown eyes showed fear as he howled.

"Give him to me!" Nick shouted, furious. "You're hurting him!"

The monstrous-looking woman held the squirming animal so tight to her bony frame that she seemed to choke Wolfy completely, still in midyelp.

Chapter 23

Five years prior
to the events of that night

RUSTY never completely recovered from his stroke. He needed a cane to walk, and even then, walking was difficult. His power of speech returned, but it was different. His words always came out with a struggle.

Nick did his best to make the Irish cottage a sanctuary for Rusty, and Rusty did his brave best to make a new life for himself. No longer would he paint his beloved landscapes and still-life portraits, having lost the ability. With help, he could amazingly play a little piano, but not with the fluidity Nick had always known.

Susie moved in. It soon became evident that the intrepid woman was more than the ideal gal Friday. The neighboring MacMurphy family was also more help to Nick and Rusty than ever.

Rusty's daughter Janette, though, never came around to visit her ailing dad. She was said to be living in California with Clive. When Jill contacted Nick by telephone after he'd made several inquiries on Rusty's behalf, she was cool.

"My daughter is a drug addict and probably a criminal," Jill said on the telephone. "And as for my ex-husband, he—"

Nick cut her off before she could insult Rusty. "Is a great man and a far better father than either of you ever considered."

"You *would* say that," Jill said acidly. "Look at everything he gave you."

"I do," Nick said. "Every day. But don't you dare think that what he gave me is something material that you could put a price on. Or that I wasn't worth Rusty's generosity and talent! Or that I didn't have something to do with the life we have together. It's not for you to judge, Jill."

"You have some nerve, Nick, I'll give you that."

"If that's how you choose to see it, I can't make you see me."

"Of all the—"

"You and your daughter have been more than compensated financially," Nick went on. "What's sad is, Janette rejected the greatest gift Rusty had to offer, which is himself and his love."

"Rusty chose himself over both of us!" Jill shrilled over the phone. "He chose you! He abandoned his marital vows, and he lived a life of indulgence."

"Is that what you think? Is that why you hate him so much?"

Jill didn't answer right away.

Nick said, "I happen to know that you ended the relationship, taking up with a certain Mr. Fitzgerald, a guy you'd been seeing for ages behind Rusty's back."

Jill sputtered on the other end.

"He told you that? That's a lie!" she cried.

"No, it's the truth. And it wasn't your first affair, either. But even if you hadn't cheated, you know damn well that what you and Rusty had wasn't right for either one of you. You both needed to move on. He did move on. Somehow, Jill, you never really have. And it's not out of some undying love for Rusty. It comes from jealousy, from the galling fact that somebody else won something you carelessly discarded. Because you also know that Rusty is one of the kindest and most loving gentlemen on this planet."

She sobbed into the phone.

"No! You've no right, Nick!"

"I'm afraid I've got your number Jill, and I don't see any reason to bullshit or play games about it anymore."

"I do love him!" she wailed. "I do want to see him! I want to see how he is... but I can't stand the thought of him in a wheelchair... or struggling on crutches... unable to communicate!"

"You're afraid, Jill," Nick said.

"Yes, yes! I'm afraid! I'm afraid of what's happened, I'm afraid for my daughter who hates me, and I'm afraid of you!"

That one pulled Nick up short.

"But I don't hate you, Jill. I have never hated you. And I want you to know something. If Rusty wants to see you, I will welcome you here in our home."

He could hear her sobbing. Then at last she said, "Nick Davanger, who the hell do you think you are?"

She hung up the phone before he could calmly answer.

"I'm Nick," he said, setting the phone down. "Nothing more. Nothing less. Simple as that." He looked up and saw Susie looking at him. She brought him a steaming cup of tea.

"I thought you might need a little refreshment after that phone call," Susie said.

Nick sat back and smiled. He felt sweat in his armpits. The call had taken more out of him than he'd been willing to admit. He smiled at Susie.

"What would we do without you?" he asked.

THAT winter was difficult for Rusty, and therefore, it was also a tough one for Nick.

After Nick's time in LA, they had worked very hard to repair the damage to their relationship, and from the scars came new strength. Now Nick understood how much they needed that trial by fire. It helped them through a time of bittersweet losses, but also some remarkable gains.

Rusty never complained. He was actually, miraculously, able to take up painting again. One day he began working on what would become a brilliantly colorful series of abstract works that seemed to help him express some of the emotions he was experiencing, in a way words could not.

The colors were bright, and the brushstrokes sometimes violent. There was a joy in this work, and therefore in his days. If Rusty had lost the ability to draw and paint realist or representational images, or to do really fine work with an oftentimes trembling brush, he took it in his stride. Nick relished a truth: creative people create, and that fundamental gift will find its expression, against any odds. The ability to make things included the ability to dream, at its heart.

There were shockingly painful days too, though. Days when Rusty's body frustratingly refused to obey his mind. Nick did everything he could to cheer Rusty, who sometimes sat speechless at his piano watching the snow fall outside the big lead-glass windows overlooking the white-shrouded gardens. Everything beyond the window looked like sculpture in marble-white coats of snow.

Rusty's power of speech continued to deteriorate badly, but his eyes could always communicate expressively to Nick. Nick understood subtleties of Rusty's communication that went far beyond head nods or shakes, or the blinking language of yes and no.

One evening, some neighbor boys and girls came visiting with their guitars and violins, singing Christmas carols. Nick and Rusty invited them in, and Susie served everyone eggnog and cookies by the crackling fire. An enormous Christmas tree twinkled in the great room of the cottage. Beyond the cheery windows, a new snow fell over a perfect, silent night. The visit felt like a tender blessing to Nick, because it cheered Rusty so. The kids came from three local families, the MacMurphys, the O'Malleys, and the Morrisons. One of the little girls, Kitty, sang with a lovely high soprano voice. Rusty was visibly moved.

"I… have an idea," Rusty said slowly, surprising everyone.

Rusty offered to give piano lessons to Kitty. That seemed incredible to Nick, but over the next few weeks, Rusty somehow summoned the strength to show Kitty where to place her hands on the keyboard and play scales. And so the lessons began. Rusty could, with some struggle, clap meter and could make signs for tempo. His ear had remained as keen as ever. And that's how their home became a place where local children and a few adults came for lessons in music, voice, and eventually even in painting. Kitty was the first of their "students."

Rusty began to show small signs of improvement. Nick never doubted it was the act of teaching and sharing his knowledge, as well as the spirit of the child "students" themselves, that helped to revive Rusty.

Over the next three years, some twenty-eight area musicians and singers made old Lord Plover's cottage a hub for music and folk art. In summer, an annual recital was held on the lawn under an awning and raised money for local charities. Nick had also joined forces with some of London and Dublin's biggest pop stars in fundraising for AIDS charities, which led to more charity projects and the opportunity to help far beyond their western Irish province. Rusty lent his best efforts too.

By this time, Nick was rarely recognized on the streets of London on those few occasions when he visited. He did turn heads, though, still. His face was as handsome as that of any movie star, and those legendary emerald eyes of his still drew appreciative notice. Nick didn't dress "flashy" like some of his contemporaries in the business still did, regardless of their age. He favored good clothes from Bond Street tailors, and for home it was simple clothes typical of any country gentleman, though perhaps a little heavy on the cashmere.

That summer, Rusty had another stroke. It aged him visibly, and took away forever all the gains in strength he had made. The music lessons were over. The children's recitals became sad affairs, in which a barely mobile Rusty sat inert in his wheelchair, a tartan cloth upon his bony knees, eyes misting over.

Nick arranged for two weeks at Wild Palms, a resort they liked in the West Indies, through the end of August and into September. With Susie's assistance, the trip was expected to be relatively smooth and perhaps reviving for Rusty, who was eager to go.

"One last time," he said in a rasp.

"Don't say that," Nick gently admonished.

It was not high season, and they seemed to have the place very much to themselves. One night, Nick sat alone on the patio of one of the smaller beachside bars, sipping a gin and tonic. He'd left Rusty sleeping in their suite, with Susie nearby reading a novel.

It was at this very resort in 1997 when Nick had heard, on radio, the terrible news about a car crash in Paris, involving Princess Diana and her companion Dody Al Fayed. That night, the few English nationals staying at the hotel gathered around the straw-thatched bar, listening to the reports as they came in. Nick simply assumed it could not have been a serious accident. But then the news reader said that Al Fayed was dead.

At last the radio newsman said that the government of France had made an announcement, saying that Diana had died of her injuries.

Nick had cried for her that night. The memory almost made him cry now.

That night, Nick sobbed deeply into his pillow. He tried to stifle his voice and shaking body so Rusty, sleeping beside him, would not be disturbed or upset. Nick cried an aching sort of silent cry into his pillow, a deeper, muffled cry than he had ever before expressed.

Nick calmed himself at last with a prayer. And after a long while, he started at last to fall asleep, feeling Rusty's trembling hand upon his head, gently stroking his hair.

THEY returned home to the Irish seacoast and got on with their lives. These years in Ireland were like an amazing gift, but not without some excruciating trials. Rusty continued to decline in health, but he was ever-present in Nick's life, always at his side. He was the center of it, and had been for so long. But it wouldn't be long enough. It could never be long enough.

The accomplished and vital young lion Rusty had been in his prime, when he'd met Nick, was now a person fighting a degenerative disease, and he was growing even more frail.

Eventually, Rusty could no longer walk or feed himself. He needed constant care, which Nick provided, barring no expense. Susie was a lifeline of critical support. And though she seldom allowed a crack to show in her Anglican veneer, the toll showed on her hale ruddy face too, at least on certain difficult days. Susie was a stoic lass of considerable strength, used to being leaned upon by her younger siblings.

But as she told Nick, "Nothing prepares you for this," which was said while wiping some tears from her eyes with two quick dashes with the heel of her hand, and getting on with it—that was Susie.

Rusty could hardly speak, and when he did manage a few words, they came with great difficulty. Yet he still surprised Nick from time to time.

"I'm… not much… fun anymore, am I…." he said one day. He smiled at Nick.

"Yeah, who says," Nick answered.

"I'm… not… a good dancer," Rusty joked. His special bed was pushed up against Nick's in their big cozy bedroom with its view overlooking the sea. "I'm not… a good c-c-c-conversationalist," he said, with considerable difficulty. He grinned and shook his head. He made these kinds of jokes frequently. Lame jokes, he called them, twinkling at the pun that made Nick wince and then laugh. "It's probably time to… t-trade me in for a *newer model.*"

Nick gently touched his fingers to Rusty's sparse beard, caressing him. It was twilight, a peaceful time. Music was playing softly in the stereo system downstairs, Mozart drifting up the stairs where the two men rested beside a cheerful glowing fireplace.

"No, I'm afraid you're stuck with me," Nick said.

Rusty was smiling but all at once his eyes filled with tears. "Nick, I want to… t-t-to *thank* you."

"For what?" Nick asked. The room was growing dark and blue, with a shadow of the window frame projected over them. The sky was filling up with stars. Nick felt relaxed, content. Calm before a storm, he told himself.

"What if… I hadn't found you?" Rusty asked.

"But you did," Nick said. "Or maybe I found you… don't you believe in destiny?"

"I've been so… so bloody *lucky,*" Rusty said in his raspy voice, punctuating his words with a fist rapping against the soft arm of his chair. He coughed. After the coughing settled, he continued. "I blew it, you know, w-with… a lot of people. My own daughter…."

He couldn't finish that sentence.

"You tried," Nick said. "You really did your best… her mother poisoned the possibility of a better relationship. Don't blame yourself."

Nick was angry that Janette had not once tried to see her father during this particularly vulnerable time of his illness. Nick had tried to locate her, but she seemed to have disappeared, possibly to America.

Nick imagined the worst about poor Janette, yet he tried to keep such thoughts from his mind lest Rusty see the worry on his face.

"Drake… all those guys who got AIDS… I n-n-never did enough for them," Rusty said.

"But you did what you could, for many, many AIDS charities," Nick offered. "We're still helping all the time. Maybe we both made mistakes and didn't speak up when we should have. When we had the spotlight. I promise you we're making up for it now, and I'll never stop trying to make up for that."

"Thank you… Nick," Rusty said. "In… the end, that's the one thing I knew… I couldn't leave unfinished." Rusty swallowed hard a few times. "And you helped make sure I wouldn't leave that business undone…."

"You've given so much, Rusty," Nick said again.

"*Not enough*," Rusty said. He closed his eyes. "It was not enough…."

Nick held Rusty's hand. He wanted to try and sooth Rusty. But he didn't want to keep pressing his disagreement, to condescend to Rusty in any way.

Rusty was the last person Nick felt had any need for regrets. And maybe what Rusty was saying and feeling wasn't merely a regret. Maybe it was a kind of summation.

Rusty was soon sleeping peacefully, to Nick's relief. Nick kissed Rusty's forehead, softly, and watched over him until it was time to find Susie and carry on with the tasks and duties that kept a house running, no matter what, and make a life.

THE end came abruptly.

Susie called Nick in from the garden. Her call was sharp, not panicky, but direct. It was a late morning in August. A pretty day. Rain predicted, and much needed. But for now, the sun was shining.

Nick ran past the blooming white hedges and inside, despite his boots being muddy after watering the gardens.

Rusty had suffered another stroke, his last.

He went into a coma and remained that way for three days in a hospital bed in Dublin, where he'd been transported by air. Nick had wanted very much for Rusty to be able to die at home. But it wasn't to be.

On August 28 of that year, Rusty Maraba passed away.

RUSTY'S funeral was held in the small chapel on the property he shared with Nick. He was buried less than a mile from their home, in a shady old churchyard and proper cemetery of picturesque beauty and tranquility. The music was provided by the O'Malley, MacMurphy, and Morrison children and their friends. Such luminaries as Marisa Tambov, Abigail Abeche, and other stars from music and show business were in attendance, including famous film actors and writers. Nick was in a daze, but he knew it was all happening like a dream when one of the former Beatles came over to shake his hand and offer a hug. He'd almost not recognized him in his sunglasses and hat, until Susie sputtered in his ear, "You know who that was!"

Rusty's ex-wife, Jill, wore black.

Janette, Rusty's daughter, did not attend and was not even heard from. As far as Nick knew, no one had been able to find her to let her know the sad news.

A MONTH later, Nick sent Susie on a dream vacation to a resort in Kauai, in Hawaii, where she'd always dreamed of going. Three weeks with kid sister Nan were, she promised, just what she needed.

"Who wouldn't want that?" she exclaimed, her face registering emotions from shock to incredulity to utter joy. "I'd be out of my mind not to!"

"That's the spirit, Susie," Nick said.

"But what about the cottage?" she asked, her face registering something akin to a comical expression of alarm. "There's so much work to be done! And what of you? Who will take care of you and keep you company?"

"I'm going to London," Nick said evenly.

"For good?" she gasped.

Nick smiled. "No, of course not. But for a time. Don't worry about the cottage. I'll have it looked after, and it will be just fine when you get back."

"Well, don't get too used to my bein' away," Susie said haughtily and laughed her big booming laugh.

He purchased a modest flat in a distinguished old building on an up and coming block in North London, and rang up his literary agent. Dawn was hoping for a long-hinted-at follow-up to the ghost stories, but Nick had something else in mind. Dawn offered her usual measured support when he told her his idea.

He set up his workspace upon a modest desk with a laptop computer and a small lamp. Slowly, he eased himself into the writing life in this flat, eating in good ethnic restaurants in the neighborhood, and stepping out into the buoyant life that brimmed throughout the great city, for London itself was having one of its most exciting resurgences.

A writer's life, it was. Walking all over the city, reading, catching the occasional play, taking solitary strolls through museums and galleries. Sometimes calling up old friends, occasionally meeting new ones. He felt like he had all the time in the world to work at whatever pace suited him. He liked the illusion, and made the most of it.

And on days when the grief became too much, Nick forced himself to knuckle down and work even harder. That's what Rusty would have done.

A year later, Nick's book, called *Memoirs*, was published to modest acclaim.

Chapter 24

The Present

NICK said, "Give him to me."

He said it forcefully and calmly.

"Hand my dog over to me carefully, you hear?" he commanded.

The strange woman who grasped Wolfy so tightly had sores on her arms. Meth sores, Nick recognized from some newspaper article about the dreadful conditions that happen to abusers of methamphetamine.

She blurted painfully, "I brought him here for you, Nick. I freed him!"

"You know my name?"

Nick was confused but took a few steps closer, and Wolfy again squirmed violently, but his barking at least proved to Nick he was not being choked to death in the arms of this vile criminal.

"You're hurting him, holding him like that," Nick shouted angrily. "Set him down gently or hand him to me. Do it now, or so help me!"

Nick had no time to more than briefly wonder if this disheveled woman was here alone. Or if the plan had changed and he was supposed to give her the money, here and now, and not at some drop location. But all he wanted at this instant was Wolfy safe in his arms.

"You've changed," the woman said, looking at him with pathos in her tortured eyes. She had an English accent. She grinned, showing badly decayed teeth. "Well, I've changed, that's for sure," she said. "We all change." Her eyes were wide now and tinged with madness and despair.

"Who are you?" Nick asked, taking another step closer. She took a step back.

"I'm Janette," she answered. "I'm Rusty's daughter."

All at once he recognized her. With horror. Recognized her through all that grime and decay and aging before her time. It had been many, many years since he'd last seen her. And time had been cruel.

"I'm Rusty's daughter, I said," she repeated with a frown.

Her English raspy voice, erupting from a constricted throat, tugged at Nick's heartstrings despite himself. He was glad Rusty would not see the specter his daughter had become. Now she held out the young dog in her arms. He whimpered and peddled his little legs.

"Here, take him," she implored. Tears ran down her dirty face.

Nick rushed up to gather Wolfy in his arms. Wolfy yelped with excitement, licking Nick's face with his pink tongue.

Wolfy could not contain his excitement and began to bark frantically.

Nick buried his nose in Wolfy's warm coat.

"Attaboy, Wolfy," Nick soothed. "Good boy, Wolfy."

He looked up at the disheveled woman. "Thank you," he whispered. Then he cleared his throat. "You came for the money, right?"

She shook her head.

"No," she whispered.

"But you kidnapped my dog! Blackmailed me!"

"It wasn't me," she cried. "Not this time! I swear it!"

"Not this time?"

She nodded, more tears streaking her dirty face. "Oh Nick, I have made such a mess of everything… I'm only here now to say how sorry I am… and to bring your doggy safely back to you."

"Janette, you're not making sense. You didn't kidnap Wolfy and blackmail me?"

"No!" she cried and stamped her foot. "I mean, I did participate in blackmailing you once, a long time ago, in England… and I was not alone. But this time, it wasn't me! I swear I had nothing to do with it this time! I was against it from the start!"

"Who did it this time?" Nick asked.

She was about to speak when a shot was fired from the bushes behind her. Nick recoiled as Janette fell forward onto the grass, shot in the back. A tough-looking white man rushed out of the thicket, his gun raised and pointed at Janette. Then at Nick. He pointed back and forth, nervously. Nick barely had time to react. He held Wolfy to his side, as if to protect him.

The ugly man showed a frightful grimace.

Even after all these years, Nick recognized Clive. He was red-faced, furious. He had also aged, deteriorated actually—drugs and alcohol abuse had made a horrendous map of broken blood vessels and dark lines upon his face. Nick took a step back. Gently he placed Wolfy down beside a boxwood shrub. The little dog scooted behind it, hidden at least for the moment.

"You stupid bitch!" Clive screamed at Janette, holding his pistol over her. A dark stain was spreading through the back of her ragged dirty blouse. Grunting with agony, she turned to her side, holding out a shaking hand.

As Clive turned to Nick, she picked up a handful of pea gravel and hurled it at Clive. Some of it hit his face. He stepped back and sputtered.

"It was Clive and Drake this time!" Janette cried to Nick. "I wanted *nothing* to do with it! Not this time, I swear! You must believe me, Nick!"

Nick was surprised to hear Drake's name. He had figured Drake would have died long ago. Was it possible what she was saying was true?

"Shut yer mouth!" Clive raged at her. "We need this sod's money, and you're fuckin' it all up!"

"Can't you see it's not going to work this time, Clive?" she hissed at him. "I'm not going along with you anymore, and I don't care if you shoot me again! In the back again, Clive! That's your way, isn't it? But now it's all finished! *You're* finished, through!"

"I'll make damn sure you are anyway," Clive growled. He stepped closer and held his handgun over her. He placed his finger on the trigger.

Nick dove forward, directly into Clive. Nick connected with Clive at the waist and knocked him off balance. Together they tumbled to the edge of the concrete pool. Wolfy hopped from the tall grass and barked and yipped hysterically at them.

Clive was stronger than he looked. Even though he showed signs of drug-related emaciation and sores, he was enraged and desperate. His eyes were wild with rage and panic, and up close in this clinch, he looked like a total madman.

He gave Nick a hard kick to the side, and sprang to his feet. Nick jumped up and dove hard back into Clive, and they struggled over the weapon.

Clive kicked and squirmed, but at last Nick was able to take hold of his wrist and wrench the weapon from Clive's hand. The handgun flew into the grass. Clive kept his eyes on the gun, A mistake. Working on sheer adrenaline, Nick gave Clive a huge right-cross to the face, smashing his jaw upward, breaking it. Clive fell backward. He landed in a heap right next to Janette, who bloodily pushed at him, trying to get away. Despite the belt to his face, Clive was fast. He sat up, took hold of Janette by her greasy hair, and pulled a knife hidden near his belt. He held the shining point to Janette's throat as she screamed with all she had left in her.

Nick had no doubt he was about to witness a horrific killing. Clive was set to draw the knife deeply into and across Janette's white throat. A sudden gun blast stopped him.

Clive's head was thrown back violently on his whip-lashing neck. He'd been shot clean in the forehead. His eyes rolled up in his head. The knife fell from his slackening fingers as he crumpled forward, blood pumping from the small bullet hole.

Nick looked across the yard and saw Anson, his weapon raised in his steady hand. A tiny plume of smoke curled from its barrel.

AN AMBULANCE came. Clive was pronounced dead at the scene. Janette was wounded but not mortally. Anson blotted her wound and spoke with her, quietly and softly, before the rescue vehicles screamed up the driveway. Nick sat nearby in the grass holding Wolfy close.

With an effort, he calmed his breathing. He tried to take in everything that was happening, and at last he found himself becoming strangely calm as he watched Anson work.

"You know what I need from you," Anson said quietly to Janette. "Whisper it in my ear. The address. Give it to me."

She moved her lips and Anson pressed his ear close.

Anson, whose surveillance strategy never took him far from Nick's place, had arrived after Clive. He'd rushed in when he heard the commotion, just as Clive drew his knife. A second later, and Janette would have been dead.

As it was, Janette was understandably in a state of shock. Her emaciation from years of drug abuse made her injury even more serious.

Paramedics were able to dress her wound and sedate her. She was loaded into the ambulance and driven to the hospital with sirens blazing.

Nick talked to the rescue team and the police. Anson stood beside him, rock steady.

"You saved her life," Nick said.

"So did you," Anson replied.

"You saved my life too, Anson."

"That's entirely possible," Anson said, flashing a momentary grin. He grew serious. "I recognized the car driven by Janette right off. It was the car I saw here the other night."

"Janette is innocent," Nick said. "Very troubled, but innocent."

Anson frowned.

"She made a decision that was very brave, but not until she'd spent a lifetime making bad decisions, Nick. She's not really innocent. She told me where Drake Atka is holed up. I'm going there."

"Drake's really alive?"

"I aim to find out."

"Anson, no… let the police officers go there."

"I am the police, this is my case, and I'm going to find this Drake character."

"Then I'm coming with you," Nick said.

THE apartment building was one of the most decrepit in downtown Los Angeles, and little more than a drug den. The forlorn palm trees beside it waved their burnt-brown fronds in the fetid breeze.

"You stay in the car, get it?" Anson said forcefully.

"Don't I have a right to confront Drake?" Nick asked.

"As a matter of fact, no," Anson said. "This is police work, not vigilante time."

"I wasn't gonna pistol-whip Drake, if that's what you mean. But I do want to talk to him."

"He's dangerous," Anson said. "You saw what his cohort, Clive, did. You stay put, and you can have a look at him when he's handcuffed in the back of a squad car."

"Anson, I don't want you to go up there," Nick said. "Let the uniformed guys go up and make the arrest. They'll be here any minute."

Anson shook his head. "If Drake was expecting Clive back by now, he already knows something is wrong. He could get away."

Nick was now really worried.

"On second thought, I don't care if Drake gets away," Nick said now. "The person I care about is you."

The two men looked soberly at one another.

"This is my job," Anson said. "Whether we like it or not, I'm going to find out if he's up there. And I happen to care if Drake gets away. I want him in front of a judge and jury, and then in a prison where he belongs."

"Anson... tell me what floor he's on in case the police come and they don't know where to find you. In case...."

Anson smiled cynically.

"They know 'cause I told 'em."

"So tell me, dammit!"

"The seventh floor."

Anson turned to go, but then he looked back at Nick.

"One thing, though, Nick, I also want you to know I feel the same way about you. I promise I'll be safe, and tonight will be a night for us to both remember. You promise me you won't leave this car."

Nick couldn't help but grin, even as he felt a surge and an ache in his heart and in his loins.

Nick nodded halfheartedly. "I... can't promise that," Nick whispered.

"Huh? I didn't hear that?" Anson said.

The front entryway door to the building opened, startling them both.

Anson started toward the door and looked back at Nick only once, his eyes angry with warnings. Two young tough guys came out of the building and looked Anson over. He charged forward, and they stepped aside in his powerful presence.

Anson entered the building. Nick waited on the street, wondering where the backup police were and why they were taking such a long time to get here. Then again, he pondered, this was Los Angeles after all, with its share of troubles.

Nick waited several more anxious minutes before he decided to follow in after Anson.

He knew that was reckless and would piss off Anson mightily.

But what if Anson was in trouble? Nick was not a man to wait in a situation like this. He needed to act.

Nick climbed the stairs of the foul-smelling, decrepit building. The security locked door had long been broken, giving him easy access.

He climbed to the seventh floor.

The hallway was long and shadowy, with small dirty windows on either end letting in muted light. Most of the bare lightbulbs screwed into ceiling sockets were burned out. From down the hallway, Nick heard a commotion and shouting coming from behind the graffiti-smeared door of one of the apartments. He ran toward the desperate scene that was unfolding.

THE small apartment stank and was littered with the paraphernalia of crack and meth addiction. Anson stood peering out halfway behind a bug-speckled kitchen wall, a large stuffed yellow envelope under his arm. His service weapon was grasped in his extended hand, held up close to his tense face.

Across the room beyond the windows and cruddy furniture, someone was hidden behind a chair beside the open window. A wan, pale, horrible figure.

Nick peered through the halfway-open door at Drake Atka.

Drake's hair was long and stringy, white against his sallow, ravaged face. His body was all skin and bones. His nails were long. He wore nothing but a dirty pale blue shirt and ragged shorts, both spotted with stains. In his hand was a long shiny kitchen knife.

From the hallway behind him, Nick heard a door slam and lock. The poor people who inhabited this neglected building were probably used to violent scenes of arrest or beatings or shakedowns by drug dealers and the like.

This place was a living hell.

And Drake had fallen a long, long way down into it.

"Go ahead and shoot me," Drake rasped at Anson in a haughty English-accented taunt.

"You come along on out from behind that chair," Anson said firmly. "Put your knife on the floor and come along peacefully. You need medical attention, Drake. You need help, man."

Drake laughed in a dry and hideous, almost theatrical voice.

"Help?" Drake asked. "Prison is where you'll send me!"

"Isn't this a prison, Drake?" Nick asked.

Anson spun around, surprised as hell to see Nick there in the doorway. If looks could kill, the one Anson shot at Nick would have been deadly.

"What the hell—I told you to wait in the car!" Anson shouted angrily.

Nick stayed put, but said, "I'm sorry, Anson. I couldn't risk something happening to you. I didn't mean to get in the way, but now that I'm here, I need to talk to Drake."

Drake's eyes slowly slid into focus, taking in Nick. A slow, evil smile crept upon his lips.

"Well, if it isn't the celebrated bare-ass idol of Soho himself," Drake mocked. "The one-hit wonder fresh off the slag heap of has-been pop nebulae."

"You would have made an artful critic, Drake," Nick said. "Shame you didn't consider that route, but it's not too late. Come on out from behind the chair and let's get you to the hospital."

"Where is Clive... what happened?" Drake said.

"Clive is dead," Nick replied.

"Did she kill him? Janette?"

Nick shook his head. "He tried to kill her, but she's okay."

"She ratted us out, didn't she?" Drake asked. "I knew she would. Hell hath no fury like a woman scorned, especially if she's a *crackhead*...."

"She did the right thing, Drake," Nick said. "It's time for you to start on that path...."

"My path is prison and hell, if there is one," Drake said.

"There's help for you...," Nick said. "Even in prison you'll be given medications and a chance to recover."

Drake smiled, showing the terrible ravages of "meth mouth" rot.

"I should have tortured and killed that little dog of yours while I had the chance," Drake said. "I would have then at least had the tiniest bit of satisfaction. Now this big black cop here has the photos and negatives in his hands, all of them, and I won't be able to make any more fun."

"Trust me, we'll make sure you ain't lyin'," Anson said. "We'll search the place and check that out real good."

Drake shook his head.

"You have it, all of it, *officer*. That particular game is over, woe is me," Drake said. He dropped the knife on the floor. Anson stood back as Drake struggled to his feet, bracing himself uneasily on the back of the chair.

"That's right... easy does it," Anson said. "Chances are, you'll be out in five years... maybe less."

"Really?" Drake asked, affecting a sympathetic clown face. It melted and he sneered. "What makes you think I have five years to spare?" He took a few steps toward Anson.

"I want you to sit down on that chair by the window and take a few deep breaths," Anson said, his gun still pointed at Drake. "You're under arrest."

"Gonna put the cuffs on me?" Drake asked.

"Sit down and be quiet," Anson said. "Don't make this any more difficult."

Drake took a couple of steps toward the rickety chair. Then he glanced down at the knife on the floor. It was still too close to him, Nick thought. *Too close.*

"I said sit down," Anson barked.

Drake turned his head and looked accusingly at Nick.

"You think you're so much better than me, don't you?" Drake asked. "You're a queer, a whore... you're nothing!"

"It's odd, then, that you wanted to have so much power over me," Nick said coolly. "That is, if I'm what you mistakenly thought I was all those years. Surely there's gotta be easier ways of getting money than blackmail. But you went and targeted me twice. Hating me has ruined your life, not mine. Because you know what? You didn't know me. That thing you hated was something in yourself. Something you created."

"And now you've got me, got me cornered and bound for prison," Drake accused.

"Wrong again, Drake," Nick said. "I don't want vengeance. I'm going to forgive you. I'd even help you... don't you get that?"

Drake's face went completely white.

"I won't let you!" Drake hissed, and turned sharply on his foot.

"Drake, no!" Nick cried.

"I won't let you forgive me!" Drake screeched. "I will *not* be forgiven!"

And just like that, Drake hurled himself straight through the window in an explosion of shards. He fell seven stories onto the dirty concrete sidewalk below.

THE story didn't even make it into the national news. Nick's name was mentioned in the local media as the focal point of an unspecified financial crime attempt. Only a little website devoted to eighties music connected him to his hit record, "Wonder What," when they reported on the crime.

The perps were written up as small-time nobodies. A local TV station reported that a drug-addicted couple trying to extort money from the one-time pop star had been subdued on the grounds of Nick Davanger's rental property, with one of the perps having been shot dead by police.

Drake's lethal fall received scant mention.

The autopsy performed on Drake's body would reveal some surprises, though the cause of death was obvious: massive internal injuries sustained in a fall. A number of substances were found in his system. Curiously, he did not, in fact, have HIV-AIDS. His remains were cremated in LA.

Rusty had told Nick that Drake had AIDS (or so Drake had claimed to Rusty). At the time of this confession, Drake had sores on his limbs that he attributed to the disease. But they could also have been sores from alcohol-related malnutrition or a dozen other maladies.

Perhaps Drake had only assumed it was AIDS. Or perhaps he had lied.

Nick cooperated with the police in every way he could, and he spoke with the few slightly world-weary reporters who had seen far worse crimes.

He owed Anson an apology, but after he was done at the police station, Anson was nowhere to be found.

Nick sure hoped Anson would forgive him, eventually, for disobeying orders. But his hopes where Anson was concerned went a whole lot further than that.

Five hours later, he was back at his luxurious rental house, in the golden light of a magnificent sunset. Marisa poured the deliriously happy and sweet-smelling Wolfy into his arms. Susie hugged him hard.

"Just look at you!" Nick said as the dog licked his face and barked with sheer joy. Nick turned his gaze to Marisa, whose eyes registered wary concern even as she smiled bravely.

"You look a little tired, Nick," she said with a grin. "Why don't you take a shower and rest up, then come on over to my place for a nice supper. Bring Wolfy, and we'll celebrate his safe return."

Nick smiled. "That sounds wonderful," he said. "It's been a rough day, a tough week, and a hell of a year, to tell you the truth."

She smiled hugely. "Then there's only one thing to do," she said. "Let's have a little party and celebrate the good things."

"Always," Nick said and kissed Marisa on the cheek. "Oh, and please be sure to invite Anson too." He hoped he didn't sound too worried.

"I already did," she said, a satisfied smile on her radiant face.

Chapter 25

THAT night, Marisa sent her cook home and gave her assistants the night off. Nick and Marisa and Susie fired up the state-of-the-art grill station built into the poolside bar at Marisa's house and started cooking up an amazing feast. And there were plenty of treats for Wolfy too, to help build up his spry little body. He'd grown a bit skinny during his ordeal, probably from not being able to eat. Nick gave him a beef rib, and he went to work on it with relish.

Chorizo sausages sizzled on the grill alongside lobster and salmon. Marisa's debonair partner Deshawn opened a bottle of white and a bottle of red. Nick decided that it was a wise decision to spend the last of the nerve-jangled adrenaline coursing through them on a celebration, despite the horror they'd been through.

There was only one thing missing. Anson's presence.

Nick dejectedly sat down and blinked his eyes in the setting sun. A form eclipsed the sun and stood before him. Nick had to shade his eyes. His heart surged at the sight of the big man.

"It could have been a whole lot worse," Anson said, stepping out of the sun's glare. He had a glass of wine in his hand. He was freshly showered and wearing a baggy pair of crisp madras shorts and a snazzy pink La Cost polo shirt. It looked damn good on him. On his bare feet were new, handmade leather sandals. Marisa had spent a couple of hours shopping for him while Wolfy was getting cleaned up and getting his clean bill of health, and she'd sent him home to change for the party.

Nick stood up and his knees felt so weak he almost laughed. He also felt embarrassed.

"I'm sorry, Anson."

Anson smiled.

"Think I wouldn't forgive you?" he asked. "I think we both know I think far too much of you to hold a grudge, even for one minute. And besides, I like a man who does what he believes is right."

Nick felt joy overflowing in him.

"Come on," he said, gesturing. "Everyone's inside."

The kitchen was stocked high with cheeses, a mountain of fresh fruit, and a huge assortment of breads and pastries. Nick filled his wine glass and grabbed a plateful. Everyone regrouped on the patio. Nick sat in a chair next to Anson, who was clearly enjoying his slices of cheese, French bread, and a sampling of grapes and berries. He ate with gusto. Nick was happy to see that Anson could completely relax and let his guard down a bit.

Nick also couldn't help but notice that Anson sported a really fine pedicure, and his manly calves and strong thighs showed evidence of his regular workouts at a gym. Anson's body was a temple. Nick smiled to himself, thinking about forms of worship.

Susie looked snappy in her linen whites. A diamond tennis bracelet flashed on her wrist, showing nicely against her newly tanned arms. A gift from Marisa. The Englishwoman was clearly taking to Southern California. He'd never seen her face so relaxed. She set down her glass of Pinot Grigio and with a smile turned the sizzling sausages on the state-of-the-art grill. The air was filled with tantalizing smells.

"I want to propose just a small prayer of thanksgiving," Nick said, "and of forgiveness."

Anson eyed him carefully.

"By the grace of God, I have Wolfy back," Nick said, looking at the cute ball of fur at his bare feet, now working intently on a leather chew toy. "And I have my dear family, you all," he added. Marisa smiled warmly and Deshawn reached for her hand. Nick looked at Susie and winked. Then he turned to face Anson. "And I have a true knight in shining armor, right here beside me."

Anson held up his glass and grinned. They touched glasses. Marisa nodded knowingly at Deshawn.

"It's very sad that Drake and Clive and Janette made the choices they did," Nick continued. "They ended up hurting no one more than themselves. May God have mercy on their souls. All of them."

Each bowed his or her head slightly, reflective for a moment. No one wanted to dwell on the tragedy. They all knew better.

"Not so sure I'd trust Janette ever again," Marisa said. "But in the memory of her daddy, our dear Rusty, I will also forgive."

"She needs to know she has a second chance," Nick said. "Just like we all have second chances."

"Amen to that," Marisa said.

"What she doesn't know yet is that her father left her a very nice nest egg, which she is entitled to," Nick said. "I'm going to do my best to make sure she gets herself on track, for Rusty, and for her. She tried, after all, in the end."

"She could still end up doing some serious time," Anson said quietly.

THE party went late. When it was time to go, Nick thanked Marisa at her door.

"Believe in happy endings?" she asked. She gestured with her eyes toward Anson.

"Happy beginnings too," Nick answered.

He and Anson and Susie and Wolfy took the short drive from the canyon back to Nick's rented house.

After Susie went off to her bedroom on the main floor of the house, to—of all things—make a phone call to a guy back in Ireland who had been calling her daily, Anson surprised Nick with another gift in a day that had begun in turmoil and ended in gift-giving. It was a large, sturdy, hand-weaved basket with a luxurious pillow in tartan plaid.

Nick raised his eyebrows.

Anson gently took Nick's hand and led him to the stairs. Wolfy followed expectantly. They climbed to the bedroom suite, where Anson positioned the basket in a corner near the bed.

"You didn't think I was going to make Wolfy sleep on the cold hard floor tonight, did you?" Anson asked with a sly grin.

Nick gently placed the sleepy pooch in the basket, and Wolfy yawned and licked his snout. He turned in a circle, wagging his tail, and settled in, with his face on his paws.

Anson stoked the fireplace across from the bed. Nick stood beside him and gently slipped his arm around him.

"I have a confession to make," Anson said, looking into Nick's eyes.

"Mm-hmmm," Nick replied sleepily as their noses touched.

"I'm serious, Mr. Sexy Green Eyes," Anson said and grinned. Anson looked deeply into Nick's eyes. "They really are emerald-green. How's the saying go? 'Where'd you get those eyes!'"

"Didn't get 'em from my Mama or her side," Nick replied sleepily. "Must be from my daddy's side."

"He had sexy green ones too?"

"Don't know," Nick said. "I never laid *my* eyes on 'em, or him."

"Hm," Anson grunted. "Sorry."

"Nah, don't be," Nick said. "I know my real Father, you know what I'm saying?" He touched the cross on Anson's muscular creamy-brown chest.

Anson nodded. "Mama always wanted me to end up with a righteous Christian fella," Anson said with a laugh. "Well, the *fella* part took her some time to get used to. But she agrees the good Lord made us all."

"He made something when he made you, Anson. Let me look at you. *All* of you."

Anson didn't waste any more time undressing. As he pulled off his socks and slipped down his white briefs, he turned around completely.

Anson showed an unmistakable sign of excited attraction.

"Now you've seen everything," Anson said. "My turn."

Nick grew rock-hard too. He peeled off his clothes, every stitch, and felt real joy in doing so.

Naked, the men embraced, sliding their hands over one another, kissing.

"Before we go much further, Anson, what's this confession?" Nick asked with a smile.

"I looked at every single one of the pictures I took from Drake's apartment," Anson answered. "The nude shots from the men's magazine, the photos on the beach, as well as stills from the film. You were hot, Nick. Still are. Hotter. And that baseball player… and by the way, he didn't look all that straight to me in those shots."

"Well, he didn't act very straight that night… guess that's obvious."

Anson went to his leather carry-on bag, resting on a comfortable leather chair. Nick watched, admiring Anson's strong young back and muscular bottom.

"What are you doing?" Nick said.

Anson withdrew a tattered yellow envelope.

"These are the shots of you and Paul Tolanaro," Anson said. "Negatives too." He took them out of the envelope. "Want a last look?"

Nick opened his mouth in surprise. He saw himself in a very compromised position with Paul Tolanaro. There were about twenty shots in all. He saw the negatives in a thin, translucent wax-paper envelope.

"Thought that all that stuff got turned over to the police for evidence," Nick said.

"The magazine shots and film stills did," Anson said. "In strictest confidence for police eyes only. As for these, with you and the young ballplayer…." Anson walked to the fireplace with the photos and negatives in his hand. He dropped them into the flames where they crackled and shriveled up and blackened, then turned to ash.

"Gone forever," Anson said.

"Now that's gotta be a violation of police procedure," Nick said with a grin. "Thought you were a by the book detective."

"I was," Anson said. "I resigned this morning."

"What?" Nick was genuinely shocked.

"I've been meaning to start my own detective agency for a long time, Nick. And I knew from the moment I met you, my life was never going to be the same. It was going to be a whole lot better."

He came to the bed and wrapped his muscular nakedness around Nick, and they shared a deep kiss.

"You see, Nick. This is Hollywood. Those pictures might have been kept under lock and key, but eventually they could get out. The magazine pictures are already out there, anyway, just like that old film. The shots of you and Tolanaro were the only ones in existence. And now they're gone forever. I figured you'd want it that way. Though the photos in the long run probably wouldn't have harmed you, they would be the ruin of Tolanaro. He'll never know what a friend he has in you. That's his loss."

Nick was thinking. "That reminds me of something I lost, a long time ago. I may have your very first private detective agency job for you. I mean, after we complete… this matter at hand." Nick traced his hand down Anson's front, over his tight abs, and onto his manhood.

That night Nick and Anson sealed their bond, making sweet love and loving every inch of their sacred bodies. In the morning, with the light coming in the window, they slept. Wolfy, happily at his master's side for good, slept through the whole thing, even the groans and cries of ecstatic delight that could have awakened the dead.

Chapter 26

A month later

NICK slipped into black jeans and a fresh shirt in his dressing room. He always took a shower after every evening performance, and this one was no exception. He felt good and completely refreshed. That was important after the energy he had conjured on stage.

Tonight's performance had gone exceptionally well, no glitches, and a packed house to boot.

All the shows had been sold out and would be for the next several months. He was still able to take an occasional Sunday off, though, and he was looking forward to it, even if he had a busy couple of days ahead, starting with this night.

He checked the plane ticket at the top of his carry-on bag beside a big bouquet of flowers from Anson and a bag of candy bars and other good things to munch on during the flight. Anson was always thoughtful that way.

There was a knock on the dressing-room door. Nick was expecting someone. His heart beat a little faster.

Janette looked like a completely different woman. Her hair was cut in a business-like style. She wore an elegant jacket and pants combination. She'd gotten some sun, and that ghostly drug pallor was gone. Still, he could see she was very fragile.

A police matron waited outside the closed door.

"Nick, I came here to thank you… and to begin to learn, with your blessing, about my father and the man he loved." She turned her face away slightly and fought back tears. "I have been such a miserable daughter, and to you, Nick… well… I don't expect forgiveness. But I want you to know that I am sorry, deeply sorry, about everything."

Nick kissed her forehead and they embraced. He'd paid for her rehab, and was now paying her legal expenses as she began the process of untangling herself from years of Clive's abuse, and her own self-abuse. He'd agreed to allow her backstage after she'd contacted him, begging to see him, and see his show, his "life," as it were, in a monologue that was both funny and heartbreaking in its honesty.

"I forgive you completely, Janette," Nick said. "You must believe that, and begin to forgive yourself."

She nodded. "I know, and I promise to try."

"As for helping you... well, you're a living reminder to me of Rusty... and I know he'd be proud of you. I'm gonna be there for you and do all I can. "

Tears rolled down Janette's cheeks.

"One of the things I've done is reach out to my mother," Janette said. "She knows how much you're doing for me, Nick. Someday she'll thank you too, if you just give her time."

"Of course," Nick said. "Janette, we still have time to get to know one another. And be friends. Or more than friends. Family."

There came a soft knock on the closed door.

"That must be the matron, so I guess it's time for me to go," Janette said.

Before she could finish saying goodbye, the door opened and in walked a handsome, athletic black man of prosperous middle age. He was well dressed in a conservative business suit.

"Please pardon me for interrupting," said Paul Tolanaro. Nick recognized him at once. Paul's hair was streaked with silver. His handsome Latin face had filled out pleasingly, showing his prosperity. But that infectious smile was the same. "I didn't know you had company."

"Please come in," Nick said, surprised. A stage hand nervously followed.

"Mr. Davanger, I apologize," the redheaded, freckled kid said. "This gentleman said he knew you, but he walked right by me when I told him he had to wait."

"It's okay, Mel," Nick said to the relieved young man.

Janette looked nervously at Paul.

"I was just leaving…," Janette said.

"Paul," he said, extending his hand. Janette looked nervously at the police matron now standing in the doorway behind Mel. Janette took Paul's hand and gave him a light squeeze. She smiled.

Janette kissed Nick on the cheek. "Be seeing you, Nick," she said, and joined the matron in the hallway.

Paul closed the door behind her and remained in the little dressing room. He turned and smiled sheepishly at Nick. "Would you believe I got my kids with me tonight? Brought 'em here to see the show. They're waiting just down the hall."

"You were in the audience?" Nick asked. "I'm surprised you'd come to a show like this."

"I'm not a complete Neanderthal, Nick… I thought it was pretty classy, actually. Honest, but still discreet. The queer stuff, I mean."

Nick wanted to say, *and the fact that your name didn't come up*, but he stayed quiet.

"I'm flattered you would think enough of me to bring your family, Paul," Nick said.

"Just the kids. I'm divorced," Paul said. "But I'm engaged to Alexandra, and she's great. Just the right kind of woman for me. Born again, like me."

Nick nodded.

"Anyway, the kids are big fans of yours. That old eighties music everybody still seems to like, you know," Paul said.

"Wonder What," Nick's singular hit record, was being used in yet another car commercial. The timing was good for publicity, even if it made Nick cringe a little.

"Anyway, when I mentioned to the kids I got to meet you at the 1984 Olympics, they just couldn't believe it," Paul said. "They've been bugging me to come to the show. I know what a pain autographs are, but would you come out in the hallway and meet them?"

"Sure I will, Paul," Nick said.

"Obviously, they don't have a clue about their poor old Papi's ancient sins."

Nick narrowed his eyes.

"Think I'd bring that up?" Nick asked.

"Bring up what? Oh, that. That was… man. A long time ago. We must have been good and drunk. You still think about it ever?"

"No," Nick lied.

"Me either. That was… boy, that was *ridiculous*… only time I ever tried anything like that. And on a public beach no less!"

"I recall," Nick said.

"Nick," Paul said, changing his tone, sounding more serious. "Nick, I wasn't going to say anything about all that, or stand in judgment of you. I know you're not a Christian…."

"Am I not a Christian?" Nick asked directly.

That quieted Paul for a moment.

"You know what I mean," he said slowly. "You talked in your show about believing… but so do a lot of stars, rappers, hip-hop people. I mean, I admire the honesty… but the play disappointed me in that regard. Whenever I thought of you, I always hoped you'd gotten over this queer thing, got married, had a more meaningful life."

"Like yours?"

"Now, Nick, don't be offended. I wouldn't say this if I didn't really care. But the lifestyle you've chosen… it's selfish. You can't really imagine what it's like to put someone else first, ahead of yourself, not in that kind of lifestyle of self-gratification. The life I'm advocating is a life of self-sacrifice."

"Wish I could have done more for you, Paul," Nick said, noting to himself the irony of his past weeks in LA. And the photos Paul never knew about, and never would know about. "How about I send in a campaign contribution?"

Paul didn't smile.

"That almost sounded sarcastic," Paul said. Then he smiled. "But I guess you heard I'm thinking of running for office. You know us politicians. I won't turn down the offer of money. Shame how much money is involved in these races. It's part of the game, though."

"The game, huh?" Nick said.

Paul came closer to Nick.

He stuck out his hand, as if to pat Nick's shoulder. But his hand kind of awkwardly froze halfway there. He let his arm fall to his side.

"Let's go out and meet my kids and help the old man look cool in their eyes," Paul said. "Let's keep it friendly."

"But not *too* friendly," Nick said and laughed without a smile. Paul laughed nervously.

"Nick... I...."

"Paul, I kept my end of the bargain," Nick said. "You said you never wanted to see me again, remember? Never wanted to hear from me... you erased me from your life. But maybe you understand now that it's not possible to make other people invisible, or just disappear."

They went out into the hallway, where Mel told them that Paul's kids had gone out of the stage door and were waiting alongside the building for their father. The theater was closing up, lights going off all around them.

They walked out the stage door into the warm night. The smell of cigarette smoke and popcorn drifted on the night air.

Paul stopped Nick before they reached the youngsters.

"As long as you embrace that lifestyle, Nick, we can't really be... good friends."

"Then let's stay old friends, Paul," Nick said. "Distant old friends." Nick smiled his high-beam bright smile at the beautiful teenage girls rushing up to their father with their autograph books open.

The car that was to take him to the airport was parked at the curb, the driver waiting.

NICK knew that Bonnie Guadeloupe was damn surprised the day she got a Facebook message from a complete stranger. She was close to forty now, and this Facebook thing still threw her off her game a little. It was something her daughter, at Morehouse, had gotten her into, she told him.

But she had explained to him that she was now alone in the modest little house in a black section of Atlanta, and she felt like she could use some friends. Even computer friends. And it was a kick hooking up again with sisters from her high school days.

But the messages from Nick in Hollywood were the real trip. He said at first he was a "friend of a friend," but it was disconcerting, she'd said, when he seemed to want an awful lot of information from her. Not just about her past, which put her guard up, but all kinds of funny, nosy details. For some reason, though, she started telling him things. Like about how she worked two jobs trying to keep Cara in school. How she was an inactive member of the NAACP these days, and single. She did word-processing in a law office at night and during the day she stood at a beverage concession (one of those on wheels) in a uniform, working conventions.

Nick could almost picture her. Most days her back hurt, she confessed to him. She didn't really like to sit at a computer in her free time. But the attention of Nick from Hollywood seemed kind of amusing at first, she thought. That is, when she wasn't wondering if maybe she was being stalked. That had make Nick laugh.

He knew she liked his sense of humor. When he sent his picture, she messaged back right away that she liked his face. But she gave no indication of recognizing him or knowing of his celebrity.

She asked him point blank one day if he was married.

Nick answered that he had a partner, that he was gay. Nick was relieved when she said that was no big deal.

He sensed that she was kind of lonely. That she wanted more out of life, but had somehow been held back.

Nick was so touched when she told him that having him as a friend on Facebook really meant a lot to her. Maybe more than she could say. Her child was grown now, and miles away. But now she had this new friend, this guy on Facebook. Maybe she was going to break out of her old shell, after all. Maybe he was going to help her reconnect to the world again, to other people, strangers, the whole world of new folks out there eager to meet each other.

That had emboldened Nick to finally say what he'd wanted to say all along, knowing it would probably floor her when he did. He wrote, "Bonnie, I think I might be your brother."

THE doorbell rang. It was already quite late in the evening. Nick could hear the chime ring behind the front door of the modest little house. It didn't surprise him that a woman living alone would have her door strongly bolted and locked tightly. At last the final lock turned and the door opened.

She was wearing a pretty dress. She had her hair styled. She was slender and attractive. Her smile trembled as tears filled her dazzling green eyes.

Nick didn't know when he'd been hugged so hard, or when he'd hugged back like that.

Like family.

"THIS was Daddy's room," Bonnie said, standing in front of Nick in the doorway of the humble bedroom with its neatly made single bed, simple side table, and plain wooden chair.

"Looks almost like you're expecting him home," Nick said.

She cleared her throat. "I left it this way… for now," she said, holding the huge bouquet of yellow roses and baby's breath he'd brought for her, along with a bottle of her favorite wine (they'd had dozens of Facebook exchanges by now; he knew some of her tastes).

"It'll be my daughter's room, if she needs it," Bonnie added. "Way Cara's going, though, I don't know if she'll need Mama's help much longer. She has a four-point grade point average. Anyway, I still haven't looked at any of Daddy's stuff. I just come in and change the bedsheets, vacuum and dust. I don't even look at his few things or the stack of books by the bed. I will someday, though. When I'm good and ready."

Nick wanted to look at the room more closely, to lie down on the bed and even smell it, take in the aroma. But he wanted to respect Bonnie's property too. And her delicate feelings.

"I have so many questions to ask you," Nick said, backing out of the room. "I don't even know where to start. I suppose for now maybe it would be best if we just have a glass of wine, together, get to know one another a little better. I can get back to my hotel early and take you to breakfast in the morning, any place you like to go."

"Nonsense," she said. "You just got here. And you'll stay in Daddy's room."

Nick's heart warmed. He'd see the room again and be in it soon enough. He popped open the wine, and she poured two glasses.

"Your Mama?" he asked.

"Gone in '94," Bonnie said. "Cancer."

"Oh, I'm sorry."

She smiled sadly.

"Funny things is, that's how I found Daddy," Bonnie said. "Like you, I grew up without him close by. He came to see my Mama when she was sick. He wasn't so well himself by then. Already had bad blood pressure and heart disease. I barely knew him when I was a child. But I loved him anyway."

Her face showed a glow of pride Nick admired in a very deep way.

"I took him in here, and he helped me raise Cara when she was at a turning point in her life," Bonnie continued. "Well, I'm glad to say he helped her turn out all right. Heck, more than all right. She loved her Granddad, and it made all the difference in the world. And… I came to love him too as the daughter he rediscovered." She looked at Nick closely. "Obviously I didn't know anything about Daddy's past, not much anyway, nothing about any other children. Maybe it sounds funny, but I still believe he was a good man, Nick. A Godly man."

"I'm happy it turned good," Nick said. "I just wish…." Nick couldn't finish his words. He started to choke up. It was so overwhelming to be beside his own sister, talking about their father.

She gently touched his arm.

"He played football up north," she went on calmly. "As a young man, he was a fine athlete. He went by the name of Ty back then. He didn't finish college, but he was very book smart, well read. He worked for the railroad. Started up in Chicago. Where I reckon he met your

Mama. Ended down here in Georgia. He had a small pension, and that helped us, believe me."

She opened a small scrapbook and handed Nick a photograph. Nick accepted it in a trembling hand.

Young Daddy looked so handsome. Proud. Intelligent and dignified in his posture. Bonnie showed him more pictures. The latter pictures showed Daddy's age. To the end, he was an elegant man. In a few old color snapshots, his eyes showed the green of his offspring.

"Do you know if he had any other children besides us?" Nick asked.

"He didn't speak of it," she answered. "You sure surprised me, I can tell you that. But I should have figured it. Your Mama… she was white? Is she living?"

"She was white," Nick said. "And she died, a long time ago. She couldn't raise me. Kind of left me. It still hurts, Bonnie. My grandparents tried with me… but they weren't really equipped to deal with a boy nobody wanted."

Nick was embarrassed by what he thought of as a note of self-pity. His eyes were blurry again with tears. Bonnie handed him a tissue.

"Bonnie, I don't know if you remember an old pop tune called 'Wonder What', but I was a singer a long time ago."

She shook her head.

"Famous?" she asked.

"You sure you never heard the name Nick Davanger?"

She looked at him, hard.

Now they both laughed. That name didn't mean a thing to her. But he could tell that he, himself, on the other hand, meant quite a good deal. He could feel her affection.

"Things have turned out pretty well for me, financially," Nick said. "And I'm going to help you and Cara along," he said.

"I ain't asking for a handout, Nick," she protested.

"Ain't a handout," he said. "It's family. I want to be a part of your life, and Cara's life." More softly he added, "Daddy's life."

She smiled and then it was her turn again to shed a couple of tears.

"We have soooo much catchin' up to do, Nick!" she laughed.

"Bonnie, I can't even begin to tell you how much I have wanted to have a sister for my very own. And now, to have a niece! I can hardly wait to meet her! No, I just can't begin to tell you." He knew he was perilously close to dissolving in tears.

She smiled and warmly took his hand in hers.

"We got time, brother Nick," she said. "We got a world of time."

She refilled their glasses, and they talked and laughed and cried late into the night.

FEELING happy and a little buzzed on the wine, Nick crawled between the fresh, crisp sheets of the squeaky but soft twin bed in which his father had slept in the last years of his life. After the night he had his heart attack, he never returned from the hospital. Nick flicked off the lamp. Morning light was already beginning to brighten the windows. The first birds of the day were beginning to sing.

Daddy had spent about a week in the hospital after the heart attack, but his condition declined. There was nothing that could be done for him, Bonnie had tearfully explained. With Cara and Bonnie on either side of him, holding his hands, he departed this life for another.

He died well loved.

Nick placed his head on the pillow. His father's pillow. He sighed, feeling much too excited to fall asleep. So he reached over and turned the lamp back on, accidentally knocking over a couple of small, framed pictures on the night table. He grabbed his cell phone from his bag beside the bed and dialed as he absently righted the upset pictures. It was way too early to make a call to California. But Nick couldn't help himself.

"Wow," Anson said by way of groggily answering his phone.

"Anyone ever tell you that you do amazing work," Nick asked with a grin. "Your first assignment, and you hit a home run. I'm here at my sister's house. Thanks to your detective work. Would you believe it? I'm sleeping in Daddy's bed."

"Nick, I think you're a brave, brave man," Anson said.

"Hell, I'm nothing without you!" Nick said, and they both shared a chuckle.

"Nick, I can hear the joy in your voice," Anson said. "I am so happy for you."

"For us, Anson. Our little family just grew a little more."

"Wow," Anson said.

"That all you can say, 'wow'?" Nick grinned.

"Nick, it's like three in the morning," Anson laughed. "You're lucky I can manage a syllable."

"I'll let you sleep. I'm gonna stay one extra day and get in Monday night in time for the performance. Hope you're well rested, because I'm looking forward to getting all over you."

"You know I will be. I love you, Nick."

Nick's heart soared.

"And I love you right back with a double helping of sugar on top of it!"

Anson laughed. He liked it when Nick talked so damn sweet it was almost silly.

"Together, nothin' is gonna stop the two of us," Nick said avidly.

"Uh-oh," Anson said in a joshing tone. "You're making plans!"

"I gotta talk to Susie first thing in the morning," Nick said excitedly. "First thing I'm gonna do is make sure my niece—my *niece*, Cara!—gets all her expenses at college taken care of. New wardrobe too, if she wants it, car, if she needs it."

"Wow, Santa Claus is coming to her town!"

"And I want to help Bonnie with her finances too. She's holding down two jobs! That's enough of that. The little house here is cute as hell. But fresh paint and a new kitchen never hurt anyone. Anson, I want to make their dreams come true."

"Honey," Anson said sweetly. "Don't you know? You already have. It's you they're gonna love. Hell, they do already, even if they don't know it."

With that, Nick bid Anson his goodnight, sweet dreams, with love and kisses on the way.

Just before Nick switched off the little bedside lamp, he took a glance at the dusty framed pictures next to some prescription bottles. Things he hadn't yet had time to inspect. He saw that Bonnie wasn't kidding that she hadn't changed anything in this room. And if she was really dusting, well she missed a few spots.

Either that, or she hadn't wanted to look too closely at the few dusty framed portraits that had been the last things Daddy must have looked at each night before he went to sleep. Before he went away.

There was a funny school picture of Cara, with a tooth missing. It warmed Nick's heart. There was a high school graduation portrait of Bonnie, unmistakable. There was a picture of an old black woman with wiry gray hair and a smile of sweet innocence. Nick just knew, with a lump in his throat, that he was looking at a grandmother he would never meet in this life. But maybe someday….

He sighed happily, his emotions getting stirred up all over again.

And there was another picture in a simple wood frame. One he'd accidentally knocked over a few minutes earlier.

It was small, and like the others, he hadn't really noticed it till now. It would have been easy to overlook among the others. At least at first. He picked it up and examined it closely, and then a funny feeling started in the marrow of his bones.

The photo was a bit grainy. But he recognized his mother. His heart pounded frantically. A little child was in her arms, his cute face peering out mischievously. It was Nick. He recognized himself from some other old photos he'd kept.

In this photo, a handsome man was posed beside him and his mother. Nick's little hand was wrapped around one of the man's fingers. Nick recognized his handsome father. But the picture grew blurry.

Nick gently replaced the framed photo in its place with the others on the tabletop. Pulling the chain, he turned off the light, then laid his head down onto the pillow where Daddy had once rested his head. He took in a deep, steady breath, then let it out real slow. A hot tear ran down his face like a precious jewel. A tear of pure joy, of hope, and of humble thanksgiving.

Yes, it was possible to be loved by a father you don't know without even knowing you were loved by him. To dare to hope for and believe in such love as this was, Nick now understood, the meaning and the truest treasure of his life. Love was there with him all this time. And love always would be.

HANK FIELDER is from Wisconsin and has lived in London and California. A passionate devotee of soulful romantic music, he has worked a variety of jobs, but his favorite occupation is storyteller. In addition to writing novels and stories, he volunteers in his community combating bullying in middle and high schools. Visit him online at http://www.authorhankfielder.blogspot.com and on Twitter at @HankFielder, http://www.twitter.com/HankFielder.

Also from Dreamspinner Press

BUTTERFLY'S CHILD

ALAN CHIN

http://www.dreamspinnerpress.com